PLIER

THE IRONSIDE SERIES
BOOK ONE

JANE WASHINGTON

CONTENTS

Also by Jane Washington

Ironside Academy

Book 1: Plier

Book 2: Tourner

A Tempest of Shadows

Book 1: A Tempest of Shadows

Book 2: A City of Whispers

Book 3: Dream of Embers

Book 4: A Castle of Ash

Book 5: A World of Lost Words

Bastan Hollow

Standalone: Charming

Standalone: Disobedience

Standalone Books

I Am Grey

Curse of the Gods

Book 1: Trickery

Book 2: Persuasion

Book 3: Seduction

Book 4: Strength

Novella: Neutral

Book 5: Pain

Seraph Black

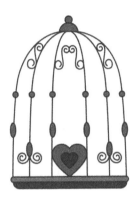

Oh, the irony of this prestigious place,
As puppets dance inside, lost in the chase.
The world applauds from outside the bars,
Iron on all sides, but inside are stars.

IRONSIDE ACADEMY MAP

To view the map of Ironside, please scan the QR code below.

IRONSIDE ACADEMY PLAYLIST

To listen to the playlist for the Ironside series, please scan the QR code below.

I

SHIPS THAT PASS

Sixteen Years Old

THE INSIDE OF THE CAR WAS THICK WITH TENSION. It shivered along the windows, raising the hairs on the back of Isobel's neck. Every time her father shifted or cleared his throat, both she and her mother froze. They winced. They waited, holding their breath, relaxing only when his mannerisms turned into coincidences instead of precursors. It was a day of celebration for many families. Isobel's family wasn't excluded from that group, but they weren't experienced with celebrating anyone other than her father. They existed to support him. To skirt around him, stepping into the bright halo of his glow only when he ordered it, sharing in his limelight only when the accessorising of his family might make him shine brighter.

This day was for Isobel, and that made him uncomfortable.

It made them all uncomfortable.

"Please," Isobel's mother dared to beg softly, her hands twisting in her lap. "I just want to walk her inside."

The car was quiet for a moment, the plea like a pencil scattering loudly to the floor in the silent examination halls where the Gifted kids were herded at the end of each year to prove that the settlement schools were teaching them how to read, write, and fear the outside world.

And then the silence broke.

He pulled over in a sudden jerk, throwing Isobel against the side of the car. He wasn't thrown—he was too big, as Alphas should be, his shoulder already touching the window. His teeth ground together as he spoke, the side of his profile visible as he leaned over the space between seats, a tiny muscle pulsing beneath the sweep of his blond hair over his forehead. "You're pushing it, Caran."

Isobel's mother shrank back, but Braun Carter didn't press forward. He simply rolled his big body from the seat, throwing the door closed in his wife's face.

Isobel watched as her mother scrambled for the handle to go after him, and she quickly reached for the older woman's shoulder, stopping her.

"Mama. It's okay."

She was used to this. Swallowing down the fear, tucking away her own pain.

It wouldn't stay buried long; it never could with her kind. Sigmas were vessels of emotion, more than the other ranks of Gifted … but she preferred it this way. She sometimes thought of herself as a little paper boat bobbing through a river of gutter water. Something people could focus on while life tried to pull them under. It was an approximation of how she was designed: to exist in the tumultuous sway of life, though she was stubbornly riding the waves when submersion was the "proper" way.

Her mother twisted around, trying to blink away the tears in her eyes, but a loud, impatient knock against the window—no doubt telling Isobel to hurry up—had her losing the battle, and soon tears were tracking down her cheeks to wobble along the edges of her jaw.

Caran Carter was always submerged.

"You be good," she said, still in that softly

trembling voice. "I'll be there at the first family visit in a month. Just ... don't let them see you cry, okay? They're going to want to see who can break you first, but you're stronger than that. Stronger than most Sigmas."

"I promise they'll never see me cry." Isobel smiled as her mother's hand covered hers, squeezing tightly. "I love you, Mama—"

Isobel's door flew open, her father's face appearing in the opening as he hunkered down. She quickly slipped away from one parent and toward the other before the situation could escalate. He didn't step aside immediately. His light, honeyed eyes slid between his wife and his daughter, the gold flecks around his iris brightening as his pupil contracted.

After a tense moment, he moved out of Isobel's way, gripping her bicep to drag her after him. He already had her bags waiting, and he turned without another word, walking them over to the path that led up the desert mountainside.

"Here." He set the bags at her feet. "Take them yourself."

She hadn't expected anything more. Her father was a rare Alpha, and she was a rare Sigma. Their society had a hierarchy, and the polar ends of it were sparsely populated, separated from the more common middle rungs simply by the reality of their minority. Her father was at the top, and Isobel was at the bottom. He had not expected his genes to be less dominant when he discovered his mate was a Sigma, and both mother and daughter had been paying for it since.

It would have been unseemly for him to escort her all the way to her dorm, carrying her bags like a porter. He had made sure she knew that during the drive. It was enough that he had driven her at all.

"See you soon," he grunted, cupping her cheek.

She flinched out of habit, and his face darkened for a moment before his breath hissed between his teeth and he spun on his heel, lumbering back to the car. It was impressive that he even had one, but then again, Braun Carter wasn't just any Gifted. He was a graduate of the very academy she was about to enter. A *winning* graduate. An Icon. This was the first thing she had ever done that he actually gave a shit about.

Not enough to walk her inside, though.

She grabbed the handle of her suitcase, shifting her backpack on her shoulder as she forced her legs to move.

You better stop acting like I'm forcing you to go. Her father's words when he found her crying over her bags that morning chased her up the hill, followed by her own hesitant bolstering. He didn't force her to do anything. It was her pleasure, her duty, to obey his every command. His, and any other Alphas. Not that she had met any others.

Don't look back, Isobel. Not all new things are bad.

She approached the first checkpoint, which had a gate for cars to pass through and a narrow path for people.

"Where are your parents?" the guard immediately asked, peering out of his small service window.

"They already left." She dug out her paperwork, handing it all over. The rest of the world had gone digital, but not all Gifted families could afford phones or computers, so the academy sent out everything in hard copy.

He glanced at her paperwork and picked up a receiver. "Can you send a car down? We've got a student walking—" His eyes caught on something on the page he was reading and he paused, leaning out of the service window to get a better look at her eyes.

She fought the urge to duck her chin down, lifting her face for inspection. Her Sigma ring was black, starkly circling the outside of her iris, which was a light gold like her father's, though the darker bronze flecks were more prominent in hers, making the rest of her iris seem almost translucent.

"Disregard." The guard set the receiver aside, directing his next words to her. "You can walk." He nodded his head toward the narrow pedestrian gate, handing back her papers, his tone dismissive. "Welcome to Ironside, Sigma."

She averted her eyes, showing no reaction. The ring around his iris was silver, marking him as a Beta. He wasn't as potent as an Alpha, but in the absence of an Alpha, the Betas were the ones who stepped up to lead. They put the *gift* in Gifted with their interesting abilities, charismatic personalities, and stubborn entitlement ... which by some miracle survived the constant subjugation of their people. Most of the graduating Icons like her father were Betas.

She pushed through the pedestrian gate, ignoring the burn in her muscles as the slope became steep, her suitcase gaining weight as it dragged behind her, the wheels threatening to snap against every step. She paused halfway to the top for a break, turning to look over the prickly, sunburnt valley, mesas cutting into the distance. She had always loved the desert, even though she rarely left the city. Her mother told her so many stories of the settlement she grew up in that Isobel had adapted it into her dreams, imagining that she, too, came from a life behind sandstone brick walls, playing in the red dirt with her siblings. They would all wear clothes too small for them, and her youngest siblings would eat mud pies not for play, but because they were hungry.

It was wrong of her to romanticise the hardships of her parents' childhoods—of the lives most other Gifted lived—but Isobel couldn't help it. It wasn't the suffering she was drawn to. It was the *community*. The family.

What was the point of an apartment in the sky, with doormen and porters and a private chef if she spent all her time hiding from weighty footfalls and lights flickering on in the middle of the night?

It took about half an hour to reach the top, and during that time, she was only passed by one other car. The rest of the new students would have travelled by private coach from their respective settlements, arriving earlier that morning.

When the academy came into view, she stopped again, savouring her last moment of relative isolation. As soon as she stepped through those big glass entry doors, her every action would be recorded and broadcast to the outside world, because that was the whole point of Ironside Academy. An opulent, resort-style school for young adults and college-aged kids. The *only* educational institution available to Gifted kids outside of the primitive settlement schools, perched in the middle of the desert where it was tucked safely away from humanity. They would be given every little luxury they could ever want, just as long as they performed for the cameras, for the humans, for the outside world.

Most kids came for their families, to send home money until they "graduated," but some kids actually came to win. It was a highly improbable outcome for her, as a Sigma, but she had lived the benefits of an Ironside Icon every day, thanks to her father. She had enjoyed days of pampering with her mother—usually on her birthday—where fashion designers brought clothes to their apartment for them to try on before they descended to the day spa that took up a whole floor of the building they lived in. Her family had a slick black town car and a beautiful home outside the settlements. Her father was a recognised citizen who was allowed to own land and vote. There were toys and clothing made in his image, and he had acted in several movies since he graduated, earning the family even more money.

She understood the appeal, but that would never be her.

As a Sigma, she couldn't even win a game of Uno.

Whenever she felt herself pulling ahead, some kind of basic instinct to make people happy took over, and she folded. She let everyone else win. She couldn't help it.

"Name?" a woman demanded of her the second she walked through the doors into the air-conditioned room.

"Isobel Carter," she mumbled, nervously adjusting her luggage. When the attendant raised an inquisitive eyebrow, she repeated it, louder. "Is-Isobel Carter."

The woman scrolled through her tablet as Isobel glanced around, thankful she wasn't the only student there before she peered up at the tops of the walls, looking for the cameras. She had consumed all the information she could find online about how to survive Ironside, and the one thing the past students kept repeating was *don't look at the cameras all the time, or your screen time will be cut.*

"Carter, Carter ..." The attendant frowned, tapping her stylus against her chin. "What dorm?"

"A-ah. Dorm S?" she stuttered. Everyone knew the dorms were named after rank, ranging from Dorm A for Alpha, all the way down to Dorm O for Omega. She hadn't actually heard of a Dorm S, but she supposed there had to be one.

"We don't have a Dorm S—*Oh. Carter.*" The woman emphasised Isobel's name this time, her attention zeroing in on Isobel's eyes. "You're our only

Sigma, and we certainly weren't going to build you your own dorm, even if your dad is an Icon." She laughed, and Isobel heard another of the assistants nearby chuckling as well. "You'll be in Dorm O. Consider it an upgrade. Here's your map and ... ah, it looks like we forgot to set aside a welcome pack for you. Can you whistle?"

Isobel nodded, her lips pressing tightly together.

"Good. Just whistle if you're being attacked or assaulted; we don't have any spare assault horns."

"That's okay. Thank you." She shuffled away, glad she wasn't going to have to carry around one of those stupid horns. They were as much of a joke as the "classes" she would be enrolling in.

A clip had gone viral the year before of the fifth-year students doing a Christmas variety show of assault-horn carol renditions. That was how seriously people took them.

She consulted the map and let a small sigh escape her lips. Naturally, Dorm O was the furthest away. Dorm A was the closest, sequestered to the side of the academy entrance. It was nestled into a hill that Isobel knew to be artificial from the *Creating Ironside* documentary. It wasn't even legal anymore, the amount of dirt they had hauled in to build Alpha Hill.

Twenty-nine thousand cubic yards.

Of *dirt*.

The documentary had shown the trucks like a line of marching ants crawling into the construction site, looking regal and proud in their new, royal-blue painted glory, the words *Ironside* stamped boldly on their sides.

Dorm A overlooked a small lake formed by an artificial waterfall tumbling from the top of the butte above. It pooled into an oasis outside the dorm before travelling through underground pipes to the main lake, which Isobel circled now to get to the northern point of the campus. There were hydraulic pumps beneath the main lake, cycling water back up to the top of the waterfall. The documentary had also explained the expansive rainwater harvesting system on the other side of the buttes, and the emergency water deliveries needed to maintain the waterfall and keep the lakes filled. She always tried not to think about the droughts in the settlements when she thought about that.

Dorms B and D were on the other side of the glittering blue expanse, separated by a small nature reserve, so they had lovely views from all sides. The government spared no expense on Ironside, just as they spared no expense on their Icons. This was one of the country's biggest industries, contributing a staggering—yet somehow undisclosed—number of billions to the yearly economy.

Meanwhile, the rest of the Gifted lived in secure settlements, weighed down by poverty and picked off by common infections and diseases that would have been treatable in the outside world. There were reasons for that, of course. Reasons the humans eagerly accepted ... but there was only one *real* reason, and that was fear.

The Gifted were different. *Other*. Unknown. The human population in general were welcoming of the *other*, curious about things they didn't understand, but it only took one bad apple to ruin the whole bunch. That's how her piano teacher had described it. She still wasn't sure if he had been talking about the Gifted or the humans, because it wasn't a topic of discussion that was allowed in their household. According to her father, the settlements existed not just to protect the humans from the Gifted, but also the other way around. It was best for everyone, and he wouldn't be told differently.

Even though he lived in a tower in the city.

"Well, *hello there*!" a voice called out, drawing her attention to a cameraman, who waved at her from one of the upper paths, winding his way down to walk beside her. "Aren't you a pretty little thing! What's your name—Ugh. Sigma? Wait, seriously?" He shook his head, his shoulders slumping. "Never mind." He lowered his camera and walked away, just like that.

It wasn't that Sigmas were hated, necessarily. It's just that they weren't interesting. They all had the same power. *Empathy*. Isobel could take on people's negative feelings, leaving them lighter and happier. The empath ability actually made Sigmas incredibly useful ... except that they could also block themselves off. They could be selfish with their powers, even if it went against their natures; because at the end of the day, there was still something self-preserving within them. Something that didn't want to exist constantly doused in darkness.

So, to the rest of the Gifted, the Sigmas essentially had no power at all, since they refused to use it with any regularity. And to the humans? That just made them boring.

The Alphas were the most exciting, of course, but they were too rare to hang your hopes on, which left the Betas and Deltas as the main sources of entertainment, and the Omegas as their main targets.

By the time she reached Dorm O, she was desperate for a shower, but she was delayed when she realised her name hadn't been included on the room assignment sheet. She knocked on the door to the office, where one of the dorm supervisors sat at a desk, tapping away on her laptop.

"Yes?" The supervisor turned her head, looking at Isobel over the top of her glasses.

"I haven't been assigned a room." Isobel shifted her weight to ease the ache in her feet. She tried to ignore the stickiness of sweat against the back of her neck and the dull ache in her calves.

The supervisor sighed, and Isobel could already tell that the woman thought she hadn't looked properly. "Name?" she asked, pushing up from her chair.

Isobel told her and watched as she scanned the list on the wall outside, finding that Isobel's name was, indeed, missing.

"Are you in the right dorm?" The supervisor nudged her glasses down further, peering at Isobel's eyes before pausing, a frown twisting her lips. "Ah, the Sigma. I forgot about you. Wait there." She disappeared into her office again and re-emerged with a set of keys. "Follow me, Carter. You can call me Professor Yarrow, by the way. I teach charcoal sketching. Each level of Dorm O has two Omega professors assigned to it. One in a room at each end, if you need anything."

Isobel didn't even have time to answer before

Yarrow was striding off. She hurried to follow, trying to make herself as small as possible in the chaos of the dorm. It was packed, people chatting excitedly, camera crews darting through the tangle of activity. She assumed there usually weren't so many Ironside staff inside the dorms, but they likely wanted to capture every face so that there would be historical footage of whichever Icon eventually graduated in five years. Not that it was likely to be an Omega.

Even when the Omegas did trend online, it was for some scene they had been involved in that featured a Delta or a Beta—or an Alpha, of course, but in that case, they were lucky they weren't cut out of the shot completely. It made Dorm O interesting to her, because it wasn't shown anywhere near as much as the others.

Yarrow climbed several stories to the top level, unlocking the first door past the office at the end of the hallway. It didn't look like the other dorm rooms, which were all labelled with gold lettering and had cute little noticeboards on the outside.

This one looked more like a storage cupboard.

The door stuck, forcing Yarrow to shoulder it open and stumble a step inside. "Ah, there we go." She wiped her hands on her skirt before handing Isobel the key. "Welcome home. The bathroom facilities are in the middle of the hall. Men's on the left, ladies' on the right. You aren't an Omega, obviously, but you are permitted to use their facilities."

Isobel wasn't stupid. She had only ever missed one episode of Ironside Academy, when she had been sick. The punishment she received from her father had ensured that the next time she was sick, she dragged a bucket to the lounge and fixed her eyes to the screen all the same.

She *knew* that even the Omega dorm rooms were fairly luxurious.

She knew that they had a bed, at the very least.

Yarrow had led her to an empty room. It was narrow and small, the window missing a pane. There were a few cleaning supplies shoved into the corner and a dusty bookshelf that housed a few rags and bottles of disinfectant. Someone had dropped a box into the centre of the room, a big sticker on top.

Welcome to your new home! Below the sticker, a name had been scrawled.

Carter.

She took all this in quickly, wary of the cameras in the hallway, not that they would have cared about her today. Not with the *other* big news on academy grounds that morning. After a quiet assessment, she thanked Yarrow politely. The woman gave a satisfied nod and walked off, snapping the door closed behind her.

Isobel took a steadying breath before exploring the box of supplies. Luxurious sheets and blankets for the bed she didn't have. A little cactus in a clay pot. An Ironside-branded water bottle, key ring, and sweatshirt. At least there were towels. There was also another map and a handbook of rules. Copies of those had already been posted to her, but this version of the rule handbook had tabbed pages. A quick glance revealed that they were trying to draw attention to rules that might affect first-years, such as the placement of cameras and the forbidden use of Gifted abilities in any way that might be considered aggressive or offensive.

After going through the box, she sat back on her heels to survey the room again. Any other person might have cried at this point, but it barely registered to Isobel. She pushed her bags out of the way and used the cleaning supplies to properly clean the floor before she laid out the bedding, folding the thickest blanket in three to use as a mattress, glad that her slender Sigma stature wouldn't need very much surface area.

She cleaned the shelf and the windowsill, picking out little bits of broken glass before packing the cleaning supplies into the empty welcome box. She unpacked most of her belongings, folding most of her clothes onto the middle shelves, lining her shoes up against the wall and piling her books and school supplies onto the top shelves. She left the rest of her clothes in her suitcase and hung her coats and towels on the hooks stuck to the back of the door.

It wasn't exactly the penthouse apartment she was used to, but she was well practised at not expecting much. The door had a lock, and she couldn't hear her father's footsteps in the hallway or her mother's quiet sobs behind the bathroom door.

This would more than do.

Isobel's classes were emailed to her the next morning.

Introduction to Musical Theory

Introduction to Language and Literature

Fashion and Design: Module One

Beginners Theatre and Film

Introduction to Applied Arts

Performing Arts: Module One

Introduction to Fine Art

She didn't get the chance to pick her own classes. The appropriate forms had already been submitted online, which meant that her father had likely dealt with it without consulting her.

Not that it mattered.

She had no delusions of becoming an Icon, so there wasn't a particular skill she was interested in honing, but that didn't mean her father was without ambition. Part of the benefits provided to her family had been free education and tutoring, and he had taken full advantage of that. Her "classes" had started at 5:00 a.m. and ended at 8:00 p.m.

At first, she had been allowed her weekends to herself, but that was before one of her tutors suggested that she had an aptitude for dance. Her father hadn't wanted to drop any of her other lessons, so he added more onto the weekend.

She wondered why he hadn't put her in any dance classes all through the first day of Welcome Week, until one of the Dorm O supervisors pulled her aside, lecturing her about booking practice rooms and not turning up, and how she was being selfish with resources.

Her father—or more likely her mother, under his orders—was booking practice time for her through her own online portal. After that, she made sure to check any changes to her timetable before setting out for the day, and she made it through the rest of Welcome

Week without anyone taking notice of her—which wasn't unusual. She was unassuming and quiet, and she always kept her head down. Being the daughter of a prior Icon was the only interesting thing about her, and she more than made up for that with her underwhelming presence and personality—or at least that was how her father had put it.

One morning in the bathroom, a few of the Omegas had even been gossiping about the "Sigma in the cleaning closet" *right* beside her, never once noticing that she was brushing her teeth two mirrors over.

Everything seemed to be going smoothly until one morning in *Introduction to Musical Theory*. There were around eighteen students gathered on the floor, taking notes while a Delta professor wrote on a board in front of them. Most of the classrooms were very casual, encouraging the students to cluster together and interact for the cameras.

It was a quiet morning. A little too quiet. The professors had dual responsibilities: to provide a way for students to up-skill if they were on the Icon track and to keep things entertaining for the show. Which explained what Professor Katz did next.

"Where's the Sigma?" Katz asked, her marker tapping against her arm agitatedly.

The others looked around, unsure, as Isobel's heart jumped up into her throat. She had been sitting by herself, slightly apart from the others, her notebook resting on her folded legs. She raised a shaking hand, earning a few surprised looks. Perhaps her black Sigma ring was easily mistaken for the navy Omega ring if people didn't look too closely.

"Right, there you are." Katz tossed the marker onto her desk. "Do you play any instruments? You're the only student in this class who didn't grow up in one of the settlements. You certainly had ample opportunity and access."

She wasn't sure, but she thought the surprise on some of the faces around her had melted into jealousy. Children of the Icons were only ever ridiculed or worshipped, depending on their likelihood of following in their parent's footsteps. There was no in-between.

"P-piano." Isobel twisted her fingers, keeping her eyes down.

"An elegant instrument," Katz murmured. "A wealthy instrument ... but we're fortunate here, are we not? To have instruments such as these?"

Isobel still had her gaze directed down, but she could hear footsteps and the quiet sound of the shiny grand piano's lid being lifted. She dreaded the professor's next words, even as she expected them.

"Go ahead, Sigma. Play for us."

Isobel walked to the bench numbly, only raising her eyes high enough to set them on the keys as she lifted her hands. She had never played for anyone before, except her teacher and her parents. Her teacher had been kind. A middle-aged man who considered himself a fan of her father, willing to do anything to please him, even if it meant tutoring a Sigma as though she might actually make something of herself at the famous academy.

Isobel swallowed, sweat gathering on her forehead.

This was it. This was the moment her father would see. This was her chance to change his opinion, to make him proud, to show that all the lessons he spent on her weren't wasted. She knew he had pulled strings to get her into the academy despite her rank.

"Ah, this is embarrassing," one of the kids murmured.

"You can do it," another one spoke up, though they didn't sound especially genuine, more pained. This was awkward for everyone. They wanted it to be over.

Why couldn't she move?

"I thought Sigmas were supposed to be obedient?"

another kid muttered before whoever he had been speaking to hushed him.

"Tell her what to play!" someone offered up loudly.

Her vision had gone blurry, and it was becoming difficult to breathe, but she tried her hardest not to let her reaction show, despite how loud and ragged her breathing sounded to her own ears. She focussed on the ivory-and-black contrast of the keys, on the red felt at the very top, the little motes of dust drifting in front of her face.

The taste of bile in the back of her throat.

"Do you know any songs?" Katz asked, tapping the top of the piano to get Isobel's attention.

Isobel tried to nod, to speak, but nothing happened.

Eventually, Katz pinched the bridge of her nose, muttering something lowly.

"Since the lesson is on tonality," a voice drawled, "I assume you want an example of tonal music, with a tonic note."

The voice was moving closer. A form settled onto the bench beside her. Isobel felt his energy—bitter, with a bite to it. It rolled over her, far more powerful than she had expected. He was angry or annoyed, and she let a little of it slip into her before she could help herself, welcoming the darkness like she was trying to punish herself.

He stilled for the briefest of moments, possibly sensing what she had done, before lifting his hands to the keys. He was warm, his shoulder set above hers, the side of his body radiating heat into hers. He smelled warm, too. Like clove and woodsmoke. Deep and rich and a little spicy. She couldn't tell if it was soap or something else. His fingers were long and graceful, his skin tone smooth and perfect, not quite pale but not quite tanned, his nails cut short and immaculate, a little scar on his thumb. She stared at those fingers, somehow knowing that they were capable of complex chords, especially from the way he arranged his hands to begin, weighing his wrists lightly.

And then he played "Happy Birthday to You."

Loudly.

Obnoxiously.

To take the attention away from her, or to rub it in?

She jerked her head to the side as everyone started laughing, catching his eyes for the briefest second before she stood and fled the classroom.

Light, bright grey, like an ice-capped ocean, ringed in heady gold.

An Alpha.

THE CLIP WENT VIRAL.

Isobel knew, because at the end of the month, she received an email from the Ironside officials, informing her of her prize. For contributing to one of the most viewed clips that week, she was to be awarded with a dedicated study cubicle in the library. Just for her, whenever she wanted it, for the entire year. It was extra generous, even as a reward, but she soon realised why when it incited the anger of the other students. The very next day, someone threw a flare through her window, breaking another of the panels and shattering glass over her sleeping spot on the floor. It scared her enough that she tried to stay up most nights studying in her cubicle ... until that, too, was taken away.

It wasn't actually removed, of course, but every time she went there, she encountered a boy leaning up against it, waiting for her. After a few days of this, she finally decided to approach him, even though she knew the cameras were probably waiting for a confrontation.

He was a little taller than she was, with wavy brown hair that brushed against his collar.

"Can I help you?" she asked as he stepped aside for

her to pass before blocking her in, notching his elbows on either side of the cubicle opening.

"Name's Bellamy." He was so confident, so strongly-spoken. "Adam Bellamy." He waited, but she didn't offer her own name. "Carter, right?" He chuckled. "We all know your dad. He's a legend."

"I believe that's the point," Isobel whispered, but he only leaned closer, having not heard her.

"What?"

"I asked if I could help you?" She set her bag down, inspecting her cubicle for any damage. She really loved it, even if it had caused her trouble. She had stuck up a photo of her parents on one of the short walls and had a few select books lined on the left, waiting to be leafed through.

"What are you doing Friday?" Bellamy displayed a row of straight white teeth. She quickly looked down.

"Studying."

He laughed like her answer was hilarious. "Hopefully not the piano," he teased.

The outside world weren't the only people who watched Ironside. Everyone did. It was a small—albeit mocking—beacon of hope for them. Every year, one of them was elevated. Sometimes, those Icons tried to change things, to make life overall better for the Gifted.

Isobel flinched, and he immediately changed his tone, becoming contrite. "Sorry, I meant no offence. I'm sure you're great at piano. So ... Friday? I won't tease you anymore, I promise."

"I don't understand. What about Friday?" She glanced up, confused, drumming her nails against the desk.

He laughed, shaking his head in a charming sort of way. "Do you want to hang out? With me? On Friday?"

She was already shaking her head before he finished. "No, thank you."

"Come on," he coaxed, not even missing a beat. "You can't study all the time. You need to have some fun, let the people see who you really are."

When she didn't look convinced, he tried a new tactic. "I'm sure your dad would love to see you making some friends, and with Betas no less."

She swallowed against the sudden lump in her throat.

"Please?" He sensed her weakness, ducking his head so that he could peer up at her, still smiling, not taking no for an answer. And maybe even showing off his silver Beta ring. "Just to hang out? Meet some nice people?"

"O-okay."

"Great." He reached into his pocket, withdrawing his phone. "Put in your number. I'll be in touch."

She did as he asked, her fingers tingling as he walked off. She sat down after he left, wondering if the cameras had seen a Beta trying to befriend her and if it would please her father. Maybe if it did, they would finally visit her, since they hadn't shown up for any of the family visits yet.

She should have known better.

That was all she could think as she stood by the lake, hair plastered to her face, her dress sticking to her skin as she dripped all over the pathway. Someone was manipulating the light, shrouding those who had pushed her into the lake while keeping her visible for the cameras perched on large posts, vigilantly recording everything. The cameras that had watched her standing there nervously, wondering if she had the wrong time or place. The cameras that had watched her seemingly stumble over a rock, right into the lake. The cameras that had watched her scramble for the bank, her entire system frozen from the shock of the cold water. Only a Beta or an Alpha could have managed that kind of light manipulation, but she shoved the thought out of her head. The *who* didn't matter.

She was the fool, and she had allowed herself to walk into the obvious trap when she should have known better. She had only herself to blame.

Bellamy was nowhere to be seen.

She wrapped her arms around her torso and raced back to the dorm, only to find all the doors locked. She tried to knock but was answered only by muted giggles. There were no emergency phones around, because at Ironside, there were no emergencies. Only highlights.

Isobel slumped into the hollow of the doorway to wait for someone else to enter or leave the building, and sure enough, a group of third-year girls approached from the pathway leading away from the lake.

"Everything okay?" one of them asked before another elbowed her.

"It's the Sigma," she informed the speaker lowly.

They ignored her after that but thankfully allowed her to slip into the building behind them. They had taken their keys with them, which Isobel took note of.

She showered quickly before locking herself into her room and curling up on her pallet of blankets with her laptop. There was no point in her checking the

Ironside website, but she did it anyway. Production didn't move quickly enough to expose her humiliation. It didn't matter how big their team was, the agency behind Ironside couldn't seem to air the drama sooner than a week after it happened in real time. They needed to review it all, cut it together, edit it, and of course, have the famous Ed Jones bringing it all together with his charismatic commentary.

The most viewed clips hadn't been knocked out of their spots yet, remaining the same as the week before:

First-year Alpha Spade is a genius!

Another Alpha? Is Hart a human lie detector?

Spoiled for choice! Dorm A has never looked so full!

Beta heartthrob: Does first-year Bellamy already have a fan club?

We don't know where to look! Braun Carter has a Sigma daughter? Alpha Reed is a low-key comedian?

The coverage was mostly focussed on the eight new Alphas who had joined that year, which wasn't a surprise. She was fairly sure Dorm A would have been empty if they hadn't managed to repopulate it—still, eight Alphas was unheard of in a single year, not to mention the two new Alpha professors.

She skipped over the highlights, clicking on last night's episode and setting the laptop off to the side. Her vision of the screen blurred, but not from tears.

She slipped into a fretful sleep, kept company by her promise.

They would never see her break.

THE LIBRARY WAS SO QUIET SHE DIDN'T REALLY NEED THE headphones, but she used them to focus anyway, channelling what she had learned in one of her art classes to sketch her own birthday cake, drawing seventeen candles on top. Things had settled down since she had arrived at Ironside, but she still didn't have any friends.

And her parents hadn't come.

Not the first month nor the second.

Not the seventh, which had just begun. Not even to wish her a happy birthday.

Still, she chose to celebrate, in her own small way.

Draw something you wish you had, the sketching assignment was titled. The professors focussed on dreams and wishes a lot in those art classes, trying to fill the students with enough hope that they started properly competing with each other.

There wasn't much point in staying any longer, not with her eyelids drooping. She wouldn't be able to concentrate on her work, so she packed up her things and tucked her headphones away, walking toward the stairs.

The top floor of the library was mostly used to store boxes of books and broken furniture. There were only three cameras, and they didn't work anymore, which was exactly why Isobel had made this her secret space, having given up her private cubicle on the second floor to an insistent Beta only two weeks after it had been awarded to her.

She had almost reached the stairs when something flickered in her periphery. Something that didn't belong in that quiet, abandoned space.

Clutching the strap of her bag nervously, she edged around the side of the staircase, peering into a darkened corner of the library, where someone was half-hidden beneath one of the blown lights, shadows enveloping their hunched shoulders.

"A-are you okay?" she asked, stepping closer.

His head lifted so slowly, like he was reaching out with his senses before he bothered with his eyes, but when they finally met hers, she found that they were completely black, the colour bleeding all the way out from his pupil, spilling like oil to the sooty lashes framing his eyes.

She froze, her breath stuttering. She had read something once, something she wasn't supposed to read based on the way her father beat her afterwards and began locking his office cabinet. It described a special Alpha ability called "ferality," where the affected Alpha became beast-like, destroying everything around them and causing harm to anyone who got in their way.

Illegal, the document had said.

Risk too high to reliably mitigate.

Deemed highly dangerous.

Must be decommissioned or destroyed.

She had never heard the term again. Not in all the episodes of Ironside or in the rare visits back to the settlement to visit her parents' families. But she remembered the image in the book and some of the terms it had used. It was seared into her mind. A nightmare on the page, coming back to life in the deepest, most disorienting of her dreams.

She remembered the deep, endless black eyes, glittering with malice. She remembered the explosion of dark veins webbing out, like the dark sickness was spreading, crawling over the rest of the head.

And now she was staring at it again, except this time, it wasn't in a book or a nightmare.

This time, it was a boy.

Flesh and blood. Only ten paces away. Deep, endless pools of dark swam in the space of his eyes, infected veins disappearing into his hairline. He seemed to be staring at her, but she had no way of telling.

"Leave," he growled low, the sound barely human. Loud and textured, his voice echoed with danger. She moved to obey without even thinking, but was stopping again just as instinctively, fighting against the strange pull the order had over her, having caught sight of something else.

His cheeks ... were wet.

He ... was *crying*?

She felt his emotion nudge at her, and she cautiously allowed it, expecting some sense of sadness or conflict, but instead, she was almost bowled completely over by the tidal wave of his despair. She dropped her bag, and his head shifted minutely so that it seemed like his black eyes were following the movement. It was oddly mechanical. Other than the tears tracking down his cheeks, no other part of him moved. He didn't even seem to be breathing.

She vaguely remembered the warnings of that book, but her nature was already taking over, driving her toward the boy, that steel door she usually hid behind creaking open, sucking in more of the horrible emotion he drowned in.

She reached the spot where he was hiding—huddled

or crouched. He seemed to want to disappear but ready to pounce all at once, like he didn't possess either a fight or flight response, but both, at the same time. She turned to sit beside him, her legs crossed like his. His head had moved to follow her, his nostrils flaring.

She pulled more of the darkness into herself, feeling it settle with sickening heaviness into the pit of her stomach as his face swam closer in her blurry vision. They were close enough for Isobel to see the way the blackness slowly bled from his eyes as she blinked away the haze from her own, still sipping on his awful, consuming emotion. The black sank into his iris, revealing a golden Alpha ring enclosing eyes of a dark, stormy grey. His dark hair was messy, strands stuck to his skin by sweat. His jaw was so tight she could see the muscles working, his teeth grinding.

"Sigma?" he croaked, those stormy eyes now flitting over her face. His chest moved, and Isobel felt herself slump a little in relief that he finally seemed to be breathing.

"Isobel," she corrected, her tone husky, a small whine of pain in the back of her voice.

He didn't seem to hear her. "You took it." His head turned, his wide stare dragging to the hands in his lap. They were broken and bloody. "Why?" he rattled, disbelieving, a hint of a growl still riding his uneven voice.

Isobel wanted to answer, but the stolen emotion was weighing her down ... and it was too much for her. It would only be a matter of time before she was unconscious, or violently ill, so she struggled to her feet, wobbling her way to the stairs.

"Wait—" he called, but she kept going, faster and faster, her vision swimming.

She was already sweating and shaking by the time she made it to Dorm O, and from there, she veered sideways into the first-floor bathroom, collapsing onto the floor, where the first seizure took her. She knew better than to go to her room. If she were in any real danger, she didn't want to think about how long it would take someone to find her.

With any luck, she would come back around to herself before the sun came up, and nobody—not even the cameras—would know what happened.

THEODORE KANE WATCHED FROM THE TOP-STORY WINDOW of the library as the Sigma hurried along the darkened pathway below, her steps tottering and unsteady. Everyone knew there was a Sigma at the school, but nobody—least of all him—expected her to show her ability. They very rarely did.

He pushed off the window, his legs aching like he had been running for hours as he pulled in a deep breath, sniffing the air. A low, faint growl carried along his indrawn breath, an after-effect of the ferality. He followed her light scent, unable to distinguish what it was just yet. It led him to a clean cubicle tucked into the very corner of the wall. Everything else was covered in dust.

What was she doing here so late at night? The question surprised him. He had enough on his plate to think about. With another shuddering breath, he tucked his busted hands into his pockets and approached the stairwell, noticing a loose piece of paper that had fallen to the ground. He swiped it up, staring at the drawing.

Draw something you wish you had.

The birthday cake had seventeen candles.

A strange little pang of something niggled in the back of his mind, but he pushed it away, folding the paper carefully and tucking it into his pocket to dwell on later.

There were far more pressing issues that needed his attention before the sun came up.

2

THE CHARIOT

One year later ...

"Come *on*, Carter." The other girls whined at her as they ran up the pathway toward Jasmine Field.

Isobel would still be hard-pressed to say she had friends, but a year and a half in, she had at least learnt that people were willing to let her tag along, if only for her last name and to boss her around.

The recreation area was to the north of Dorm D, with a little stream running through it from the main lake. It was separated into four squares by jasmine-choked fences and connected over the stream by adorable little footbridges, electric lanterns attempting to capture every little misdeed the students got up to beneath the weeping willows. The garden oasis was entirely out of place in the desert, and she tried not to think about how much water they piped in to keep the foreign plants so lush, green, and happy.

Some of the Betas had organised a party for Bellamy, whose father had just landed a new movie role. It took a few months for Isobel to connect the dots, that Adam Bellamy was *that* Bellamy. The son of her father's greatest rival. Both of them were Icons, with Bellamy's father graduating the year after her father.

It explained his little trick on her in the first year, and she had steered well clear of him ever since. Not that it stopped him staring and smirking whenever he caught sight of her, despite her best efforts.

The group of Omega girls she trailed branched off as soon as they spilled past the jasmine fence, some of them going into the left square and some into the right. Isobel faltered for a moment before following Eve Indie, who seemed the nicest of the group. Almost like a friend.

Eve smiled when Isobel sidled up to her. "Here, drink this!" She passed Isobel a paper cup, and Isobel took it without a fight, tipping it to her lips as the girls migrated to a cluster of wooden benches, huddling around a Delta with a guitar. Pomegranate burst over her tongue, the cocktail lacking alcohol, which she was grateful for. It wasn't allowed on grounds, but that didn't mean it wasn't often snuck into the drinks that lined the tables at these sorts of parties.

"Cheers to whoever gets the prizes this month," Eve said, tipping her cup toward Isobel's.

Eve was a tall girl, her slender form always looking fashionable in anything she wore. Her hazel hair hung loose about her shoulders, her bright blue eyes peaceful as she hummed along to the song.

The classes at Ironside centred exclusively around the arts. The government was only interested in producing Icons who would contribute to the global economy by boosting their cultural sectors. That was why they accepted Gifted refugees without complaint, unlike the other countries, who had very strict border rules.

Isobel settled in against the fence, her head cushioned by the thick, fragrant vines as she listened to the Delta strum away, several of the surrounding people joining in his song. It was about a boy who had lost his mate and how the mate-bond haunted his sleep every night, reaching for someone who would never reach back.

Mates were rare—usually only occurring in the Gifted with the strongest abilities. It was more common for people to go their entire lives without ever finding out they had a mate, especially since the conditions for finding their mate were deadly.

Quite literally.

One had to be right beside their mate and reach the brink of death before the bond was revealed. Some believed the bond was formed by the near-death, while others believed it was all the machinations of fate. Fate brought people together, and fate put them in danger at exactly the right moment.

Isobel's parents had a complete mate-bond, but they never spoke about how it happened. For some people, the stories were extremely private.

Somewhere nearby, a fight broke out, and everyone glanced over, asking who it was. Apparently, it wasn't anyone worth their attention, because they quickly resumed their easy conversations, even when there was a loud crash.

When Bellamy walked into their circle, flanked by two other Betas, Isobel slipped backwards off the bench and lost herself in the crowd, letting the bustle of students pull her to the other end of Jasmine Field. She was almost clear when a hand suddenly landed on her shoulder, spinning her around.

"You weren't going to congratulate me?" a smooth, easy-going voice asked.

She knew who it was before she even turned, so it was easier to stick the polite smile on her face and keep it in place as she looked up at Bellamy. He was smiling back at her, flashing those straight white teeth, one hand wrapped around a paper cup.

She could smell the pomegranate, but she could also smell the alcohol in his cup.

She tried to shrug his hand off, but he held tight.

"Congratulations," she said, hoping he would release her once he got what he wanted.

Instead, he dragged her closer. She could see the pores along his straight nose and smell his tangy deodorant trying to hold back the stickier smell of his sweat. He was usually doing some kind of sport, swimming or running in the afternoons, so he usually smelled a little sweaty. His chest almost brushed hers, so she hunched her shoulders in, making herself smaller. She heard the echo of something tickle her mind before his voice suddenly burst into her head.

You look good tonight.

Her eyes widened and he noted her reaction, his smile stretching, his light green eyes narrowing in victory. He leaned down, his breath against her ear. "I've been practising. Are you impressed?"

"Y-you're not allowed to—" she spluttered, but he cut her off, raising a finger to hover over her mouth. She was glad he didn't actually touch her.

There was somewhat of an unspoken rule at Ironside. Some students actively practised their abilities, trying to hone them ... and the rest of the students didn't say anything about it. So far, the Ironside officials hadn't interfered—or tasked any of the professors with interfering. They were all walking a fine line, thinking their fan clubs on the outside gave them some sort of immunity.

They couldn't just *disappear* from the show, could they? Popularity lent a strange kind of security in that sense.

She immediately yanked herself out of his grip.

"Hey now, no need to overreact." His smile was charming for the cameras. "We're allowed to have a friendly moment. You won't get in trouble."

There are a few Betas who wouldn't mind having a friendly moment with you, if you ever want to stop slumming it with the Omegas. We could use a Sigma in the dorms to pick up after us and make us feel good.

"Get out," she demanded, holding her hands over her ears.

He chuckled, directing his attention to the nearest camera.

"She's shy," he said with a charming wink for his viewers before brushing right by her to rejoin the activity.

Another set of hands landed over her shoulders before her breath had even returned to normal. The boy—who she thought she recognised as one of Bellamy's friends—spun her around.

"Oh, are we leaving already?" he asked, the expression on his face one of a casual friend. Except she had never spoken to him before in her life. She barely even categorised his features, since she was edging closer and closer to panic.

She tried to squirm out of his grip, but he only tucked her under one of his long, heavy arms and began to steer her away. He smelled worse than Bellamy, like burning clay, sweat and vodka.

"Make a scene and you'll regret it," he whispered, a chemical stench on his breath. "You don't know what I'm capable of, and I doubt your daddy wants *this* to be your next viral video. Word is, he hasn't even come to visit you yet. Is he still mad at you for jumping into the lake last year? It was a pretty desperate grab for views."

She twisted just enough to try and catch sight of anyone she knew, anyone who might actually respond if she shouted out to them, but there was no one, so she let him steer her to the back of Dorm D, where he promptly pushed her up against the wall.

It was a common misconception that Sigmas would do anything asked of them, which was why people often acted like they had no power at all, because if a Sigma could help someone lift the dark and heavy thoughts that weighed their family, friends and peers down, then surely they would? They wouldn't be able to help themselves, right?

Well ... people were wrong.

"Kiss me," the boy demanded, planting his hands either side of her head and ducking down, his lips trying to push against hers.

He didn't even wait for a response, he just assumed she would.

She twisted, ducking from beneath his arms, but he grabbed her and pinned her again. "Kiss me, Sigma." This time, it was less of a suggestion.

If he had been an Alpha, he could have used Alpha voice.

He could have made her.

For a horribly weak moment, she considered obeying just to get it over and done with. In her experience, it was easier to go along with what people wanted. The torment didn't last as long as when she fought against it ... but this was a different kind of torment.

This was her first kiss.

Isobel let her body drop straight down, grabbing two rough handfuls of dirt as he captured her and dragged her upright again, but when he came for her this time, she mashed both handfuls of dirt into his face, making sure to focus on his eyes. He shoved her away and she cracked her head against the wall, feeling the sharp stab of pain as she caught herself upright and bolted away. Being small and slight was a distinct advantage, as she easily slipped through the students still enjoying their party.

Her dorm was too far, so she ran to the library instead, sequestering herself away in the familiar little corner where nobody ever bothered her. She laid her throbbing head on her arms and closed her eyes ... but still, she didn't cry.

Not now.

Not ever.

THEODORE FELT A PUNCH AGAINST HIS ARM.

"What the hell is wrong with you?" Moses demanded, slitting a look to him as people scattered out of their path.

"Nothing," he lied, shaking his head to dislodge the image of a familiar girl running toward the library.

He rarely saw her around, but he had been thinking about her today because it was Mikki's birthday. Which meant ... it was also *her* birthday. The girl who had drawn seventeen candles. He could never forget what had happened on this exact day a year ago, after he went feral, ruined Mikki's birthday, and forced everyone to cover up his mess before the production crew discovered it.

He couldn't forget her, either. The little Sigma who took it all away without a second thought. He *should* have forgotten her, especially after he had forced Kilian to stalk her for a good week to make sure she didn't tell anyone what she had seen. Just so that he could put her from his mind.

"Head in the game, Theo." This had come from Niko, who slung a muscled arm around Theodore's shoulders, shaking him. "It isn't every day Moses agrees to show his face outside of Dorm A. Let's make the most of it."

"Right." Theodore tried to focus, but his eyes kept drifting back to the library. *Was that blood on her face? Don't do it, Theo. Don't—* "Actually ... just give me a sec, okay? I'll meet you guys there."

"I'll come." Moses immediately moved to follow

him, but Theodore pushed him back playfully.

The other boy had features similar to him, but not similar enough to make it clear that they were the twins they publicly claimed themselves to be. More like brothers … which was closer to the truth.

"I'll be quick," Theodore promised, trying to ignore the frown that furrowed between Moses' brows.

Niko was right. This was a special occasion, and Moses needed all the support they could manage. He hadn't learned to control his ability anywhere near as well as Theodore had. It caused anxiety to twist in his gut as Theodore jogged toward the library. He should have stayed back. He should be there to make sure everything went smoothly.

He checked the first floor, but when he didn't find her, he skipped the others and went all the way to the top. He hadn't been there in a year but he still remembered where her little hidey-hole was, and he approached it now, finding her slumped over the desk, her face resting on her arm.

She wasn't crying, not like he had been the year before, and he wasn't a Sigma, but the despair was easy to read in the slump of her shoulders.

"We should stop meeting like this," he suggested gently.

Her head jerked up, fists raising like she might

clock him, her pale, elegant fingers covered in dirt. She had light gold eyes, glinting with darker specks in the shitty library lighting, and they were wide with a manic spark of alarm. They were so big they swallowed her whole face and made her seem tiny.

"You're bleeding." He knelt beside her chair, reaching toward her hairline, but she flinched back, cowering in the corner of her cubicle as far away from him as she could get.

Her fists were still up, but they trembled before crossing her chest, latching onto her shoulders in a tight hug. He only waited, hoping that she would remember him, and eventually she seemed to, her hands falling. Her eyes focussed on his, squinting, before dropping over his features.

"Theodore Kane," she muttered, relaxing in her chair a little.

"I never told you my name," he said lightly, trying to reach for her head again. This time, she allowed him, though she still went very stiff, her eyes tight with wariness.

"Everyone knows the famous Kane twins." She tried to lift her gaze to see what he was inspecting.

"Trying to find where the blood is coming from," he muttered.

She turned, pointing to the back of her head.

"Ah." He located the gash, checking it carefully. "It doesn't look too bad. Wait here, I'll grab something from the bathroom."

Isobel sank back in her chair, watching him walk off with no small amount of caution. He had grown, his shoulders filling out, but he still had those wide, innocent eyes she remembered. The dark irises flooded with all sorts of heavy emotions.

When he returned, he had a pile of damp paper towels, and he set them on the desk as he knelt in front of her again. "May I?"

She just blinked at him stupidly. "Why?"

"You know why." His voice dropped, his eyes glinting with the briefest flash of darkness, almost like he was trying to remind her.

For a horrible moment, Isobel actually expected the dark colour to expand again, to swallow his eyes entirely and spill out along his veins. She had almost convinced herself that she had imagined it the first time, no matter how many times the image visited her in her dreams.

When it seemed she wasn't going to push the matter, he picked up one of the paper towels and started to gently clean away the blood on her face. He looked so focussed, his eyes narrowing, his tongue appearing between his teeth. He sniffed lightly, and she knew he was trying to scent her. Alphas all had heightened senses and could read scent the same way some people could read words, but scenting a stranger generally wasn't done. It was almost rude.

"You have ferality," she whispered, just to test him.

His hand froze, his attention slamming back to her eyes. "That's ... how do you even ..." He paused, shaking his head. "Your father is an Alpha. But you shouldn't know that word."

"That was made clear to me."

He stalled at the tone in her voice, before sucking in a short breath, some of his heavy Alpha influence nudging against her skin. "You can't repeat that word, Sigma."

"Isobel."

"Isobel, sorry. You need to keep that word to yourself, just like you kept that night to yourself, do you understand?"

"How do you know I kept that night to myself?" she shot back, showing a remarkable lack of fear, considering he was an Alpha, she was alone, and there were no cameras on that level of the library.

He pulled back, his hand dropping, but when he raised his eyes to hers, they weren't threatening. The grey storm was carefully restrained, his expression guarded.

"Who did this?" He waved the bloodied paper towel, a subtle warning in his tone. It didn't really sound like it was for her.

"I don't want to tell you," she said quietly.

"That makes two of us." He smiled, looking satisfied, switching the used paper towel for a fresh one. "Let's keep our secrets, then."

He had big hands, but they were surprisingly gentle as he finished cleaning the blood from her face. He shifted her hair, tucking it behind her ears, and then he surprised her by taking her hand and cleaning the blood off her arm, where she had been leaning her head when he came in. She knew that Alphas were supposed to be overpowering, their heady magic and influence spilling out of their pores, but it was something different to experience it in person. His touch almost made her dizzy, every brush of his skin making the hair on her arm prickle in response.

He set her hand back on her lap and then folded some of the paper towels, gently pressing them to the back of her head as he sat back on his heels, examining her face. She knew he had grown since last year, but the way he was curved around her really made the difference seem extreme. That was the way with

Alphas. They were always the biggest, the strongest, growing rapidly in their early adult years, around the same time the Sigmas stopped growing at all.

"Cherries," he suddenly blurted, his lips lifting into a small grin. "That's what you smell like."

Isobel chuckled despite herself, his little smile forcing it out of her. "Is that a good thing?"

He stared at her. "I like cherries."

"What do you smell like?" She tried to surreptitiously discern his scent. She didn't have an Alpha nose, but *something* between them had a warm fragrance: rich and musky, it wafting over her sweetly.

"People say I smell like amber," he answered, watching her with a hint of amusement, as though he knew she was trying to scent him despite being a Sigma.

"Does your twin smell the same?"

His expression shuttered, a metal door slamming over the brief glimpse of warmth that had sparked from their conversation. He pulled back instead of answering her, lifting her hand to press it against the paper towels at the back of her head.

"I should go," he said, his attention drifting to the windows. He stuffed his hands into his pockets as he stood, but paused again, those dark eyes pulling back to her. "Happy birthday, Isobel."

"Th-thanks."

She wasn't proud of it, but she followed almost immediately after he left, keeping his shadow in sight until he veered off toward the party. She was acting like he might actually come to her rescue if she was attacked again, even though it was unlikely. She checked the time on her phone as she slipped back into her dorm, noting that it was an hour after midnight.

It was the first time since her mother snuck a birthday cake into her room three years ago that another person had wished her happy birthday, and as much as she tried to disregard it ... it *meant* something to her. She checked out her head in the bathroom after her shower to make sure the wound wasn't still bleeding before she settled in her room, staring at the bad patch-job she had done on the broken window.

With itching fingers, she reached for one of her notebooks, scribbling out a note before tearing it out and scrunching it up, a sound of frustration in her voice. There was no point. With a short growl, she flopped onto her makeshift bed and turned to face the wall, tugging a blanket up around her hips and succumbing to the throbbing headache that tugged her under.

She didn't even notice the light from the hallway

briefly filling her room, or the door that clicked closed again.

Kɪʟɪᴀɴ Gʀᴀʏ ʀᴀɪꜱᴇᴅ ʜɪꜱ ʜᴇᴀᴅ ꜰʀᴏᴍ ʜɪꜱ ᴄᴏɴᴠᴇʀꜱᴀᴛɪᴏɴ ᴡɪᴛʜ a Beta when Theodore re-joined them, but he didn't miss the waif of a girl who darted out from behind Theodore, or the strange scent clinging to his friend. He couldn't put his finger on it right away, but he had enough protective sense to break away from the group and follow it. Follow *her*. The Sigma from last year. There was a tinge of copper trailing behind her. She was injured.

Had Theo ...? No, he had been calm and relaxed when he reappeared. Surprisingly so.

Someone else had hurt the girl.

Kilian trailed her to Dorm O, activating his ability after the inconvenience of the first few brave students who were drunk enough to try and approach him. He was completely invisible as he caught the door that tried to swing closed behind her, and remained so as he waited outside the bathroom for her to finish whatever she was doing. She re-emerged without the copper tang, and he lazily followed her to her room, pressing his ear to the door until he felt certain she had fallen asleep, and then he slipped inside.

Cherries.

It hit him all at once, and he breathed in deeply. He had almost forgotten. After following her for a week the year before to make sure she didn't blab about seeing Theodore going feral, he had gotten acquainted with her rich, tart and almost chocolatey scent, but he didn't bother with her after that, and he was glad for it.

Her existence wasn't a happy one.

It was ironic because he had come from a settlement and she had come from the life of an Icon's only child. And here they were, stripped down to their rank. He had been elevated to luxury, and she had been pushed into misery.

He glanced around at the room he hadn't found reason to enter last year, only to find that it wasn't quite a room. More like a storage closet, though she had tried to make it homier. He frowned, taking in the plastic taped over the broken window panes and the old record albums stuck to the walls. They were faded, busted up and torn, like the music department had tried to throw them out, but there was something beautiful about the way she had arranged them. There was a strange, mismatched curtain pulled to the side of the window, secured at the top by tacks. He figured it was probably different squares of discarded material from another of the school's departments. The stitching was appalling, and that made his lips quirk slightly.

There was only one bookshelf in the room to house all of her belongings, though she had collected a few boxes along the wall for her school things. Very neat little rows of clothes decorated the shelf, folded up as small as she could make them to utilise the limited space.

She didn't even have a bed. She was curled up on a mat of blankets, one of them tugged up toward her hip, her phone face down on the floor beside her.

He knelt down, pulling the blanket up another inch until the bare skin at her hip was covered, and then he leaned over further, gently brushing the long strands of hair out of her face. He remembered thinking the year before that she had nice hair. Some strands were lighter blonde, some darker, until he could barely even tell what colour it was. He could see gold tones mixing with strawberry, the whole mess damp and starting to wave. He found the wound at the back of her head and winced, his brows pinching in. *How did that happen?*

She had a cute face. Cheeks that puffed out a little and long black lashes fanning against skin so pale it should have highlighted every single little imperfection. Her freckles were stark, some darker than others, isolated unlike the spatter across her nose. There was one below her brow, another above it, two below her eye, and another one outside her lip. He dragged his attention from her pillowy strawberry-red lips because that was totally fucking inappropriate considering she didn't even know he was there, and pulled away from her curled form.

She looked like strawberries and cream, but smelled like cherries and chocolate. It was … *wow*. He didn't want to think it, but there it was.

She was a little Sigma dessert.

Still, he didn't quite understand. Why had Theodore snuck off to see her? Kilian was missing something.

He made to leave, but the sound of paper crunching beneath his boot had him pausing. He bent to retrieve the note, moving to the window to read it.

Thank you for remembering my birthday.

Do you want to be friends?

At the bottom of the note was a phone number, but it was crossed out. She had obviously decided not to deliver the note. Kilian pulled out his phone and took a picture before laying the paper back where he had found it and slipping out of the room.

It took all weekend for Isobel to gather up the courage to eat in the dining hall on Monday morning, and it was mostly because she had run out of protein bars. Someone had left a packaged cupcake outside her door the morning after the party, but there was no note with it, and none of the Omegas on her floor remembered seeing anyone leave it there.

It had been a cloud-like vanilla cake with white vanilla bean frosting and a plump, shining strawberry on top, packed into a little white box. She could only assume it was for her birthday, but couldn't think of a single person who would go to that effort for her. There was a faint, trailing scent that seemed infused in the wrapping, making it even more heady and delicious than the cupcake itself, and it wasn't until she was licking crumbs from the paper that she realised what she was doing and tossed it out. She was probably just dying to eat something other than granola.

Bolstered by the decision to face the rest of the world again, she tied up her long blonde hair, tugged on her lucky ripped jeans, and finished the outfit with her favourite T-shirt. She tried to gather as much confidence from her clothing as she could before she shuffled to the hall, grabbing a tray and making a beeline for the breakfast bar.

The food tower in the centre of the room had a different theme every day, but she barely lifted her eyes enough to gather what the theme was as she blindly shoved a few pieces of fruit and an apricot pastry onto her plate and hightailed it to one of the more private tables.

The hall was decorated like they were catering a high-profile wedding every single day, with crystal vases full of fragrant flowers and delicate, ivy-tossed chandeliers. All around the outside of the room were semi-private booths, made cosy with oak panelling and rice-paper screens that could unfold to enclose the space, not that anyone ever did that.

She had arrived early enough to claim one of those booths, and it hid her while she hurried through her breakfast, proving a welcome sanctuary when she was forced to duck back into the hall for coffee. She paused when she slid back in, glancing at her phone as it vibrated on the table. Frowning in confusion, she checked the message that popped up on her screen.

Unknown: I want to be friends.

Her frown deepening, she hesitantly texted back.

Isobel: Who is this?

The reply was instant.

Unknown: Theo.

Theo?

Theodore?

Theodore Kane?!

She scoffed, but then paused. How could this be a prank? Nobody knew about the two times Theodore had spoken to her. She shuffled to the edge of the bench, sticking her head out of the booth like she might find a group of snickering students with their heads bent together over a phone.

Instead, she found herself peering into a booth directly across the room from her, where Theodore Kane sat.

Staring back at her.

Phone in hand.

She jerked back, her heart racing, her fumbling fingers dropping the phone several times before she managed a reply.

Isobel: How did you get my number?

Theodore: What's one more secret between us?

Isobel: Friends don't keep secrets from each other.

Theodore: Don't they?

She lowered the phone, something in her chest pinching. She didn't have any friends. She didn't know. Was he trying to point that out? Her mother was her best friend, and no woman in the world seemed to hold as many secrets inside her, barricaded behind a shaky smile and watery eyes.

Isobel slipped from the booth, intending to get to her first class early, but found three Betas blocking her way. Bellamy, a girl whose name she knew to be Kiki Rayne from her recent popularity on the Ironside website, and ... *him*. The boy from the party. His eyes were still red and a little puffy, a couple of scratches marring the sensitive skin around them.

"Where are you going in such a hurry?" Bellamy asked cutely, scrunching his nose up. "You asked Crowe to take you behind Dorm D and then had some sort of panic attack on him. He was really hurt, you know."

"You shouldn't play games like that for attention," Rayne added, shaking a slender finger in Isobel's face. "You should show some respect to your Betas."

"You can make it up to me right now," Crowe suggested, his smile crooked. Isobel hadn't noticed on Friday night, but he was big. Big enough that a fresh wave of fear rolled over her. He had stringy black hair and large, focussed eyes. He wasn't even blinking. "Let me walk you to class."

"Move it," a rough voice barked, forcing the Betas to skitter away.

Alpha voice.

Everyone within hearing range perked up, craning their necks to see what had upset one of their precious Alphas enough that he had used his inherent ability to command people with his voice alone.

Cold, light grey eyes locked with Isobel's, and she quickly categorised his slender, aristocratic features and the silvery blond hair that drifted across his forehead before she ditched her tray and hurried out of the hall, running away from Elijah Reed the same way she had the first time he placed himself that close to her. She didn't bother wondering why he had moved all the way around to her side of the hall just to ditch his tray and leave, but that's what it had looked like. It was the second time Reed had interfered in her life, after that day in Introduction to Musical Theory during her first year, where he sat beside her on the piano.

The Ironside website said he was a genius. And she had been right, back then. He played the piano beautifully. The few recordings of him that had popped up online hadn't even been him showing off, though—more like taken by sneaky students through the cracked doors to private practise rooms—and she found that confusing. With his talent, he could be an Icon. Wasn't that what everyone wanted? He seemed to avoid the cameras and the other students at all costs, to the extent that he even skipped some of his classes, preferring not to be seen at all. Then again, he was supposed to be a genius, so maybe it was a strategy to generate mystery and make everyone even more interested in him. Maybe it was even working.

Her phone buzzed again as she made it to her first class for the day, and she pulled it out to check the message.

Theodore: Reed hates bullies.

Theodore: There, I've told you a secret, now you tell me one.

She found herself smiling as she drifted to her seat.

Isobel: That was Reed's secret, not yours.

Theodore: Fine. I can't swim.

Isobel: Most Gifted can't swim. They don't have pools at the settlements.

Theodore: Can you swim?

Isobel: Yes. Do you want me to teach you?

Theodore: I don't need you to do anything for me, Sigma.

She frowned, unable to form a reply as Professor Vega walked into the room, calling for the students to take their seats and start working in their assigned groups. Isobel should have dropped the class since none of the other students wanted to sit with her for the group activities, but unlike most of the classes where they could actually learn some useful skills if they wanted to, *Fortune Telling and the Mystic Arts* wasn't likely to teach her—or anyone—anything useful anytime soon, so it wasn't like she was really missing out.

She didn't know why her father had put her in the class, since he still hadn't turned up to any of the monthly family visits since dropping her off on her first day … but she assumed it was strategic. He might have been trying to force her in front of the cameras, and anyone could have guessed that one Alpha in particular would be taking this class, which guaranteed coverage of it.

Speak of the devil.

"Professor?" An arm shot up to question Vega before she gave out assignments for the day, a folded sleeve falling down to reveal hard, streamlined muscles. Everyone fell silent. "Can we separate into pairs today?"

Cian Ashford didn't need a reason. He didn't even need to ask, really. It would have been ridiculous that an Alpha was taking such a stupid class … except that everyone knew his ability was divination. So instead, it was just borderline illegal. Still, there was only so far Ashford could hone his skills by shuffling the same dozen tarot decks and flicking the individual cards into people's chests, hitting them with "truth bombs." Mostly, Isobel assumed they kept him in the class because the viewers found his antics entertaining.

"Of course!" Vega exclaimed, clapping her hands together. "A wonderful idea. You should all have memorised the meanings of the cards by now." *They hadn't.* "So please go ahead and find a partner and do an expanded reading on each other."

Isobel sighed, picking up her desk as everyone else did, moving it from the group cluster it had been in— not that anyone had been sitting with her. She found a private corner of the room and began shuffling one of the decks, surprised when her phone vibrated again.

Theodore: But actually, yes. Teach me how to swim.

Theodore: I meant to say please in there somewhere.

Isobel snorted despite herself.

"Boyfriend?" a voice asked as a desk was dropped opposite hers, a tall body falling into a seat behind it.

Confused, she looked up.

Cian Ashford had a dark brow arched, his eyes flicking between the phone she was trying to hide and her face. "Is that your boyfriend?" he pressed. "I can ask the cards if he loves you."

Isobel cast a quick glance past him, taking in the rest of the class, who were all staring and not even trying to be subtle about it.

"N-no." She slid her phone away, twisting her fingers together in her lap. She really wanted to ask *what do you think you're doing*, but instead, she managed to say, "I don't think you want to be my partner. I'm really bad at this."

"Ah." He clucked his tongue. "But I've done a reading for everyone else in the class, you want to be left out?"

She felt a pinch of something from him, something like annoyance. Thankfully, she was used to having an Alpha around, so she wasn't thrown off by the increased strength of their emotions ... but she wasn't exactly used to having so *many* of them around. The other ranks couldn't slip their negative emotions past her barrier unless she consciously chose to open herself to them, but the Alphas were stronger, and she always felt their heavy emotions knocking up against her walls.

Ashford lazed back in his chair, waiting for her response, his lips in a neutral position despite the emotion she had felt from him.

"Okay." She slid the deck across the desk to him. "Whatever you want."

He didn't deal the cards straight away, choosing instead to remain leaning back, his head tilted to the side. He didn't look her age, but it was always hard to tell with Alphas. Still, he could have easily passed for someone older. He was taller than Theodore, his dark blond hair just long enough that he could have secured it behind his head, but he left it loose, constantly tucking it behind his ears with tattooed hands.

He wasn't the only eighteen-year-old in the entire academy with tattoos, but they were too random to be ... well, random. There were ten of them, and they were small, the subtle symbols decorating spaces just above his knuckles. They were all in the same style, thinly-drawn and minimalist. She spotted a sun, a skull, a wave, a lightning bolt, a sprouting plant, a mask, a set of wings, an hourglass, a crescent moon, and some sort of harp-like instrument—that one was on the pinkie of his hand turned slightly away from her, so it was difficult to make out.

Isobel tried not to stare at him, but it was difficult. He was *very* handsome. She had seen all the posts about Ashford, clicked on all the freeze-framed images of his face, with eyes a stunning aquamarine so clear they hardly seemed real, golden skin and pretty pink lips that were almost always drawing the eye. He was doing it right now, his white teeth peeking out to catch his lower lip, giving her a look like he was trying to figure her out as he absently shuffled the cards. He could have passed as one of the fifth-years getting ready to graduate.

"Are you checking me out, Sigma?" he asked, lowering his voice to a soft purr.

His voice was almost an ability in itself, but not in the way of Alpha voice. This was different. His timbre had reached right into her throat, tickling its way down her stomach until it had something low in her belly in its fist.

And then it squeezed.

"I don't think I've ever done that," Isobel whispered. *To anyone.*

Suddenly, he smacked the deck down, making her jump. He picked up the top card, covering it before she —or anyone peeking over his shoulder at them— could catch sight of it.

"Just as I suspected," he drawled, slipping the card into his pocket. "It says to keep your distance, Sigma. Stay in your lane, you understand?"

I understand you're a bit of a dick.

He smiled after that, the slightly crooked grin that made her classmates swoon. Isobel frowned, reaching for the deck and going through the motions of her own reading, which he sat for patiently, though the look in his eyes wasn't quite friendly, and that annoyed thump of his emotion against her only increased.

When it was time to go, he lifted gracefully from his chair, stretching his arms above his head, making his shirt lift enough to have one of the girls smacking into a desk when she got distracted by the few inches of tight golden skin on display between the raised hem of his shirt and the waistband of his pants.

"Remember what I said." Ashford levelled a finger at her before smoothly dropping his arm over the clumsy girl and lowering his head to whisper something teasing into her ear. She giggled, her ears turning red as he steered her from the room.

He didn't have the confidence of an eighteen-year-old, either.

Isobel waited until everyone had left before she gathered the deck again, comparing the remaining cards to the guide Vega had handed them until she narrowed down the one Ashford had taken with him.

The Chariot.

She traced the description of the card in Vega's guide, her mouth pitching further and further into a frown.

Should you prepare for an adventure or a battle?

The figure in the chariot sits beneath a celestial canopy, carrying a crescent moon on their shoulder. They are guided by their own intuition, which can serve them well. There is a crown on their head, showing that they are both enlightened and pure of will, the earth element on their chest grounding them and their actions.

But the figure is only a passenger, and they could be pulled in many different directions. Note that there is a sphinx of light pulling their carriage but also a sphinx of darkness.

Isobel stood up, shaking her head. The entire card-reading had just been made-up drama for the cameras. It seemed some of the Alphas were here to win, after all.

3

SPLIT CHERRIES

She didn't text Theodore for the rest of the day. She tried to make herself invisible as she endured the rest of her classes and the two solo practice sessions she had booked that afternoon—one in a piano room, the other in a dance practice room. She had learned that if she booked them herself, whichever of her parents was booking them for her would stop. Unless she tried to take an afternoon off, and then there would be double the practice time the next day.

After dance practice, she dragged herself through a quick shower and changed into comfortable tights and a sweatshirt, leaving her hair loose to dry. She slipped into the dining hall to make a quick sandwich, having missed the dinner service, and then she sequestered herself into her corner of the library.

Only then did she bring out her phone again.

She was behind a wall of books that she had carried up from the lower level, most of which she had already scoured for information. She didn't find anything because she didn't actually know what she was looking for.

The Alphas she had encountered at Ironside weren't like what she expected. They acted nothing like her father, and that confused her thoroughly. She had come across a few interesting texts, which she hoped to explore further, but mostly it seemed that the subjects covered within the shelves were focussed on arts and culture—and the history of the great people who shaped many of the cultural industries around the world.

Most of the books on the Gifted people that she had managed to hunt down were actually on the top level of the library, stacked without categorisation on the dusty, forgotten shelves. After procrastinating for so long that her eyes began to droop, she finally shook herself awake and replied to Theodore's message.

Isobel: Okay, I'll teach you. When?

His reply came quickly.

Theodore: What are you doing right now?

Isobel: Studying.

He didn't respond after that, so she set her phone

aside, dragging one of the books back into her lap. It mostly covered the Alpha growth cycle, but it was still interesting to read. Having grown up watching Ironside, she had always been fascinated by how she could never correctly guess the ages of the Alphas.

She was shocked when Theodore's face popped over the top of her cubicle, causing her to drop her book with a heavy thud. She managed to jerk her foot away just in time.

"How about now?" he asked, those wide, stormy eyes peering down at her as he ducked to retrieve the book, placing it on her desk.

"Oh ... okay." She quickly gathered her things, acting more on instinct than anything. "Are you sure? It's late."

"The fitness centre doesn't close," he told her, like she didn't already know. He reached for her bag, wiggling his fingers at her until she hesitantly handed it over. He immediately slung it over his shoulder, striding for the stairs.

His walk was long-limbed and leisurely, a vision of strong, confident lines and light, airy movement. It was oddly graceful, but she couldn't put her finger on exactly how or why.

"That's not really what I meant." She frowned, quickly tucking the books she had sourced up along the back of the desk before following him. "I mean … are you sure you want to be seen with me?"

He cast her a sideways look, that happy curve to his mouth falling away. "Because you're a Sigma?"

She nodded, and he stopped suddenly, his arm blocking her path, his hand curving around the stair railing. "Do you even know what your own kind are capable of?" he asked, his voice almost a whisper.

Isobel flicked her attention to the bottom of the stairwell, where a camera waited to catch them. He had stopped her progress just before they would be seen. He was so close to her, but he seemed miles away from the boy she had found in her first year, huddled up and black-eyed, tears flowing freely.

He was bigger, more confident, his stormy grey eyes clear and focussed. He had lovely eyelashes, as coal-black as his hair, which was wavy and messy, the style young and fashionable, the sides so short they were almost shaved, the strands longer on top, mostly falling messily around his face. He had a very angular face, eyes that tilted up at the sides, and a few little scars that she could see, little nicks spread over his skin. His lips were on the thin side, light pink, hiding the most perfect smile she had ever seen. She was fairly sure he even had dimples, but she couldn't stop staring at his perfectly straight teeth whenever he smiled, so she wasn't sure.

"We can help people," she allowed, matching his quiet tone. "We can take away their bad emotions and feelings."

He waited, and when she didn't say any more, he sighed, backing off. "You don't think that's valuable?" he questioned as they continued down the stairs. "You don't think that's worth as much as a Beta like Bellamy, who can talk inside people's heads?"

"He wouldn't like the comparison," she answered.

Theodore didn't respond immediately because there were still some people lingering inside the lower levels of the library. They passed two Delta girls in the stairwell, and the frenzied whispering shadowed them all the way to the ground floor.

"What's your ability?" Isobel asked boldly, as soon as they stepped foot outside. She wanted to take the question back immediately. *Ferality* was an ability, and Alphas could only ever have one ability, outside of their generic Alpha talents.

"I only have the Alpha voice." He didn't even skip a beat. "And the Alpha senses." He shot her a grin. "We can't all be lucky."

"Even that is impressive," she said quietly, still

kicking herself internally. "Betas are very proud when one of their abilities is like an Alpha sense. The improved hearing, or the sense of smell, or taste, or sight. You have all of them. Plus, you're bigger, stronger."

"Ah, stop it." He grinned, his cheeks growing a little red.

She stared at him as they walked, utterly fascinated. The Alpha was *shy*. And kind of cute, the way he widened his eyes all innocently. He was making her think that she really didn't know anything at all ... except the Betas, Deltas, and Omegas she had interacted with so far had all been quite predictable.

Maybe he was different.

"Do you think most Alphas are like you?" she asked. "I didn't spend much time in the settlements, so ..."

He bit back his answer as they passed a group of students by the lake. They all stopped their chattering and immediately turned to stare.

One of them even whispered: "Who the hell is that? Did anyone see her eyes? Was she a Beta? Did anyone recognise her?"

When the path was clear again, he spoke up.

"I think all Alphas are different. Just like all the other ranks are different. I bet there are some bossy Sigmas tucked away somewhere."

Isobel giggled, and his whole face lit up, but he quickly ducked it down, his dark hair slipping forward to shield his eyes.

"I've only met one other Sigma in person," she said. "My mother." And then she quickly changed the subject, glancing up at the nearest camera and deciding her family wasn't a topic for the Ironside show. "Which settlement did you come fr—"

"Here we are!" he suddenly declared, striding forward to hold open the door to the fitness centre for her.

She had no idea if he had intended to dodge the question or if he was just really excited for his swimming lesson, but she decided to let it drop in either case. The fitness centre was really more like one of the luxury spas her mother had taken her to in the city. There were exercise rooms, of course, but there were also steam rooms, saunas, plunge pools and an indoor and outdoor saltwater pool. There was also a connected building for people who wanted to train in dance, acrobatics, or any physical art form that couldn't be classified as "offensive."

They stopped by the shop first and gave the Omega attendant their sizes for swimwear. She didn't look away from Theodore once, even while Isobel muttered her size.

"I'll be right back," the attendant said, touching Theodore's arm. He slid it back from the counter, but she hardly seemed deterred.

Alphas were considered a catch in the settlements, but within Ironside, the Gifted took it to a whole new level, because if they were a student, then there was a chance they would one day be an Icon. That was a guaranteed ticket to a better life, and only one thing could possibly ruin it.

A mate-bond.

"That must be annoying," Isobel whispered lowly.

It was maybe a little too low, because Theodore had to bend close to hear her. When he realised what she said, he snorted.

"You have no idea."

"Want to wait by the bathrooms?" she offered. "I can bring the swimsuits."

His eyes widened, giving him that innocent look again. He was the kind of boy who wore his emotions on his face for everyone to read. That didn't seem like a very good attribute for an Alpha. At least not with how her father lectured her on how Alphas were required to act.

"Actually ... yeah." He smiled, and she forgot all about how he should and shouldn't be acting, because his smile was *seriously* beautiful. It was actually one of the best smiles she had ever seen, and that included her mother's.

Her mother always tried to smile with kindness, but no amount of empathy could hide a pain as long-standing as hers. Theodore seemed less ... tainted. His smiles were pure. And purity was such a rare thing in their world. It made her itch to know who his family was. Who had raised and protected this boy so well?

"Isobel?" He touched her arm. "Are you sure?"

"Sorry." She laughed awkwardly. "Yes, I'm sure! I'll meet you there."

He smiled at her gratefully and then disappeared with only a few seconds to spare, as the Omega attendant returned. She placed two folded towels and a set of swimsuits on the counter, glancing around like she couldn't even see Isobel standing right there.

"Ah, thanks." Isobel reached for the pile, feeling a little awkward that there was no exchange of money.

Everything was free at Ironside. Humiliation included.

"Were you here with Kane?" the attendant asked, scratching her head in confusion.

"Yep." Isobel gathered everything into her arms and tried to leave, but the other girl suddenly shot a hand out over the bench, her eyes narrowing on Isobel's face.

"It's you," she said.

"It's me," Isobel answered, without inflection.

"The Sigma," the attendant insisted.

"The Sigma," Isobel confirmed calmly.

"With *Theodore Kane*."

"He needed someone to teach him how to swim," Isobel offered, hoping the reason would make the whole situation easier for the Omega to swallow.

She really wanted her arm back, because the other girl's nails were beginning to dig in.

"The academy offers swimming lessons," the girl insisted, her nails digging in even further.

Growing tired of the conversation, Isobel ripped her arm away. She didn't need to look down to know that the attendant's nails had drawn blood.

"Thanks for your help," she said, hurrying out of the shop.

The hallways were misted with steam from the indoor pool, making her squint a little as she stopped outside the bathrooms. Theodore was still, his nostrils flaring as his eyes raked over her. His attention snagged on her arm and stayed, his eyes narrowing.

"Here." She thrust out his swimsuit and towel, pushing it against his chest.

He took it wordlessly, still staring at her arm.

"You wanted to be friends?" she asked him, trying

to ignore the battering of his anger against her walls.

He nodded once, short and sharp, the rest of him still eerily frozen.

"Then get used to it," she suggested, brushing past him to enter the female bathrooms.

The second she was inside, all the bravado dropped straight out of her, and she set her things down on the counter with shaking hands, twisting her arm to see the scratches. They weren't serious, but they stung enough to be a reminder to her.

Keep your distance, Sigma. Stay in your lane, you understand?

Ashford's voice swam back to her, but it was soon drowned out by a more insistent, more familiar voice.

That of her father.

A Sigma is not to be seen or heard. They are only to be felt. It is your privilege to be of service to the other Gifted ranks. If you cannot even do that, your best hope is that the burden of your existence goes unnoticed.

"Carter?" Someone stepped into view from the direction of the shower cubicles, their voice soft and concerned. *Eve Indie.*

"Eve. Hi." Isobel hated that her voice shook, and she quickly busied herself with turning on the taps to run her arm beneath the stream of water. "Were you swimming?"

"No." Eve laughed, but she still sounded concerned. "I can't swim. I was at the gym. Are you okay? What happened to your arm?"

"Nothing." Isobel smiled, trying to reassure her. When it didn't seem to work, she opened herself up just a little, syphoning off the other girl's worry.

Eve froze, her dark brows jumping up, her lips parting in surprise. "Wow, so it's true." She immediately schooled her face, looking embarrassed. "Oh my god, I'm so sorry, I can't believe I said that. Of course it's true. I'm not one of those people who think the Sigmas don't have any power. Me and my parents, we're always telling people it's true, I swear."

Isobel was a little shocked herself. "It's fine. I shouldn't have done it without your permission. I can't help myself sometimes. My mom says I need to hold back more."

"Your mom is a Sigma too, right?"

"Yeah." Isobel pulled her arm from the water, drying it off.

"Oh, here." Eve propped her gym bag onto the counter, rummaging inside for a couple of Band-Aids, which she handed over. "I'm always getting blisters," she explained. "Shoes don't like my feet, it's a fact."

Isobel laughed softly, feeling her smile pull at the sides of her mouth. She had naturally puffy cheeks and a narrow mouth. When she smiled, she always felt it pushing at her cheeks. "Thank you."

"You know you can come and talk to me if you need to, right?" Eve asked gently. "I know plenty of places other than the bathrooms where they haven't put cameras. Just saying." She shrugged lightly before exiting the bathroom, leaving Isobel feeling torn.

Could she really have discovered the potential of two real friends all in one day? It seemed impossible. She covered the scratches on her arms and quickly changed into the swimsuit, stepping out of the change stall to check her appearance in the mirror.

Someone like her was usually invisible, but anyone who stood next to an Alpha was guaranteed to feature in the next episode. She wasn't sure how she felt about the entire world seeing her in a swimsuit, but it wasn't too revealing. A plain black one-piece. Still, she wrapped her towel around herself, unsure about the pale line of her legs and the barest swell of cleavage pushed up by the tight suit. She hung her bag inside one of the lockers and walked back out to the hallway.

Theodore was already waiting for her, leaning up against the glass wall of the indoor pool, his arms folded over his bare chest. He hadn't huddled himself into a towel as she had, but that wasn't the detail that really struck her.

There wasn't a single ounce of fat on his body. Only honeyed skin wrapped tightly over muscle. She could see ridges where his ribs should have been. She could see little muscles under his arms. She could see the beginnings of a defined V leading down to the plain black swim shorts she had given him.

"What the hell are they feeding you?" she blurted, blinking at him.

He snorted again, but this time it turned into a laugh. Bright and sunny, as beautiful as his smile. He brushed his fingers down his stomach, obviously knowing exactly what she was talking about. "God," he laughed. "You should see Sato's abs. You never will, though. It would break the internet. Which pool are we going to?"

Isobel dragged her eyes away from his bare torso, her face flaming. "I don't mind," she muttered to the ground, like she was searching for a hole to crawl into and die.

"Are you okay with the cold?" he asked, motioning to the door outside. "It's too quiet in here."

And less private.

"Not at all." Isobel hurried to lead the way, happy that the cameras outside at least wouldn't be able to hear her humiliating herself, though it would be a pretty safe guess if all the viewers just assumed it was happening anyway.

They both approached the steps leading into the pool, and Theodore tossed his towel onto one of the sunloungers that were usually populated by the senior students during the day. He already had the body of a swimmer, which made Isobel clutch her towel even tighter, because she didn't. She was pale and small, but she wasn't skin and bones, either. She danced a lot and she ate a lot. She wasn't chubby and she wasn't thin; she was just ... normal. Healthy, maybe. When she finally unwound her towel, throwing it beside Theodore's, she couldn't help but look down and take note of her gentle, subtle curves, so unlike his body.

If she had been serious about trying to win the Ironside show, those natural curves would have to go. The female champions were nothing short of perfect, with perfect bodies. Some of them even arranged "sick leave" from academy grounds to get surgery done, and nothing was off limits when it came to imperfections.

Arms. Necks. Ears. Fingers. Ankles. Skin pigment.

There was no argument that their fans loved them the way they were and would support them no matter what they looked like ... because their fans were the ones sponsoring the surgeries through crowdfunding campaigns.

She glanced up at Theodore, finding his eyes waiting to catch hers. He had already taken a step into the water and was closer to her height. He was near enough that she could see the way his pupils had expanded, even with the dimmed outdoor lighting.

"Your smell gets stronger when you have more uncovered skin," he said lowly. "I can smell cherry wood, crushed leaves, split cherries ..."

Isobel didn't even have a chance to think of a cool reply. She was too busy choking on her own saliva. He laughed at her, holding out a hand to encourage her to step down into the water beside him.

"What's first?" he asked, surveying the rippling surface as she quickly placed her hand in his and stepped into the water.

The wind was picking up, teasing against the surface of the water and causing the hair on her body to stand on end. Theodore dropped her hand as she stepped further in, shivering at the temperature.

"You can come in further," she suggested. "You'll be able to stand just fine."

She barely remembered her own swimming lessons. Only that her father had insisted on them and that her mother had been terrified, trying to learn alongside her.

Theodore stepped down to the base of the pool

without an ounce of fear, but he was holding his hands up above the water for some reason, like he was ready to grab onto the side of the pool if something happened. She was glad he had reached for her hand earlier, because it made offering hers to him a little easier.

"Have you tried to swim at all?" she asked.

He slapped his hand into hers and she pulled it down, dipping it beneath the water, moving just a few steps further in, drawing him behind her.

"My first day," he admitted, biting back a smile. "It was the first thing I wanted to do. I walked through the water just like this, but I didn't know what to do when it got to my neck." His smile escaped, his hand twitching in hers. "I googled it, obviously, but I didn't want to look like a fucking idiot in front of the cameras."

She was pretty sure the cameras couldn't hear what they were saying, but he didn't even *try* to lower his voice. She couldn't help but wonder what it must be like to have that much unfailing confidence.

"Hey." He tugged on her hand and she stopped moving deeper into the water, turning to glance at him. "Sorry about before. The whole scenting you thing. I can't help it sometimes."

She cracked a grin. "It was weird, not gonna lie."

He groaned, looking up at the sky. "It's just that ... well, you know everyone has a scent signature, but most of them are harsh and they hurt my nose. Yours can be a little bitter—I smelled bitter cherries when you came to give me my swimsuit—but most of the time it's sweet. It's a nice break from everyone else."

She felt her grin collapsing, melting into a frown. "Yeah, I know. My father ..." She dropped her tone, unable to help the instinctual whisper that took hold of her words. "He has a sensitive nose. He doesn't like when I'm upset. He says it smells sour."

"Maybe a little sour," Theodore agreed thoughtfully, though he was wearing a frown to match her own. "But still edible." Almost as soon as he said it, he seemed to regret it, his hand going stiff in hers, his face struck emotionless for a moment, until it melted into another of his easy smiles. "I meant because you still smell like food—just more like sour food."

"Thanks," she managed, taking on the embarrassment he had managed to shed. "Do you want to try and float now?"

"Can I do it without looking like a cat trying not to drown?" he asked with a sigh. "I've seen all the videos of people trying to swim when they get here. I might have grown up with other Alphas—so you'd think I'd be used to being shown up—but I actually have a hard time not being amazing at things on my first try."

A snort escaped her lips before she could stop it, and he quirked a dark brow at her, though there was still a smile hovering around his mouth.

"Sorry." She tried to contain the laugh. "That must be hard for you."

"Let's make a deal." His eyes narrowed on hers, his tone suddenly serious. "You don't apologise to me unless you've lied to me, okay?"

"Why would I lie to you?"

"Self-preservation." He shrugged. "I'm not an idiot. I know how this world works, but I also meant what I said this morning. I want to be friends."

Sigmas aren't friends with Alphas, her mother had told her once, after she asked why her father seemed to hate her. *Sigmas only ever mate with Alphas, and even then, it's rare.*

"Why do you want to be friends?" she asked, dropping his hand now that the seriousness of his voice had wrapped around her. The night seemed to grow colder, her skin peppered with gooseflesh, her teeth gritted against the chill.

He considered her, his head tipping a little to the side, his dark grey eyes shifting into a stormy haze, like ominous clouds rolling over an overcast skyline. It gave him a strangely menacing presence, no matter how hard she focussed on his perfect lips, imagining the way his smile tended to stretch wide and innocent.

"Honestly?" His voice was low. "I don't know if it's you or your ability, but I'm jealous. I figure there's something I can learn from you, and maybe there's something you can learn from me, too."

"Like what?" She shivered, glancing toward the immaculate towering hedges that ringed the pool area. She was a little disappointed, but of course this beautiful boy wanted something from her. *Of course there was a reason.*

"How to stand up for yourself, for starters." He stepped forward, his expression analytical like he was observing her the way a scientist might observe an animal they were experimenting on. "Like right now. Why don't you say what you really want to say?"

She considered brushing past him and climbing out of the pool. Running back to the dorm. Deleting his number. Finishing up her stint at Ironside as barely more than a clerical error on their enrolment records.

"Come on." His hand brushed against her thigh under the water. She wasn't sure if it was accidental or not. His face had become unreadable, those stormy eyes boring into hers.

"I don't want to stand up for myself," she blurted,

the words expelled from her chest on a shaky exhale. "I know my place."

"And where is your place?" he asked immediately. "Below us all? A Sigma slave? A sponge for all the shitty things we think and feel?"

"Yes." Her smile was tight. "Exactly."

"That's fucked up, Izzy."

"I hate that name."

He grinned, his eyes flashing. "Good. What else do you hate?"

"Shouting."

"And?" He was creeping closer, his eyes on her mouth, his touch hovering over her thigh again. With anyone else, it might have been sexual or intimidating. With Theodore, it was magnetising. He was a perfect Alpha specimen—tall, dark, *ripped*, and handsome. A smile to block out the sun and sky. A power so vast and terrifying it was quite literally classified as a national threat. And he was channelling all that power and magnetism at *her*. Surrounding her with it, giving her his undivided attention, and allowing his presence to draw out the exact words and reactions from her he wanted, without needing to explain why he wanted them.

"Alphas," she whispered.

"Ah." His smile broke free. "And?"

"Betas," she continued. "And Deltas and Omegas. And *humans*." The last word was barely more than a breath, but he was staring at her lips so hard he definitely would have known what she had said.

"And?" he whispered.

"Myself." She was shocked at the word that escaped, her eyes widening on his.

"And there it is," he breathed out quietly. "That's why me and you will be friends. Because underneath the yards of nonsense that puts you down one end of the ladder and me up at the other end ... we both still just straight up despise ourselves."

It was like she had pushed past some kind of barrier, seeing past the Alpha persona he wore to the wounded, devastated boy she had found on the top floor of the library in their first year. Whatever had made him cry that day still affected him. It was a soul-deep wound, and it made sense to her, in a strange kind of way.

She was wounded, too.

"Illy," she said, swallowing against the emotion butting up against her chest. It was the only nickname anyone had given her. "My mama ... It's ..." She closed her eyes for a moment, allowing that crack in her chest to widen, to suck in his pain so she wouldn't have to deal with her own. "You can call me Illy."

4
THE UNDERDOG CLICHÉ

"I'T'S GETTING LATE." ISOBEL WADED THROUGH THE WATER to the pool's edge, stepping out and hastily wrapping herself in a towel.

"Sure," Theodore replied, sounding like he *knew*. He knew she was freaking out over giving him her nickname and was embarrassed about freaking out over something so small to top it off. His smile and his voice were light and soothing, but his eyes were heavy as they met hers. "We can continue the lesson another time, if you're still up for it."

She nodded, hoping he could still hear her even though she lowered her voice enough that it wouldn't carry to any of the cameras now that she was moving toward the door leading back into the fitness centre.

"That would be nice. Night, Kane."

"Theo," he corrected her, a large hand skimming over the surface of the cold water. "Only the producers call me Kane."

Isobel snorted. "Everyone calls you Kane."

"Except anyone who matters. Goodnight, Illy."

She nodded slightly and pushed through the door, catching sight of the clock on the wall. 2:00 a.m. She had to be up in three hours for dance practice. After a hasty shower, she got dressed again and hightailed it back to the dorm, tucking her head down at the sight of Ironside doused in darkness and solitude, even though it was something she might have paused to admire at any other time.

She unlocked the front door of Dorm O and skipped up the stairs two at a time, skidding to a stop in her open doorway. The door was shoved wide, the light from the hallway spilling in to illuminate the mess within, and a single form crouched in the middle of it.

"Eve?" Isobel asked, swallowing down the tremble in her voice. "What happened?"

Her room was wrecked. The record covers she had salvaged from the pile of items left outside the music department for trash pickup were in tatters, the records they had housed snapped into halves. Her makeshift curtains were torn apart at the very messy seams she had laboriously stitched by hand.

She had salvaged trash, trying to make something beautiful from the discarded items, but someone had taken it upon themselves to reverse her efforts, relegating it all to a brand-new trash pile in the middle of her room.

Her personal belongings had been pulled from the shelves and were in broken fragments or tattered pieces. Her clothes had been cut up, her shower bag emptied, the bottles of toiletries squeezed out onto her makeshift bed.

"I'm sorry, Isobel." Eve had tears in her blue eyes, making them look like big oceans of sorrow. "I tried to stop them, but it was me against a whole group of fourth-years."

"Fourth-years," Isobel echoed, trying to piece together what she had done to deserve this particular cruelty. It was methodical, purposeful. As mean and impactful as they could have made it.

STAY IN YOUR LANE was scrawled over the wall in lipstick, jerky and messy, like whoever had written it had been particularly upset.

"Someone told them about where you were

tonight." Eve pulled to her feet, approaching carefully, her hands wringing together. "I saw Kane waiting for you outside the bathrooms, so I guess other people saw as well."

The girl at the shop.

Isobel deflated, glancing down at the Band-Aids on her arm. "How did they get a key to my room?"

"They didn't." Eve pointed to the door. "They busted the lock."

"Then I can't sleep here tonight. Thanks for waiting for me. I'll just ... go and tell one of the dorm supervisors and see if there's anywhere else I can sleep."

"I already reported it." Eve stared at her shoes. She was wearing sneakers with her pyjamas. Probably because of the mess of broken things on the floor. "And ... well ... I asked for an extra mattress in my room. It's all set up, if you ... I mean, no pressure—"

"Please." Isobel cut her off, realising just how nervous and unsure the other girl was. "If you're sure."

"Definitely!" Eve seemed to gain a few inches of height, her smile snapping across her face like it had been an effort to hold back. She was a naturally bubbly person and seemed to struggle when she had to see others in pain. "Should we try to pick through this to see what we can save?" She looked around at the mess.

Isobel's stomach sank, thinking about the photos she had brought from home, her notebooks, her favourite piano music, even things she would have considered replaceable, like her favourite T-shirt and ripped jeans. She could see a cut-up section of the shirt on the floor. The pretty flower design on the front, like album art, sliced into triangular pieces.

"I'll do it tomorrow," she eventually said, turning her back on the chaos.

"Come on, then." Eve slipped an arm around her shoulders, leading her out of the room. "Those bitches never would have dared if you had cameras inside your room like the rest of us."

"Lucky me," Isobel muttered.

Eve steered her down the hall and into her own room. The noticeboard out the front was filled with cute messages because everyone loved Eve. It was impossible not to. There was a mattress on the floor, already made up with sheets, pillows, and blankets. Isobel immediately went and sat on it, dropping her bag down beside her. She fiddled with the edge of the top blanket, her eyes trained down like she hadn't yet been given permission to see the rest of the room.

"Do you need to change or shower?" Eve prodded gently. "I can come into the bathroom with you."

"You don't need to feel sorry for me," was all Isobel said, her eyes finally lifting. "I'll be fine."

"I used to think that," Eve answered immediately, like she had pre-empted the statement. "I used to watch you sometimes in our first year, always alone like you didn't really want to mix with anyone. You never try to talk to the other kids in class, and you only ever come out in the evenings when the other girls drag you. Sometimes you seem sick, too, and I thought maybe that's why you don't want to be close to anybody, but then one night I came home from tennis practice really late and you were passed out in the common room, all pale and sweaty. I sat with you for a while, and you eventually just woke up and shuffled off to bed like nothing had happened. You were so out of it you didn't even see me. Now, I think … I've been stupid all this time. You're not alone because you want to be."

Isobel couldn't help it. She glanced up toward one of the cameras, and then forced herself to look down again. *Don't ever let them see you cry.*

"No," she whispered. "I don't want to be alone."

"Then it's settled." Eve looked happy. She even clapped her hands together and bounced against the edge of her bed. "You're staying with me until we can get your room sorted, *and*—" She held up a finger to cut off Isobel's protest. "We'll eat our meals together in the dining hall from now on, too. The food here is too good to eat by yourself every day."

"You really don't have to—"

"I'm not finished." Eve frowned at her. "You're a dancer, right?" She waited for Isobel's wary nod. "I'm a singer!" she exclaimed. "We could do some work together! Maybe even submit a collab!"

Isobel chuckled despite herself. "You don't want to submit a collab with me. Getting a Sigma to dance to one of your songs is the easiest way to send it straight into obscurity."

"Oh, *pfft*." Eve flapped her hand. "That just makes it more of a challenge, and I'm a firm believer in taking the hard way. How else will I get noticed in this place? In case you haven't realised, I'm a nice-girl Omega. I'm not dramatic, sexy, scandalous, or insanely powerful. I have nothing else to offer but my skill."

"Then I guess we aren't so different," Isobel said, suddenly thinking about Theodore. How they were the same, too. But then she was thinking about how his angular jaw had sparkled with drops of water while his eyes darkened with intensity.

Eve was a *much* safer friend choice.

Eve thrust down her hand, offering it to Isobel. "Shake on it. No take-backs."

"No take-backs?" Isobel smirked, shaking her head as she slipped her pale hand into Eve's tanned one.

"What?" Eve pouted. "I'm wholesome. It's adorable. I'm the perfect best-friend candidate."

"I've never had a best friend before."

"Oh thank god." Eve tightened her grip like a vice. "Then you won't know the difference."

SHE DIDN'T SLEEP AT ALL, THOUGH SHE CLOSED HER EYES SO the cameras wouldn't see. Just in case anyone cared. When her alarm went off, she slipped out of the room with her bag, changing into the same clothes as she had worn the night before, thankful that they were at least comfortable to train in.

The fitness centre was quiet but not empty. This was the time reserved for people who actually cared about winning ... and Isobel, who didn't have a choice. Not that she minded. She had figured out at some point during her first year that her father hadn't enrolled her into any dance-related classes because they were all too elementary for her. She was the daughter of an Icon and had been dancing with private tutors and choreographers since she was old enough to prove that it was a worthwhile investment. He enrolled her into dance classes in her second year, but didn't ease up on all the private training time.

She dropped her bag by the door, plugged in her phone, and scrolled through for a playlist, deciding on something slow and calm, even though she felt the opposite. Once the first heavy, dragging song started to creep through the room, she pulled back the long curtains from the glass windows, allowing the natural morning light to spill in. She squinted, fighting off a headache as she slipped her sweatshirt over her head, dropping it beside her bag. In just her tights and a sports bra, she dragged a yoga mat into the middle of the room and started her stretches.

She eased herself into her warmup, increasing her heart rate and pushing the limits of her muscles until she felt looser, her breath deeper, more settled. She rolled up the mat, returning to the centre of the room. She spun to face the mirror and started to move.

Dancing was the easiest thing in the world for her. It was the only thing that didn't make her pause, or stumble. It was the only thing she trusted, the only thing that gave her confidence—but at the same time, it wasn't an immediate thing. It was something she had to work for. It was a gradual act of self-soothing, to make her steps lighter, to make her arms extend further, to have her chest rising or falling exactly in time with the beat. It was finesse and control and everything she lacked as soon as the music stopped and the rest of the world rushed back in.

And in this moment, it was the only way to release the dark, endless feelings that built up inside her, swirling around an empty well that always seemed a few drops away from spilling over and years away from ever being too full. She was a Sigma. A never-ending vessel for pain, sorrow, fear, and anger, but as much as she could take it away from other people, she couldn't ever seem to expunge it fully from herself.

Eve had said she often looked sick, and Isobel would have to agree with her.

She *was* often sick. Weighed down by the little sips of suffering she stole, hoping to ease the frustrations of the very same people who chose to take their very same frustrations out on her. She was too pale, too weak, too addicted to pain.

Until she danced.

Then, suddenly, she was strong. She could extend herself instead of hunching inward to avoid being seen. She could let her steps make a sound. She could make her movements as angry, as frustrated as she felt inside.

She barely even noticed when the hour was up, and she might have continued to dance if her music hadn't stopped playing, her timer interrupting the haunting melodies. She stumbled to a stop, like a ballerina doll at the end of a puppet show, limbs limp, lights out.

Her brain was foggy and distracted as she padded over to her phone and switched off the alarm, so it took her several moments to catch sight of the two boys leaning up against the wall either side of the door.

Gabriel Spade and Elijah Reed.

She froze, and they all just stood there for a few seconds, staring at each other. Reed's light grey eyes were the exact same shape of coolly-pissed off as they had been the previous morning when he used his Alpha voice in the dining hall. Spade had his blond hair combed impeccably into place, his colouring a few shades darker than Reed. He had dark brown eyes that appeared a little reddish and an incredibly symmetrical face, which she imagined would probably please him, as everything else about his appearance was exact and symmetrical too. He stood with his arms crossed, the barest frown on his lips.

"We did knock," Spade finally said, those reddish-brown eyes of his drifting over to the speakers before snapping back to her. "You didn't hear."

She shifted nervously on her feet, glancing between them. The only thing she knew about the two Alphas, she had learned from the Ironside website. They were best friends and notoriously hard to get interesting footage of. They kept to themselves, skipped classes ... and also happened to be dancers, like her. Which would explain why they were standing in one of the practice rooms, but not why they were standing inside *her* practice room.

"How long have you been there?" she asked.

"Approximately twenty-four and a half minutes," Spade answered, without looking at his phone to check the time.

Wasn't Reed supposed to be the genius?

"You're in our practice room," Reed supplied coldly.

Isobel felt her face heating, panic tripping through her system. "I'm so sorry." She grabbed her bag but dropped it and had to quickly snatch everything up again as the zipper was pulled open and a few of her books tumbled out. "Shit. Fuck. I'm sorry. I haven't slept—you don't care. Sorry."

She managed to get all her stuff together and hurried to the door as they both kicked off the wall in an eerily similar movement and began walking toward the bench and shelf where people could set their things down and hook up their phones.

ELIJAH REED SLOWED HIS PACE AS HE NEARED THE SIGMA, examining her in the moment she passed them, just as he had the previous morning. She had seemed frazzled then, and she seemed frazzled now. There were deep, dark bruises under her eyes, and her long blonde hair, hanging in a thick rope over her shoulder, was tousled, with silky strands escaping everywhere. She would have looked like she had just rolled straight out of bed and into the practice room if not for the light sheen of sweat on her pale skin and the choppy breath that was coming out of her mouth in little bursts.

The girl was in bad shape. Not that it was his problem.

He tore his eyes away, dumping his bag down on the bench as he shared a look with Gabriel. His friend seemed to be wondering the same thing as him. *Why had they stood there and watched for so long?* They could have spoken up earlier, but they didn't. They didn't even knock, like Gabriel claimed. They walked in, prepared to watch her scatter at the sight of two Alphas, to apologise profusely and trip over herself in her haste to leave as soon as she realised she was in the wrong room—exactly as she was doing now.

But she didn't even notice them.

She just kept dancing, slow and hypnotising and heartbreaking, her face creased in pain, her hands often flinging up or reaching out, like she needed help, before retreating back to protect her body.

She was good. *Really* fucking good. Shockingly so.

Elijah was saying that in the look he shared with Gabriel, who lifted both brows in surprised agreement. Honestly, it was the first time they had been able to tear their eyes from her. It was purely an appreciation for her dance, though. Isobel Carter was damaged with a capital *D*, and he didn't have time for that kind of drama. He noticed her sweatshirt on the bench and picked it up without thinking, calling out to her.

"Carter."

She stopped, her arm frozen in its reach for the door. She took her time turning around, like she couldn't believe he knew her name, but when she saw the sweatshirt he was holding, her face flooded with colour. Again.

"K-keep it," she choked out, reddening further as she took in the expression on his face, obviously realising he had no use for her sweatshirt, but she didn't want to come anywhere near them. She just gave a slight, embarrassed nod and hightailed it out of there, slamming the door behind her.

Gabriel chuckled. "Where did all that gracefulness go?"

Elijah hummed in his throat, tossing the sweatshirt back onto the bench. He should leave it there. They both just stood there, looking at it, until he finally picked it back up, passing it beneath his nose. There were rules, amongst Alphas. It wasn't polite to scent someone without their permission or knowledge. It was a very invasive thing to do without being in full view of the person, and it was *not* something he should have been doing in that moment.

He sensed a strange mix of sweet and sour. Like bitter cherries wrapped in glistening toffee, with the lightest tinge of two other scents that drifted apart from hers. One, he was unfamiliar with, and it was too wispy for him, so he immediately moved on from it, narrowing in on the second.

Amber.

"Theo," he growled, reaching for his phone.

He tossed the sweatshirt in Gabriel's direction, who immediately lifted it to his nose as Elijah searched for Theodore's number. He answered on the fourth ring, and by that time, Gabriel had hooked up his phone to the speaker system and was playing music loud enough to drown out their conversation for the cameras. People often said that Elijah was a genius, but he was hard-pressed to see how Gabriel was any less intelligent than he was.

"Did you forget something?" Theodore panted through the phone. "Because I'm out running. Call Mikki, he has nothing better to do."

"We decided last year you were going to stay away from the Carter girl," Elijah snapped, turning the phone on speaker.

They could practically hear his sneakers grinding to a halt on the pavement. Silence met the accusation.

"Theo ..." Gabriel sighed, his perfectly symmetrical face suddenly scrunching in a way that threw all the perfect lines and angles off. Gabriel *hated* when things didn't go according to plan.

"No," Theodore snapped, sensing something Gabriel had yet to say. "I like her. She's funny."

"Seems like a bucket of laughs," Elijah stated dryly. Gabriel smirked.

"Okay, fine," Theodore grumbled. "She's having a tough time here—"

"Not our problem," Elijah interrupted.

"She could really use a friend," Theodore tried again, only to be interrupted by Gabriel.

"You can't afford friends."

"When have I ever asked for anything?" Theodore demanded. "I agreed to the plan. I'm here. I do everything Kalen demands and I'm asking for *one* thing."

"And what if she overhears something?" Elijah growled out. "We aren't playing high school games here. Knowing *anything* puts all of us at risk—and her, as well. If she makes even the slightest move to report us, Kalen will dispatch Oscar. She'll be over, do you understand? And if she finds out something and *doesn't* report us, she's just as liable as us."

"She helped me," Theodore whispered back. "She could have walked away and left me there to slowly go insane, but she helped me. Helped us *all*, in case you've forgotten, because that night could have gone worse. And now she needs a friend, and I'm going to be that friend."

Gabriel was shaking his head, but he sounded resigned when he spoke. "Then you can hang out with her in Dorm A. If she really wants to be your friend, she won't mind. And that way, there will always be someone around to intervene—"

"If I go feral?" Theodore's voice was so soft, but also hurt and a little sour.

"It's for the best." Elijah forced the anger and

frustration from his voice, gentling it with understanding. "And for her safety. If it happens again, it might not be like last time. And I have the cameras in Dorm A rigged. If anything happens, we can just switch them off like last time. We don't have that control anywhere else."

"Fine," Theodore grunted. "I'll see what I can do."

He hung up, leaving Gabriel and Elijah to look at each other, silently sharing the concerned thoughts they didn't want to voice.

Isobel didn't bother showering since she had nothing to change into but her swimsuit. Luckily, it was still early enough that nobody batted an eye at her walking around in tights and a sports bra. They likely just assumed she had gone for a run. She dropped her bag inside the door to her room, crossing her arms to survey the mess.

"Just in time, Miss Carter." The voice behind her belonged to Professor Yarrow, who was brandishing a heavy frown and a roll of garbage bags. "I'm afraid we don't have any cleaning staff available, since individual rooms are the responsibility of the students inhabiting them." She grimaced, looking around at the chaos, before handing over the garbage bags. "But I've asked them to drop around some supplies during the day for you to use after your classes this afternoon. A locksmith will also be attending to fix your door. Is there anything else you'll be needing?"

Isobel knew better than to ask if any action would be taken against the girls, and in all honesty, she didn't think she could bear to hear the answer right at that moment, so instead, she said: "I don't have any clothes."

"No clothes?" Yarrow repeated, eyeing her sports bra. "Well ... of all the things." She frowned. "As you know, Market Street only becomes available in your third year, so there's nowhere to buy clothes on campus. Might that be something you can sort out with your parents? Most first and second-year students have new clothing brought in by their family."

"My parents haven't attended any of the family visits since I started here."

Yarrow tipped down her glasses, her frown softening somewhat as she peered at Isobel's face. "Do you have a way of contacting them?"

Isobel's hand shot into her pocket immediately, wrapping protectively around her phone. She didn't want to admit to the constant, unanswered saga of messages she had sent her mother.

"I haven't succeeded," was all she said.

"Very well." Yarrow pushed her glasses back up. "I'll contact them today and sort something out. The next family visit is this weekend, so you'll have to borrow some clothes from a friend until then."

Thank you for your help. That was what she was supposed to say. It was what her father would have wanted her to say.

So why did the words stick in her throat?

Why did she swallow them down, watching silently as Yarrow left?

She picked up her bag again and closed the door, returning to Eve's room, where she found a message written on the noticeboard. *Door is always open for my brand-new bestie, Isobel Carter.*

She shook her head. The girl was downright crazy. Did she *want* to be ostracised by all her friends? Isobel tried the handle and found the door unlocked. There was another note on the bed on the floor, which she had carefully made that morning before slipping out. It was Eve's phone number, and another message beneath.

Good morning, early riser! Did you sleep at all?! Help yourself to any clothes, as long as you promise never to return the underwear. Meet me in the hall for breakfast! I'll save you a seat.

P.S. I foresaw you being too uncomfortable to just go through someone's closet and try on their clothes, so I already picked them out for you. They're on my bed.

Isobel laughed reading the note. It felt nice, having the attention of a happy and bubbly girl like Eve. It was like she suddenly belonged somewhere. She wasn't just the Sigma anymore. She was Eve's friend. There was yet another sticky note on the folded pile of clothing, and she picked it off.

Show up. Be fierce. Don't let them know they hurt you.

She wasn't planning on hiding away, but she also wasn't exactly planning on being *fierce*. The note seemed to be referring to the outfit more than anything else. Black high-top boots; high-waisted army pants with random pockets and hanging straps; a loose, off-the-shoulder shirt cut off at the waist. It definitely wasn't her usual style, but in a weird sort of way, she understood what Eve was trying to do. It was a storyline she had seen play out on the Ironwood show many times over.

The underdog cliché.

At some point, they *always* got a makeover. Some sort of revenge outfit—though they were usually third-years by that stage, with access to the Glow-Up Bar and Market Street to get fully made over for their big entrance. Nobody cared about Isobel's revenge outfit or her underdog entrance. Nobody except Eve, who was silently cheering her on even though she wasn't in the race. And that was why Isobel grabbed the clothes and took them to the bathroom to shower and get dressed for the day.

5

ANGELS AND DEMONS

HER FIRST CLASS FOR THE DAY WAS FORTUNE TELLING AND
the Mystic Arts, and it wasn't until she sank into her
seat, cushioning her heavy head onto her folded arms
that the words written on her wall floated back to her.

STAY IN YOUR LANE.

Ashford had said those exact words during his
tarot reading. With anyone else, it would have been a
coincidence, but she couldn't help but stew over his
words as exhaustion tugged at her, threatening to
send her under.

At some point, the class must have started,
because a desk bumped up against hers, jolting her
upright. A surprised sound squeaked from her throat.
Ashford was sitting across from her again, his mouth
pressed flat, his arms loosely crossed over his chest,

117

his hips low in the chair as he kicked out his long legs. Thankfully, he had set his chair far enough back that his shoes didn't touch hers.

"Ashford?" she croaked, glancing around the rest of the room.

This time, the other students weren't paying them any attention. They were paired off in twos, heads bent together, talking and laughing quietly. She glanced to the clock, her frown deepening. They were halfway through the lesson already.

"Good morning." Ashford unwound one of his arms to inspect his fingernails. "Nice of you to join us. Vega decided to make yesterday's pairings permanent for the rest of the year."

She dragged her eyes back to the table, taking in the tarot deck. She reached for it, her fingers shaking, and he suddenly dipped forward, his hand catching her wrist. He held her hand up before his face, his aquamarine eyes hyper-focussed. She found herself distracted by his own hand for a moment, peering at the feather-thin tattoos decorating his golden fingers before she quickly pulled her hand away.

"You're shaking." He tipped his head to the side, re-crossing his arms. "Long night?"

"Don't you already know?" she suddenly snapped, surprised by the acid in her own tone.

He blinked and leaned forward again, his pink lips parting. "Ah." The sound barely escaped him, it was more of a sigh. "Something happened to you and it reminded you of what I said. I get it. It happens. You understand that doesn't make me responsible, right?"

She did, but she wished she didn't. She just wanted to *blame* someone. The fourth-year girls would have been preferable, but Ashford had predicted it in some way, and he was the one sitting in front of her right at that moment.

Still ... She sighed. *He's right.*

She reached for the deck of cards again, her shuffling unsteady.

"What happened?" he asked casually. "You're a little shaken up, but you don't seem hurt."

Hurt? She dropped half the deck, watching as the cards scattered over the desk.

"Did you see me getting hurt?" she asked, gathering the cards back up again.

He tucked his dirty blond hair behind his ears, his chest swelling with a breath. "If we're going to keep answering questions with questions, we might as well not talk at all."

Ashford had a stubborn streak. She could see it in the set of his eyes, in the way his lips pressed together and firmed. He had a little dimple close to the side of his mouth that appeared only when he was hardening his lips the way he was now.

"Nothing happened." She broke first, but she broke with a lie.

That dimple deepened and he corrected his posture, dragging his chair forward and stretching his legs out again. She could feel the heat of his long limbs either side of her ankles, his shoes knocking against the legs of her chair.

"Why bother lying?" he asked conversationally. "I'll find out when whatever it is airs."

She stumbled over a surprised laugh. "You think the show is going to air my day-to-day existence?" she asked.

"It can't have been that bad, then." He shrugged.

The statement had her bristling, and she angrily slapped the deck down onto the table, pulling a card at random. "Or it wasn't on camera," she ground out. She didn't want to confide in him, but it rankled that he was dismissing something that was still pecking slowly away at her, like a loose thread she had yet to tidy up.

It had created a wound, and she didn't like the way it was festering.

Ashford plucked the card out of her hand, rolling

his eyes and tossing it back to the desk without looking at it. "You're terrible at this. Try again."

She picked another card and had only slid it out a few inches before he was snatching it off her. "No." He tossed it. "Again."

This happened several more times until one of them finally made him pause. This one, he actually turned over. He looked from her face to the card and back to her face, his unhappy dimple appearing again. It was the deepest she had ever seen it—even on the Ironside show.

He laid the card down on the desk, face down, his fingers tapping against it.

"Can I see it?" she prompted, when it seemed like he was just going to sit there, so deep in his own thoughts that she momentarily ceased to exist.

His attention shot back to her, and he hesitated before flipping the card. She watched as his entire demeanour changed, a slow smile spreading over his face. It seemed oddly forced, but she wasn't sure how she knew that exactly. She didn't *know* him. She turned her attention to the card instead.

The Lovers.

It seemed innocent enough. It certainly didn't seem to predict any sort of doom or death, or anything else that should have had him frowning so hard.

"Hardly news, is it?" He winked at her, releasing a low chuckle, his blue eyes sparkling, his teeth flashing.

"No, I suppose it isn't," she said mildly, gathering the cards and handing them over to him. "You're always with girls."

He *tutted*, pushing the cards back to the centre of the desk. "One reading a day, you heard Vega. After the first, the powers of divination aren't nearly as accurate."

"Did you draw my card while I was sleeping?" she asked, glancing at the desk.

"No." He levelled her with a look, that smile and sparkle melting right away.

"Then—"

"We've done each other already." He cut her off, but not harshly. "Now tell me what happened last night. You're bruised." His hand shot out, suddenly cupping her face, his thumb stroking beneath her eye. "All purple and black. This is more than a sleepless night."

His hand snapped back to his lap just as quickly, making the side of her face prickle with strange heat.

"People don't like it when Sigmas are friends with Alphas." She used those words deliberately and watched as he mulled them over, not a single tic in his impassive expression.

"Hmm." It wasn't quite a response, more like an acknowledgement.

He didn't ask which Alpha she was talking about.

Which meant he already knew.

"You told me to stay in my lane." She chewed on the inside of her cheek, waiting to see if he would react to her words. He only nodded slightly, his eyes flitting over her features. He didn't usually sit so still, holding his attention in place for so long. It was beginning to unnerve her. "Was that a reading or a warning?"

He pulled in air through his teeth, his shoes knocking against the legs of her chair again, jostling her just slightly. "All of my readings are warnings."

He wasn't exactly being rude, but she was beginning to feel the thump of his annoyance against her chest again, though it was now tinged with something else. Something like ... panic.

It didn't make any sense.

She was tempted to open herself to it. To taste it, to see if it might tell her the secrets he was keeping so close to his chest, but Ashford didn't seem like the type to take that sort of intrusion lightly. Of all the Alphas she had met at Ironside, he seemed the most like her father, though he was still worlds apart. Even so, those few qualities they had in common made her extra wary of him. She wondered at his secrecy, his pride, his short, cryptic answers, and she wondered how he might find ways to harm her.

"Ignore that," he said, a second before her phone vibrated.

She had reached for it out of instinct, but she paused, her hand halfway to her pocket. "Why?"

"Because." He regarded her coolly. "As you just said: Sigmas shouldn't be friends with Alphas."

"That's not what I said."

"Now *mates* on the other hand," he continued. "Sigmas can most certainly mate with Alphas. In fact, it's widely regarded as the most fortunate pairing, as you must well know, your parents being who they are."

He must have said that a little too loudly, because several people turned to peek at him. You didn't simply toss the word "mate" around in a casual fashion at Ironside. It was equivalent to mentioning explosions in an airport. Even if the conversation was innocent, everyone's hair still stood on end and a target popped up over the speaker's head. *Observe carefully. Possible love terrorist.* She slumped back in her chair, too exhausted to put her usual walls up and keep her expression neutral.

"I disagree," she said flatly.

His dark gold brow quirked, and she wanted to say

more, to just let it all out, to tell the whole world about her mother's quiet, invisible pain and her father's quiet, invisible wrath. She wanted to speak the dark thoughts swirling inside her like she had done last night with Theodore, but she didn't dare.

She sat back. She deflated. She pressed her lips together and turned her eyes from Ashford, disengaging from the conversation.

"I see," was all he said, and the thumping against her chest shifted, leaking through a small taste of pain.

"Do you know who your mate is?" She blurted the thought as soon as it popped into her head, and several more students turned to watch them. "Have you ... you know." She tapped on the side of her head.

His lips twitched. "I don't see flashes of the future. Nothing so concrete."

"Do you have any straight answers inside you?"

It was the first genuine smile she thought she had seen on his face, and the little dimple was back, almost disappearing into the creases either side of his mouth.

"Tell you what ..." His shoes bumped her chair again. "You unlock your phone and put it on the desk here." He tapped the surface before him. "And I'll give you a straight answer."

Thinking it had something to do with not wanting to be overheard, she did his bidding, unlocking her phone and sliding it over the desk to him. He picked it up, tapped something out against the screen, and then slid it back.

"I'll text you," he said as Vega signalled the end of the class.

He got up without another word, leaving her behind to frown at her phone. The message from Theodore was still there, on her lock screen, and she picked it up to tap on it.

Theodore: Can we move our lessons to the lake?

Just as she started to wonder why the hell he would suggest such a thing, several more messages came through.

Theodore: Not the main lake, I meant Alpha Lake.

Theodore: It's heated, like a swimming pool, and the water is really nice.

She quickly gathered up her things, not wanting to be late to *Dance Acrobatics*, and tried to text him back as she navigated the corridors.

Isobel: What's wrong with the pool?

Theodore: I really want to be your friend, but people might start talking.

She halted so fast someone almost smacked into her from behind. They let out a disgruntled murmur, sidestepping her and hurrying away as she stared at her phone, trying not to feel the pang of hurt.

Theodore: I don't want people thinking we're trying to force a mate-bond. They might come after you.

She started walking again, chewing on her lip.

Isobel: I hadn't thought of that.

It was common for couples who wanted to be mates to spend a lot of time together to try and force a bond, and Sigmas and Alphas were generally considered to be a well-matched pair, since the less-important Sigma could emotionally support the all-important Alpha in a way no other could. They were also the rarest ranks, making them more even in numbers.

If people thought they were trying to force a bond, not only would it increase the attacks against her, it would bring unwanted attention by the government and the Ironside officials. Nobody tried to force a bond unless they were planning on almost-killing themselves—since the near death of one of the partners was the only time a bond would actually begin to form. Those sorts of rumours brought a lot of scrutiny, and she wasn't equipped for that kind of attention.

Theodore: I'm not trying to lure you to my dorm.

Isobel: Yes, you are.

Theodore: Okay. I am.

Theodore: But my intentions are pure as the water in

Alpha Lake. Entirely athletically-motivated. Plus your
swimsuit helps.

    Theodore: Forget I said that. So, tonight?

    Isobel: I have to clean my room.

    Theodore: That's the worst excuse I've ever heard. Am I
that hopeless of a student? I have the soul of a dolphin, you
just need to give me a chance.

    Isobel: It's not an excuse. Someone trashed my room
last night.

His response didn't come immediately, and she
kept checking her phone as she arrived to the dance
hall and began stretching, nervously looking at her
phone every chance she got. When Professor Lye
entered the hall and called for everyone's attention,
she tucked her phone back into her bag with a sigh.
Dance Acrobatics was by far her most difficult class
and the most taxing on her body—outside of her
private practices. Luckily, they had a morning tea
service in the dining hall after the second period, so
she might be able to sneak in a quick nap somewhere
before attempting to tackle the rest of her day.

"Good morning, everyone." Lye moved to the
mirror at the front of the hall, an excited bounce to his
step, his lilting voice carrying impressively across the
vast space. "Since we've mostly covered the basics,
we're now going to pair up and tackle some acrobatic-

duo work. Gender and size mean nothing to me. Pick someone you have chemistry with, and the rest will work itself out. I reserve the right to switch out the pairs if I think something isn't working. This is a serious class. You aren't just here to look good, you're here to hone your skills, so if you have any complaints about the pairings I change, you're welcome to take it up with the beginner's dance professor, who you'll be finishing out the rest of your year with."

Immediately, people started pairing up, like they had known this was coming. She supposed it was happening in a lot of their classes by now, after four months of being taught the basics for whatever module they had chosen.

She resigned herself to waiting in the back until the last person needed a partner, but it was equally humiliating when she realised there were an odd number of people in the class, and she was now the only one standing by herself. As soon as Lye noticed, he frowned. He was a no-nonsense sort of person and didn't care for the rank politics that plagued the students.

"Is anyone willing to take on a third?" he asked. His frown deepened when everyone avoided looking at him, and he hurriedly motioned her over to his side. "You can partner with me for now, Carter."

Great.

Still, Lye was better than one of the Omega girls, who was glaring at her from across the room, or the Beta smirking cruelly at her, probably counting down the minutes until he could relay her humiliation to Bellamy.

The lesson was particularly gruelling, since Lye decided to use Isobel to demonstrate all the positions for the other students. They laughed every time she messed up, and Lye's ire turned from them to Isobel. She wasn't usually this clumsy, but she also wasn't used to so much attention on her and she was bone-tired, her limbs imbued with a tremble she couldn't contain.

He pulled her aside at the end of the class, lightly clasping her elbow. "I know you can do better than that, Carter." He released her, his expression displeased. "Whatever you've got going on, you need to learn to leave it at the door. Acrobatic work—especially partner work—can be *very* dangerous if you aren't focussed."

"I understand," she said. "I'll do better next time."

"Make sure you do. Practise your balance before next lesson." He walked off, dismissing her.

She didn't even check her phone when she reached the bench where she had left her belongings. She simply grabbed her bag and stumbled to the library, finding solace in her lonely cubicle on the top floor, where she laid her head on her hands and sank into a fretful sleep.

She awoke to her alarm exactly twenty-five minutes later and dragged the phone under her face, mashing the screen to turn it off. She found herself staring at a message from Theodore, and she sat up straight to reply.

Theodore: I'll help you.

Isobel: You can't come to Dorm O and just walk into my room. See reasons above.

Theodore: I know. I called in a favour. It's my fault your room got trashed.

Isobel: No, it's not.

Theodore. Now you have to apologise.

For a second, she didn't understand what he meant, until his words the night before came back to her.

You don't apologise to me unless you've lied to me, okay?

She chuckled, shaking her head.

Isobel: I guess I'm sorry.

Theodore: I guess you're forgiven. See you later, Illy.

She hauled her bag over her shoulder and pushed herself through the rest of her classes, giving everything she had left to her dance practice in the afternoon. By the end of the day, she had sweated through three dance classes and two hours of practice in the clothes Eve had lent her, and she couldn't bear to wear them for a second longer. She stopped by Eve's room on the way to the showers, thankful to find the other girl inside. Since they didn't share any classes, she hadn't seen her since breakfast.

"There you are!" Eve tossed her arm around Isobel's shoulder but then immediately retreated. "Oh my god, you're so sweaty." She backed off, grabbing a tote from her bed. "Here, I put together some essentials. Workout clothes, a pair of jeans, another top. I'm sorry I couldn't spare more, but I don't have much myself. You can keep the pyjamas I gave you yesterday."

"It's just until this weekend," Isobel assured her gratefully. "Yarrow is organising my parents to bring clothes to the family visit. I'll wash everything then and bring it back to you."

"No rush." Eve smiled, forcing the tote into her hands. "I need to shower too, then we can head to dinner?"

Isobel held her tongue as they made their way into the bathroom. Having lunch with Eve that day had been awkward at best. Eve carried on being her usual sociable, bubbly self, but all the other girls sitting at the table couldn't seem to wrap their heads around the fact that she had invited Isobel to sit with them. They ended up talking around the two girls, almost pretending they didn't exist. Eve tried to hide it, but it clearly bothered her.

Still, Isobel couldn't refuse the invitation. Not after everything Eve had done for her. She tucked herself into a shower stall and extracted one of the amenity packs she had swiped from the fitness centre that afternoon. It contained a small fold-up plastic hairbrush and hair tie; a mini toothbrush and toothpaste set; mini bottles of shampoo, conditioner, body wash and body lotion; and even small cleansing serums and moisturiser packets for the face.

She usually languished in her showers, since even the bathrooms in Dorm O were luxurious. Each shower stall was the size of a small room, with marble floors and ceilings, and small teardrop chandeliers. There was a changing area with fluffy robes hanging up that were refreshed by the attendants that slipped in and out of the stalls between uses to clean and prepare them for the next person. This time, however, she hurried. She was nervous about making Eve wait. She extracted a pair of jeans and another crop top from the bag, slipping on her only pair of shoes remaining intact. The clothes were exactly the style she usually wore, and she wondered if Eve had noticed.

She dropped her stuff off in her room, noticing the fresh lock and the key waiting for her on the other side of the door. The mess inside hadn't been touched.

"Ready?" Eve asked, her face shining, makeup free, and her hair pulled up on top of her head. She looked comfortable, happy ... not at all like she was worried her friends were about to ostracise her.

Isobel began to follow her out but paused, glancing down at an envelope beneath her sneakers. She picked it up, reading her name across the front. She tucked it beneath her arm as she locked up the door, flipping it over as she followed Eve out. Some of the other girls had caught up to Eve and chatted with her on their way out of the dorm, leaving Isobel a few steps behind.

The letter wasn't stamped and didn't have a return address.

"Fan mail?" one of the Omega girls asked, whispering low as she passed Isobel. "For *you*?" She laughed, skipping ahead, her words trailing behind. "Must be a weirdo."

Isobel tore open the envelope, unfolding the letter within. It was typed.

Within these walls, there are true *Gifted and those who simply have the blood.*

You have the blood, but do you have the guts?

She slipped the letter into her bag, hating that the Omega girl had been right. She had no reason to expect her mother would have written to her, so she gathered up the pervasive disappointment and shoved it down hard. The letter wasn't even stamped, which meant it had been slipped into the dorm's letterbox by another student.

She had allowed herself to slip too far behind the group of Omega girls and found herself pushed to the end of the table when Eve took her seat, several of the other girls scrambling to sit around her, turning their backs on Isobel. Eve frowned over at her, but Isobel quickly stood to get her food, tossing the concerned girl a reassuring smile. As soon as she got up, someone slid into her seat, blocking her from the table completely.

She sighed, pulling out her phone to send Eve a quick message as she approached the food bar.

Isobel: I'm going to take some food back to my room and get started on cleaning up. I have a friend helping, so just enjoy your night.

The theme of the food bar today seemed to have something to do with bread, since there was almost every type imaginable on display. Different loaves, rolls and slices from all cultures of the world, with samples of dishes to go along with each kind. There was bolognaise to compliment the Vienna loaves, Greek staples surrounding knots of sesame-crusted bread, and savoury rolls that looked to have been baked with pieces of cheese in baskets between samples of Brazilian stews.

She grabbed a takeaway container, putting a couple of salted pretzels into it since they were accompanied by little containers of different dips, all with lids and easy to take with her. She also snatched up a bottle of mineral water and a sweet scone before slipping out of the hall and returning to her room. She unlocked the door, pushing inside and settling against one of the walls, opening her laptop to play the latest episode of Ironside as she ate her dinner. She had only just finished when the door opened and closed completely at random.

She jumped to her feet and then scrambled back against the wall as Theodore and another boy materialised before the closed door.

Kilian Gray.

The Alpha with the power of invisibility.

Theodore took a step toward her but then stopped, his stormy eyes taking in the destruction of her room.

"I ..." She faltered, staring at Gray. "I was just about to start cleaning."

"Hello." He gave her a half-smile, his lush lips curving. "You don't mind if I help, do you?"

"You don't need to." She shot a panicked look to Theodore, but he was standing still, staring at the mess. As soon as she got over the shock of seeing Gray inside her room, she felt Theodore's emotion, heavy and dark, tapping against her chest. He was eerily still, reminding her of the way he had stared at the scratches on her arm. He was staring at her ruined belongings like they were his, like someone had personally offended him.

Gray's pale, beautiful eyes shot to him, that half-smile disappearing. "Theo," he snapped, his silky tone transforming into a whip.

Theodore straightened, his shoulders tense as he spun around, his teeth gritted. "Who did this?"

Gray didn't wait for her answer—to either of their questions. He walked forward, frowning at the torn album covers and flicking his eyes up to the wall where they had been hanging, though he couldn't have known that.

"I don't know." Isobel shrugged. "Some of the Omegas. It doesn't matter."

"You don't have cameras in here," Gray argued,

though he didn't even look up at the walls to check. "Of course it matters. They'll just come back."

He pulled his phone out, tapping something out against the screen. He was just too beautiful. Him being inside her room was just too *weird*. She shot another look at Theodore, but this time, he caught it. He looked amused, and he just barely shook his head.

Whatever that was supposed to mean.

"Problem fixed," Gray announced. "I'll be back. Just need to meet Elijah outside for something."

"Elijah Reed?" she asked once Gray had turned invisible, slipping out of the room. "Here? Outside Dorm O?" She moved to the window, but it wasn't facing the front of the dorm.

Theodore chuckled, navigating the debris on the floor to shift behind her. The warmth of his body skittered across her spine. "You know I'm an Alpha too, right?"

She spun around, her face warming. "I agreed to be friends with you. I didn't agree to be friends with half the Alphas at Ironside."

"Kilian is probably a safer friend than I am." His eyes dropped from her face to the window. "All anyone talks about is how much of a gay icon he is and how he's completely disinterested in everyone. They won't suspect you two of trying to force a bond."

She allowed her attention to crawl over his face while he was still looking out the window, taking in the tense way he was holding himself and the hints of darkness creeping around the edges of his pupil, despite the ease in the set of his lips. It wasn't like the darkness of his ferality, but more like a shadow from the top of the window. Still, she couldn't help but be reminded of that black-eyed look again. His hair fell forward over his forehead as usual, almost obscuring one of his eyes, and she fought against the insane urge to brush the dark strands back, away from the faint gold tinge of his skin.

"Is he?" she asked, fighting to stay still when his eyes suddenly snapped back to hers. "Gay, I mean?"

"Might be." He shrugged, and she felt his emotion brush up against her, so faint she couldn't tell what he was feeling. "Does it matter?" For the first time, he sounded mildly defensive.

"Of course not."

The easy set to his mouth softened further, his perfect smile flashing. "Good. Let's get started."

At first it was a little awkward, but then Theodore set his phone against the shelf in her room, an easy, upbeat song piercing through the heavy, silent space and dissipating the tension. She tried to shake off her unease at the Alpha sorting through her private, ruined possessions, but he never lingered on anything unless it was to hold it up to her. When he did that, she directed him to the "keep" pile or the "trash" pile.

They had been at it for almost half an hour before Gray returned, and she was beginning to realise that she really liked Theodore's company. He was like a bolt of sunshine, sometimes warming the cold recesses of her body and sometimes burning a little too hot, threatening to singe her from the inside, to punish her for being silly enough to let him in. Either way, he made her feel tingly and alive, bringing an unfamiliar smile to her lips more often than not.

He had just held up one of her ruined crop tops when the door opened.

"Can I borrow this sometime?" he asked, flicking a look to the door as it closed again.

"If you plan on wearing it as a bracelet," she teased. "I don't think it'll fit otherwise."

They both watched as Gray materialised, but she froze as *yet another* Alpha appeared beside him.

ELIJAH TOOK IN THE MESS OF THE ROOM, FINALLY FINDING the answer to the dark bruises beneath the Sigma's eyes.

"Reed." She seemed to have choked on his last name.

He gave her a short nod. "Carter. I'm here to install a camera."

She opened and closed her mouth, and he took advantage of her shock to better examine the room. Whoever was tormenting her had aimed for maximum impact. No item seemed to have escaped their ire. Her underwear was in tatters, her school notebooks shredded.

STAY IN YOUR LANE was scrawled across the wall.

He frowned at the words, slitting a look to Theodore.

"N-no thank you." Isobel had found her voice, her wide, pale honey eyes only growing wider as he approached her. He tried to control his inhale, but his chest swelled, filling with the scent of bitter-sweet cherries. He brushed past her, going to work immediately.

"It isn't an Ironside camera," he explained. "It just looks like one so anyone will think twice before trashing your room again."

He didn't promise that it wouldn't be turned on. He should have. Then he would have had to keep to his word. But he bit his tongue and felt a surge of frustration because of it. It roughened his movements, making him seem annoyed as he set up one camera in the corner, high on the wall. He should have trusted Theodore, but he didn't. He didn't trust anyone, except maybe Gabriel.

They were dangling an opportunity in front of him. An opportunity to take control of the situation, to monitor it. Because Isobel Carter was *definitely* a situation.

The Sigma just kept staring at him, her small brow furrowing. She seemed overwhelmed with three Alphas crowding up her closet of a room, but she needed to get used to that if she wanted to be friends with Theodore.

They were a unit until they graduated.

That was non-negotiable.

Every one of them had to be protected, even if it was from themselves.

6
STUPID FUCKING HAPPY FAMILIES

ISOBEL BACKED AWAY FROM THE ANGRY ALPHA IN THE corner, drawing closer to Theodore without really meaning to. He slung a heavy arm over her shoulders, his breath stirring her hair.

"Don't worry, that's just Elijah. You haven't done anything wrong."

"No," Reed agreed beneath his breath. "*She* hasn't."

Isobel shivered, her eyes drifting over to Gray, who was staring at Reed curiously. She got the feeling Gray didn't miss much. It was probably a side effect of his ability, like how Isobel had gotten somewhat adept at reading people over the years. He was invisible by choice, and she was invisible by everyone else's choice.

Gray met her eyes, like he could feel her staring at him, and his soft lips lifted into another half-smile.

She was a little star-struck. Gray was an angel, complete with skin as pure as glittering snow and hair like the palest spun gold. He had the lushest mouth she had ever seen, and she truly couldn't tell the shade of his irises. They were so pale, so full of light, they could have been yellow, amber, brown or even green. She couldn't bear to meet his eyes long enough to decipher it. Gray was different to Theodore. Theodore might have looked like a perfect Alpha, but it was the way he held himself that really made him attractive. It was his confidence and easy determination. It was the focussed, intent look in his eyes and the way they sometimes widened when he flashed his stunning sunshine smile. It was how his strong, dominant features grew tight, the angular lines in his cheeks and jaw flexing when he spoke or frowned. He had an impressive body, but his posture was a little lazy, often slumped when he was relaxing. Still, he walked and held himself with an easy grace, transforming every movement into something charismatic and compelling.

Gray was different in every way. Even with a terrible personality and a complete lack of grace, he would still have looked like an angel. He had perfect posture, his head always held high, his wide shoulders always straight. The Ironside cameras always tried to catch him dishevelled, unawares, but they always failed.

He was too perfect and perfectly composed. It was impossible to read the emotion in his pale eyes or catch any tension in the sure way he moved his limbs.

He might have been the most beautiful person in their year—including all of the girls.

"Are these to save?" he asked, pointing to the small bundle of clothes she and Theodore had managed to salvage. They would only need minor mending.

She nodded, watching as he picked up a shirt dwarfed by his hands, even though his strength seemed more streamlined than the other two Alphas in the room. He sat on the floor, folding it with careful, gentle precision, the care in his touch more or less hypnotising her.

"I can ask them to leave?" Theodore's voice grew even softer as he ducked down beside her face. "If they're making you uncomfortable."

She shook her head mutely. She would have preferred to know *why* they were helping her, but she couldn't ask that while they were still there.

Theodore dove into the mess again. He was gathering up all the record fragments and tossing them into the trash pile. Isobel shook out one of the garbage bags, filling it and then another, the chaos inside the room beginning to morph into ordered little piles.

Gray folded her clothes onto the shelf, Theodore stacked her remaining usable books, notebooks and textbooks, and Reed had a tablet out, fiddling with the camera he had set up. His phone rang as he was packing up his stuff.

"Gabe," he said by way of greeting. He listened for a moment, and then, "In Dorm O." A pause. "Carter's room." He snorted, the sound sarcastic. "Yes, she's here with me." He sought her out, his cold eyes freezing her to the spot. His lips immediately dipped down. "Yes, he's here too ... No, don't. I'll come to you. Be there in ten."

"Is the camera turned on?" she asked him when he grabbed Gray's arm like he was just going to leave without a word to her.

He looked over his shoulder at her and then back to the camera. "Yes," he said plainly.

"But it isn't feeding back to the production team?" she pressed.

Gray was giving Reed that curious look again.

"No." Reed didn't extrapolate, forcing her to press further.

"Who's going to be watching it, then?"

He lifted a shoulder. "Hopefully nobody. Possibly

me."

Theodore let out a sound that was halfway between a grunt and a growl. Reed rolled his eyes at the other boy before returning his attention to her. "If you spend your time with Theo in Dorm A, I won't have any reason to check it."

With that, he jerked his head at Gray, and the two of them disappeared. Isobel waited until the door closed behind them before she spun to face Theodore, folding her arms. "What does he mean?"

Theodore's eyes shivered, the gold of his Alpha ring swelling slightly before he visibly shed whatever was niggling at him, the pressure of his emotion no longer hard against her chest. He shook out his shoulders. "He's just protecting me."

"From me?" she scoffed.

"From myself." His grin was wolfish this time. "I'm not always in control, and that's why I haven't made many friends outside the Alphas. This is just ... new for them. They'll get over it."

"They all know?" This time, she was definitely nervous.

"We don't have many secrets. There are only ten of us in the dorm, if you include Professor Easton and Professor West—even if their names are ridiculous. Did you know they assigned themselves the rooms at the eastern and western ends of the dorm when we moved in?"

She forced a laugh, her tongue thick in her mouth, allowing his sudden change of topics.

Having Theodore's attention on her was nerve-wracking enough. If she added Elijah Reed, Kilian Gray, Gabriel Spade and Cian Ashford to the mix, she would probably have a nervous breakdown by the end of the week.

Not to mention the others. The ones she didn't see so often. Moses Kane, Niko Hart and Oscar Sato. The shy Alpha, the social butterfly, and ... the dangerous one.

The one even the cameras shied away from.

Theodore even sounded like he was close to the Alpha *professors*. Did they know, too?

It was on the tip of her tongue to voice her concerns, to say *maybe it isn't worth it*, and tell Theodore she couldn't be friends with him after all, but then she looked at what he was doing. He had seated himself on the floor, tongue poking his cheek as he smoothed out pages torn from her favourite books. Slowly, he began matching them to the tattered covers, and with each book he recognised, a whole new piece of her heart thawed into a puddle of pathetic ... something. Maybe she idolised him. Maybe the Ironside show was getting to her head, making this Alpha seem larger-than-life so that even his small actions sparkled with significance.

"Are you going to start competing next year?" she asked, folding to the floor beside him. "Out of everyone, you probably have the best chance at winning. You're very charismatic."

The first two years at Ironside gave everyone a chance to find their feet and start building up skills. The final three years were when things really started heating up. It was when most people chose a specialisation.

His grin was perfect. "Did the Illy-stone just compliment me?"

"The what now?" she asked.

He chewed on his lip, looking her over in darkly glittering amusement. "You're as emotionless as a stone, sometimes. You actually kind of look at me like you hate me."

"I did tell you I hate Alphas," she reminded him, though there was absolutely no acid in her tone. There was actually nothing in her tone.

Maybe he was right.

"You did." He bumped her shoulder, letting her know that he didn't really think she hated him. "But yes, I do plan on competing next year."

"What will you be specialising in?" she asked curiously.

He could change it at any point, but most people didn't. With only three years to become the best at their chosen specialisation, they didn't want to waste time by switching it up halfway through.

"Singing." He stood up, pulling her to her feet as they surveyed her room. The only thing missing was a bed, but there was a new "welcome box" by the door, containing the same items she had been given when she moved in.

"Why haven't I heard you sing?" she asked, squinting at him.

He arched his brows at her. "Have you been looking me up?"

She flushed, quickly shaking her head. "No, no. I mean ... you haven't sung in any Ironside episodes."

"We're saving it." He froze, like he had accidentally said something wrong, and then began stacking the books they had put back together on the shelf.

"Who's we?" She opened the new welcome box, drawing out the fresh bedding. "And why are you saving it?"

"For maximum impact." His answers grew short, but his easy smile was still there, never far from the surface, like bright light peeking through the clouds. "Looks like you're all set up. I should probably get going. It's already pretty late and Moses has been texting me for a while." As he spoke, he glanced at his phone, scrolling for a few moments before switching off the music.

"Thank you for helping." She stood before him, unsure what to do. "I owe you."

"No, you don't." He touched her shoulder, his face serious and thoughtful. "You're teaching me to swim, remember?"

She nodded, and then the pad of his thumb shifted against the soft skin of her collarbone. He drew his touch away, his chest swelling as he breathed deeply. For the briefest moment, his eyes closed, and then his smile was back and he was walking to the door. He knocked once on it, and it opened a second later, Gray appearing. He was carrying a small pile of folded clothing.

"Just in case," he said, holding it out to her.

She took it, stunned, and barely managed to mumble her thanks before they disappeared. With them gone, her room seemed bigger than ever, and strangely cold. She put the pile of clothing on her makeshift bed, shaking out the top item. A T-shirt. Far too big. She pulled it close to her face, catching a hint of a soft, calming scent. It was bergamot and bark, woodsy and complex, but sweet and gentle.

They were all T-shirts. All smelling the same.

Gray had folded her clothes—even her underwear —and had noticed that her tops had suffered the most damage. They had been able to salvage the tights and jeans by cutting off the damaged legs and turning them into shorts—some of them with slashes she would have to pretend were deliberate.

Since Bellamy was the only other student who had joined from an Icon family in their year group, Gray likely didn't have that big of a wardrobe to spare— though the settlements certainly pooled resources to support the Alphas more than the other ranks, as they had a better chance of winning.

She carefully put the pile of shirts on her shelf before unpacking her bag and dragging the trash to the refuse room. It was late enough that most of the Omegas were either in bed or getting ready for bed, so she was left alone as she had her shower and locked herself inside her room, falling into her blankets.

Wind blew in through the newly-opened window panes, her makeshift curtain tossed out, the tape covering the broken panes ripped away. She snuggled further beneath her blanket, trying to turn off her thoughts.

Stormy, dark eyes swam into her mind, the heady gold Alpha ring piercing her. She swept them away but they materialised again, ice-cold, light grey, rippled with little bolts of white. Ringed again in gold. She groaned, turning over, accidentally kicking the wall. The eyes shifted again. Pale, pale, yellow-green, darkening to the dark gold of his Alpha ring.

She was star-struck.

It was a shock to her system.

Alphas being *nice* to her.

That was why it felt like she had touched a live wire. That was why she felt tilted off her axis. Dizzy and disorientated, grasping the memory of their eyes, warm and cold and gentle, like it was the only thing that made sense in the world—which obviously made no sense at all.

She was definitely star-struck, and she needed to get a handle on it before she made herself the biggest fool the Ironside show had ever featured.

SHE MANAGED TO PUT OFF HER SECOND LESSON WITH Theodore until the weekend, stating that she had too many training sessions booked, though the truth was that she was simply terrified of the way her thoughts filled with him when her head hit the pillow every night. And it wasn't just him, though she certainly thought of Theodore the most.

She found her stomach in knots every morning before her first class with Ashford, and she crept through the hallways linking the private training rooms every afternoon, smelling the clove and woodsmoke scent of Reed on every shadow, or seeing the strange reddish tinge of Spade's analytical stare in every face.

After her evening training, she hid away in the library, trying to learn whatever she could about Alphas, resorting to books about the Gifted in general when she couldn't find anything more specific. She wasn't sure what answer she was seeking, but she couldn't shake her unsettled feeling.

On Saturday, she woke with the feeling intensified, her skin sticky with sweat, a strange mix of dread and anticipation swirling around her stomach. She borrowed a dress from Eve and stopped in at the office on the first floor of the dorm before leaving.

"Carter," Yarrow greeted her knock, shuffling around the room. "Shouldn't you be at the family centre?"

Isobel chewed on the inside of her cheek. "Will anyone be there?"

Yarrow lowered the papers in her hand, her tone changing. "Of course. I told you I would organise it."

"I just mean …" Isobel shifted uncomfortably. She couldn't bear to turn up and wait all morning, only to leave disappointed. She had promised herself she wouldn't do it anymore. "Did my parents confirm they were coming?"

"They did." Yarrow checked her watch. "And you'd better hurry or they might leave."

Isobel nodded, walking out with a snap to her step. The weather was warming up, the sun coming out with a vengeance as she wound around the lake, noticing all the flowers that were just starting to come out in little buds, basking in the warm, sunny air. Everyone seemed happy and excited, like they did every weekend. Saturdays were for the first and second-year students, whereas Sundays were for the older students. She spotted a group of second-years hurrying down the path and chattering, sharing peeks of the packages their families had brought for them. She spotted a bundle of the almond cookies that they made in the settlement her mother had come from, and stacks of letters from fans or friends back home.

The nerves tugging at her increased, building and building until she reached the family centre. She gave her name to the attendant at the door distractedly, scanning the faces.

"Go on to the chapel," he told her, already waving for the next student.

She faltered.

The chapel?

That was for students whose family members were …

No.

It wasn't possible.

She stumbled out of the way, pushed by a first-year desperate to fly into the arms of an older man who could have been a father or uncle. The path grew hotter as she rounded the family centre, coming up to the chapel shrouded in the shade of towering oak trees. It was quieter there.

She stepped inside, a cool air-conditioned breeze teasing the sticky strands of her ponytail. There were two small groups gathered around small confessional-style booths, quietly spending time together as they paid their respects to whatever member of their family they had lost. She also spotted a boy alone in one of the booths and a familiar man near the front of the dais, standing before an unlit candle. He was huge, with blond hair, his hands held behind his back.

"Father?" She stopped behind him, her heart beating out of her chest.

She felt him before he turned, the assault of his grief and anger beating into her ribcage. He was also annoyed and uncomfortable. Unlike the other Alphas she had encountered at Ironside, her father's emotion didn't just batter against her, it threatened to roll right over her. To flatten her. He faced her, his hands disappearing into his pockets, his honeyed, gold-specked eyes hard on hers.

"Isobel."

She waited. Like her mother was about to step out from a side door, having left to go to the bathroom.

She waited until his face crumpled and his fists clenched in his pockets.

"Pay your respects to your mother," he said, nodding toward the candle.

Finally, she saw her.

Caran Carter's beautiful, angular face was inside a small frame, wavy blonde hair reaching the edges of the glass, the heart-rending, familiar smile unwavering. The likeness sat before a candle.

Her mother was now a photo in a frame.

Her mother was now a candle in a chapel.

Her mother was …

Isobel took a shaky step backwards, her head

whipping from side to side, but her father strode forward, his grip like iron wrapping her bicep and dragging her forward.

"I told you to pay your respects," he growled, holding her against the little podium.

It had been some time since she had felt his grip. That strength that made her bones feel small and fragile. She still remembered the snap in her wrist from the last time she had fought against him, so she didn't attempt it now. She stood there, forced to confront a face that had become nothing more than a memory, all without her knowledge.

"When?" she croaked on an exhale that threatened to break her.

But she wouldn't allow it.

Not in front of him.

Not in front of the cameras.

Not yet.

"Just before Thanksgiving last year," he answered. Adding, "I wanted you focussed on your studies."

Not yet. *Please, fuck, not yet.*

"But now that you know, I'll be visiting when I can, and I'll be expecting regular, detailed progress reports, especially with your third year approaching. You've flown under the radar too long."

"Okay." It was barely a word. More like the sound

of a wounded animal, slinking away pitifully beneath the table.

"I've brought your clothes, as the dorm supervisor requested." His grip on her arm loosened, only slightly. "They said they would take the suitcase to your room."

She waited, the smiling face in the frame becoming blurry. She couldn't drag her voice up from her throat, couldn't deliver the gratitude he expected, even when his grip tightened again, making her whole body flinch.

"Isobel ..." he warned. "This is not how you treat your father."

She reached down inside herself and tore her walls open, revealing the bleeding chasm of her chest, raw and screaming out in sorrow as she sucked in all the ugly darkness her father threw at her, consuming everything he had built up since her mother's death. The loneliness, the rage. *So much rage.*

And regret.

Usually, this was her mother's job. But he had nobody left. He had been saving it up.

It tasted like acid washing down her throat, but she didn't step away until she was finished, until he was as strong and impeccable as he expected himself to be—as pure and untarnished as his wife had made him every single day, sipping away at his darkness and taking it into her own heart.

Isobel refused to meet his eyes, fighting off the sickness that now roiled inside her, threatening to eat her alive.

"Very well." He spoke softly, unemotionally, answering something he saw in her face. "I'll see you soon. Make me proud, Isobel."

He reached out to cup her cheek, and she jerked back so violently she knocked over a candlestick on the dais behind her. Her eyes were almost unseeing, barely categorising her father's frowning face and the way he flicked his eyes about the chapel, noticing the attention they were receiving before he turned on his heel and strode out.

The boy who had been in the booth beside theirs swam before her rapidly fading vision, and all she caught was the deep, weightless darkness of his eyes before he caught her arms.

They were ringed in heady, vibrant gold.

"Sigma?" His voice was a low rumble, rough around the edges.

"Not here." She was talking to herself, closing her eyes and fighting with everything left inside her. "Not yet. Not yet ..."

He wrapped his arm around her waist and tugged

her arm over his shoulder, dragging her to a door and up a set of concrete stairs. She didn't open her eyes until she felt the breeze on her face, and she took only one look at the blissfully bare rooftop before she crumpled to her knees, a wail keening from her chest. It was pitched low and painful, all of her agony breaking into the sound. She curled into herself, rocking from side to side, her tears making her skin slippery.

"I'll kill him," she whimpered, overwhelmed by the mixing of grief within her, the too-hot rage that built and built until she had no idea who it belonged to anymore.

Her father's, or hers?

Her limbs were weakening, her stomach cramping, her head spinning, the heat of the sun only making it all worse. She vaguely recalled the gold-ringed eyes of whoever had dragged her up there, but she was weakening too fast to lift her head and check if he was still there. She tried crawling back toward the blurry door she could see, hoping it led back downstairs.

She couldn't pass out on a roof with no cameras or people.

What if she didn't wake up?

It had happened, before. She had taken too much from her father when she was too small, and the fit had stopped her heart. Her mother had rushed her to the emergency room, and they had told her how lucky she was to be the daughter of an Icon, to have access to their services. Because of him, she lived.

The twitching started, worse than usual, and her reaching hand recoiled, grasping the cloth over her chest.

"Oh god," she groaned against the concrete. "It's happening."

OSCAR SATO KNEW EXACTLY WHAT WAS HAPPENING, BUT HE hadn't seen it hit so violently before. He ducked down, slipping his arms beneath the Sigma's back and legs, lifting her easily. She was light as a feather, trembling like the wind was strong enough to blow her away. He carried her to the rooftop air-conditioning unit, sitting back against it, using the shade it provided to get her out of the sun.

Her skin was covered in a light sheen of sweat, loose tendrils of golden hair sticking to her neck, chest, and forehead. He brushed them back, her eyes briefly fluttering open, staring sightlessly at him, searching around like she couldn't tell where she was. Her pupils were blown out, almost meeting her black Sigma ring, leaving only the barest hint of tawny colour. She was flushed, breathing hard, her eyes closing again. And that was when the fit started in earnest.

He set her down, cushioning the back of her head as he pulled out his phone with his other hand, debating whether he should text Theodore or not. They were trying to be friends, or something stupid like that. It was a hot topic in Dorm A, causing enough drama to keep Oscar amused from sunup to sundown. Maybe it would be best if there was a friendly face here when she woke up. Or maybe it was better that she woke up alone.

Her breath stuttered, becoming a soft rasp before spluttering out, her body growing still.

"Oh fucking hell." He tossed his phone aside, tucking his face against her chest, trying to listen for her heartbeat. She didn't seem to be breathing.

He set his hands against her chest, interlocking his fingers and pressing down, shifting his leg to the other side of her hip until he could lean his weight over her. He counted thirty compressions and then ducked his head to hers, pinching her nose and gripping her chin to pull her mouth open. He had watched her throughout the week as the Alphas argued about her existence, just for the fun of it.

She was small and sweet, and he would have bet that she had never been kissed.

She would probably have a whole new fit if she ever found out his mouth had been on hers.

Even if it was filling her chest with air.

He didn't even realise that he had licked his lips, subconsciously tasting her as he went back to pressing against her chest. He counted out another thirty compressions and then dipped back to her mouth, breathing into her twice, his hand light against her chest to feel the way she expanded slightly with his breath.

Still, she didn't seem to be making any movements of her own. A lick of panic crawled its way along his spine, and he went back to his compressions with perhaps a little too much weight, because when she breathed again, it was on a desperate gasp of pain. He quickly rolled her over, crouching behind her as she curled into herself, arms wrapped around her chest. She was breathing raggedly, slow, sluggish sobs catching in her throat. He kept a hand against her back, reassuring himself with the rise and fall of her shuddering body until she seemed to get her wits about her, her sobs dying off as she began to struggle upright.

He jumped to his feet, using his Alpha speed to get

past the door before she could fully turn around. He raced down the steps and left through the back of the chapel, looping around the family centre so she wouldn't even see him leaving from her vantage point on the rooftop.

He made it back to Dorm A, stopping in the common area, where Theodore and Kilian were lounging on the couches, talking quietly while they went over last night's episode of the Ironside show.

"How was it?" Kilian asked, catching sight of him.

He shrugged, his attention switching to Theodore, who arched a dark brow in silent question.

Oscar opened his mouth, but caught the taste of her on his tongue again.

She had smelt like deadly nightshade, bitter and acidic, but she had tasted like the sweetest pain, a poisoned cherry, and he liked that kind of thing. He closed his mouth again, shaking his head and continuing on down the hallway. He knocked on Elijah's door, propping it open before the other boy could answer.

"Hey," he said, as Elijah looked up from his books, pushing a set of black glasses up his nose. "Let me know when the Sigma gets back to her room."

Elijah just stared at him. "I said I wasn't going to activate the feed, Oscar. Not unless it was necessary."

Elijah was the master of half-truths.

"I already checked your computer." Oscar gave him a bored look. "You must have found a necessary reason."

Elijah sat back, ripping his glasses off and tossing them onto his desk. "What's *your* necessary reason?" he asked.

"Just let me know." Oscar slammed the door, continuing to his room. He closed himself in, but the restless energy inside him refused to dissipate. He was like this every other Saturday after he visited the chapel, after he was forced to watch all the other students giddily returning from their family visits. He paced around for a few minutes before bursting from his room. Theodore and Kilian watched as he left the dorm again, and as much as their concerned looks annoyed him, he couldn't dredge up the effort to snap at them to stop treating him like a wounded animal.

He jogged down the stone steps winding up Alpha Hill and walked back to the family centre. The tablet-guy at the front door tried to ask for his name and information, but a single baleful look had the man stepping back and turning to the next student instead.

He dragged a chair to the middle of the room and looked toward the door with a fake, hopeful expression, like he was waiting for some long-lost relative to enter. His ability knew his real purpose, however, and it rose to the surface, infecting the room like a slow, invisible fog, reaching vaporous tentacles into the chatty mouths and brightly-flushed ears of all the stupid, fucking, happy families.

It took only a moment for chaos to break out, and he sighed as he tipped his head back to look at the ceiling, basking in the cacophony of sound that rose up around him. The gathered people were playing happy families no longer. Chaos had them gripped. People were tripping over their words, accidentally insulting their closest loved ones. Someone caught a takeaway coffee to the face. Bags ripped, people tripped, and a girl screamed in outrage.

It was music to his ears.

7

DORM A

Isobel spent all day and night in bed, letting her phone die as she stared at the wall. She refused to cry again, a haunting numbness creeping through her, making itself at home inside her mind and body. Eve had knocked on her door a few times, calling out to ask if she was okay, and her room was the first place Isobel stopped by after dragging herself through a shower.

"Isobel!" Eve jumped off her bed, scattering notebooks and loose papers. "Oh my god, you look terrible."

Isobel found a tremulous smile as the other girl gripped her arms, leaning back to take her in before setting a hand against her forehead. "You were sick again, weren't you?"

"Yeah," Isobel croaked. "I'm sorry."

"Don't be silly," Eve chided. "But you should have answered my messages at least! I could have dropped off some food for you."

Isobel gently extracted herself, patting Eve's hand. "I'll do that next time. I should go and see Theo. We were supposed to have another swim lesson, but I let my phone die."

Eve bit back her smile. "He must be upset. I doubt anyone has stood him up before. You should eat before you go, though."

Isobel only nodded, because she wasn't going to make any promises she couldn't keep. She grabbed her dead phone and stuffed her swimsuit into her bag, hoisting it over her shoulder as she slipped out of the dorm, walking back toward the lake. She probably should have paused long enough to charge her phone, but by the time the thought occurred to her, she was already at the base of the steps winding up Alpha Hill.

She sighed, adjusting her bag and walking up, her head hung low. She was a little nervous, but the great big chasm of numb disassociation still had her firmly in its dark grip, carrying her through the movements her mind deemed necessary until she was at the entrance to the dorm, her hand dropping back to her side after knocking loudly against the door.

Dorm A wasn't anything like Dorm O—whose doors usually hung open in the daylight hours, a steady stream of activity bustling through the corridors. Dorm A was eerily silent, a single polished slot beside the door for mail.

The door opened after a minute, a man filling the opening. She had to search through her frazzled mind for a moment to recall his name. Mikel Easton, one of the Alpha professors—and, she supposed, one of the dorm supervisors. There were always at least two dorm supervisors for every level of the dorms, and since there were only two Alpha professors, she assumed they both likely doubled as supervisors.

"Carter," he greeted immediately, knowing exactly who she was. He stepped forward, easing the door half-closed behind him. "I wasn't expecting you today."

She shifted her weight from foot to foot. "Professor Easton." She cleared her throat of the husky, too-quiet tone. "I-I'm sorry. I was sick."

"Did you let Theodore know you were coming?" His body language seemed at ease, open and friendly, but his voice was a little sharp, just like his features. She had seen his profile and the few promotional reels of him on the Ironside website, but nothing could have prepared her for the litany of scars that scattered across his skin. What had *happened* to him?

She focussed on one in particular, dragging through his lower lip, before forcing her eyes up to his. His golden Alpha ring hugged sharp, dark blue eyes with splotches of black in them. They didn't exactly match—one of them blacker than the other. She winced, focussing on another scar slicing his eyebrow in half, but she couldn't hide from the thrum of anger that radiated out of him and into her.

He didn't like people flinching at his appearance.

Who would?

She sucked in a breath. "Sorry." She exhaled on the word. "I'm still ... a bit sick. And I haven't charged my phone yet, so I haven't reached out to Theo yet."

"Theo," he echoed softly before stepping back, flinging the door open wide. "Well, you're lucky, he just came back from a run. He's in the last room on the left." Easton pointed down a long hallway, stepping aside for her to pass by him.

She kept her head lowered as she slipped past, fighting off a shudder as his red-hot emotion followed her, a tinge of resentment licking up her spine.

"I'll be in my office here if you need anything." His voice followed her, light and easy. Completely at odds with his emotion.

"Thank you." She turned to look at him, but he had already disappeared.

Her steps slowed as soon as she realised she was alone. Her eyes crawled around the dorm, her jaw dropping open. On-screen, it had seemed vast and luxurious, but that was nothing compared to how it felt to be standing within the embrace of those high oak-panelled walls, with sunlight slanting in from giant windows and strategic skylights. The stone beneath her feet was polished to a bright sheen, the wide hallway opening into a common room blanketed by a thick, plush carpet and several deep couches and armchairs. The dorm was designed like some sort of luxury woodland chalet, with mile-high ceilings and log pillars framing walls of glazed glass looking out onto the beauty of Alpha Lake. The walls were painted royal blue, with darker oak accents scattered about, and the doors further into the hallway were a rich cherry oak.

She crept forward, feeling like an intruder as the twisted, polished wooden chandeliers cast glittering light patterns down over her. The first door swung open before she made it past, a bare chest appearing before her face.

She *never* thought she would ever be three inches from the naked muscles of Gabriel Spade's sternum, but there she was, blinking at the light sheen of sweat covering his skin. He had a towel slung over his shoulder, his nostrils flaring.

"I thought something smelled out of place," he said, crossing his arms and leaning against the doorjamb. "Weren't you supposed to be here yesterday?"

"In any other dorm, you wouldn't know that," she found herself replying, at a loss for what else to say.

"This isn't any other dorm." He gave her a quick once-over, and she took the opportunity to do the same, though she only categorised his face.

There was no way she was going to check out a shirtless Spade. No way in hell.

His usually impeccable, dark blond hair was mussed, his tanned face a little flushed, his russet-eyes filled with a sort of detached curiosity. He was usually tucked into one of the training rooms in the mornings with Reed, even on the weekends. Maybe they jogged home. She caught a hint of sunscreen mixed in with his scent, and figured she was right.

"Something happened, didn't it?" he surmised, finishing that calculating sweep of her person.

"What do you mean?" She feigned ignorance, glancing over as another door opened. Reed appeared across the hall, not the least surprised to see her.

"Could you really smell me from inside your room?" she added, a little surprised.

"Spade is sensitive to things that aren't in their proper place," a voice drawled, drawing her eyes over to yet another door. She hadn't even noticed Ashford appearing. He smiled at her, but the motion was stiff, almost harsh. He brushed past her without another word, Reed and Spade both glancing after him.

"What did you do to Cian?" Reed asked, a hint of humour to his question.

"Nothing," she grumbled, easing back from Spade's doorway. She wanted to continue past them but didn't want to be rude.

They weren't exactly being unwelcoming, but they were watching her warily, and Reed especially seemed to be staring holes through her, like he was trying to figure something out.

"Okay, well ..." She started to awkwardly step away. "I'm sorry to disturb you both."

They just silently watched her as she approached the last two doors, hesitating over which one to knock on. She turned to the right, but a sound from Reed had her pausing.

"Not that one." His smile was small, secretive. "You don't want to knock on that one."

She frowned, hearing something on the other side of the door.

"Uh-oh." Spade chuckled. "Better run, little Sigma."

She stared at the door handle, which had begun to turn, and quickly spun to the other door, shoving it open and falling inside.

"Where is she?" a rough voice asked on the other side of the door, sounding so close. So familiar.

"Just missed her." Reed clucked his tongue, the sound faint through the door. "Are we playing games or not?"

"Gabriel hasn't even showered," the rough voice razed back. "Call me when you're actually ready."

"Illy?"

She tore herself away from the door, staring at the boy who had just walked out of an adjoining bathroom, a pair of track pants hung low on his hips, a towel dragging through his dark hair. Theodore dropped the towel, his eyes widening. "You're here."

She nodded dumbly.

His eyes crawled over her. "What's wrong? What happened?"

She immediately looked up, searching for cameras, even though she knew the private rooms in Dorm A weren't filmed. Theodore stepped into her personal space, his thumb against her chin, easing the tremble that had taken up residence there. "Illy?"

The nickname her mother had given her almost sent her to her knees again, but she pushed away the despair, forcing the words out of her mouth in a mindless rush.

"I'm sorry, I got sick. Let's go swimming."

He inhaled, licking his lips. "You don't smell sick. You smell hurt."

She scoffed, but the sound lacked confidence. "You couldn't possibly know that."

"Maybe I shouldn't," he admitted. "We haven't spent that much time together." There seemed to be a *but* that he didn't expand on, and she was happy for it to remain unspoken.

"I got some bad news," she finally said. "Can we go swimming?"

He must have sensed or *smelt* her urgency to avoid the conversation, because his whole facade shifted, his beautiful smile blossoming as his touch dropped from her chin. "Sure thing, pretty. You can get changed in the bathroom." He directed her through the still-open door, closing it behind her as the word he had called her hung between them.

He seemed to have said it without any thought, but it nipped at the back of her mind, demanding to be acknowledged and dissected. She tried to swat it away as she shucked her clothes and extracted her swimsuit, stepping into the one-piece. As she pulled the straps around her shoulders, she turned to face the mirror, sucking in a breath at her appearance.

Her hair lacked its usual bounce, her eyes flat, ringed by dark bruises, her skin pallid.

Pretty, he had said.

She frowned, dragging the towel from her bag and wrapping it around herself. She hesitated, unsure where to put her bag. The bathroom was the most intricate room she had stepped into yet. The walls were designed in a wave pattern, curving around and flattening in places, dark blue panelling on the lower halves and pure white marble on the upper halves. The taps, handles and fixtures were varnished dark gold, the mirror ringed in soft, hidden lighting. The shower was a curved vestibule of tiny glittering tiles. There were jets above and to the sides, with a very complicated control panel in the wall.

She left the room feeling a little dazed, which only worsened as she came face-to-face with Theodore again. He had swapped the sweats for his swim shorts, showing off that surprisingly muscular body again.

"These rooms are so different to the other dorms ..." She spoke breathily, the awe in her tone obvious.

"I know." There was just a touch of bitterness in his voice. He had grown up in poverty, unlike her, and his family remained there.

"Let's go." His hand engulfed hers and he pulled her after him, pausing when he reached the common room, where Reed and Spade had gathered with three more Alphas. Oscar Sato, Niko Hart, and Moses Kane.

"You've already met Elijah," Theodore began, and she realised he was about to introduce her.

She drew back a step and half-hid behind him, trying to avoid the five sets of eyes that were now fixed unwaveringly on her. "That's Gabriel." He motioned to Spade, whose lips twitched.

"We've met," he said.

Theodore grunted. "Right. When? Never mind." He shook his head, pointing at Hart. "That's Niko—don't call him Hart, he hates that."

Niko regarded her slowly, his usually infectious smile absent, his almond-shaped eyes, usually large and heavy, narrowing on the way her hand was wrapped in Theodore's. She tried to pull it away and Niko's perfectly shaped brows jumped slightly, passing an inquisitive look to Theodore, who gripped her even tighter.

"Hello, Isobel," Niko drawled. He surprised her with her first name before turning back to the screen before them, twitching a few buttons on the controller in his hands.

"This is Moses." Theodore tapped the back of the armchair closest to them, where the side of Moses' profile was only just visible. His dark hair was curlier than Theodore's, his grey eyes so dark they reminded her of the first time she had seen Theodore in the library.

He had a bruise blossoming across the side of his face, and his lips—a little fuller than Theodore's—were swollen and split.

He nodded at her, dark eyes fixing on Theodore's hand. He had a more visceral reaction than Niko, flinching back and focussing on the TV, anger radiating out of him. Isobel didn't need to be a Sigma to feel it.

"And that's Oscar." Theodore nodded his chin toward Sato, who was staring unblinkingly at Isobel, quietly taking in her reactions to the others.

She knew the rough voice belonged to him. The others had warned her away from his room, and Sato was the only Alpha who inspired that amount of fear and caution. He hadn't declared an ability, but that didn't stop people from suspecting, and their guesses weren't good. It would have to be an illegal ability for him to have not declared it, which drew plenty of wary and watchful attention to him, though the production team seemed to shy away from airing any of the footage they captured—either that or he was remarkably good at avoiding the cameras.

Sato didn't greet her, and the longer she stared at him, the more his eyes appeared familiar. It swam back to her in a haze, the deep dark depths ringed in gold. The rough voice in her ear. The touch against her back, measuring the rise and fall of her breaths. The rooftop door slamming before she managed to find her feet.

Her hand raised instinctively, touching her chest. Those gold-and-obsidian eyes flicked to focus on the movement, zeroing in on something. She glanced down, catching the hint of a bruise that crept out past the edge of her towel. She swallowed, tearing her hand from Theodore's and striding outside.

She hadn't looked down at herself as she showered in a daze after waking up, and she had been too focussed on Theodore calling her pretty to look at herself in the mirror until her swimsuit was on, but now she was desperate to tear it all off. To discover what Sato had done to her.

Or done *for* her.

She pushed through the door, spilling outside with Theodore behind her.

"Illy." He caught her hand again, but he was gentle. "Isobel."

She paused, her eyes on the lake. "My mom died," she whispered. "Last year. My father only told me yesterday."

He tugged her hand, surprising her by drawing her tight to his bare chest. His skin was warm, his touch so soft, gentling against the back of her head.

"I'm so sorry." He breathed the words into her hair, taking a deep breath like he could suck away her pain through her scent. "Oscar—*Sato* was at the chapel yesterday. Did he see something?"

She pulled back, resisting the urge to burrow against his rich amber smell. She didn't know him that well, even if he had offered the hug in the first place. He kept his hands on her arms as she loosened the towel, pulling down the top of her swimsuit to reveal the mottled bruising to the both of them.

"I think he saved my life," she whispered, staring down at what seemed to be the beginning of a hand print.

Theodore swore, touching the tender skin before extracting her grip and tugging the top of her suit back up. "You're going to need to explain that," he suggested, his tone off.

She glanced up, catching the darkness shivering over his eyes.

"Some part of me feels responsible for you," he ground out. "Maybe because of what you did in our first year, but ... I tried to fight it, but I feel defensive of you, now. Like I owe you my protection. I don't like ..." His breath shuddered. "I don't like feeling out of control. I don't like ..."

A shudder travelled up the entire length of his body, and he cast a quick glance back to the dorm, his emotion pushing through to her.

Alarm.

She tried to open herself, to suck it in, but the wound inside her was too raw, refusing to crack, nothing able to staunch the bleeding inside her.

"I get sick," she hurried to say, her shaking fingers reaching for his. He gripped her tightly, his eyes swinging back to hers. They were still darkening, the colour bleeding very slowly outwards. "Very sick," she specified. "When I take on too much of people's emotions."

"I know," he croaked, clearing his throat. "My mom was a Sigma." The darkness jumped inward, almost swallowing his eyes. "She died the day you found me in the library. She took too much and her heart stopped."

His attention drifted down to her chest, his breathing ragged. She pressed forward, pulling her hand from his to cup his face, forcing his eyes to hers.

"If I could take this from you, I would—"

"No." He covered her hands, but his voice was harsh and grating. "Don't you dare."

"What can I do?" she whispered. "Theo? I'm okay. Nothing happened."

"Apologise," he growled low. *For lying.*

She sighed, wishing she could bump her forehead against his, but he was too tall. "I'm sorry. But I'm here. I'm fine. My heart is still beating."

He stared at her chest so hard she almost believed he could see through skin and bone to the beating organ beneath, and then he suddenly swept her up, breaking her grip on him. One arm banded behind her legs, the other against her back, pressing her chest against the side of his face. He was listening, trying to seek out her heartbeat.

She hesitantly touched the tousled dark hair atop his head before tracing her shaking fingers through the strands. He shuddered, sinking into her, his arms tightening around her. He smelled heady, his scent wrapping all the way around her, his warmth burning through her skin, but the sensation of his breath, short and sharp, blowing right against the top of her swimsuit, was so shocking she could only grip onto his hair and wait for him to gently place her back on her feet.

She looked up into his face, seeing that his stormy eyes were back, colour high in his cheeks.

"Fuck." He toed the ground, the tremble still in his limbs as he dug his hand through his hair, messing the strands up even more. "I'm so sorry. That was ... I should have ..." He groaned, the pinkish colour deepening. "Forgive me?" he asked, dipping his head in shame and peering at her through the fan of his dark lashes.

"Okay." She laughed, unable to help herself. His change from growling and dangerous to blushing and cute was just too much to handle. Nobody could stay immune to that.

He surveyed the dorm, letting out a sigh. "At least they didn't see." He began rounding the lake, slowly coming into view of the high glass walls of the dorm. "Since when were you friends with Spade? He never mentioned he knew you."

She picked up her towel, scrambling after him. "I'm not, really. Sometimes I pass him and Reed in the practice rooms."

"Well." He spun around, tossing his towel to a bench set amongst a little flower garden, edged by rocks. "It's probably best they don't know what just happened."

"You're my friend," she said with a frown. "They're not my friends."

He smiled, kicking off his flip-flops and walking into the lake. He had been right about the water—it was so pure it was almost transparent. She watched the little fish darting away from him as she followed, both of them pausing when the water lapped at her chest and his stomach.

"What now?" he asked.

"Now, you float," she told him. She didn't want to admit that she had researched how to teach someone to swim in preparation for this. She stepped back up the rocky slope of the lake, gaining some height over him as she gently pushed against his chest. He walked backwards into the water, his eyes on her, like he didn't even care if he stepped off a sudden ledge and drowned. It was unnerving.

"Okay." She stopped, and so did he. She touched his stomach, the muscles twitching beneath her fingers as she turned him sideways, her other hand flat against his upper back. "Now just lean back into my hand," she instructed. "Like you're trying to lie down on the water."

He obliged, and she shot a quick look to the glass

walls, unable to see through them. Still, she could *feel* their eyes.

Watching.

Judging.

"Perfect," she said, even though his hand had shot out, gripping her hip beneath the water. It seemed like an unconscious movement. "You won't go beneath the water," she reassured him, earning a disbelieving snort.

She bit back a laugh. "Okay, now lift your legs up and I'll hold them like I'm holding your back."

He tried to right himself in a wild splash of movement, pushing her back a few steps until they weren't in such deep water. His wet hair was plastered to his face, his dark eyelashes spiked with perfect little teardrops.

"No way," he growled. "There is no way in hell you're going to carry me bridal-style through the lake. I will *never* hear the end of it. And there are cameras out here," he added, jerking his head to the side, where a long pole stood at the top of the steps to Alpha Lake. It was too far to hear them, but close enough to view the entire lake. Luckily, the spot where Theodore had almost lost control of his ferality was blocked by the towering cacti edging that side of the lake.

She giggled, quickly biting down on her lip to cut

off the sound. He gave her a rueful look, and the sound escaped again.

"There has to be another way to teach me that won't make national headlines," he pleaded, squeezing her hip.

She hadn't even realised he was still holding her.

"I could get you floaties," she suggested.

"You're so cruel," he groaned, finally releasing her.

She walked back to the edge of the lake, still biting back her amusement. "Okay, I have an idea. Do you have any rope?"

"Why would I have rope?" he asked, pausing when his hips hit the water, his arms crossing over his chest.

With a light shrug, she stepped out of the water, peering around. Dorm A was so separate from the rest of the campus, almost like its own little world. Surely, they would have a separate maintenance shed so that the groundskeepers wouldn't have to cart things up and down those stone steps every day.

"Where are you going?" Theodore called out as she started to walk away.

"Be right back!" she tossed over her shoulder, slipping her wet feet into her flip-flops. She squelched back to the front of the dorm and spotted what she was looking for tucked away into the side of the building. A small attached room, a padlock hanging open on the thick, barn-style door. She pushed inside, giving her eyes a second to adjust to the sudden shade. Everything was arranged neatly on benches and shelves. Garden tools and equipment, maintenance kits, and bags of soil organised almost obsessively. She grabbed a long rope from where it was coiled evenly around a hook, hefting it over her shoulder as she returned to the lake.

Moses gave up pretending to give his attention to the game they were playing when the Sigma returned to his view. He heard Theodore's loud laugh through the double-glazed glass, and he fought down the twinge of his own amusement when he saw what had caused it. The looped length of rope could have wrapped Carter from ankle to neck and completely covered her, but she was holding onto it like some kind of prize. The shadows beneath her eyes seemed to have lifted somewhat, the sun glinting off the water that sparkled on her skin.

Moses was the only one who was *actually* her age, though she wouldn't know that. It was hard to tell with Alphas, and they had used that fact to their advantage. He liked the way her narrow mouth tried to smile, her pillowy lips stretching back over straight teeth, poking into the sides of her cheeks. She had dimples, not just two in each cheek, but another two right at the sides of her mouth, two that dug into her chin, just beneath the sides of her mouth, and two high up, stretching between her eyes and cheeks. It was like her whole face rearranged to accommodate her smile, her skin dimpling everywhere.

He could see why Theodore wanted to be friends with her when she smiled like that. She had helped him in his darkest moment, and that was no small feat.

Still ...

He hated it.

He hated the way his brother laughed at her like he had never seen anything so funny. He hated that he couldn't go out there and join them. Laugh with them. Share in this surprising friendship that Theodore was risking so much to entertain.

"Just go outside," Kilian sighed. He had appeared while they were all staring out the window, controllers forgotten in their laps.

The others were playing again, but Moses was still staring.

"You know I can't." Moses forced his eyes from the glass. "I might mess up."

"You won't," Kilian promised gently, touching his shoulder.

He really believed that, but he was the only one. Elijah shot him a sharp look, warning him away from encouraging Moses to do anything he wasn't ready for. The only problem was ... he wasn't ready for anything. And it wasn't getting any easier.

"Well, I'm going outside." Kilian drew everyone's eye as he stalked toward the door, and then they all stood, unashamedly walking over to the wall to survey the scene.

Everyone except Sato, who threw down his controller, cast a single glance to the laughing girl outside before prowling out of the room, a hint of his scent trailing behind. Moses' nose was the most sensitive out of all of them, so he was able to pick up on the slight variation to Oscar's usual oleander signature. It was usually mild, like sweet nectar carried on a breeze, but there were times where that nectar thickened, darkened with a smoky flavour. That was what Moses smelled as Oscar disappeared, and it made him uneasy.

Theodore breaking out of their norm was one thing, but if something was affecting Oscar, then things really had tipped out of balance.

With a short, stabbing sigh, Moses pushed up from the armchair and joined the others at the window.

Carter had tied one end of the rope around the base of a palm tree, walking the other end around to the other side of the lake. Theodore was turning in the water, following her with his eyes.

"He likes her," Elijah commented.

"Obviously," Gabriel snorted. They should have been the pretend twins in the group instead of Moses and Theodore. They acted like they shared a single brain cell.

"Theo likes everyone." Niko was frowning at the scene, his eyes fixed to Carter before drifting over to Kilian, who had pulled off his shirt and was sitting on the bench by the lake, teasing Theodore about something. "And so does Kilian."

"So do you, usually," Elijah pointed out. "But you're not out there."

Niko shrugged lightly. "I don't see what all the fuss is about. Let the guy have a damn friend. She's pretty, she has a nice smile, and she has no chance of winning the game. Where's the harm?"

Even as he tossed out the question so carelessly, his eyes flashed quickly to Moses. *He knew what the harm was.*

They were balancing together, but it was precarious. Moses was always one slip away from exploding, and Theodore wasn't too far behind him. *Anything* could set Oscar off, and the rest of them were under constant pressure to keep the whole operation together.

She should have picked Kilian or Niko, and then they wouldn't have had to worry, but she chose Theodore. Theodore, who had become the glue binding them—and their plan—together. Theodore, who was now pulling himself across the lake by the rope she had strung up, proving to them all that he would always be the first one to jump in, to face the unknown on his own, and they would have no choice but to follow.

8
WELCOME TO THE GAME

A WEEK LATER, ISOBEL TRENDED IN EVERY SINGLE HIGHLIGHT on the Ironside website.

Sigma Carter and Alpha Kane sneak away for a midnight swim!

The most unlikely friendship in Ironside history doesn't sink like a stone in water? Carter and Kane together again!

Carter and Ashford partnered for the mystic arts, but what's this mysterious tension?

The Sigma and the Beta—are Carter and Bellamy friends or foes? Is a feud brewing?

Carter—an Icon reborn. Watch her dance! (Reed and Spade certainly did.)

She stared at the screen for a full ten minutes until the banging on her door shocked her out of her stupor.

"It's me!" Eve called out, knocking again. "Isobel!"

She quickly jumped up, unlocking the door and letting the other girl spill inside. Eve quickly shut and locked the door again, leaning back up against it with her hand on her chest.

"Have you seen it yet?" she demanded, her eyes a little wild. "You're trending. You're *everywhere*. You didn't tell me you've been going to Dorm A!"

Isobel fell back to her bed on the floor, turning her numb face to stare at the screen again. "When they didn't show us swimming the first time, I thought they were just going to ignore me," she admitted.

"No," Eve groaned. "They were just saving the footage for when it would have the most impact. What the hell is going on?"

Isobel chewed on her lip, looking back at the screen. "I don't know."

"You haven't seen it yet?" Eve gasped. "Any of it?"

Isobel shook her head, a cold trickle of trepidation dripping through her. Trending was a *good* thing. In the third year, it was essential to play the game, but Isobel wasn't there to play the game, and she wasn't even in the third year yet. She was there because her father had put her there.

He intended for her to play the game, but she only intended to escape him.

"This is good news." Eve reached over Isobel and

started last night's episode of Ironside, the opening
sequence filling her room with sound.

"Is it?" Isobel whispered back.

"Yes." Eve gripped her hand firmly. "This is
amazing."

"And when they come after me?" Isobel jerked her
chin toward the door.

Eve's lips twitched. "Make sure it's on camera."

The first ten minutes of the show followed around
the fifth-year candidates who were pulling ahead in
the popularity race, shadowing their antics through
Ironside Row, which was tucked along the back of the
academy on the other side of Market Street. It
consisted of interconnected buildings rigged to the
teeth with cameras and full of film-worthy activities.
It was carnival-themed, complete with wet and dry
obstacle courses, photo booths, carnival rides, a
haunted house, dance machines, and karaoke rooms.
There was even a "reaction" cinema screening the
latest movies and shows. It streamed the daily
Ironside episodes during the day and the Friday
specials in the afternoon, the same times they were
released to the public.

After exhausting themselves on that day's Ironside
Row antics, the scene suddenly switched, Ed Jones'
voiceover lowering to a conspiratorial whisper.

And what do we have here? he asked, as the camera panned in on Theodore. *Is that one of the Kane twins in the pool? I guess tonight is a very lucky night for Ironside fans—is that ... who is that?*

The camera angle switched, zooming in on Isobel's face.

Well well well. He chuckled. *If it isn't little miss Carter. You might remember her from last season, but she was only in one episode, isn't that right, Jack?*

Jack Ransom, the secondary voiceover for the show piped up. *That's right, Ed. I didn't think we'd be seeing her again. What are they doing in the pool? Can you tell?*

Looks like they're just talking. Jump on the website and comment on the episode, everyone! Let us know what these two could possibly have to talk about. Hold on, Jack. Are they holding hands? This looks like a very intense conversation. Is it possible some drama slipped under our radar? We might have to deploy our resources to get to the bottom of this. What do you think, viewers? Do we care? If your answer was yes, then you're in luck. Because that clip was actually from last week's footage, and we've been following our little Sigma around very closely since then. And, boy, *do we have a surprise in store.*

Just one? Jack chuckled gleefully.

What do you think of this, Jack? Ed spoke as the scene changed, showing Isobel slipping out of her booth in the dining hall to be immediately confronted by Bellamy, Rayne, and Crowe.

Looks like the Sigma landed herself in a little hot water with the second-year golden boy, Jack noted.

Uh-uh, Ed tittered, *not that. This.*

Reed stood from the other side of the room, and the cameras zoomed in on his face, showing the dark frown twisting his lips. He seemed to be staring at the three people crowding her against the booth. He picked up his tray and stalked his way to her side of the hall, the sounds from that morning suddenly crystallised through her laptop speakers, so that when he used his Alpha voice, it rang loud and clear. The other second-years scattered, leaving Reed and her staring at each other. In reality, it had only been a fraction of a second, but they slowed everything down, making it drag on, filling it with meaning and tension.

Well, that *was intense,* Ed breathed. *I have goose bumps.*

You get goose bumps over everything, Ed.

Oh, did you need something a little more titillating, Jack?

You wouldn't dare. Jack fake-gasped. *You can't broadcast what was clearly a private moment they decided to play out in front of obvious cameras on the most popular reality TV show in the world?*

Ed cackled. *I know, how naughty of me. Can you tell who's dancing there, Jack?*

I do believe it's little miss Sigma Carter.

Isobel flinched at the image of herself on screen, dancing like nobody was watching.

And she's astonishingly good too, Ed commented. *Do you know who else thought so?*

Don't tell me! Jack gasped. *No, don't tell me! I can't watch!*

Well, maybe you can cover your eyes. Ed had his gleeful tone back. *But these two certainly couldn't.*

The camera zoomed in close to Spade's and Reed's faces. They had walked into the room, seeming surprised to see her dancing there, but instead of knocking on the door or leaving, they quietly closed it and leaned up against the wall. And they watched. And watched. For far too long. There were enough cameras in the room that one might have been able to pick up their words if they had been talking, but they didn't say a word. They didn't even look at each other. It was like they could read each other's minds.

She's really quite good, isn't she? Ed commented, the camera angle regularly changing to show off her dance. *Maybe we were too quick to dismiss the Sigma. She is the daughter of Braun Carter, after all. Does he seem like the kind to send her into the academy without any training, do you think?*

Jack laughed ruefully. *No, Ed. I wouldn't expect that of him, but not even Braun Carter can pull enough strings to make these kinds of connections.*

Oh, you thought that was all? Ed asked. *I can assure you, the Sigma doesn't do things by halves. She seems to have connected with half the Alphas on campus. That would be an achievement even for a Beta.*

The scene changed after a dramatic slowing-down of the moment she passed by Reed and Spade on her way out of the room, showing her sitting alone in her Mystic Arts class. She knew what was coming next, but she still winced when Ashford knocked his desk up against hers and proceeded to do her tarot reading, slipping the card he had chosen into his pocket. Ed and Jack spent a few minutes speculating on why he would hide the card from the cameras when he was usually very showy with his readings in class, and that was followed by an embarrassing dissection of her every blush and fumble in Ashford's presence.

Can you blame her, though? Ed asked. *Half the world is in love with Ashford. Didn't your wife tell you Ashford was her new celebrity crush, Jack?*

Jack snorted. *She said that to your husband, Ed, and*

he agreed, but ... He seemed to shift closer to the microphone. *They're willing to wait until he graduates.*

What about your daughter? Ed shot back.

No way in hell, Jack grumbled. *That boy can stay the hell away from my daughter.*

Ed laughed good-naturedly. *Let's hope Braun Carter doesn't share your position, because it looks like these two have been partnered for the rest of the year. What do you think of that, Jack?*

I think things are about to get very interesting in Ironside. But I wonder how Kane feels about all these other connections our sneaky little Sigma is weaving?

Well, Jacky boy, I saved the best for last. Can you tell me what this building is?

It's Dorm A, of course.

Of course, Ed purred. *So what might our little Sigma be doing there?*

"Okay," Isobel croaked. "That's enough." She quickly clicked off the video, her mouth as dry as the desert. She licked her lips a few times, but it made no difference.

"Check your emails," Eve demanded. "You took up all five highlight spots for the week. I *need* to see what your rewards are! This is so rare, even for a Beta!"

Isobel navigated to her inbox, ignoring the other messages to zero in on the one from the Ironside officials. She clicked on it, and they both stared at the message, mouths dropping open.

Congratulations, Isobel Carter! You featured in all five of our trending spots this week. As a special gift, we would like to offer you an early accumulation of popularity points.

These points are special, as you know. They can be used in Market Street and Ironside Row in your third year, but they will also be serving another purpose we have created just for you.

If you reach 2,000,000 popularity points before the end of your second year, you will be moved from Dorm O to Dorm A, where you will be given a private room and bathroom, along with the benefits enjoyed by our resident Alphas.

Your current point status stands at 250,000 points.

After a moment of blank staring, Eve suddenly pounced off the makeshift bed, dashing over to the shelf and extracting a notebook and pen, which she then began to scribble in, mumbling to herself. When she finally looked up, there was a wildness in her eyes and a croak in her voice.

"That's fifty thousand points for every highlight, and we only have fourteen weeks left if you don't include spring break. It breaks down to forty highlights before the end of the year. That's almost three highlights a week."

Isobel sank back against the wall, understanding the game they were playing. They wanted her to cosy up to the Alphas to create drama, and they were dangling an impossibility in front of her to try and make it happen.

"I can't do it." She shook her head. "There's no way."

"Of course there is." Eve waved off her statement. "The weekly highlights aren't the only way to gain popularity points. Anything you post on social media will earn you points for views or likes—"

"I don't have social media," she interrupted.

Eve frowned. "Yes, you do. I follow you." She dug out her phone, flashing it in Isobel's face. It was a picture of her. And all the posts were old videos of her dancing. It looked like they had been professionally edited. She groaned, rubbing at her face.

"My father must have set it up."

"Ask him for the password," Eve suggested, though her brow was scrunched in confusion. "You need to try to do this, Isobel. If you want to keep being friends with ... Is it still only Theo?"

"Just Theo," Isobel muttered.

"Well, if you want to be friends with *Theo*, who, by

the way, is like some kind of Alpha *masterpiece*." Eve pointed at the laptop, her brows jumping up, a small smile twitching across her mouth. "Then you need to get out of this dorm. They will tear you apart if you keep this up."

"I just want to be left alone," Isobel whined, dropping back against her blanket, though she added in a lower voice: "Not that my father is going to let me after this."

"Welcome to the game," Eve sang, pulling on Isobel's arms to lift her up. "First things first, we need to figure out what you have to offer. You're not very funny—no offence."

"None taken." Isobel deadpanned.

"And you're not very sexy—"

"Is this a very long list?" Isobel asked, wincing.

Eve laughed, a light tinkling sound. "Sorry, I meant you don't dress sexy and hook up on camera just for the sake of a scandal like some of the other girls."

Isobel waited because she knew there was more. Eve frowned around her room. "You're not very loud and you can't even enter Ironside Row, yet, which gets more screen time than any other building here." She hummed, her eyes catching on one of Isobel's leotards, hanging out of her bag.

"You can dance." She snapped her fingers. "And probably other things, right?"

Isobel toed the ground. "I ... I can play piano."

Eve smiled. "Anything else?"

"I like to sing, but my father didn't think I was good enough to pursue it. He wanted me to focus on dance."

"We'll see about that. Anything else?"

She sighed, brushing hair away from her face. "He made me learn some obstacle courses, like the ones on Ironside Row."

"Hmm." Eve's eyes took on a faraway, almost detached look. "We could work with that. How do you feel about breaking rules?"

"I don't know. Will it get us kicked out?"

"Highly unlikely." Eve grinned, showing all her teeth. "I have a plan, but I'm going to need a few weeks to put it together. You're sticking around here for spring break, right? I don't think I've ever seen you go home."

Isobel nodded, her father's face flickering into her mind for a brief, haunting moment. She would never be with her mother for any holidays ever again, and her heart wanted to blame him. Thanksgiving was her mother's favourite holiday. Isobel could still remember their quiet giggles as she snuck away from her lessons early to help with the special vegetarian dishes her mother snuck onto the menu just for her.

"Leave it with me, then." Eve clapped a hand on her shoulder, ducking to catch her lowered eyes. "By the end of March, you're going to beat out Bellamy for top place in our year group."

After the episode aired, she hid herself away in the library. Theodore must have assumed that she would be too busy with her dance practices to see him in the afternoons, because he mostly left her alone that week, only texting her on Monday to ask if she would come back to Dorm A on Friday night. She had agreed, but that was before she checked the headlines, and now, on Friday afternoon with only twenty minutes to spare before she was supposed to be at Dorm A, she found herself digging out her phone and offering up a pathetic excuse.

She abandoned her usual Alpha research after that, opening her laptop to create a new practice playlist. It took less than ten minutes for Theodore to show up, which meant he hadn't bothered going anywhere else to look for her. He had known exactly where to find her. He strode from the staircase, heading straight toward her cubicle, a faintly exasperated look on his face as he leaned up against the opening of her cubicle, folding his arms and regarding her silently.

"Sorry," she offered with a small smile. "I shouldn't have lied."

"Yeah," he drawled. "You don't look sick."

"Have you seen the latest episode yet?" she asked nervously.

"We all have." He gathered up some of her books, making room to perch on the edge of her desk. "Is it too much for you? I don't want the Omegas attacking you again."

He didn't offer to stop seeking her out, but it seemed to hang, wordless, between them. He bit on his lower lip, his stormy eyes soft on her face.

"I can handle it." She was lying through her teeth, but he didn't seem to care, for once.

He smiled his perfect, melting smile. "Great, then let's go. Kilian wants to see you, too."

"Maybe it should just be me and him," she joked. "He's probably the only one the production crew can't make a fuss over, because there couldn't possibly be anything going on."

"But there could possibly be something going on with us?" Theodore shot back, watching as she fumbled with the book she was trying to shove into her bag.

"I ..." She peeked up at him before quickly looking away. "I didn't mean ..."

"Relax," he teased. "I have a girlfriend now."

She froze, her knuckles turning white as she gripped another notebook. "Now? Girlfriend?"

Why did his smile look so forced?

"Yep." His lips popped on the word. "Sato introduced me to one of his Beta ... friends earlier in the week."

Why? she wanted to scream. *Why now? Why me? Why did he hesitate over the word "friends?"*

"Oh." She coughed to cover up the weird crackle in her voice. "Yeah. Okay. And she's your girlfriend already?"

He shrugged. "Stranger things have happened, right?"

Like the weird way her heart was thumping and the uncomfortable prickle of heat across her face.

"Actually," he added. "Reed and Spade have met people, too. It looks like things are heading in the right direction."

Another weird jolt ran through her, and it took her a good, long moment to realise all the weird sensations didn't belong to her.

Some of them belonged to him.

"Is this something I really needed to know?" she asked, stuffing her bag full and pulling it over her shoulder.

He immediately swept it off, hooking it over his own. "No. I don't know why I said all that. Sorry."

She wanted to scowl at him and declare she hadn't been trying to *date* him, to remind him that he was the one who had texted her, he was the one who invited her to Dorm A, he was the one who kept turning up, dragging her out of her shell ...

But he always seemed to know when she was lying.

And she would have been lying, because he was ... perfect. She *liked* him. She liked his beautiful smile and ridiculous muscles and the way he stared into her eyes, so focussed, so intent. She liked the way his full, unabashed laughter tickled all the way into her, and she liked his protectiveness. But she didn't need any more. She didn't need to belong to him to still enjoy his smile and laugh. She didn't need him to belong to her.

"Don't worry about it." She grinned at him. "What did you want to do tonight?"

"You didn't know?" He pushed his hair back from

his face, but it only flopped forward in perfect disarray again. "We're having a party."

"Oh, cool. So ... the Betas will be there?"

"Don't worry, Illy." He tucked her under his arm, the familiar feel of his breath warm against the top of her head. "It's outside, around Alpha Lake, in full view of the cameras."

They left the library, but to her surprise, Theodore didn't drop his arm from her shoulders, leaning down to quietly drawl sarcastic anecdotes to her every time they passed a group of students, putting her a little more at ease with all the staring and frantic whispering. He released her at the base of the steps, following behind her as she climbed up to Dorm A.

"Oh, you're here already," Theodore said, almost running into Isobel's back. His hands dropped to her shoulders, and the small group of Beta girls standing around the entrance to the dorm fixed their eyes to the movement with a laser-like focus.

One of them stepped away, her silver hair floating around her shoulders as she smiled up at Theodore. "Sorry, we're a little early. I thought you might want some help setting up." She glanced at Isobel before quickly returning her attention to Theodore.

She was stunning, and familiar. Renee Wallis. One of the best dancers in Isobel's *Lyrical Ballet* class. And the longer she stared at Theodore, the more he edged away from Isobel, finally dropping his hands from her shoulders and reaching out to Wallis instead. She smiled brightly, slipping her hand into his.

"Yeah, thanks, that would be great." He glanced back at Isobel. "Come on, Illy. I think Kilian had something to give you."

Isobel trailed them, ignoring the smug looks the other Betas were throwing her, like they had won some sort of battle against her and her kind. Inside the common room, Reed and Spade were crouched over a laptop on the coffee table, their expressions perplexed. Reed reached over and snapped it closed, both of them straightening up to survey the group.

"They were waiting outside," Theodore tossed out, chastising the two boys.

"Didn't hear the knock," Spade stated blandly. "Hello, James."

"You can call me by my first name." Another of the Beta girls broke away from the pack, sweeping a handful of smooth braids over a dark cocoa shoulder and flashing a dimpled smile at Spade, who just stared back impassively at her.

"Okay, Alissa." He was so toneless.

"Please." She laughed, stroking his arm. "It's Lissa. We've been through this."

"Must have forgotten." He turned a little, sharing a look with Reed, whose mouth twitched in amusement, before he fixed his attention on Isobel. "Nice to see you, Carter. Kilian had something for you."

"So people keep saying." She flicked her eyes around the room, but Gray was nowhere to be seen, and Reed's attention had already shifted, landing dispassionately on the third Beta girl to separate from her friends. Another blonde, her eyes a shimmering blue, her petite form so small beside Reed that he had to bend down a little for her to kiss his cheek.

Isobel spun, seeking out Theodore, who was looking down at Wallis indulgently, answering all of her questions about what had and hadn't been done for the party. He didn't look like he adored her. He looked ... well, the same way he always looked. Like a nice, attentive person.

"Where's Gray?" she asked when his eyes flicked to hers, feeling her stare on him.

"Middle door on the right," he said, pointing to the hallway behind him.

She felt his eyes on her even after she walked away, but she shook off the sensation, knocking on the door he indicated. It swept open, revealing a harrowed-looking Gray, who pulled her immediately through the opening.

"Isobel, I'm so sorry." His hand slid down her arm in a strangely comforting way. "Are you okay?"

"Why wouldn't I be?" she asked carefully.

He rolled his eyes, giving her some space as he dropped onto the window seat in his room. The Alpha rooms were so big, with enough space to fit a small living area and a study nook. He patted the seat beside him, and she wandered over, sinking into the soft cushions, turning her eyes toward the window. She spotted Moses struggling with a string of fairy lights out by the lake.

"Because those assholes sprang this on you without any fucking warning," Kilian growled, his usually soft tone taking on a grittier quality.

She assumed he was talking about the sudden appearance of three girlfriends she—and likely Ironside—had no idea about. "What does it matter to me?" She sounded a little defensive. "Theo is my friend, and I barely even know the other two. Or you," she tacked on, sweeping her eyes over him.

"I've folded your underwear," he pointed out. "That has to count for something."

She flushed bright red, clearing her throat.

"And it matters because ..." He tossed his hands up, suddenly rising from the bench. "Look, you don't know me, you're right. But I'm fucking sensitive, okay?"

She couldn't help the smile that threatened her lips. "Okay. You're sensitive."

"Exactly." He levelled a pale, graceful finger at her. "And I can't keep a secret."

She nodded. "Of course you can't."

"And I like you. We get along. Hanging out at the lake with you was fun. You have a nice laugh."

"That hardly seems relevant, but okay. Thank you."

He shot her a look, and her smile broke free again. Gray's angelic looks made him seem intimidating at first, but the more he worked himself up, the harder it was to bite back her laugh. He was messing up his beautiful pale hair, a tinge of agitated colour creeping across his perfectly snowy skin, his elegant hands gesturing all over the place.

"We have a ... special friend," he explained, falling back to his seat. "He warned us about the episode coming out. We held a meeting, like we do whenever there's some heat on one of us, let alone four of us. Kalen suggested Theo, Elijah, and Gabe be seen with some other girls. Spread the attention around a little, so all of it isn't on you."

"Kalen?" she parroted, realising who he was

talking about a little too late. Kalen West was the other Alpha professor. "Why does it matter so much?"

"Theodore doesn't want you punished for hanging out with him, and the rest of us agreed, mostly."

"What does Sato have to do with it?" She looked down at her fingers. "Theo said he was the one who introduced Wallis to him, but he said it in such a weird way."

"Wallis is …" Gray grimaced, looking at the window.

Moses had given up on the fairy lights and was violently yanking them from the palm tree.

"Well, actually, Wallis tried to hook up with Sato a few weeks ago. She literally snuck through his bedroom window."

She reared back. "What?"

"Yeah." He sighed. "It was messed up. But Sato didn't report her. He kept her on the hook, knowing he would be able to exploit a favour out of her at some point."

"Her and her friends agreeing to date three of the Alphas is a favour?" she asked, a little sarcastically.

"Without saying a word about what really goes on when they're alone, it is." He reached down to a bag at his feet. "Anyway, I got something for you, for your first Alpha party. I wasn't sure if you've managed to fix your clothes situation yet."

She stared at the bag and then dragged her eyes up to his beautifully pale gaze. "Why would you do that?" she asked.

"Because I'm a nice person, dummy. Here." He dangled the bag between them. "Hurry up and try it on."

She shook her head, dumbfounded, and took the bag from him. There was a pretty blue dress inside, light enough that she could even dance in it if she wanted to. She held it up against her chest, staring down at the slightly flared skirt fluttering against her shorts.

"It's beautiful," she whispered. "How did you get this?"

"Another special friend," he admitted. "She has a shop in Market Street. Put it on!"

"Do you mind?" she asked, gesturing to his bathroom.

"I wouldn't mind even if you changed right here." He shrugged, his lips curving in another of those soft, pillowy smiles.

He had probably meant it as a joke, but she was suddenly feeling the pressure of having to make a decision. Staying in the same room and getting changed seemed like some sort of gesture of trust between them as friends. Of course, if he hadn't been gay, the situation would have been different, but she decided to treat him like Eve, or any other of the Omegas girls in their shared bathroom.

She slipped her shirt over her head, diverting her eyes to the window, where Theodore had appeared to rectify Moses' butchering of the lights. "They can't see in, can they?" she asked.

"No." His voice was a little deeper than she expected, but when she glanced back to him, he was staring out of the window with her. "I expect the surprises will keep on coming tonight."

She stepped out of her shorts and then pulled the dress over her head, twisting to try and reach the zipper.

"Come here," Gray offered, his expression shuttered, that low tenor still riding his words.

She stepped closer, turning so he could reach the zipper. "What about Ashford?" she asked. "He was in the highlights as well. Why doesn't he have a pretend girlfriend?"

"Because he's already a man-whore in training," Gray muttered, smoothly sliding the zipper up. "Nobody cares." His hands landed on her hips, spinning her back around to face him. "You're really fucking beautiful, Isobel."

She flushed happily, her stomach twisting at the compliment even as some part of her brain registered how much he liked to swear. She smoothed down the material of the dress over her stomach, fluttering out the little skirt. "It's the nicest dress I've ever worn. You have great taste."

"No." He smiled tightly. "Not the dress. You."

She laughed, the sound coming off awkward. "I'm pretty average."

His eyes flashed, that strangely intense expression never shifting. He carefully released her hips. "Say that again in a year or two." He cleared his throat. "Maybe you don't see it, but you're going to break some serious hearts."

She gave him a flat look. "I can't even break a piñata."

His lush smile twitched halfway into existence. "Didn't you just say I have great taste?" he teased. "Trust me on this."

"You're into guys," she shot back. "Your taste in this department doesn't count."

Something raced across his expression, and all of a sudden his head was thrown back as he released a deep, husky laugh. "I get it now," he eased out between chuckles. "I was wondering why you were so comfortable whipping your clothes off in front of me."

"Oh my god," she rushed out. "I thought ... I didn't make you uncomfortable, did I?"

"You couldn't if you tried. I just forgot that was ... popular knowledge these days." He smirked. "Shall we head out?"

She quickly slipped her shoes on, bending to pick up her bag, but he gently caught her wrist. "You can leave that here. And you can stick with me tonight, if you want. Theo's loss is my gain. And I am into guys after all, so nobody can have a problem with it." He seemed highly amused by that prospect.

"Okay." She watched as his hand slipped down her arm, closing around her fingers, his touch so soft and gentle she was momentarily mesmerised by it.

He let out another breathy laugh, drawing her from the room.

9
LITTLE RABBIT

THE PARTY WAS MOSTLY SET UP, WITH BIG HEART BALLOONS and streamers. Pink and red drinks decorated the table, heart-confetti all over the place.

"Gray." She tugged on his hand, her feet refusing to go any further.

"Kilian," he corrected.

"What's with all the ... hearts?" she hissed out the last word.

"Valentine's Day?" He looked at her like it was obvious. "Dorm A always holds the annual Valentine's Day party?"

"Oh." She burst out laughing, drawing the attention of Moses, who was on his way back inside.

He stopped, looking at them, shoving his hands into his pockets and staring at the ground awkwardly.

"Have fun," he muttered, looking up once, his eyes narrowing a little, like something upset him.

"You should stay," Kilian suggested. "Just for a little while."

He grunted. "Would rather have a tickle fight with Oscar."

Kilian chuckled. "One hour," he bargained.

Moses lifted his head, brushing a dark curl from his eye before searching out Theodore, who was sitting lakeside, surrounded by the entire group of Beta girls, except for Reed's and Spade's girls, who were hovering nearby on the outskirts of the best-friend duo, looking like unwelcome third and fourth wheels.

"Theo is too busy," Moses said plainly.

"But we're not." Kilian arched his brows.

Moses slid Isobel a look. "Yes." His eyes darkened, fixing on Kilian. "*You* are. Hang out with the Sigma if you want, but I won't be joining. This is all because of her." He spat the words out, twisting on his heel and striding away.

"Lovely." Kilian shrugged off the entire interaction. "Everyone's on their best behaviour, I see."

Niko crested the top of the staircase, then. He seemed to lead a whole stream of Betas, with some Deltas thrown into the mix. They crowded around him like he was already an Icon. Like they just needed to touch him, to bask in his presence. Isobel scanned the rest of the faces gathering, mentally taking stock of who was missing. Sato, of course, but he never did social things.

Ashford.

Just as she thought his name, her phone vibrated in the pocket of her new dress. She pulled it out when Kilian released her, trailing him without really looking as she checked the message.

Lover: Do I detect Kilian's handiwork?

Lover? She frowned, almost bumping into Kilian, who had stopped, plopping down into one of the wooden chairs stuck into the sand sloping into one side of the lake. Reed and Spade were taking up two of the other chairs, and Ashford appeared out of nowhere, holding his phone as he stole another of the chairs. He raised a dark gold brow at her, resting his phone on his thigh.

Lover, as in *The Lovers*. The card he had pulled. Or ... she had pulled?

She glanced down at her dress, smoothing her hands over it again, painfully self-conscious.

"Sit," Reed told her, kicking out a long leg, nudging the only remaining free chair, between Spade and Kilian.

She sat on the very edge, looking around warily.

The two girls—James and the other one whose name she didn't know—were still hovering nearby, holding drinks they had apparently fetched for the boys. They had paused on their way back, counting the new bodies before sighing and heading back to the table to fetch more drinks.

Isobel fiddled with her phone, feeling a few too many eyes on her. She busied herself replying to Ashford's message mostly just so that she wouldn't have to make eye contact with anyone.

Isobel: Yes. He's very kind.

His reply was immediate.

Lover: A very saintly notch for your belt.

Her brows pinched in as she contemplated the message.

Isobel: You waited so long to text me I forgot what you were supposed to tell me in the first place.

After sending the message, she changed his name, far too conscious of all the eyes, all the cameras. The last thing she needed was someone to notice that she was texting someone called *Lover*.

Ashford: I told you I would give you a straight answer.

She chewed on her lip, glancing up at him from beneath her lashes. He was talking to Reed, somehow carrying on a conversation even though he was also texting her, his phone still open on his thigh. Kilian seemed to be following on with their conversation—something about a tennis match—but Spade was completely disengaged.

He was staring downward, his posture straight, tapping out a pattern on the wooden arm of his chair. The way he glared at the sand, it was like it had personally offended him. The longer she watched him, the more focussed she became on his tapping. It followed a distinct pattern. Three taps, break for one second. Three taps, break for two seconds. Three taps, break for three seconds … and then he started over. He lifted his boot, shaking off the sand, and then sighed, forcing himself to look away from the ground.

Her face was the first place he looked.

"How are things going with James?" She just said the first thing that popped into her head. "You two look cute."

"If glaciers can be cute," Ashford muttered, causing Kilian to snort out a laugh.

"Is that her first name?" Spade shrugged. "She's satisfactory."

"I'm sure that assessment will make her very happy." Isobel was teasing, but some of the humour bled from her words as her eyes drifted over the unhappy look on his face.

There was so much stimuli around, so many

people flitting to and fro, and it took her a moment to narrow down which thump of emotion belonged to him. He was *very* uncomfortable. *Because of the party, or because of her?*

She gripped the arms of her chair, easing her wall down until all that discomfort, unease, and frustration spilled into her. His breath was heavy and long, his eyes widening on her. She managed a tremulous smile as she turned away, sitting with the new twist of emotions in her gut and tucking her hands beneath her thighs to hide the sudden tremble in her fingers.

The two Betas returned, drinks bundled between them. They handed one to Spade, Reed, Ashford, and Kilian before settling on the sand either side of Spade and Reed, tipping their own drinks to their lips.

Kilian rolled his eyes, taking a quick sip from his cup before handing it to Isobel. "Here." His voice was loud. "Have mine. I'll get another one."

Reed started to frown, those cold eyes icing over. "No," he said, a slight command riding his rough voice. "Ellis and James will get it."

When the two Betas just looked at each other, eyes wide and disbelieving, Isobel quickly jumped up, shoving the cup back at Kilian.

She could feel the beginning of a growl in the back of Reed's throat, that biting precursor to his Alpha voice. She had heard it enough in her father to understand what it meant. She was a little shaky on her feet as she dashed away, making a beeline for the drinks table. Once she was there, she leaned against the edge, pulling in a deep breath.

She moved to grab one of the plastic cups, but a hand appeared, extracting it from her grip.

"Allow me, Sigma."

Bellamy.

She sighed, rubbing her temples. *Could her night get any worse?*

"Not happy to see me?" he guessed, a sly smile twisting his mouth. "But we make such great headlines together." He leaned in close, light green eyes searching hers. "Friends or foes?" he asked, the smile never wavering. "Don't you want to keep them guessing?"

"Not really." She folded her arms, propping her hip against the table.

"Oh?" he chuckled, his gaze sweeping over her. "Grew a great big pair of Alpha balls, did you?" He began pouring a drink, dropping his voice low. "Don't get too comfortable in the wolf's den, little lamb. I'd hate to see you eaten before I get a chance to play with you."

He handed her the drink and she fought the urge

to snatch it away, instead accepting it with a false smile. "Keep dreaming, Bellamy."

She turned on her heel and strode back to the circle of wooden chairs, only to find that Theodore had claimed her chair, Wallis sprawled over his lap. She was about to turn away when Kilian caught sight of her. He shook his head, crooking his finger at her. She approached, keeping her eyes from Theodore as Kilian's gentle grip wrapped around her wrist, pulling her toward him.

She had never sat on a boy's lap before, but Kilian was so graceful he made it seem natural, catching her hips when she would have lost her balance and sitting her across his thighs easily.

"Cheers," he muttered, knocking his cup against hers. "This Valentine's Day punch is awful. Who the fuck made it?"

"Moses did." Reed sighed. "I think he was trying to poison us."

"His mission was successful." Ashford frowned into his cup. "Where are our problem children anyway?"

Reed pointed up without even looking, and they all turned, peering up to the rooftop of the dorm. Sato and Moses weren't visible, but Reed seemed sure they were there.

"They'll come out to the edge when it gets dark," Reed advised. "Like vampires. Picking out which of us they would most like to torture, and how."

He seemed to be joking, but Isobel still shivered, her eyes scanning the rooftop. The bruises on her chest had faded, but she still remembered the distinct, mottled handprint.

Only Sato could turn saving someone's life into something frightening, like he was marking her for later, for something more sinister.

Kilian traced light fingers over her arm, soothing the shivers he must have felt, and she melted a little further against his chest. "Is this okay?" she whispered, so only he could hear. "Is this weird?"

"Is it more or less weird than me manhandling your underwear?" he asked.

"We can't use you manhandling my underwear as a gauge for our entire friendship."

His pillowy lips quirked. "Is it more or less weird than you getting almost naked half a foot away without so much as a warning?"

She choked on the mouthful of punch she had just taken, and Kilian laughed, patting her back. "It's completely fine," he reassured her. "I already told you, you can't make me uncomfortable."

Because he's not interested in you, she reminded

herself, as the flush of the drink spread through her body. The punch was so bad she hadn't even been able to tell there was alcohol in it until she started drinking it. She contemplated the cup and then sighed, resigning herself to only two more mouthfuls. She still had to get home and avoid being caught in a rush of vengeful Betas.

Headed by Ellis and Wallis, probably.

Reed's and Theodore's girls were doing the majority of the glaring, which was surprising since Theodore had barely spoken to her. Although ... he *was* staring. At her. At Kilian.

And he was frowning.

And he was ignoring Wallis, who eventually got up and sat beside Ellis, the two of them bending their heads together to whisper.

Isobel tilted her chin up, asking Theodore wordlessly what his problem was, bolstered by the few mouthfuls of alcohol she had indulged in. He ran his tongue across his lips, his nostrils flaring.

She knew him well enough to know that he was scenting her ... but she didn't know him well enough to guess why.

"Do you know the biggest tradition of the Alpha Valentine's party?" he asked her, his voice coated in gravel.

Isobel had to think about it for a moment, wondering if it was some sort of trick question. "The love lottery?"

"*Love letters*," Ashford drawled the words with a touch of ire, mimicking Ed Jones' commentary. "Are delivered to the Alphas in residence. A favourite is chosen, and the winner gets to choose one of the Alphas for a kiss."

Isobel already knew the tradition. She had no idea why it was being explained to her. "Okay?" she asked.

Theodore's usual smile flashed across his face. "So have you thought about what you're going to write?" he asked.

She blanched, and she was pretty sure she heard Kilian and Ashford laughing at her.

"No," she bit out. "I'm not participating."

"You're here." Theodore spread his hands. "You have to participate."

"Isobel?" a familiar voice called out, causing her to twist in Kilian's lap, searching over her shoulder.

"Eve." She smiled, hopping off Kilian and setting her cup down as she hurried away from the boys and into the arms of a much safer—and less moody —friend.

Eve laughed at her enthusiastic hug. "You're shaking. Are you sick again?"

Isobel shrugged. "Only a little. I'm so happy you're here."

"You are?" Eve bit back her smile, ushering Isobel away from the group of girls she had arrived with. "What were you doing on Gray's lap? Isn't he gay?"

"That's exactly why." Isobel rolled her eyes. "Theo and the others managed to snap up emergency girlfriends to knock back any rumours from the episode tonight. I was kind of ... left out a little. Kilian was just being nice."

"He can be nice to me any day." Eve sighed wistfully, looking over at the circle of chairs.

"Don't drink the punch," Isobel advised, tugging her arm to get her moving in a different direction. "It's horrible. And very alcoholic."

"Ah." Eve chuckled. "That explains the enthusiastic hug."

"I could be a hugger." Isobel pushed out her lower lip.

"Sure you could," Eve indulged her. "An adorable, prickly hugger. Oooh, the love lottery! We have to enter!" She suddenly dragged Isobel over to the lottery table, which was already drawing the crowd of Omegas that had arrived at the party.

"No thanks." Isobel tried to disentangle herself, but Eve held firm, shooting her a chastising look.

"Don't forget the plan, Carter. We need to get your popularity points up, and whoever wins this lottery is a guaranteed headline next week."

Isobel chanced a look toward the chair circle, noticing that Theodore was basically hanging off his chair to watch her get dragged to the table. He was laughing, too. He winked at her, giving her a quick thumbs up.

Theodore could be a bit of a dick, but he got away with it because his smile was so amazing and his eyes crinkled just mischievously enough to give him a free pass. It was a little bit infuriating.

"Here." Eve shoved a slip of paper and pen into Isobel's hand.

She stared down at it, completely at a loss. She wasn't in love, so how could she write a love letter?

With a quiet groan, she put the pen to paper and scrawled out something lame.

Roses are red, violets are blue, try to kiss me and I will actually kill you.

Folding the paper, she tossed it into the big glass bowl, peeking over Eve's shoulder to catch her already on her second paragraph. Something about luscious lips and eyes like dawn sunshine. Kilian, then.

It was hard to guess who would get the most letters between Kilian, Theodore, Niko, and Ashford.

While Theodore seemed to have an impressive fanbase —if the Ironside website was anything to go by— Kilian, Ashford, and Niko were all commonly dragged into the online debates about who was the hottest Alpha at Ironside. Kilian's striking pale perfection had most people comparing him to all sort of mythical creatures, like angels and vampires. Ashford's dusky gold colouring, messy, tarnished locks and confident smirk was to blame for the comment sections of Ironside clips being spammed by thirsty emojis. Niko seemed more like a comfort food for the fans— someone they could rely on to always be showing cocky smirks and flashes of skin at all the right moments to keep viewers engaged. And they *loved* his laugh. Niko had the most engaging laugh she had ever encountered—even if she had only encountered it on screen. It always started off as a low, throaty rumble before exploding into a sound so infectious it was impossible not to smile. The deep, velvety timbre resonated in a warm, tingling sound that could influence the tone of the show like the flick of a button.

She paused, glancing back to the bowl, realising she completely forgot to put a name on her slip of paper. Both a name for who it was to and also who it was from. She shrugged, stepping back to wait for Eve.

Except Eve didn't seem to be finishing up anytime soon. With a small sigh, she moved back to the ring of chairs, perching on the arm of Kilian's chair when he smiled at her.

"That was quick," he noted. "I suppose we shouldn't expect long, flowery lines of poetry."

"It was poetic as fuck." Isobel glanced longingly at the cup she had set onto the ground, wishing she could just let loose like the other students.

"Bold Sigma," Ashford chuckled, sounding delighted. "I knew you were hiding a filthy mouth and a backbone in there somewhere."

"Deep down," Isobel shot back, looking at him over her shoulder. "Very deep."

For some reason, his eyes darkened, and he moved an inch forward in his seat.

"Weren't we supposed to be serving food?" Theodore suddenly asked, standing up from his chair. "Who was in charge of that?"

"Moses," Reed said, his smile sharp. "Did none of you idiots think it was strange he volunteered to do *everything*? I don't even want to see what he deemed worthy for us to eat."

Theodore groaned, shaking his head. "I'll go check."

"I'll help!" Wallis jumped up, attaching herself to his side.

"I'll go help too." Kilian stood, stroking her arm. It was just enough of an invitation for her to escape the others and follow the gentle Alpha back into the dorm.

When Eve glanced up from her letter, Isobel caught her eye, miming that she was following Kilian inside. Eve flashed her a thumbs up and went back to scribbling, her tongue in her cheek.

"Who's your friend writing to?" Kilian asked. "She's covered both sides of the paper."

Isobel laughed. "You."

"Me?" He touched his chest, turning backwards to face her as he pushed open the door with his shoulder. "How touching. And unsurprising."

Isobel shook her head at his complete lack of modesty. Kilian led the way to the very end of the corridor, taking the stairs to the second level. They had barely reached the top step before Wallis was tearing back past them, her face as white as a sheet as she ran away.

They stepped into an undercover kitchen area, facing the rest of the rooftop, which was laid out like a luxury desert oasis. Leather bucket-seats were scattered around a wide, tiled fire pit, and there were other little areas that Isobel caught sight of out of the corner of her eye, but she was too focussed on the Alphas standing in the kitchen area to fully take in the rest of the space.

Sato was in the middle of the aisle between the island and the bench, his arms folded, the dark void of his eyes drilling into the back of Wallis' head until even her footsteps had faded away, and then those eyes switched to Isobel.

Moses looked to him, waiting for something, before that dark expression fell over his face again, and he turned the full, thundering force of it on Isobel.

"This area is off limits," Moses snapped.

"Oh stop it." Theodore shoved his arm. "Where's the food?"

"You're looking at it." Moses bared his teeth, but all the ire dropped out of his tone when he addressed his brother. There was even a hint of a smile at the corners of his mouth.

Sato hadn't even moved an inch, his eyes still fixed on her, like his gaze alone could somehow swallow her whole. It occurred to her that maybe he was waiting for her to thank him, but it wasn't like they were ever alone together, and she didn't want to bring up the uncomfortable topic of her breakdown in front of anyone else.

Especially Moses.

Theodore moved away from the kitchen island, giving Isobel an unobstructed view of the trays lined up. There were ten of them, in total. All of them piled with burnt-to-a-crisp ... somethings.

"Everyone's down there getting wasted," Theodore complained. "We need to feed them, or Mikki and Kalen are going to fucking flay us."

Isobel swallowed, her tongue feeling weirdly thick. She blinked as a wave of dizziness came out of nowhere. She shifted to lean against the stairwell wall. Sato's eyes crept after her, narrowing slightly. He sniffed the night air.

She pulled her shoulders back, pretending like nothing was wrong, but the longer Theodore and Moses argued, the worse the dizzy spells got. This wasn't the kind of sickness she was used to.

This was something else.

"I'll be downstairs," she mumbled, quickly turning and catching herself against the stair railing before she could fall. She ducked into Kilian's room, thinking she could just grab her bag and rush back to Dorm O, where she could sleep off whatever this weird feeling was, but as soon as she spilled outside, she pitched to the side, the world around her spinning violently.

"Let's try this again, shall we?" The voice in her ear was familiar, the hand around her waist pinching.

Someone had been waiting for her just outside the dorm. She smelled something off, something sour and chemical, but she couldn't place it. Whoever dragged her was big, towering. So strong. Her back hit the wall, the sounds of the party a little too far away. She groaned, fighting against the fog pulling her under. Her limbs weren't working. The strong person was holding her up.

"I knew you'd give in eventually," he whispered, his hand creeping between her legs before it jerked away. She pitched to the side, suddenly without the support holding her up, and slammed into the ground.

"We'll see what gives in first," a second voice taunted. "Your ribcage or your fucking spleen?"

And then there was thumping. Groaning. The cracking of something hitting the wall beside where she had fallen.

"Pick." Someone's Alpha voice pierced right through her haze, vibrating against her bones.

"Ribs," was the pained reply, torn from a throat by the Alpha command.

It was followed by another heavy thump, and the sound of a body cracking violently against the wall, a voice hitched with pain.

It seemed like an eternity before her body was moving again, shifting with sickening speed, becoming weightless as some sort of cloth dropped over her head. It smelled like leather, but there was another scent there, clinging and cloying. Nectar. Sweet and smoky. The mildest poison.

She was sure it was familiar to her somehow.

She heard a door opening and closing, and then a new voice.

"What the fuck, Oscar?"

"Just reverse it," the rough voice demanded. "Take her body back an hour or something."

"What happened?"

She was passed from one set of hands to another. The softness of a rug cushioned her back as she was laid carefully down.

"Oscar?" the voice prompted harshly. The door closed again, and a whole litany of swearwords followed it, all of them growled out ferociously.

The leather item slipped off her face, and rough hands cupped her temples, a trickle of energy working beneath her skin, skipping along her veins like electricity. She could feel breath against her face and then the warmth of the body close to hers. Her vision began to clear, but the leather suddenly dropped back over her head.

"Don't move," the voice demanded. It was smooth and deep, velvety and rounded. It made her

shiver, her twitching fingers falling back to the
soft rug.

"Good girl," he whispered, his touch falling away.

She heard the sound of the door again and quickly
sat up, a leather jacket falling from her face to her lap.
She was in an office. It dripped in precise opulence,
without a single personal touch in view. There was
nobody else in there with her.

Her vision was clear, her body back to normal, but
she was *very* confused.

Take her body back an hour or something.

She stared down at her hands clenching in the
leather jacket. The leather jacket Sato had been
wearing earlier. The memories tried to swim back, but
they were prevented by some sort of weird block, like
none of it had really happened and she was trying to
recall a fading dream. She stood on shaky legs,
stepping toward the door, her breaths choppy as she
moved out into the empty hall. She looked at the door,
a flash of memory threatening at the edges of her
mind, and then she glanced the other way, toward the
stairwell. Her decision made, she started that way, her
mouth set into a firm line, but she barely made it one
step up before the door to her right suddenly opened.

Sato stood there, his hand outstretched.

"My jacket," he prompted her.

She held it out, but he made no move to grab it, so she pushed it into his hand. His fingers brushed hers as he pulled it back, twisting his body and tossing it back into his room. "And now you," he demanded, holding his hand out again. She swallowed past her refusal, but she didn't take his hand. His lips crooked, not really a smile, and the darkness in his eyes seemed to grow deeper.

His emotion felt different to other people's. It wasn't a singular feeling, more like maelstrom, a tornado of possibilities, just out of her reach. He reached forward, grabbing a handful of the flared skirt of her dress, and then he dragged her into his room.

He closed his door, pushing her lightly until her back hit the cherry oak, though he didn't press up against her or invade her personal space too much. Not with his body, anyway. Those dark pools of his eyes were a different story. They tunnelled right into her.

"We have a little problem," he whispered silkily.

"We do," she agreed, her voice trembling. "I feel like my memory was just tampered with."

"It wasn't." His room was unlit, but the flash of his teeth was clear. "Your body was taken back in time to before it was drugged."

"Drugged?" Her forehead crinkled.

"The big fucker." Sato loomed just a little closer. "The second-year Beta with the oily hair."

"Crowe," Isobel breathed, horror in her tone. She frowned, a hint of the incident coming back to her. *No*. Bellamy had given her the drink.

Sato made a soft, dangerous humming sound. "He's lucky I didn't kill him. Back to the problem, Sigma."

"Isobel," she corrected.

"Little rabbit," he countered. "Always slipping beneath the fence line into where she isn't welcome. Always getting caught in snares."

Isobel felt for the door handle. "Tell me what the problem is."

"The problem is your mouth." His eyes dipped, fixing to her lips. "You need to keep it shut about what just happened."

"Or?" She wasn't actually planning on telling anyone, she just wanted to know exactly what she was up against.

"Or the next time I rescue you ..." His body brushed hers, his head ducking, his lips against her ear, sending shivers racing down her spine. "It'll be so I can go in for the kill myself."

"Noted," she breathed, turning the handle and

spilling into the hallway, where she collided with Kilian.

"There you are!" He gripped her arms, throwing a concerned glance at the door that had slammed behind her. "What happened?"

"I ... Sato dropped his jacket. I was returning it."

"Oh." He did a quick assessment of her face but didn't seem to like what he found there, the concern deepening. "We should go out; they're about to draw the love lottery."

They started for the door, but Kilian stopped her before they made it outside again. "If Sato does something ..." He didn't seem to know how to finish the sentence.

"Like what?" she asked, keeping her expression calm.

Sato hadn't exactly been subtle in his threats, so she wasn't willing to find out if *keeping her mouth shut* included whatever she might say to the other Alphas.

"Never mind." He forced a smile, shoving open the door. "But next time you find something of his ... just leave it."

IO

THE GOODNESS OF SATO'S HEART

"Isobel!" Eve broke away from her group as soon as she spotted them, and Isobel branched off from Kilian, who seemed to be looking for the others. "What happened?"

"Nothing," Isobel quickly brushed off the question.

"Well ... the Alphas are going to race across the lake," Eve told her breathlessly, dragging her back to the crowd huddling around the lake.

"Why?" Isobel asked, her concern spiking. None of them could swim.

"To decide who will draw the lottery!" Eve shouted over her shoulder, the bodies jostling them as they tried to push forward. When they broke out in front, Isobel saw that Theodore, Reed, Spade, Ashford, and Niko were standing at the other side of the lake, already half naked. Kilian jogged up to join them, pulling his shirt over his head.

This time next week, the Ironside fans were going to have an aneurism.

She had seen Theodore's muscles up close, but nothing could have prepared her for the sight before her. They were each so different, but they were all strong and fit. They could have filled out six pages in a textbook of the different variations of a perfect Alpha specimen. Theodore and Ashford had a little more bulk, but Spade's and Reed's torsos looked like they had been chiselled out of marble. Their endless hours in the practice rooms were clearly paying off. She didn't know what Kilian did to keep fit, but his was a more lithe, graceful strength, his muscles jumping and twitching as he bounced around, warming up.

Niko looked the strongest, his arms, chest, and thighs thicker than the others. It was both surprising and not, because Niko was on his way to specialising in tennis, and he spent a good deal of time outside in the sun, practising different types of sport. But Niko didn't really have the persona of an athlete, and his face was so beautiful, his features so sharp and delicate, she sometimes couldn't merge the two sides of his personality that the Ironside show aired.

Ashford stepped forward, gripping one of the—

now many—ropes that climbed across the lake, testing it. He looked like the old gods in the Gifted books—the ones their ancestors had believed in—with golden skin, eyes like sapphires, and dark blond hair that he had managed to twist into a knot, thick clumps of it falling free to frame his face.

"In three!" he yelled as the others stepped forward to grab a rope. "Two!" He scanned the faces, licking his lips. "One!"

They raced into the lake in a tangle of limbs and splashes, laughing as they tried to shove each other, utterly uncaring of what would happen if one of them released their rope. Isobel couldn't help but chuckle as Reed used the rope to hoist himself up, wrapping his strong thighs around Theodore's torso and tearing him away from his rope. Theodore grabbed Reed's rope instead and then switched back to his own, shoving roughly at the other boy.

Kilian was fast, Ashford was sly, and Spade was methodical, but they all had one thing in common: they wanted to stop Theodore from winning. They did everything in their power, but he only laughed at their efforts, dodging and wrestling and at one point grabbing as many as three of their ropes to keep himself secured. It seemed that any one of them could have won, but Kilian mysteriously lost his speed a few feet from the edge of the lake. Reed subtly pulled back, and Niko slipped, taking Spade down with him. Luckily, they landed in shallow water and stood back up, laughing and shaking off droplets as Theodore reached the bank first, turning and shoving Ashford—who was coming up behind him—back into the water for fun.

"The winner!" Ashford bellowed, emerging from the water like some kind of god-of-the-seas, shaking out his hair and grabbing Theodore's arm, punching it into the sky.

Everyone cheered, but Isobel only stood there, her brows pinching in. Everything they did seemed so *deliberate*, like they weren't just playing the Ironside game. They were playing a different game, with different stakes, against everyone else there ... except they were the only ones who knew about it.

Which meant the rest of them were destined to lose.

When Theodore looked her way, she quickly pasted on a smile, and he walked up to the bowl, sticking his wet hand inside and shuffling it around. He seemed to grip one of the papers, but Ashford shook his head, leaning up against the lottery table.

"Nah," he said casually. "Not that one."

Everyone laughed, cheering at his playful nature,

and Theodore released the paper, catching another one. Ashford shook his head, and this continued a few more times until Ashford and Theodore locked eyes.

A message seemed to pass between them, Ashford cocking a brow, almost like a challenge, and then Theodore drew out the paper.

"Roses are red, violets are blue, try to kiss me and I will actually kill you." He lifted the paper, and she knew he was scenting it, even though it might not have been apparent to the rest of the crowd. "Isobel Carter."

Eve—who had taken her hand in a death grip at some point—released her in shock and then shoved her a little too hard in the direction of Theodore.

There was a chorus of sound all around her, like something particularly dramatic was happening. The timing was ... not great. The Ironside show had insinuated that she was trying to cosy up to several of the Alphas only a matter of hours ago, and now she was in a position where she would have to choose between them.

She could choose Theodore. Her friend.

Or Kilian, who wouldn't make it weird ... but that would be unfair on him. And uncomfortable.

But ... it was her first kiss.

"Well?" Ashford goaded, aquamarine eyes glinting. "Pick an Alpha, Sigma."

The longer she took, the quieter it got. Some people had their phones out. Students were allowed to post photos prior to Ironside episodes airing, to try and get popularity points or grow their social presence, but videos were only allowed if they depicted personal projects.

They were waiting.

Hoping to catch a photo.

She grimaced, glancing up to the roof, where two more Alphas looked down at her, surveying the scene with cold looks on their faces.

"Moses," she said, a small smile on her lips. It was the one Alpha she was *sure* would refuse. "I pick Moses."

"Moses isn't here," Ashford drawled.

"Yes, he is." She pointed up to the rooftop.

"Moses!" Reed snapped.

Both Alphas disappeared from above, and Isobel grinned, feeling like she had won some sort of personal victory. Until she heard Eve hissing against the back of her neck.

"What are you doing?" she asked. "He isn't going to come out!"

"I know," Isobel complained quietly. "But this is too far!"

Eve groaned out a frustrated sound. "Can you just pick someone else?"

Isobel shook her head, trying to avoid the looks of the other Alphas as everyone around them shuffled nervously. The rest of the academy didn't know much about Moses, since he kept out of the spotlight and didn't attend any social events, but it was clear that Theodore's twin had aligned himself with Sato.

"It's getting late," Isobel said loudly, checking her phone. "Guess I should be heading off."

A few people snickered.

"Cool party," she said by way of goodbye.

"Not so fast." Ashford laughed a second before Moses walked out of the dorm.

Well, that backfired.

MOSES COULD HAVE JUST STAYED INSIDE. HE COULD HAVE PUT his headphones in and ignored the desperate people outside calling his name, hoping for a photo opportunity.

But the Sigma thought she could use him in her little game with the other Alphas, and he was just annoyed enough to call her bluff. Let them all see her tuck tail and run, because he sure as fuck wasn't going to.

She stood there with squared shoulders and a clenched jaw, and for the briefest moment, he allowed himself to feel just a little bit of pity for her. Her night had been a rough one. She didn't let it show, but the beast inside him always recognised turmoil. Her pretty blue dress was a little too wrinkled. Her blonde hair was tangled, strands of strawberry catching on strands of gold, darker wisps tickling her face. Her hair had been in a ponytail earlier in the night.

She also carried scents that weren't her own. Bergamot and bark, and burning oleander. Kilian's complex, pleasurable scent coiled around the smoking poison of Oscar. There were others, too, but Oscar and Kilian had drenched her.

Oscar, who had disappeared for a short amount of time earlier, returning with a scowl instead of his jacket.

Oscar, who conveniently disappeared whenever Kalen appeared on the rooftop, that familiar prowl in his step when he was hunting someone down.

That only increased Moses' anger. Now, even Oscar was getting involved with the Sigma—even though the most likely explanation was that he had pulled her aside to threaten her. It might explain the harrowed, crushed cherry scent of her skin as he drew close.

"You can still run away," he told her quietly, close enough that only the people immediately surrounding them would hear.

"So can you," she shot back, eliciting a round of gasps and laughter.

Theodore was spoiling her. Making it seem like Alphas weren't dangerous, when they most definitely were.

A growl built up in the back of his throat, and he felt two of his friends drifting closer, alarmed by the sound. Elijah and Gabriel, always the first two to clue on. If he went feral, the Sigma was dead. And not just her—anyone around them too weak to defend themselves against him.

Which was all of them.

There were too many witnesses and it would create too big of a mess for the others to cover up. He would be executed, and everything they were working toward would be lost.

But she was just an annoying little Sigma. She couldn't make him break.

He cupped her cheek, and her breath stopped, her skin flushing, those pale gold, black-ringed irises disappearing from view as she lowered her eyes. She was staring at his chest, her beautiful lips pressed tightly together. He didn't like that he thought her lips were beautiful, but there was nothing to be done about that. There was another scent on her. Chemical and sour, unfamiliar to him. He used that to guide his thoughts away from wondering if he might actually want to kiss her or not.

He had never kissed anyone before, and the rest of the Alphas knew it.

"The last person who tried to kiss me got a handful of dirt in his eyes," she warned him quietly, the words barely making any sound as they formed on her lips.

But he was already staring at her lips, so he heard her.

"You picked me," he reminded her.

"You weren't supposed to come out."

"Why did you put your name in the draw?"

"I didn't," she bit back. "I just wrote something stupid and didn't put my name on it."

He blinked, drawing back a little. *Those assholes.* He glared at Cian, who had a towel wrapped around his golden shoulders, his sapphire eyes filled with equal amounts of humour and trepidation. He had known which letter was hers and had challenged Theodore to pick it.

Theodore wanted to prove that Carter wasn't a threat, so he had.

And now Moses was being punished.

He sighed, his eyes drifting back to her. She was staring him full in the face, a tinge of confusion in the way she was examining him. He felt something brush against his mind, and the smallest sliver of his annoyance melted away.

She was trying to figure him out.

Trying to read him. Trying to taste his emotion.

He couldn't have that.

He ducked down, fusing his lips to hers. A burst of sensation followed, almost too quick for him to absorb it, but it was like being kicked viciously in the stomach. An immediate, violent reaction that he hadn't been expecting.

So this was what it was like?

Her breath tasted like the awful punch he had made, but *she* had a sweeter scent, so strong he could taste it over the juice and alcohol, like a tingle against his tongue. She was syrup and she was sour. A heady, vanilla-scented cherry liqueur that had his head spinning. Her lips were soft and plush, impossible for him to kiss lightly. She was so soft his harder lips sank right into hers, his hand flexing as he tried to anchor himself, slipping away from her cheek and toward the back of her head. His other hand rose, hovering by her neck, the silky strands of her hair brushing against his knuckles, the velvet texture of her skin soft beneath his palm, hitting him with the need to spread both hands out. To touch more, to drag her body into his and see if it had the same give against his hardness as her lips did.

And then there was the familiar fury.

It took over completely, driven wild by the way his skin grew tight, by the softness of her lips, by her small shocked gasp and the desperate, driving need to shove his tongue in and indulge in her properly that knocked him off balance.

Isobel immediately gasped, and that somehow deepened the kiss, his lips slipping either side of her lower lip, capturing it, his teeth lightly grazing her flesh. But still, it was over as quickly as it had happened. He tasted bitter and hot—burning, actually. And even though it had lasted only a fraction of a second, the kiss had been hard, leaving a strange imprint when he made a low, furious sound and ended it.

Moses eased back, and it seemed like he wasn't even there anymore. Those dark grey eyes, a few shades stormier than Theodore's, were bleeding black ink. He tucked his face down before anyone else could see it, turning and striding into the dorm without a word. Theodore broke away, running after him. Reed followed at a slower pace, focussed intently on his phone.

The rest of the Alphas stayed, pretending nothing weird was happening. Niko hyped up the cheering crowd, and Ashford made out like he was going to draw another name, causing an almost-stampede.

Isobel slipped away from it all, ignoring Eve calling her name as she made for the stairs leading away from Alpha Lake.

She was confused, emotionally-wrought, and she just wanted to be alone. She intended to go back to Dorm O, but found her feet carrying her in another direction instead. She tried the door to the chapel, finding it unlocked, and slipped inside.

It was quiet and dark, a stark contrast to the party she had left behind, and the chapel was one of the only buildings in the academy entirely free of cameras. She took what felt like her first full breath of the night, padding between the aisles. She found a box of matches on the dais and approached one of the vestibules. She lit the candle and closed her eyes.

"Mama." She let the word hang there for a

moment as she struggled to form the words that seemed forbidden to her, like speaking them was the gravest betrayal against her remaining parent. "What happened to you?"

The chapel door creaked, jerking her out of her thoughts as she spun toward the sound. Crowe was hobbling, blood leaking down the side of his face, one big arm wrapped around his torso, like he needed to hold himself together.

"That was silly," he croaked. "Coming here. All by yourself."

She didn't even think, she just ran to the only other door—the one heading to the rooftop. He darted after her, suddenly forgetting his injuries. She slammed the door, setting her feet against the second step to brace her back against it. It bowed inward, the force of him hitting the other side making her teeth smack together.

"Come out, little Sigma," he growled. "I'm hurt. Isn't it your job to make me better?"

He collided with the door again, and her right leg crumpled painfully, her knees smacking against the steps as she was shoved forward. He grabbed the back of her dress, dragging her back into the chapel, where he tossed her over the dais like she weighed nothing at all. He bodily twisted her around, looming over her as he batted her arms away.

"Look at what you did to me," he spat. "Look at me!" He pinched her cheeks, his face hovering over hers. Sato had knocked a few teeth out and cut through his eyebrow.

Crowe's other hand had captured hers, the bulk of his body pinning her to the ground. She couldn't move, couldn't break free. With a steadying breath, she reached for the only power she had left. She cracked herself open and pulled in his darkness.

It was gritty and hard to swallow. There was so much pain, so much untethered anger, racing around and building momentum, like a crazy person shouting at a wall. But there was more, too. There was something insidious, and it seemed an endless well, something that she could draw on forever. She cut herself off with a pained gasp, watching as his expression smoothed. He smiled, and all that was left in his eyes was that hint of never-ending evil she had tasted.

"I think it's time you gave me that kiss," he whispered, shifting his body to press more solidly into hers.

His grip on her wrists had loosened just enough for her arm to fling out, her fingers grappling with something hard. She gripped it, swinging it toward Crowe's head.

He seemed surprised when she made contact with a sickening crack, his mouth opening and spraying blood across her face. His body went limp, his eyes rolling back, and she shoved him off, scrambling to her feet, glancing down at the candlestick in her hand. It didn't even have any blood on it, and it wasn't damaged at all. Those details seemed safe to grasp as she tried to talk herself around to assessing the entire situation.

Crowe was ... unconscious.

She knelt beside him, her hand trembling as she tried to hold a finger under his nose. *Please be breathing*.

She couldn't feel anything.

"Fuck." She stood up, tears tracking down her face. "*Fuck!*" She fell back, crawling up against the wall, a silken sash brushing her shoulder from where it had been hung up on the wall behind her.

She pulled out her phone, sobs beginning to break through her body with the violence of a hammer hitting her ribs. She thought about who to contact. *Her father? The police? The dorm supervisor? Eve? Theodore?*

She clicked on the last message she had received.

Ashford: I told you I would give you a straight answer.

It took her three attempts to reply, her fingers slipping over the screen.

Isobel: I need an answer.

She waited, her eyes fixed with eagle-eyed intensity on Crowe, like he might suddenly reanimate himself and come after her again.

Ashford: What's the question?

Isobel: What's Sato's phone number?

The reply took a little too long, and the darkness she had taken from Crowe was beginning to make her dizzy.

Isobel: You promised me a straight answer.

A few seconds later, he sent the number through, following it up with another message that she didn't read, instead clicking on the new number. She raised her shaking hand to her ear, trying to calm her sobs.

"Yes?" Sato's rough voice asked, the sounds of the party faint in the distance.

"If you want me to keep your secret, you have to help me," she managed to get out. She tried to sound assertive, like she held all the cards, but she knew she sounded wounded and terrified instead.

"Share your location." He hung up.

She stared at her phone through a fresh wave of tears. She was beginning to question the sanity of her choice, but she still shared her location with him. And then she darted forward and picked up the candlestick again, holding it out in front of her with both hands, her eyes switching from the door to Crowe.

Sato pushed through the door ten minutes later, wrapped in his leather jacket and a dark expression. He took in Crowe with a cursory, uncaring sweep of his black eyes before focussing on her—or on the candlestick in her hands.

"Sigma does it in the chapel with the candlestick," he muttered, shaking his head.

"Th-this isn't funny." She gripped her weapon harder, curling a little more into herself.

"Do you see me laughing?" he asked sharply before kneeling right in front of her. He knocked the candlestick out of his way but she didn't release it as he leaned over her to grip her chin. He glanced between her eyes, his nostrils flaring.

"He didn't make it far," he surmised, inching back to include the rest of her in his assessment. The strap of her dress was torn, hanging off, and there was blood smeared along the front of it, but it wasn't hers. He picked up her wrists, frowning at the bruises beginning to form, touched just below the scrapes on her knees, and then he gently took the candlestick from her, setting it aside.

"Clean-up usually isn't my forte." He left her

curled there, walking back to Crowe, who he toed with his boot, shoving the bigger boy onto his back. "I might have to call Gabriel in."

"No need," a voice announced from the doorway. Spade stepped through, carefully closing and locking the door behind him. "Cian said the Sigma asked for your phone number."

"So naturally a murder has occurred." Sato rolled his eyes. "Not even you're that smart."

"Aren't I, though?" Spade asked glibly.

Isobel ignored them, her eyes on Crowe again. "Murder?" she whispered.

Spade knelt by Crowe, a finger pushed into his meaty neck. He seemed to be counting. "Pulse is there, but it's sluggish." He then began touching Crowe all over, checking his ribs, his head, his legs, his chest. When he drew back, he was looking from her to Sato. "You did all this?" he asked her, trying to hide his scepticism.

She hesitated before nodding.

He frowned, glaring over at Sato, who just shrugged. "She's clearly stronger than she looks."

"Strong enough to break several ribs and almost choke him out?" Spade shot back, annoyed. "Can she even reach his neck?"

"I stood on a ... on here." She pointed to the dais. She sounded ridiculous.

"Smart thinking," Sato commented.

Spade grunted, sitting back. "We can either call Kalen or we can sneak him into the medical building. It's close enough." He was looking at her. "Professor West," he specified, just in case she didn't know who Kalen was.

"You don't want to know what happened?" she asked faintly.

"Sure." He stood, pulling a small pack of sanitary wipes from his pocket. He cleaned his fingers methodically, waiting for her answer.

Sato was looking at her with arched dark brows. His hair was a rich, deep oak colour, streaked through with hints of mahogany and darker ink, and just like Professor Easton and Moses, he sported a few scars— though not quite as many as Easton. They mostly littered his arms and hands, with only a few ticking over his face. He had deep-set features, shadows beneath his eyes, and a cutting jawline that made his firm mouth appear even harsher.

"He tripped," she found herself saying.

Sato's lips twitched.

"That's quite a fall." Spade was utterly toneless.

"And you?" He looked up, setting focussed russet eyes on her. "Did you trip too?"

"No, I'm fine." She tried to jump to her feet, as though to demonstrate such, but her leg buckled, and she pitched straight down again.

Sato jerked forward, catching her at the last second, his fist twisting in her dress. He slipped an arm around her waist and then picked her up, sitting her on the podium in the middle of the dais.

"Where does it hurt?" he asked as Spade stepped up beside him.

"Ankle?" Spade's cool touch slid around the body part in question, both of them completely ignoring Crowe.

She winced, nodding her head. He gently slipped off her sandal, setting it on the podium beside her. He lifted her leg, propping it on one of his arms as he traced his fingers up her calf, squeezing gently.

"Any pain?"

She shook her head, and he slid his touch back down, gently clasping her foot, his touch warming up a little against her skin. He slowly turned her foot to one side. "Now?"

She shook her head again, and he delicately turned her foot the other way, immediately stopping as she winced and tried to jerk her leg back.

"You're swelling up a little." He released her leg. "But it's just a sprained ankle." He flicked a look to the side. "Oscar ..." He drew in a sharp breath, hesitating. "Can you help her back to her dorm?"

Sato returned his look flatly. "I believe I can manage it."

"Wait." Spade held out his hand to her. "Give me your phone."

Sato rolled his eyes, walking away. She eyed the tension in both boys before handing her phone over quietly.

"Why are you helping me?" she asked quietly.

"Because Oscar is here," he responded automatically. "And he's one of us. The real question is why is *he* helping you?"

She nibbled on her lip. "Out of the goodness of his heart?"

Sato laughed darkly. Spade frowned, handing her phone back. "Text me when you get home. I'll be checking in until Oscar returns to Dorm A. Make sure you respond."

She didn't think she could feel any worse, but a fresh skitter of fear travelled over her already-shaking limbs.

"Okay," she whispered faintly.

Sato materialised in front of her in seconds, his

arm slipping around her waist. He helped her off the podium and then drew one of her arms around his shoulder, flicking his hair out of his eyes. He smelled like sweet, poisonous nectar, and she thought the scent suited him. His eyes were a snare, his movements like a striking snake, his words dripping with poison.

"Don't take too long," Spade warned, his rust-coloured stare tracking them all the way to the door.

She was suddenly, unbearably grateful to him.

Sato, however, pretended not to hear him. As soon as the door closed behind them, he bent and knocked her knees out from under her, lifting her against his chest. "Quicker this way," he grunted, stepping toward the path that would take them the long way around the lake.

She understood why, when he left the path to go around the back of Dorms B and D, where there weren't any cameras.

He didn't speak until they spilled from the edge of Dorm D, and he sat her on one of the fences inside Jasmine Field. They could hear students travelling back toward Dorm O from the party along the main path up ahead, and he apparently wanted to wait them out.

"If I have to get a fake girlfriend because of this,

I'm going to ..." His whispered words trailed off against her collarbone, his hands cinching in her waist as he surveyed what he could see of the path over her shoulder, peering through the trees.

"Going to what?" she asked, also whispering. They were tucked beneath one of the weeping willows, where students infamously squirrelled away to avoid the cameras.

He drew back, his eyes dark as the night around them. "Use your imagination," he suggested.

"I'd rather not."

His lips twitched. "I'm happy alone," he told her. "If you ruin that happiness, I'll fucking ruin yours."

"Noted." She sucked in a breath as he hauled her back into his arms without any warning. "Or you could just not care. Have you tried that?"

His exhale was a groan. "Sweet Sigma, you really do overestimate me."

"You must care about something, or you wouldn't be so desperate to keep what happened at the party a secret."

He scoffed, just about to step out from Jasmine Field when another group of students approached. He ducked back beneath another willow, setting her on the edge of the fence again. "Are you really so clueless?" His tone was flat.

She bristled, shoving against his chest. "Just let me down, I'll crawl if I have to."

He grinned, and it was the first time she remembered seeing him smile properly. His canines were a little pointed, the smile transforming his entire face. It made him seem almost boyish, until it melted away, replaced by his usual, terrifying blank mask.

"What would Theo do if he found out some Beta Behemoth had dragged you, *drugged*, behind Dorm A and was trying to shove his hands up your dress?" he asked pointedly.

She shifted uncomfortably, seeing the answer more than thinking it.

His eyes would bleed black. He would be in danger.

She hadn't managed to find a single mention of ferality in all the library books she had combed through, but she had felt Theodore's emotion in their first year. She knew the taste of it. The violence, the endless darkness and despair.

"He would be upset," she admitted. "He feels responsible for me because I helped him out once."

Sato gave her an exasperated look. "That's a convenient way of putting it."

"He might surprise you, you know. He might have more control over it than you realise."

Sato frowned at her like he pitied her. "Theo went

after Moses tonight. Take a good look at them both tomorrow and tell me if you think this is something we can play around with. If they're both still walking, that is."

"Moses went fer—" she began to question, but he loomed so close all of a sudden that the words died off.

He was right in her face, his hand cupping her jaw, his lips an inch from hers. She could feel his breath and see nothing past the darkness in his eyes. They swallowed her right up, dangling her over a precipice.

"Never say it," he warned in a whisper. "I don't care who can or can't hear you. *Never* say it."

Suddenly, she didn't know who she was looking at. The shadows drowned out the rich tones of his hair and deepened the sunken set of his eyes, making the dark circles beneath seem heavier. He had seemed almost handsome back in the chapel, with his mahogany locks and hard, smirking mouth—but now he looked haunted. A vengeful thing from a world separate to hers, a world where Alphas prowled through the rest of them, forcing them to cower and bow.

For the first time, he really truly scared her.

And he noticed.

His hand on her jaw hadn't been rough, but he dropped it like he had hurt her somehow, his mouth twitching down at the edges. "Let's go," he said, though he didn't try to pick her up again. He just stood half a foot away from her, watching her with those blank, burning eyes.

"It's not far from here," she croaked out. "I can manage it."

He nodded, still unmoving. Waiting. She shifted off the edge of the fence, attempting to put a bit of weight on her foot. When it didn't immediately collapse beneath her, she stood, looking up at him. He still hadn't moved, and they were so close now. Close enough for another skitter of fear to make its way through her.

He sniffed, like he could smell it, and she couldn't tell if he liked that she was afraid of him or not. He was so *still*, so emotionless.

"I'm sorry I sort of blackmailed you." She crossed her arms over her chest, fighting off a shiver and skirting her eyes to the side.

"Ah, don't take it back now." His voice was a low, deep rumble. "I like it when people owe me favours."

"Okay." She sucked in a quick breath, chancing a quick look up. "But I'm not going to fake girlfriend any of your friends."

He swept his eyes over her. "That would be a favour for *you*, little rabbit."

She grimaced, turning away from him and hobbling to the edge of the cover provided by the tree above them. She glanced over her shoulder, seeing that he still hadn't moved. He had saved her. Twice. Maybe three times. "Thank you," she forced out, wondering why it was so hard to be grateful to him. "I owe you."

"And I'll collect," he promised darkly.

And that was why.

II

DANGEROUS THINGS

HER DANCE SESSION THE NEXT DAY WAS A PAINFUL ONE. SHE
had gone to the medical centre to have her ankle
wrapped, but it still twinged and twitched with little
bolts of pain throughout the two hours of practice
time she had booked. She was sweating more than
usual when she finished, so she dragged herself out to
the pool and stripped off her sweats, since she was
wearing a leotard beneath anyway. She dove into the
cold water, immediately soothed as she slowly swam a
few languid laps before propping herself on the side
and reaching for her phone.

There were messages that she hadn't read, as well
as an inbox full of emails. Some were from the tutors
her father had hired over the years, probably offering

veiled advice in the hopes that she name-dropped them on television, now that they thought she might have a chance at getting famous. If they could make a Sigma famous, they could make anyone famous. It was enough to have her avoiding her phone like the plague, though there was also an email from her father buried amongst them, and the bold subject line had been niggling at her all morning.

Well done, Isobel.

She ducked beneath the surface of the water, sinking to the bottom where her phone was out of sight, before finally kicking back up and reaching for it again. She opened her messages, scrolling to the newest.

Theodore: I found your bag around the back of the dorm. Thought I was going crazy, smelling you every time I stepped outside.

Isobel: Sorry. I'll come and get it.

He replied after only a few seconds.

Theodore: Have you eaten, yet? I'm heading to the dining hall.

Isobel: Meet you there.

She navigated out of the message, clicking on another one. It was from last night, after she asked for Sato's number.

Ashford: Whatever you've gotten yourself into, do yourself a favour and back the fuck out.

She sighed, resting her forehead against the edge of the pool. What had Sato done that had all the other Alphas convinced he was some kind of monster? Since she didn't know what to reply, she quickly exited the message and clicked on the last unread message.

Spade: Check in.

Spade: Check in, Carter.

Spade: For fucks sake.

Spade: Oscar is here—late, by the way—so what part of check in didn't you understand?

Spade: Never mind Oscar, now I'm the one you have to worry about.

She butted her head against the tile again, this time a little harder.

Isobel: I'm sorry. I was about to text you but I passed out with my phone in my hand.

She climbed out of the pool, wrapping herself in a towel and picking up her bag to head back inside. Spade's reply came through when she was rushing through a shower in the fitness centre.

Spade: I know. I checked Elijah's camera.

She frowned down at the message as she dried herself and dressed in a pair of tights and a cropped shirt.

Isobel: How do I turn it off?

She waited for a reply as she walked to the dining hall, but it never came. The food theme seemed to have something to do with cheese this time. There was fondue, croquettes, toasted sandwiches, antipasti, pastries, savoury muffins, pasta, and great big wedges as decoration. She grabbed a toasted sandwich and a juice, peering into the booths along the side of the hall until she found Theodore. He was sitting with his head in his hands, looking exhausted, but he quickly sat up when he saw her. She relaxed immediately at the sight of his smile, warm and wide.

"Hey." He waved at the seat across from him. "Where did you go last night?"

She slid her tray onto the table, sitting opposite him. "I ..."

He dipped to the side, unfolding the thin rice-paper screen so they were blocked from view, even though the hall was relatively empty. He sat back again, quirking a brow at her, waiting for her to find her voice.

"I ... left," she tried again.

"I noticed." His smile dimmed, some of that exhaustion peeking through again. "I fucked up, Illy."

She leaned back, ignoring her food in favour of folding her arms loosely. "How so?"

His smile dipped completely, a troubled look fleeing over his features. He scratched his jaw, and that was when she noticed the cuts. They were deep and red, some of them held closed with surgical tape. He was wearing a light jacket despite the weather, so she could only spot the lacerations that poked out of the edge of his sleeve, but it was enough to have her jerking forward, reaching for his hands.

He smoothly slid them under the table, pretending not to notice. "I should have told you about ... you know." He leaned forward, tilting his head away from the cameras in the corners of the booth. *The girlfriend thing,* he mouthed before straightening again. "Kilian said he explained why we did it."

"He did," she confirmed, staring at the edge of the table, where he was hiding his hands. "And it's fine. You don't owe me anything, Theo."

"Except the truth." He smiled at her again, and this time, she could tell it was entirely forced. "I made things weird for no reason."

"Stop it," she grumbled, folding her arms again.

His smile shifted, a genuine glint of amusement peeking through. "Stop what?"

"You had a good reason to be acting weird." She rolled her eyes. "I was teaching you how to swim, and the Ironside show made it look like something super angsty and dramatic, and then they combed their footage for every minuscule moment I spent in the presence of other Alphas and twisted it all to look like I've been desperately trying to find an Alpha boyfriend or something. Of course it was strange."

He chuckled lowly, pulling his tray closer. It was stacked with more crepes than she could eat in a week, but he looked down at them sceptically, like he worried they wouldn't be enough, before he began to dig in.

"So we can keep going with the lessons?" he asked between mouthfuls.

She nodded, picking up her sandwich. She couldn't look away from the cuts. *Had Moses done that?* She wanted to ask if he was—if they were *both*—okay, but knew that she couldn't.

"As long as you don't care that I kissed your brother," she said instead.

He dropped his fork, his head snapping up. He swallowed and then cleared his throat. And then swallowed again.

"You could hardly call that a kiss," he said. "Happened so fast I almost thought I hallucinated it."

"Hmm," she agreed, taking a bite. It tasted like nothing. She was so nervous, but she didn't really know why. Her face felt hot, her stomach twisting. "But it's okay, right? I mean ... he's your brother. And I feel like I kind of forced him or something. He didn't want to play the game."

"Neither did you," Theodore shot back, picking up his fork again. "So maybe I'm the one to blame." He laughed, short and sharp. "Moses doesn't do anything he doesn't want to do." He seemed to be about to say something else when the screen suddenly folded back, Wallis appearing in the opening.

"There you are!" She slid right in next to Theodore without waiting for an invitation, her hand landing on his stomach as she leaned over to bite the little bit of crepe left off his fork. "Yummy!" she exclaimed.

Isobel choked on her juice, almost spraying it everywhere. She slapped a hand over her mouth at the last second but still managed to make a mess. Theodore edged over on the seat—looking like he was making room for Wallis—and grabbed one of the serviettes from the table setting, handing it to Isobel. He did it all without blinking an eye.

And *that* was when she realised just how good of an actor he was.

She mopped at her face while Wallis slid her a quick, pointed look. Almost as if to say *do you really have to make my job harder?* Isobel looked down at her juice-soaked sandwich and sighed, glancing over at her bag, which Theodore was holding hostage, sandwiched between his body and the wall.

"Hey, babe." He smiled at Wallis, easy and warm just like always, though he slid another inch away to give her even more room. "Want me to go get you something to eat?" He was also inching his plate away from her, and he put down his fork, glancing at the untouched cutlery on the edge of Isobel's tray.

Wallis peered out of the booth, considering the food bar, and Isobel quickly slid him her fork. He slid the other one her way and had resumed eating by the time Wallis turned back to pout at the tray that was now out of her reach.

"That's okay," she said, frowning slightly as Isobel dropped the contaminated fork onto her tray. "I'm trying to avoid carbs. If I gain any weight, Francis won't be able to lift me in class anymore, and he's the best male dancer we have. I can't afford to give him up."

"Makes sense," Theodore muttered around his crepe.

Wallis grew quiet, looking at her lap, and Isobel wanted to groan out in frustration. The other girl wasn't an Alpha, so her emotional spikes didn't batter against Isobel's chest, but she didn't need her ability to know that Wallis had been expecting a compliment. She kicked Theodore under the table, and his head jerked up and then to the side, taking in Wallis' dejected appearance.

"But you know ..." He curled his arm around her shoulders, giving her a little shake. "Frankie is probably hoping for a better workout; I bet he can barely feel you when he lifts you."

Wallis flushed, a slow smile creeping across her face.

"Francis," Isobel corrected beneath her breath, making Theodore smirk, but Wallis didn't seem to care. "Can I have my bag?" Isobel added, standing up and edging her tray to the end of the table. "I'm late for ... studying."

"Studying what?" Theodore asked, releasing Wallis to drag her bag into his lap.

"Musical theory," she bluffed. It was a class she didn't need to study for since her tutors seemed to have already covered everything they were learning in the second-year module, but Theodore couldn't possibly know that.

"Perfect." He stood, dragging the strap of her bag

over his shoulder. "I need some help. I was thinking of picking up a music class next year."

"You're leaving?" Wallis' chin snapped up, her eyes darting between them. "I just got here."

"You're welcome to come along." He smiled, unaware of the sinking dread his offer had conjured in Isobel. "We'll be in the library—you have something you need to study for too?"

Wallis' lips dipped down. "Well, no. I don't. I guess I'll just see you later."

"Perfect!" He edged out when she finally stood to make room for him, and then he leaned over the table and dragged his tray of leftover crepes right in front of her. "Enjoy some carbs," he suggested. "They're good, and you deserve them."

Wallis melted, smiling up at him, her colour deepening to a plum blush when he bent down to kiss her cheek. Isobel didn't know why it was so uncomfortable to watch. Theodore was being sincere, for the most part. His concern over Wallis not eating was real. He had made the effort to soften the blow of him leaving her as soon as she tracked him down, but on the other hand ... he was still using Isobel to escape.

"If you're that uncomfortable ..." Isobel began, her voice a whisper as they passed into the hall.

Theodore only grinned sideways at her, interjecting with: "You haven't heard my new song, yet. You have no idea just how much help I really need."

She chuckled, but immediately afterwards, she was chewing on her lip nervously. "It feels wrong," she admitted as they hit the pathway leading to the lake where the outside cameras were less likely to pick up on their words. "Even though she knows, it still feels like we're making fun of her."

Theodore shot her a look, brushing a few strands of dark hair out of his eyes. "She's free to walk away whenever she wants; I'm not holding her hostage."

"Not with your words, but maybe with your face," she muttered.

His smile was sudden, wide, and utterly disarming. "Did the Illy-stone just compliment me again?"

"No." She almost smiled. "I'm just calling it how I see it."

"And you see a lot." He touched her elbow gently to draw her away from the library, which she was heading toward. "Why is that?"

She shrugged a little, peering toward Alpha Hill, where he was no doubt leading her. She felt no small amount of trepidation, but just like Wallis, Isobel wasn't being held hostage. She could stop walking or turn the other way whenever she wanted. But she didn't. She followed Theodore, even if it meant possibly running into Sato, or Ashford, or Spade, or Moses.

Or, *hell*, any of them except Kilian.

"I'm used to being invisible," she answered after they walked in silence for a little while. "My father said Sigmas shouldn't be seen or heard, only felt. I got very good at picking up when people need me."

Almost as soon as she said it, she wanted to take it back. Last time she had reminded him of his Sigma mother, he had almost turned feral. But when she peered over at him, he was only wearing a tight frown, his eyes their normal dark grey as he scanned the students milling about.

"I suppose that makes sense," he said quietly. "Kilian is like that, because he actually *is* invisible. More than most people realise."

"You mean in more than one way, or ..." She trailed off.

"I mean he spends more time using his ability than people realise," he specified, motioning for her to climb the steps to Alpha Hill ahead of him. She pondered over that statement right up until they were walking through the door to Dorm A, and then some sort of survival mechanism kicked in, and she huddled close behind Theodore's back, hoping she could pass by unnoticed.

"There you are," a voice greeted Theodore before pausing. "I thought I told you to visit the medical centre?"

It was a deep voice, textured and rich, familiar and foreign at once. It swam back to her in a haze, Sato's voice mixing in with it.

Take her body back an hour or something. That was what Sato had said, she was sure ... but who had he been talking to?

She froze, huddling closer. The body she was pressing against vibrated with a low laugh.

"Isobel," Theodore crooned. "You can come out now."

"Fuck's sake, Theo," the voice growled out before a tall body brushed past, stalking off toward the front room that Easton had disappeared into the first time she visited the dorm.

She stared after the man, cataloguing the cropped dark hair with the barely-contained curl against his collar. He was huge. Bigger than any other Alpha she had seen. So tall that he barely cleared the doorway he ducked through. She tried to dredge up a memory of the other Alpha professor Ironside had hired, and an image of a broad, chiselled face flashed into her mind. Kalen West was even more unfriendly than Sato, if that was possible, and he swore as easily as Kilian. She wondered, not for the first time, why it seemed like these boys were friends with their Alpha professors— except now, it seemed like they were even more familiar than casual friends.

"Come on, cutie." Theodore felt behind his back for her hand, drawing it into his and gently tugging her toward his room. They were only two steps into the hallway when Spade's door swung open, the russet-eyed boy appearing in the opening. Theodore didn't even pause, but Spade watched with a narrow-eyed look that she couldn't quite read, until she was safely behind Theodore's bedroom door.

He dropped onto the edge of his bed, shrugging off his jacket with a wince. Isobel sagged back against the door, her heart racing a mile a minute ... until she saw Theodore's blood-soaked shirt, and then it felt like it jumped right up into the back of her throat. She stumbled over, trying to figure out exactly where he had been hurt and with what.

"You look like you've been attacked by a bear," she whispered, drawing closer, a look of horror falling over her face.

"Moses looks worse." Theodore gritted his teeth in a show that was somewhere between a snarl and a smile, as though she had somehow insulted his fighting prowess.

"Is he in the medical centre?" she asked, watching as he drew out a first aid kit from beneath his bed, slapping it onto the covers beside him and rummaging through it.

"No." He uncapped a tube of disinfectant powder with his teeth, spitting out the cap and opening his shirt, shaking the contents down over his chest and stomach. "He's here. Mikki will take care of him. They're sleeping in the same room right now."

"Mikki?" She stepped closer, drawn by some invisible string as she watched the haphazard way he tended himself. She held out her hand, hesitant.

"Mikel." He stared at her hand, his stormy eyes crawling up to her face. "Professor Easton." He seemed frozen with indecision, and then he handed her the tube of powder.

She curled her fingers around it, plucking at the blood-stained neckline. "You should take it off."

"You weren't supposed to fall into my trap that easily," he joked, grunting in pain as he peeled the shirt away, tossing it to the floor.

She sucked in a breath, her fingers tingling as she

looked him over. There were bruises and lacerations *everywhere.* Some deep, some shallow, some jagged, some clean. Interestingly, they seemed to be focussed on his front and didn't rise above his neck. His flawless, sun-burnished skin and all those perfect ridges of muscle and sinew were now horribly marred.

"This is what happens?" she asked, her voice wobbly.

He grunted out a sound that could have meant anything. She stepped even closer, and he spread his legs, allowing her to move between them. He leaned back on his hands slowly, watching her as she picked a cut on his shoulder and shook out the powder, carefully covering it. He gave no indication that it stung in any way.

"I can't feel anything," she noted, astounded. "None of your pain."

"Can you usually?" he asked, his voice tight.

"Mm-hmm," she hummed distractedly, moving across his chest. "It only happens with Alphas, but any strong feeling they have, I can feel. You must have a *very* high pain tolerance."

"I guess ..." He shrugged, dislodging some of the careful lines of disinfectant powder she had drawn. "You can feel *anything*? Our mom didn't like talking about it."

"Only the bad things. The negative things. But I've seen you, you know ..." She drew back, changing the subject as she chewed the inside of her cheek before spitting out, "Half naked. More than once. You don't have many scars." *Like Moses, Easton, and Sato,* she wanted to add, but didn't.

"You've never seen your dad heal?" he asked, watching her carefully.

She shook her head, and he pointed at one of the smaller scratches. "That one," he said, dragging his finger to another, deeper cut, "was like that one, last night. Alphas heal quicker, and we don't scar easily."

She baulked, her mind racing back to Easton's face. She opened her mouth to ask what could have possibly happened to the heavily-scarred professor, before deciding better of it. "Why isn't that common knowledge?" she asked instead, putting away the disinfectant and searching his first aid kit—which seemed thoroughly picked-through—for some bandages. There were no dressings or bandages left, only half a roll of surgical tape.

"Because we aren't allowed to learn about our abilities," he said. "And there aren't enough Alphas around for people to see all the things we have in common unless they're obvious. It's the same reason people don't understand Sigmas, or mate-bonds. They're too rare."

"It doesn't make any sense." She was too busy closing the worst of his cuts with the surgical tape to fully censor what she was saying. "They say all the people accidentally killing themselves to try and force bonds are one of the main reasons we're too dangerous to be allowed out of the settlements, but if they just let us learn more about it, maybe we could come up with another way."

"Those are dangerous things to say," he said lowly, causing her to jerk upright. She sucked on her lower lip, edging back slightly, immediately wary of him. Her father would have beaten her fiercely for those words, and most Ironsiders would likely feel the need to report her for anti-loyalist speech.

"Relax." His fingers brushed hers where they now hung by her thighs. "I'm just surprised. That isn't a common attitude, even in the settlements. And you didn't grow up in the settlements."

She curled her fingers into fists, drawing away from his touch. "Being a Sigma is dangerous unless we refuse to use our abilities at all. Having a little more information about how it all works could literally save lives."

His throat vibrated with a deep humming sound.

He seemed to be agreeing with her. "But we don't have the information." He covered her fist with his warm hand, gently unclenching it. His fingers slipped between hers, making something slow and hot uncurl in the pit of her stomach. They were both staring at their interlocked hands, locked in a frozen moment of slow heat and skittering awareness.

Theodore cleared his throat and pulled away, standing to fetch a fresh T-shirt. He cleaned up the first aid pack and his discarded, bloody shirt and then walked over to his desk. Above it was a polished wooden shelf, with an antler bookend on each side, a long line of books sandwiched between.

"This is all I've got." He touched one of the books, looking at her with his brows dipped down. "All the books my mom could find on the Gifted. You're welcome to any of them." At her incredulous look, he just chuckled, shaking his head. "I've seen the books you're hoarding in your library cubicle, Illy. I know you're trying to do research."

She drifted over to the desk, perching on his chair with all the hesitation of an animal being invited into a trap, but Theodore only grabbed his notebook and retreated back to his bed, leaning up against the great big wooden headboard to frown down at the page he opened to.

"C-can I take one back to my room?" she asked.

"No." His frown melted away immediately, and he regarded her with amusement. "If you want to read my books, you have to read them in my room. With me here to supervise."

"It's like you don't have any friends." She shook her head, relaxing a little at his teasing tone.

"None like you." He scribbled something and then resumed frowning down at his work, tapping his pencil against his chin, like he hadn't just said something that made her heart skip a few beats.

She stood and reached up, her fingers drifting across the spines of the books. She chose one at random, drawing it down, surprised to find that it wasn't so much an educational text as a collection of articles written about the Gifted population and published in popular journals worldwide. The most popular topics were, of course, Alphas and bonded mates, though there seemed to be a few scattered articles about dangerous abilities, which she skipped. She didn't need to read about all the examples the humans used to keep them locked away in settlements, living as secondary citizens. There was one on Sigmas, debating whether they truly had abilities or whether their empathy was just a heightened sense, like the heightened senses of the Alphas.

She skipped past that one and settled on an article about bonded mates from a BBC journalist, since her mother loved the BBC channel.

Had loved.

Past tense.

Her fingers shook as she flattened out the page, biting back the sudden prickle of despair. She had allowed herself to break that day, but it wouldn't happen again.

The phenomenon of mate-bonds within Gifted communities has always been a fascinating topic, but the NATO ban on experimentation and study of the Gifted people has made it typically difficult to gather data on how such bonds occur.

It took me five years to win an amnesty pass to visit the settlements around America in a restricted journalistic capacity. They allowed me a set of ten questions, with absolutely no deviations, and I was forced to agree to submit the tapes of my interviews to the government, but nonetheless, we were finally given the green light, and several years ago, our study of the Gifted mates began.

Three days into our tour of the settlements, one thing became abundantly clear. The Gifted didn't want to talk.

They thought I was there to entrap them into admitting they were trying to force bonds—a pervasive and dangerous rumour that hovers around many of the settlements and often leads to serious consequences. Since we only had one shot at this, we decided to pull out and apply for a further ten questions. A preliminary interview to put our subjects at ease. We asked questions such as: "Have you ever heard of the BBC?" and "Do you understand that the BBC does not act on the behalf of any government agencies?" And the question that caused almost three months of back-and-forth arguing with the Official Gifted Governing Body (more commonly referred to as "the officials"): "Would you like to remain anonymous during the course of your interview?"

Finally, we had our new set of questions approved, and we went back to the settlements. Of the hundreds of people we spoke to, none of them were willing to go on the record with their identities, but they were talking, and that was all we needed.

Isobel skipped down a few paragraphs, eagerly searching out the journalist's findings.

It seems that the bonding process can be split into two or three phases, the first stage being the most controversial, as most seem divided about whether it exists or not. This goes back to the belief that the Gifted are a product of their gods and that their "abilities" are divinely-ascribed. Those beliefs, while dwindling, still have a grip on some communities—the communities who believe in the first stage of the mating process. The Fated Stage, as we've decided to label it, calls together the "Anchor" of a bonded pair with the "Tether." It assumes that mates are fated from birth and cannot be forced, avoided, or changed. And it is the workings of fate that are believed to bring together those destined to be bonded.

In the other camp are the people who believe love, proximity and familiarity are the precursors to a bond, refuting the existence of the first stage. They believe the bond doesn't even begin to develop until the "Tether" approaches death.

This, we have decided to call the Death Stage. The first camp of people believe that when one of the Gifted destined for a mate dies, fate ensures their "Anchor" will be nearby, giving their soul something to latch on to, allowing them to live on. The second camp believes this is all coincidence. The "Tether" latches onto whoever happens to be closest in their Death Phase, turning them into an anchor of convenience. This school of thought has led many a young couple to attempt suicide with their lover by their side, hoping to force a bond.

She pushed the book away, shaking her head. There was no point. The article wasn't telling her anything she didn't already know. Nobody could decide on whether mates were fated or not, but they always happened to be beside each other when the Tether had some sort of random—or deliberate—accident. And then a bond half-formed, wreaking absolute havoc on their lives with all sorts of chaotic mayhem until they completed the bond with a permanent marking. Sometimes, it was in formal tattoo ceremonies that were carried out like weddings, but sometimes it happened by accidental scarring.

She closed the book, deciding it wasn't going to tell her anything useful. Every article was going to be a careful, cautionary tale, toting the delicate line between what they were allowed to say and what they knew, but all ending with the same sentiment: The Gifted were too dangerous to be allowed to live freely amongst the humans. The Gifted believed they were created by *gods* and were willing to hurt themselves and others to prove it.

Nothing screamed crazy like believing you were some kind of chosen one.

She reached for another book, settling back into the chair to read a collection of stories compiled by settlement writers.

THEODORE WATCHED HER OUT OF THE CORNER OF HIS EYE, amused at the way she discarded the book she didn't like and sank into the one she did. She didn't seem to notice when he abandoned his work or when he left the room. He headed up to the outdoor kitchen, starting up the coffee machine.

It was Sunday afternoon, so everyone was relaxing and getting ready for the week. Elijah, Gabriel, and Niko would have been sorting through mountains of laundry in their rooms, since they all exercised so much during the day. Kalen was likely still trying to hunt down Oscar, but Theodore didn't know why. Either way, it seemed serious. It always was with Oscar. Mikel was on bed rest after coming between Theodore and Moses again, but he would be fine. His body had adjusted to the constant abuse. He healed faster than anyone, even Niko.

Theodore sighed, pulling out two mugs. He had already dropped off food to Mikel and Moses after Spade treated their wounds. They needed sleep now more than anything. There was nothing he could do.

"Is she still here?" Kilian asked, coming up the stairs with Cian. He sat at the island while Cian hunted through the fridge. Both of them had wet hair, and towels were wrapped around their hips.

The ropes they had tied over the lake were getting constant use now that the other Alphas were facing the possibility of Theodore being the only one of them able to swim. They were fiercely competitive.

"Yeah. She's reading." He poured the coffee and then hesitated, hunting down one of the trays they used to take food to one of the boys if they were too injured to get up. He added a few things to the tray, like cream and sugar, and then hesitated again.

"No cookies?" Cian asked, peering over his shoulder. He was being sarcastic.

Theodore stalked over to the cabinet of snacks anyway and tossed a packet of chocolate chip cookies onto the tray.

"Can I come?" Kilian asked. He was leaning back on his stool, his arms crossed and a pale brow arched in challenge, like he already knew the answer.

"No," Theodore growled. "She thinks you aren't into her, asshole."

"I might not be." He shrugged a shoulder. "You never know. I'm always evolving. I'm not set in stone. I could change my mind tomorrow."

"I know you liked having her in your lap, even if it was just because she wasn't in mine. *Nothing* romantic is going on, so the lot of you can just back the fuck off. And *you*." He jerked a finger at Kilian. "You can stop trying to steal her away just so that she'll stop hanging out with me. We agreed I can be her friend as long as I keep up the show with Wallis, and that's what I'm doing."

"Maybe I just like her," Kilian suggested, narrowing his light, green-gold eyes. "She's considerate. She's dry. She's the meekest, most unintentionally savage girl at the academy. It's delightful. She's different to the suck-ups that usually hang around us. If it's so surprising to you that someone else might enjoy her, then you can't like her all that much yourself."

"That's not what I'm questioning, and you know it," Theodore snapped back before visibly shaking off the tension that lined his shoulders. Kilian was his *friend*. They had no reason to be fighting. He had no reason to feel so on edge. "Sorry," he grumbled, picking up the tray. "Of course you're welcome to join us."

Both Kilian and Cian kept quiet as he left the kitchen, but most of the tension lifted when he shouldered back into the room and Isobel didn't even glance up. She had moved to the end of his bed and was curled against the thick wooden baseboard, a blanket pulled into her lap as she turned the page.

"Do you always read like this?" he asked, setting the tray down in front of her.

She ignored him but must have smelled the coffee,

because her little hand lifted, drifting over the tray until it curved around a cup. She sipped the coffee, sighed, and went back to reading.

"So you like it black," he noted, picking up his own coffee. She ignored him again, which had a laugh building up in his chest. "Wouldn't expect anything less from the Illy-stone."

He sat back against the headboard, reaching for the remote for the drop-down projection screen over the window on the opposite wall. As it lowered, he caught sight of Isobel's hand sneaking out toward the tray again. She caught the packet of cookies and dragged it back to her chest as she stretched out onto her stomach. She never even broke pace, carefully flipping the page again while her other hand tunnelled into the packet.

He was unreasonably pleased that she was on his bed, that she had made herself comfortable, that she liked his mother's book. She had picked the single book on the shelf that wasn't just a part of his mother's collection ... it was the one his mother had written. And she was completely engrossed, unaware that her cropped shirt had ridden up, the smooth arch of her spine drawing his eye before he shook his head and forced his attention to the projection screen.

He pulled up the latest episode of Ironside, setting

it to play. Usually, the entire dorm watched it together, but he couldn't bear to disrupt her. Besides, it was Sunday. Nothing important ever aired on Sunday. It was an unspoken rule—just like the explosive episodes that came out every Friday.

And it was nowhere near interesting enough to keep his eyes off her.

12

Nice Alphas

Isobel emerged from her book in a daze, sitting up and stretching out her limbs. Theodore was resting back against the pillows on his bed, watching a projection screen as it played the ending credits to the latest episode of the Ironside show. He flicked her a look. "Good book?"

"Yeah." She rolled her shoulders back and stretched out her neck. His eyes seemed to follow the movements. "I love hearing stories from the settlements. We weren't allowed to visit much."

She finally caught sight of the evening sky peeking around the sides of the projection screen. "Shit, it's late. I should get back."

She scrambled off the end of his bed, and he clicked on a remote, sending the screen back up and turning off the projection. "Are you going to the hall for dinner?"

She grinned up at him, slinging her bag over her shoulder. "Stop using me to avoid Wallis."

He groaned, his hand brushing down his face. "Okay, fine. But I won't be responsible for what I do to the next person who steals food off my plate."

She chuckled as she left his room, her steps light as she neared the common room, where she could hear the credits for the Ironside show still playing and see the faint lights from the TV spilling into the hallway. When she passed by, she kept her head ducked down and picked up her speed, hoping to pass by unnoticed. She really thought she made it until something caught her backpack only a few steps from the front door, pulling her up short. Moses stepped around her, opening the door and using his hold on her bag to drag her through.

As soon as the door closed, he pushed her up against it, his fingers wrapping around her upper arms. It was the only point of contact between them, his body held stiffly a few inches from hers. He didn't look good. His eyes had heavy dark bags beneath them, his hair was mussed like he had just rolled out of bed, and his mouth was pinched so tightly it was only a cruel slash.

"Stop coming here," he warned her, his growl so low it reverberated through her bones. "Whatever you think you're doing with Theo, you need to end it."

He smelled like crushed petals, with the acidity of sap eating through the sweet, powdery perfume of a flower. It was complex, but underrated and subtle, like something you had to keep smelling to properly identify. His emotion, however, was not hard to identify. It crushed against her ribs, thumping into her like he was swinging a dumbbell at her, and it felt ... awful. He was confused, ashamed, *hurt* ... but most of all, he was furious.

At her.

"I'm sorry about the ki—"

He didn't even let her finish. He ducked his head down until his dark eyes were tunnelling into her. "He thinks he's invincible around you because you took it away—but that was *one* time, Carter. Next time, you'll be fucking dead, and we can't have that hanging over us right now."

"Twice," she corrected with a frown.

He froze, something awful flashing in those eyes. It was too dark to tell just how black they were getting, but she could only imagine the injuries he was hiding beneath his clothes. She didn't want to put him into another volatile situation.

"What?" he breathed, looming closer. His chest brushed against hers, and for one insane moment, she found herself staring at his mouth, remembering their brief kiss.

"Maybe this is something you should talk to him about," she suggested, trying not to sound afraid.

While Theodore and Moses didn't look like twins, they still shared similar features. They had the same wide eyes; the same strong, regal nose; and the same wide, angular jawline, where they carried most of their tension. It should have been easy to look at Moses and think of Theodore, to convince herself he wouldn't hurt her. But it wasn't. Moses was a different breed to his brother. He didn't entirely seem in control of himself, and he didn't possess the good-natured softness Theodore sometimes did.

"What's it going to take?" Moses breathed out the question against her temple, his scent wrapping around her, tinged with sweat and the tangy hint of blood. His fingers trailed down her arms. "I don't want to threaten you, because I always keep my word. So tell me what it's going to take. Are you trying to win the game, Sigma? I can make you more popular than Theodore."

She scoffed lightly, but the fear inside her grew. Moses was serious. For whatever reason, he really wanted her to stay away from his brother, and he was willing to offer her anything for her to keep her distance. And if she didn't accept his offer ... the menace shivering along the hard slash of his mouth spoke volumes.

"I'm not after anything." She pulled her head back as far as it could go, feeling the door bump behind her. "You just have to tell me why. I don't want to cause you any pain or Theo any trouble. I don't want him to pretend to be in a relationship with the girl who tried to assault Sato. Just give me a good enough reason, and I'll stay away from him."

Moses dropped his touch from her arms completely, taking a step back from her. His eyes were blank and he levelled her with a stare, looking down at her in surprise. "You know I can't talk about it."

It.

Ferality.

"Just give me a good reason," she pressed, crossing her arms over her chest. She was surreptitiously hugging herself against his cold gaze, but he didn't need to know that.

"You could get hurt," he said, still scraping his eyes over her like he was trying to figure her out.

"Bit late for that." She smiled tightly. "He isn't the first Alpha I've known. Anything else?"

He set his jaw, his emotion cracking against her. There *was* more, but he wasn't willing to say any of it. "I'll make your life hell," he whispered into the night, taking another step back.

"Was that a reason?" She edged away from the door, moving slowly out of the camera blind spot in front of Dorm A.

He noticed, his brow pinching together, though she couldn't read what emotion sank into his eyes as they swept over her. He shook his head. "No. You've already decided. It's a promise."

"Do your worst." She smiled, but there was no humour in it. No warmth. She was cold all the way through to her veins.

She walked away, letting the moonless night swallow her up. She had already been standing outside, so thankfully her eyes were adjusted enough to hurry down the steps set into the hill, with only the dim, twinkling lights that lined the path to guide her. They were set into the rocks lining the path, staring up like they were trying to impersonate the stars—just like the students within the academy. The temperature had dropped, making her shiver as she passed the lake, and it seemed that the night grew darker, thicker, as she ducked through the doors to her dorm.

WAKE UP, ILLY.

The voice was her mother's. Calm and soothing. Unwavering in a way it rarely used to be.

Isobel's eyes flew open, her breath catching in her chest. Her room was pitch black, filled with the heat of bodies all around her. Her cheek was against her blanket, her arms pulled behind her back as someone planted a knee against her spine, digging it painfully into her flesh. She tried to pull her arms away, still sluggish and confused, but the rope around her wrists only pulled tighter.

"She's awake," someone whispered. "Get her legs."

Before she could even react, several sets of hands gripped her ankles, and just like that, she was immobilised.

She tried to scream, but someone slipped a thick hood over her head, muffling the sound.

"Better shut up," a female voice warned. "Or we'll tape the hood over your mouth and you might suffocate."

She bit her tongue as they hauled her upright, dragging her to her feet.

"Got the shadows, Kiki?"

"The cameras won't see us," someone responded.

"But let's hurry."

She had no sense of where they were taking her, but after a whimper escaped her as she kicked her toe on the metal door trim leading out of the dorm, she heard the sound of thick tape unwinding from a roll, and she made sure not to utter another sound.

Suffocating outside in her pyjamas with a hood taped over her head wasn't the best way to die.

"What is this?" she whispered instead, just loud enough that one of the people dragging her by the arms would be able to hear.

"You ignored our warning." Another female voice. "We told you to stay in your lane, but you decided to one-up us, didn't you? We're just escalating the game you've decided to play."

She decided not to answer, taking stock of her situation instead. Her ankles were tied with rope, but they had given her just enough slack to take small steps and stumble along as they dragged her. Her arms were secured so tightly behind her back, it felt like one of her assailants was one more tug away from popping her shoulder joint out. She couldn't tell how many there were, but she had only heard female voices. The two on either side of her were both bigger and stronger—which wasn't hard since she was a Sigma.

Still, there wasn't much of a chance of her fighting

her way out of this. She could try to talk her way out of it, but she decided to wait to see what they had in store for her first.

Maybe they were just trying to scare her.

"Hurry," a somewhat-familiar voice hissed. "The sun is almost up."

She was tossed suddenly, landing heavily against a curved wooden floor. It rocked beneath her, swaying as water lapped at her back.

A ... *boat?* It must have been small, like the rowing boats some of the fourth and fifth-year students used in the lake, because she could feel the sides against her knees.

"Since you're apparently better than all our swimming coaches, this should be easy for you," that vaguely familiar voice taunted her.

And then they were ripping at her clothes. She flailed against the bottom of the boat, but as soon as she felt the cold metal of the scissors they began using to cut away her pyjama bottoms, she stopped, shuddering in fear.

When the metal slipped under the waistband of her underwear, she grew as cold as ice, wishing she could hold her hands over the apex of her thighs as they laughed at her.

"She's trembling," one of the girls laughed out.

"How pathetic."

"Shut the fuck up," another one muttered. "The cameras will hear you." The voice grew closer, a length of duct tape wrapping around the bottom of the hood covering her head. It drew the material tight against her neck, some of it sucking into her mouth as she gasped for breath.

"Better start swimming, bitch," the voice sneered. "This boat is broken. And by the way, Sigma ... say anything about this to anyone, and we won't give you a boat next time." The bodies drew away, and the boat suddenly jerked, bobbing unsteadily.

Drawing away from them.

She stopped gasping for breath, struggling to sit up with her limbs still tied. The boat swayed to the side and she whimpered, falling still again. This was bad.

This was really bad.

Keeping as still as possible, she began to feel around the damp wood that she could reach with her hands. She discovered that the seats for the rowers had been ripped out, leaving a few rough sections of wood. One of them still had what felt like a rusty nail sticking out of it that had probably already caught against her arm if the extra sting was anything to judge by. She twisted her body to start rubbing the rope up against the nail, measuring the way the water rose around her face, which was pressed into the bottom of the boat.

Whoever had been shielding her in darkness had retreated, because as she frantically rubbed against the nail, a muted light suddenly slipped through a torn fibre in the hood. The sun was rising.

She tried to turn her head as the water rose further, the hood growing damp and weighing down heavier over her mouth. Her wrists slipped against the nail, the boat tipping a little too far to the left. She eased her body against the right of the boat, a sob raw in her throat as she closed her eyes tightly, waiting for the boat to right itself again.

She positioned the rope against the nail again and returned to work, the rasping sounds of her panicked breathing so loud inside the hood, even with the material trying to escape into her mouth with every inhale. Enough water had pooled in that she had to raise her head, her neck straining, her arms almost locking up in pain as she finally felt the rope give way. She reached for the hood immediately, tearing at the tape and ripping it away.

Her feet were next, but as soon as she sat up to reach for them, the boat tipped again, and this time she wasn't able to steady it. She crashed into the water and immediately began tearing at the ropes around her ankles, fumbling several times as the panic gripped her, making her fingers shake.

When she kicked the ropes away and broke the surface of the water, she saw that the boat had flipped itself upside down, revealing several small gashes ripped into the base of it. She laid herself over it, using it to keep herself afloat as she took in her surroundings. She was in the middle of the lake.

Right in the middle of the academy.

And the sun had risen.

She was too far away from any of the lakeside cameras for them to see her in any detail, but she would need to swim back to land at some point, and she didn't have any clothes. The group of girls who had dragged her out of bed were nowhere to be seen, but there were a few early-risers setting out for their run around the lake or walking from Dorms B or D toward the fitness centre. She spotted five people in total, and while two of them seemed to look her way for a moment, none of them paused.

"Fuck," she growled out, some of the lake water spitting from her lips. "*FUCK*!"

There was no way out of it.

She began to swim toward the shore, determined to get it over with before even more people woke up.

Her tears mixed with the lake water as she thought about running all the way back to Dorm O without any clothes, and she paused halfway across the lake, her chest squeezing in a tight panic that made it hard to breathe and even harder to stay afloat.

Swim, Illy.

It was her mother's voice again. Familiar but unfamiliar. She sounded so *calm*, so peaceful, no longer chased by the demon who hunted them both through the halls of their own home.

Freed from Braun Carter.

"I'm going insane now." Isobel ducked her head beneath the water, closing her eyes and letting out a silent, desperate scream. She didn't want to do this.

Swim, Illy.

She pushed back up again, gasping for breath. Her chest hurt so much—not from the exertion, but from the panic.

She kicked forward, her arms cutting through the water, trying to move quickly but quietly. She didn't look up or take stock of the people out and about until she was clasping the boat dock and hauling herself up to sit on the edge. She gritted her teeth, struggling to her feet as she fought back the need to vomit.

She imagined there was a girl out there who would square her shoulders and toss her wet hair back, thrust her chin up, and strut forward, burying the humiliation and turning this whole thing around. There was a girl who might be able to hide her shame and insecurities, who might be able to walk all the way back to Dorm O like she was a bad bitch and nobody could touch her, even when they *did* touch her. There was a girl who would use this for views or popularity points—and in fact, she could think of at least two similar situations right off the top of her head in which girls or boys *had* used nudity for a quick popularity boost.

But Isobel wasn't her, whoever that girl was.

The best she could do was swipe away the water from her cheeks, refusing to let any more tears fall while the cameras could see her. She took wobbly steps across the dock, almost kicking into a run as she tried to cover herself with her hands.

"Carter?"

The voice was familiar, but her ears were full of a sound like a roaring waterfall, and she didn't turn toward whoever had spoken.

"Carter, what the fuck?" A hand caught her arm, whipping her around to face a chest. A lightweight, cream-coloured sweatshirt. It was very close to her. So close, her nose almost brushed against it. The fight melted out of her before she even had a chance to summon it as the light scent of clove and woodsmoke hit her senses.

"What the fuck?" Reed repeated, now holding both of her arms. "Gabriel," he snapped out. "Help."

A second later, a body was pressing in behind her, and a second scent wafted over her. Since it smelled so much like fresh linen, she wasn't sure if it was Spade or his clothes.

"Why aren't you answering?" Reed demanded.

They were pressing uncomfortably close, until she could feel the hard muscles they had shown off at the Valentine's party through the loose, oversized clothing they preferred to dance in ... but that same loose, oversized clothing was now doing a remarkable job of making her feel covered and protected.

"Answer, or we back off," Spade said, his tone cool.

She swallowed, her eyes drifting up to Reed's.

Say anything about this to anyone, and we won't give you a boat next time.

"I w-was s-sleep-walking," she managed to get out through chattering teeth. She wasn't exactly cold, but she might have been going into shock. Reed's light grey eyes seemed even brighter than usual, the tinges of blue and white overtaking his pupils, which had shrunk to pinpricks. His slender features were heavy with anger, and she could hear the start of a growling sound building up in the back of his throat. His gold Alpha ring seemed to swell.

He released her but didn't step away as he pulled his sweatshirt over his silvery-blond head. He was wearing a thin T-shirt underneath, but it rose up a little as he pulled off the top layer, and his bare, hot skin pressed against hers.

She felt overloaded, her nerves fried, her entire body shuddering, but he didn't give her any time to react. He dragged his sweatshirt over her head, pulling it down to her thighs as she fought to free her arms through the sleeves.

"Th-thanks," she mumbled, trying to sidestep them as soon as she was covered. They backed off immediately, and her face flamed at the wet patches on their clothing as she backed up several paces.

"Keep moving," Reed growled out, his Alpha voice vibrating along her bones.

She waited for the command to take a hold of her, but it didn't. Instead, two Delta girls skittered away from them down the path, their phones in their hands as they bent their heads together and whispered furiously.

"Not you," Spade spoke softly as Isobel backed up another step, his reddish-brown eyes fixed to her with an unwavering calm. "You stay. Explain."

"I already explained." She managed to expel the stutter from her voice this time. "And what the hell does it matter to you anyway?"

They didn't answer, and she backed up another step, waiting to see if Reed would use his Alpha voice on her, since she could still hear that low growling sound vibrating from his chest.

He didn't, but she could feel his stare burning into her back as she turned and hurried away.

GABRIEL SPADE DIDN'T LIKE WHEN THINGS SURPRISED HIM. He liked order and predictability. He liked getting up at the same time each morning, wearing the same clothes for each day of the week, and knowing exactly what would happen wherever he went.

The Sigma liked to pop up when he least expected it, and he *hated* that. He hated that she had invaded his personal space, her rich cherry scent drifting beneath his door—never at the times Theodore warned him she would be there, but always when he wasn't prepared for it. He hated that she had interrupted his practice time and that he hadn't been able to stop watching her. Usually, something like that would have triggered him and he would have ordered the disruption gone, remaining agitated until he could go through one of his soothing routines and reset, like it had never happened.

But he was struck, routines forgotten.

Just like he was struck now, though this situation wasn't so much awed shock as pure disbelief.

"Whatever that was ... it was fucked up," Elijah growled out beside him.

He barely nodded, his eyes fixed to the retreating Sigma. Elijah's sweatshirt covered her like a dress, falling almost to her knees, but it was too thin, and it stuck to her wet body in places, the white material turning transparent. He tried to blink away the flashing images that tried to gain traction inside his head, but he failed, forced to face each one of them.

He had watched her swim toward them. Had watched her pull herself onto the dock.

Seeing her sitting there, hunched over, her wet hair covering her, she reminded him of a painting. Dripping, long blonde hair; lashes hiding her downturned eyes; pillowy, strawberry lips; scattered, deliberate-looking freckles stark against translucent skin; arms curled over her chest like she was wilting; and only the slight curve of her ass against the dock visible above that waterfall of hair to tell them that something was wrong.

He and Elijah had stepped forward

simultaneously, and even though the others joked that they shared a single brain cell, he had no idea what his best friend was thinking.

He only knew that he had convinced himself he was drawn by the weirdness of it all.

Not *her*, but the situation. The anomaly.

It wasn't that she looked like a painting, but that whoever had painted her had put her in the wrong frame. She belonged somewhere ... else.

Safe.

The obtrusive word broke through his thoughts for the second time that morning, and he shook it off.

"Not our responsibility," he said to Elijah, who grunted back.

"When has that ever stopped me?"

Gabriel twisted to look at his best friend, noting the narrowed eyes, the swollen Alpha ring, and the flaring of his nostrils. Elijah despised bullying in any form, and this had *torture* written all over it.

"It's not a good idea to get involved." Gabriel adjusted his tack, softening his tone. "You'll only make the target on her back even bigger—and draw attention to us."

Elijah looked down, brushing his hand over his shirt, some of the violence edging out of his expression. "She's too young for this shit." He spoke so lowly that Gabriel wouldn't have caught the words without his Alpha hearing.

He only grunted out a sound of agreement. They were only two years older than her—not that she knew it—but she seemed especially innocent, even for her age.

"I think I need to add a sensor to her door," Elijah added, striding off toward the fitness centre.

They were already late for their scheduled practice time, so Gabriel followed with an agitated snap to each step. "That sounds like getting involved."

"Not if I hook it up to Oscar's phone."

"That sounds downright danger—actually, that's brilliant."

"I know."

"He'll be so annoyed, and you know what happens when he gets annoyed."

"I know."

"He'll be in such a bad mood he'll scare off anyone who tries to mess with her."

"Gabe. It was my idea."

"Only one problem," Gabriel said, searching out the nearest cameras to make sure their conversation was still private. "He'll fucking kill you."

. . .

Reed hates bullies.

Isobel remembered what Theodore had told her as she ran back to Dorm O. Reed must have known on some level that she was lying to him ... but she didn't realise her real mistake until she was pushing into her surprisingly undisturbed room. She swiped up her phone as a fresh wave of alarm swept through her. Since she had Spade's number, she clicked on his name to send him a message.

Isobel: Please don't tell Theo about this morning.

She chewed on her lip, her hands shaking as she fought against what she knew she should say next.

Isobel: And thank you for helping me again.

He didn't reply immediately, but she didn't expect him to. She slumped back against her pile of blankets on the floor, her head hitting the wall behind her, and closed her eyes.

She felt like she could finally breathe again, but the feeling didn't last long as she realised the situation she was in. She opened her eyes and glanced toward the door. The lock wasn't busted this time. It must have been picked, or else they somehow got hold of another key.

As long as she stayed in Dorm O, she was never going to be safe.

Which left her with two options: go home and face

her father or do the impossible and get herself a private room in Dorm A.

She hauled herself from the bed, checking the time as she grabbed her toiletries bag and a change of clothes. She was already late for dance practice, and if she needed to win almost two million popularity points before the end of the year, then she couldn't afford to slack off now.

Spade's reply came just as she stepped into one of the shower rooms.

Spade: That's two favours.

She turned on the hot water and stripped off Reed's sweatshirt, stepping under the stream until the shuddering of her body melted away, and then she stepped partially out of the spray, drying off her hands and replying to his message.

Isobel: Two favours?

Spade: One, for saving your ass by the lake. Two, for keeping it a secret.

Spade: And that's just me. You still have Reed to answer to.

She hit her phone against her forehead, getting droplets all over the screen that she had to wipe off.

Isobel: Hi vh kk sriyckg V mg necktie

Spade: Are you having a stroke?

She swore, her face flooding with colour.

Isobel: Got water on my phone.

Spade: You better not be back in the fucking lake.

Isobel: The shower.

Spade: Alone?

She reared back a little, giving her screen a funny look, even though he couldn't see her.

Isobel: ...

Spade: What?

Isobel: Why would you ask that?

Spade: To gather information.

Isobel: Why?

Spade: ...

Isobel: What?

Spade: I'll be calling in those favours soon. Stay out of the lake.

She quickly finished off her shower and hurried through the rest of her day with her head tucked down. Eve tried to draw her out a few times, but it wasn't until three days later that she finally broke through.

Forcefully.

"That's enough, Iz." The hazel-haired beauty slammed her lunch tray down opposite Isobel's, her blue eyes full of fire as she snatched Isobel's phone from beneath her nose. "You've been avoiding me, and there are rumours going around the dorm that the

Omegas and Betas teamed up to teach you a lesson. You better tell me what happened before I have to watch it on the show."

Isobel sighed, dropping her head into her hand as she picked up her fork to stab a piece of pasta. "I can't tell you."

"Bullshit," Eve replied happily. "You don't think I can keep a secret? Did they threaten you?"

Isobel gave her a small smile, and the other girl sat forward, her brows pinching in.

"Tell me," Eve demanded. "What the hell did those bitches do to you?"

Before Isobel could even think of responding, several of the Omega second-years were approaching, hoping to crowd around Eve the way they usually did ... but this time, Eve waved them off, shaking her head.

"Everything okay?" one of them asked, shooting a look at Isobel like she was somehow forcing Eve to sit there without them.

"Yeah, I'll catch up with you guys back in the dorm." Eve turned back to Isobel, waiting until the other girls had wandered away before her hand shot across the table, grasping Isobel's fingers.

"You have exactly thirty seconds to start talking before I start threatening you with things I haven't been able to come up with yet, so in reality you have a minute."

"Fine." Isobel laughed slightly, shaking her head, and then she quickly skimmed over what had happened. She wanted to leave out the part where Reed and Spade had helped her, but if the Ironside show was going to dramatize anything about the incident, it would be that part.

"Oh my god." Eve fell back in her seat, her eyes wide, her hand slipping away. "Are you okay?"

"I will be," Isobel answered, lowering her voice as she scanned the hall, taking in the group of Omegas, who had found a table close by and had all arranged themselves so they could stare over at her table. "As soon as I win all those popularity points and get the hell out of Dorm O."

"Yes!" Eve slammed both palms down on the table, her blue eyes lit with determination. "Finally! There's the competitive edge I've been waiting for. Let's not waste any more time talking about what they did to you and start strategizing about how we're going to spin it."

Isobel bit down on another laugh, cutting it off. "You're a little scary. You're like an eighteen-year-old version of my father's publicist. Mom used to whisper to me that she was a ballbuster—" She cut herself off, tensing up. "Not that you're—"

"I could be a ballbuster." Eve shrugged. "Most people think I'm nice and boring, but I have a dark side."

"Sure," Isobel indulged her. "Somewhere."

"Probably." Eve toyed with her water glass. "Ugh, whatever. I have an idea."

"You do?"

Eve smirked. "No, but I'm pretending I do because I work better under pressure—*oh*, I have something. What if we pretend it was a dare?"

"How?" Isobel scratched at her chin, her skin suddenly crawling as she realised her father was part of their audience. It wasn't like he would see her naked on television, since they would have to blur out her nudity, but he would *know* ... and whatever way they spun the story to try and get popularity points, he would likely believe. He didn't think she was smart enough to come up with any strategies of her own.

"Okay, how about this ... you start some sort of dare competition and start posting about it on your socials ..." She paused to think, tapping the handle of her fork against her cheek. She had a small beauty mark there, and the utensil kept hitting it like a target. "If Theo is still friends with you after he finds out two of his buddies saw you naked, then maybe you could ask him to help you out? If he's the one competing against you in this dare competition, it might just get you enough social media attention to generate the popularity points you need, as well as smoothing over the whole lake incident."

Isobel wrapped her arms around her stomach, glancing around the hall to peer into the booths along the sides of the room. The Alphas were tucked away inside one of them, but she couldn't see any sign of them.

"I could try and ask him."

"You do that." Eve grinned at her. "He owes you. You agreed to teach him how to swim, even though it got your room trashed."

"But then he had to get a fake girlfriend because of me."

"Say what now?" Eve leaned forward, darting her eyes around. There was too much noise at dinnertime, and they weren't in one of the private booths, so it was highly unlikely the cameras would be able to pick up on their individual conversation.

Still, Isobel also leaned forward, letting her hair fall over one shoulder to shield her face as she rested her chin on her hand. "You're taking all of this to the grave," she instructed the other girl.

Eve nodded eagerly, and Isobel only hoped that she wasn't making a terrible decision to trust the bubbly brunette.

"Reed, Spade and Theo's new female companions are all for show. Wallis owed Sato a favour after she broke into his room and tried to hook up with him. He blackmailed her into pretending to be Theo's girlfriend to take some of the heat off him after last Friday's episode. She brought her friends along for Spade and Reed."

"What about Ashford?" Eve asked, tilting her head with wide eyes before a huge smile spilled over her face. "He's too much of a man-whore, isn't he?"

Isobel nodded, chuckling. "That seems to be the consensus."

"Wow," Eve expelled on a breath. "That's ... wow, okay. So maybe you might have to do a little bit of convincing, but I have faith in you. And if Theo says no, maybe you could ask Kilian? If he let you sit on his lap just to include you, he must like you. I mean not like *that*, obviously. But he never lets anyone near him."

"I think he's just a really nice guy."

"Uh-oh." Eve chuckled, winding spaghetti around her fork. "It's always the nice Alphas you have to be suspicious of—haven't you heard?"

13
WICKED GAMES

ISOBEL: I NEED A FAVOUR.

She stared down at the message she had sent three days ago. Since then, Theodore had tried to call her three times and sent a question mark in response, but she was still working up the courage to actually ask him, so she hadn't replied or called him back. Instead, she spent her evenings with Eve, developing a comprehensive plan to get all the popularity points she needed to escape Dorm O. She would have felt guilty for all the time Eve was spending on her if it wasn't so obvious that the other girl *lived* to plot and plan up schemes.

Promising herself she would finally reply to Theodore after she finished her session, she hooked up her phone to the sound system in the training room and began running through her stretches. Eve had taken over her social media after Isobel finally gathered the courage to ask her father for the passwords, and all of her past posts had been wiped, replaced by a single picture. It was Isobel, half-hidden behind one of the columns in the dance practice room, with the morning sunlight filtering over her legs as she bent into a stretch, the light missing her face to cast her half into darkness.

The caption of the image said: *Welcome to the game ...*

Eve had chosen the song "Wicked Game" from one of the dances in Isobel's old profile and had ordered Isobel to revamp the entire routine and have it ready by Sunday.

Two days left.

Isobel rolled up her yoga mat, started the song on her phone, and began the routine she had come up with, watching herself in the mirror. She examined every extension, every arch and jerk of her body until sweat was soaking into her loose shirt. She heard slow clapping when she finally finished, and she quickly rushed over to her phone, stopping the music as Theodore kicked the door closed behind him and stalked toward her.

He was wearing his trademark easy smile, but his stormy eyes were guarded.

"You really don't notice anyone else when you're dancing, do you?" He slumped down onto the bench next to her bag, his legs spread, his arms crossed. His body language was so easy, so casual, but the look in his eyes never changed. "Why are you avoiding me, Illy?"

She frowned, crossing her arms and trying to make her eyes as guarded as his, though she had no idea if it worked or not. His lips quirked a little, so it probably didn't.

"I was just trying it out," she said.

"Ah." His fingers tapped against his arm. "How did it go?"

She grabbed a towel, wiping her face. "Well, you're here."

"So, successful then." He quirked a brow. "If I didn't know you better, I'd say you get a kick out of this. Not that I blame you. Sigmas aren't usually painted in the most alluring light. It's an entertaining change for the rest of the world, watching an Alpha run around after you like a puppy."

"Are you sure you know me better?"

He reached forward suddenly, grabbing a handful of her shirt, the material twisting into his fist. For a moment, neither of them moved, and then he tugged gently, drawing her forward. One step, and then two, until her legs were almost between his, and then he released her. "Yeah, I'm sure. What's your favour?"

She reached for her phone, restarting the song and turning the volume up loud so their conversation could remain private.

"It's about the game," she started in a hesitant way, twisting her fingers together.

He tipped his head back against the wall, his eyes melting from a hard block of dark grey to something softer, until she could make out the little tinges of blue seeping between the dark of his iris and the gold of his Alpha ring. "What game?" It was like watching a little bit of morning sunshine peek through the blanket of a heavy summer storm.

"*The* game." She waved her hand around the hall. "The Ironside game. I need to start playing it."

That seemed to get his attention. His broad shoulders tightened and his mouth snapped shut before he forced his body to relax again. "Tell me exactly what you mean."

"They offered me a private room in Dorm A next year," she forced out, even though some part of her desperately wanted to keep the whole thing to herself. "And they've started scoring me with popularity points early. I need two million before the end of the year, or I have to stay in Dorm O."

His pink lips parted into the perfect bow shape, and the hand that tried to comb back the heavy sweep of his hair from his forehead shook slightly. He directed his eyes to her feet, giving up on his hair, his hand falling to his lap as his hair flopped right back into place, a few strands falling over one of his eyes.

"Something happened, didn't it?" His narrowed eyes flicked back up, his fingers twitching before he flexed them out, rubbing them against the tops of his thighs. "There's no way you would consider this unless something bad happened. Or several bad things. What the fuck did they do to you?"

Isobel somehow managed to keep the cool mask over her features. "What makes you so sure they did something?"

He stilled. "Am I wrong?"

"Yes. No." She folded her arms tightly, tapping one foot in agitation. "Nothing happened. You don't *have* to help me."

"I want to help you." He rolled his lips between his teeth as he considered her.

"But?" she prompted.

"I need to win," he said plainly. "There's no other option."

"You don't seem like the type?"

"The winning type?" He grinned at that.

She didn't fall for it. "The type who cares whether you win or lose."

"That's because you've never seen me lose. I'm a very, very, *very* bad loser."

She still didn't quite believe him, but she accepted his answer with a shrug. "Well, I'm not trying to win, I'm just trying to get out of Dorm O. And this could benefit you, too, if you really want to win."

"Hm?" he asked softly. "How?"

"Well ... you see ... something is going to air about me next Friday—"

"They *did* do something," he growled, his eyes flashing with the briefest shadow of darkness—if she hadn't been paying attention, she would have missed it.

"I was sleepwalking," she said, keeping her tone calm. Unwavering. Just like the voice she had heard in her head. The voice that sounded like her mother. "Naked," she added. "Ah ... in the lake. But anyway," she quickly barrelled on, fidgeting with her fingers again as that darkness flashed in his eyes and a low rumbling sound emanated from his chest. "My friend came up with an idea to help me. She said I should start an online dare competition with you, and we can pretend that the whole … being-naked-in-the-lake thing was a dare. But for that to happen, we need to start publicly posting and acting out dares, and they can't be timid either."

"Your friend is smart." His voice was rough, his eyes slitted, not even the slightest curve at the edges of his mouth to hint at his usual smile. "Not only does it cover up whatever happened to you, it also earns you the popularity points you need."

"Especially if you're involved," she added quietly, staring down at his shoes. "If you'll help."

"Well then." He clapped his hands together, leaning forward. "First dare." He whipped out his phone and reached over to hers, turning off the song. He held up his device, like he was recording, his stormy eyes watching her over the top of his screen. "Isobel Carter. Truth or dare?"

What?

"Ah …" She almost choked on her own tongue … but this was very *Theodore*. Jumping into things head first. "Dare?" she asked.

"Call the last person you texted and tell them you had a filthy dream about them," he ordered.

Isobel made a face, snatching up her phone and white-knuckling it. "The last person I texted was you."

He chuckled. "Fine. The person before me."

She unlocked her phone and looked at the second person in her inbox. Spade. She winced but pressed the call button. Theodore jumped up, filming her screen as he hit the speaker button for her.

He didn't hesitate over the name that flashed up on her call screen, but she saw the slight twitch of his eyebrow.

"Carter," Spade answered on the third ring, sounding a little out of breath. He was probably training in one of the rooms down the hall with Reed. So now she could be doubly embarrassed, knowing that Reed might overhear.

"Carter?" he repeated when she didn't say anything.

Theodore's smile was back, like he enjoyed watching her squirm ... or maybe like he thought she was about to back out. Maybe this was his way of subtly refusing to help her—by making it clear that she wasn't cut out for this type of game. Or for *the* game.

"I had a dream about you last night," she quickly rushed out, her words almost a whisper.

There was silence on the other end for a moment before he said, "Okay."

Isobel bit back a groan. "A dirty one," she specified and then quickly tried to hang up, but Theodore grabbed her finger, tugging her hand away from her phone.

"You don't sound terrified," Spade answered, utterly unbothered. "So nobody is threatening you to make this call by force ... and yet there's no other explanation."

"Hey." She stepped away from Theodore and his phone, slightly insulted by how fast Spade had accurately assessed, and then dismissed, the situation. Theodore was biting back a laugh, his eyes dancing with light, as if he had known exactly how this call would go. "You should take this seriously. I really ... ah ... mean it."

Spade sighed, and she could almost picture him pinching the bridge of his slender nose. "You've interrupted my practice now. What room are you training in? It would be more efficient if we discussed this in person."

"I'm not training!" she squeaked out, forgetting all about Theodore's recording as she rushed over to her bag and began stuffing all her things inside. "And this is ... a ... matter of the heart. Efficiency shouldn't come into it."

"Of course you are," Spade answered. "It's seven o'clock on Friday morning. You're always training at this time."

Isobel paused, her bag sagging on her arm until it caught against her wrist. "I'm sick today. I'm in the medical centre actually. Super high on drugs. Don't even remember why I called you. Bye!" She hung up, turning to fix Theodore with a stare as he ended his video and slid his phone away.

"Spade knows your routine?" he asked.

He was still smiling, but it was ... off.

"It's news to me," she grumbled. "I need to leave before he finds me. Christ, that was fucking embarrassing."

"It must have been." He chuckled, stealing her bag from her and looping it over his shoulder. "You're swearing and you're sober. Come with me."

He grabbed her hand, tugging her down the hallway.

"Carter!"

Shit. Spade. She knew that voice. It was cold and smooth. Deep and clear. It reminded her of the chilling chime of thick metal striking against even thicker metal.

"Theo!" he called again. A little sharper.

"Can't hear you!" Theodore shot over his shoulder, pushing through the doors to the practice rooms and breaking into a jog.

Isobel felt a laugh exploding out of her as he pulled

her along, her shorter legs struggling to keep up with him. He didn't slow down, though. Just like how he had jumped straight into things earlier, he wasn't going to coddle her. He wasn't that type either. He was going to push her, pull her, force her to keep going, force her to leave her doubts behind as he made the world rush right by her ears.

"Where are we going?" she gasped out, her lungs beginning to struggle as they raced past students.

"Music department." He didn't slow down until they were at the double glass doors and he was tugging her through, stealing her away into one of the studio rooms that she had only ever seen on the Ironside show.

"What are we doing here?" She leaned against the desk full of instruments, one hand cradling the stitch in her side.

"We're making this endeavour mutually beneficial." He directed her to a chair, pushing her into it, and then he dropped both of their bags, setting up a laptop in front of her. "What was that song again?"

"What song?" She peered past his shoulder, looking into the recording room on the other side of the thick glass.

"The song you were dancing to like someone had just broken your little heart into a thousand pieces."

"'Wicked Game.'"

He did a search on his computer, printing out lyrics and sheet music before plopping a set of headphones over her head. He tapped his ear, pointed to the glass, and then disappeared through the connecting door with his printouts. Her heart started to race, her palms turning clammy.

She didn't know why she was so nervous, but it only got worse when he positioned the microphone over the piano, sat down, and pulled it toward his mouth.

"You were practising that for a reason, right?"

His voice filled her headphones, and she jumped several inches in the chair. The sound of a husky chuckle filled her ears.

"Y-yes," she answered. "Is this a collaboration? I promised Eve she would be my first."

"Pretty sure Moses was your first. Better let her down gently."

"Very funny," she grumbled as he began to play around with a few chords on the piano, warming up as his eyes scanned the lyrics.

"Wow." She leaned over the desk, the sweet sound seeming to surround her. "You're really good at that."

"Not as good as Elijah." His voice was so amplified.

She could hear his every breath and the soft curse when he made a mistake.

"How?" she asked. "You've only been here two years. Most settlement kids ..." She trailed off, wondering if what she had been about to say was insensitive.

"Kalen wanted to teach us all." The lines along his brow smoothed out. He was getting the hang of it, refining the song until it sounded flawless and silky. "But only Eli and I picked it up."

She bit down on her lip, fascinated at the unguarded way he was speaking, his nickname for Reed slipping out as he tried to concentrate.

"Okay." He sat back, flexing his fingers and rearranging his papers. "You're going to be late to your first class, but it'll be worth it." He cut his eyes to the glass. "You in, Illy?"

"Yeah—" Her voice cracked. "Yes. I mean ... I think."

"Click record," he said, only giving her about ten seconds to find it on his laptop screen before he started playing, and she started falling.

She fell into the softness of his voice. It was clear and surprisingly steady. Unfaltering and easy, just like his smile. There was so much control in every nuance, in the slight grittiness he let slip through, in the high, angelic notes that rang so clearly, and in the vibration of his deeper tones. She immediately got goose bumps. She couldn't stop looking at his mouth, listening to the breaths he stole between words. She had never thought that breath could sound sexy before, but now she was convinced the sound would haunt her. His hair was falling forward, hiding his eyes from her as he leaned into the microphone. She thought she saw his lips brushing it, and wondered what they would feel like against hers.

Would they feel like his brother's? Firm and angry? Stiff with shock, but briefly insistent, tinged with a fury she could taste?

Or would Theodore's kiss be sad and deep, like his perfect voice? He sang the way he described her dancing. Like he was slowly ripping his heart out of his chest to lay it on the studio floor. Like he was mourning it as he watched people walk all over it like they didn't notice it was there. He was never far from the wide-eyed boy she had found crying in the library, but in moments like those, her heart hurt for him all over again.

She rubbed her hands over her arms, drinking him in as he shared his incredible talent with her. It wasn't until that moment that she knew, without a doubt, that he would win the game.

He was the Icon of their age.

Like he said, it was the only option.

When he finished, he got up without any fanfare, taking his papers with him as he pushed back into the studio, where he found her frozen with tears in her eyes.

"Aw, Illy." He opened his arms and she rushed into them without a second thought. She wasn't sure exactly where she was aiming, but he ducked at the last second, wrapping his strong arms around her back as he lifted her, leaving her to hang onto his neck.

She pressed her face into his collarbone, using his shirt to catch her tears, because she was determined that the cameras wouldn't watch a single one of them falling.

And then she remembered the cameras.

HOLY SHIT.

Theodore thought she would laugh at him.

He never expected the Illy-stone to run at him, and he reacted before he could think better of it. It was the shock that did it. It was the shock that made him pick her up, and it was the shock that had his heart suddenly racing like he was about to dive off a cliff. She was warm for a girl so cold. And she was crying into his shirt, her nails digging into his shoulders.

Her candied cherry scent gave her away. The tartness of her shattering control wrapped in something sticky and sweet. *Pleasure.* She liked listening to him, and that shouldn't have made his blood feel so hot. He gently set her down, forcing his hands away from the hypnotising curve of her spine as his eyes dragged down to the oversized, too-thin shirt she had been dancing in. Her scent was so strong it masked the hint of sweat against her skin.

"Are you okay?" he asked her, thankful his voice sounded calm.

The last thing he needed was for things to get complicated with the little Sigma. He was already making sacrifices to keep her as a friend, and he was running out of reasons to justify that to the others. She was making other friends now. He wasn't the only one. And he got the feeling he was causing her more trouble than good.

But he couldn't stop.

Maybe at first it was a simple matter of familiarity. He had been closest with his Sigma mother growing up, and Isobel was just as sweet, but with an edge that drew him in, because she wasn't *all* sweet like his mother had been. She was different. She had teeth.

She bowed, just like the Sigmas were taught to—but she refused to break.

She had just used him—an *Alpha,* a *predator*—to hide her tears from the cameras, to conceal her momentary weakness.

She wasn't looking at him when she answered. "Yeah. Sorry, it's been a hard ... day. I'm kind of exhausted." She straightened her shoulders, spinning around while her hand still tightly clutched the back of the chair she had been sitting on. "I should head to class. I'm late." She didn't make a move.

"I'll finish up with the song over lunch and send it to you," he told her.

"Thanks, Theo. This was ... really special. I'll make sure you aren't wasting it on my dance." She still didn't move.

"You couldn't." *It's a gift.* "I'll benefit from the exposure either way, so don't worry about me."

Her nails were digging into the chair, her eyes fixed to the desk.

"What is it? Another favour?" he teased.

Her teeth sank into her lush lower lip, biting back a small smile. Those perfect little teeth were connected straight to his gut, and he watched her nibble the plump flesh with a little too much focus.

"No." She finally looked up, gracing him with the

full force of those large, gold-specked, doe eyes. "It's just that ... it's Friday. They're going to air the Valentine's Day party."

Don't ask. You don't want to know. "Are you worried about Moses?" He wanted to hit himself. "Don't be," he continued quickly. "It was part of a game the Alphas play every year."

"He didn't want to play."

"He never does anything he doesn't want to do."

"He hates me."

"He might."

She gave him an exasperated look. "He ..." She flicked her eyes to the camera in the corner of the room. "I'm late to class."

"So I've been told." He wanted to reach out and shake her, to cause all those hesitant secrets to clatter out of her mouth, but instead, he ruffled her hair.

"Let me know when you want to film that dance. I'll be there. There's a practice room with a piano in it."

"Okay." Her eyes went wider, like she hadn't expected that, and he tried not to feel a spark of satisfaction at having managed to surprise her. He had no business being pleased by stupid little things. He had nine close friends back in Dorm A, and he didn't feel a warm spark whenever he managed to surprise one of them.

It was bad.

It was explosive.

Or, at least that was how the Ironside commentators described it. An *explosive* episode. The commentators speculated on how Isobel had managed to nab the infamously "untouchable" Kilian as a friend, even going so far as to sit on his lap, which Ed Jones joked had just made her a target for all the gay men on campus as well as everyone else. Now *everyone* had a reason to hate her—including all the soon-to-graduate students she was stealing screen time off.

Coverage of the Valentine's Day party took up most of the episode, which they were calling a "Valentine's special." It dove into the politics of the current fifth-year students as they had their own drama at the party that Isobel hadn't even noticed. And, saving the best for last, it showed her kiss with Moses.

In painstaking, excruciating detail.

It slowed down, zoomed in, and focused on the moment their lips locked. She saw the freckle on the outside of her lip in clearer detail than she had ever seen it in a mirror—and she noticed details about Moses that she hadn't in the moment, too. There was a small scar cutting into his upper lip, in the shape of a hook. Another scar marked his chin, thin and white. His eyelashes were thick and dark, hiding his emotions from the cameras as he hooded his eyes. His hair, a little wilder, a little curlier than his twin's, brushed her cheek as he tilted his head.

They had been whispering to each other before the kiss, so quietly that the cameras weren't able to pick up the audio, but that somehow made it even more dramatic, as the production team layered the moment with heart-thumping music, like it was some kind of life-changing moment. It was effective, because her heart was racing by the time she finished watching.

As soon as the episode was over, her phone started blowing up. She knew she shouldn't look at it, but she opened her emails anyway, clicking on the bold notification from her father.

It's working. Keep playing the Alpha angle.

Her stomach turned and she quickly tossed the phone away. She wanted to curl up and go to sleep, but she was in Eve's room, sitting on the other girl's bed—and Eve was chattering a mile a minute about everything they had just watched.

"This is a good thing, Iz." She finally seemed to notice the pallor that had fallen over Isobel's face. "I know it's scary to think about what they might do to you next, but all this attention is the only way to get you out of here."

"I know." Isobel clutched at her turning stomach. "I think I need to go lay down though."

"Not in your room," Eve said sternly, patting the other side of her bed. "You're in here until we can be sure that no mobs will drag you out of your bed again."

Isobel groaned, flopping onto her back. "I can't do that to you."

Eve visibly bristled and then put on her best impression of Bellamy's posh accent. "Did you just argue with your better, Sigma?"

Isobel snorted, throwing a pillow at her. "Shut up. You're the worst."

"I have snacks." Eve tossed the pillow back, rolling over to her stomach and reaching beneath her bed.

"You keep snacks under your bed?" Isobel asked.

"Yeah?" Eve dragged a tote onto the bed, upending it to reveal several containers. "Where else would I put them?"

"You don't share your room. And all the food here is free. Why are you hiding an entire stash of it?" Isobel knelt over the pile, watching in amusement as Eve opened up all the containers, arranging them in the middle of the bed before she set her laptop up again, this time switching to a movie that had nothing to do with Ironside.

Thankfully, it wasn't one of her father's movies.

"I don't own anything in here, except the clothes, and most of those were donated to me." Eve rummaged through her snacks, picking out some candy and a few caramel chocolates. "That laptop?" She nudged it with her foot. "They assigned it to me on my first day here. It's second nature to hide and hoard in the settlements. I'm not the only person who does it—but you know who doesn't do it? The Alphas. I guarantee. It doesn't matter which settlement they came from, they were the top of the food chain there, and they're the top of the food chain here. Whenever they win the game, they're the top of the damn food chain out there in the human world too." She waved her hand toward the window before stuffing one of the chocolates into her mouth.

"Eve." Isobel reached for the other girl's free hand, squeezing it gently. "Even though you have so little, you always share it with me. You're a really good person."

"I know." Eve flipped her short hair back, giving Isobel a confident smile. "You're pretty lucky to have a friend like me."

Isobel rolled her eyes. "And you ruined it."

The pillow fight started all over again, and Isobel ended up shoved off the bed, laughing up at the ceiling.

"Um, Iz?" Eve's head popped over the edge, her eyes wide, her hair tousled. "Why is *Sato* texting you?"

Isobel scrambled up, accepting the phone Eve handed to her and quickly opening the message.

Sato: I'm collecting.

"I owe him a favour," Isobel squeaked.

"You *what*?" Eve yelped, almost falling off the bed. "Are you *insane*? You do *not* want to owe that boy a favour. Isobel! What's wrong with you!"

Isobel shoved her phone into her pocket without replying, rolling over to mush her face against the soft rug. "Just leave me alone to die," she whined.

14
DO IT GENTLY

THEODORE: WHAT DO YOU WANT ME TO WEAR?

Theodore: Come over and choose.

She stood outside Dorm A on Sunday morning, staring at the perpetually-closed door, wondering if she should knock or not. If Theodore had been the only one to text her that morning as she was trying to force breakfast into her unsettled stomach, she might have texted back that he could wear whatever he wanted.

But he wasn't.

Sato: Come.

She hadn't replied to Sato's first message two days ago, but she had been walking around like there was a ticking time bomb in her pocket ever since receiving it, and when she read the second message that morning, she knew her time was up.

So she had come.

As she stood there deliberating, the door opened. She skittered backwards, staring up into Kilian's soft, pale eyes.

"Isobel." He sounded surprised, but then his pillowy lips shifted into a beautiful smile. "I heard about your collab today. Mind if I watch?"

Struck too dumb to speak, she quickly shook her head.

"Good." His smile slipped a little, his hand warm as it traced down her arm. "Are you all done up?"

She jumped a little, because she somehow hadn't noticed him moving closer. It was like he hypnotised her.

"Yes." She glanced down at her tights and oversized T-shirt. "Should I have picked something else?"

"How do I say this?" His smile slipped even further, his head tilting as those beautiful, light-coloured eyes ran over her. "You don't look surprising. This is your first upload. Your first real bid for attention. You want to surprise people."

"It's all I've got." She shrugged.

"Luckily, you're a pretty good blank canvas." His

touch slid down to her hand, his fingers winding slowly through hers, and then he dragged her through the door without any warning.

She stumbled after him, her eyes wide as they connected with Moses, who was sitting in his usual armchair, a game controller in his hand. Reed and Spade were also there, both of them in swim trunks, standing at the glass wall with wet hair like they had been talking while looking at the lake. The trunks were short enough to convince her they were actually workout shorts, showing off beautifully toned thighs and even more streamlined abdominal muscles. Their skin was smooth, rippling tightly over the contours and ridges of their wide chests and narrow waists, lit by a subtle sheen that could have been lake water or sunscreen but on *their* skin it looked like tanning oil for a billboard advertisement.

"H-hi," she squeaked, eyes wide.

They just stared back. Silent. Thankfully, she found herself stolen off into Kilian's room. He deposited her on the edge of his bed and stood over her, his arms folded. "What's the song?"

Isobel dug into the tote she had brought, pulling out her phone and headphones. She passed him the earbuds, starting Theodore's version of the song, a little embarrassed that her phone was already open to it since she had been listening to it constantly. Kilian put in one of the earbuds, leaning over her to stick the other one in her ear. He listened to Theodore's rendition with a slightly arched brow, but his expression didn't change until he caught her mouthing the words, and then he seemed to go still.

She also went still, peeking up at him.

He was looking at her mouth, both elegant brows drawn low over his eyes. He must have really liked the song, because his pupils had expanded, and she suddenly thought that his eyes were somewhat serpentine, with the yellowish hue that seeped into the green of his irises. His eyes weren't wide and circular like a snake's, but they were hooded, tagged at the corners in a beautiful shape that made him look all-knowing and possibly even sly.

"You have snake eyes," she said without thinking, reaching up to touch the outside of his cheek.

He caught her hand, dragging it down over his face and neck until it rested over his chest, where his heartbeat pounded.

"He's amazing, isn't he?" she asked, smiling a little at Kilian's reaction to his friend's voice.

"I always thought so." His voice was a little deeper. He dropped her hand, pulled out the earbud, and walked into his closet. "I know what kind of look you need. What panties are you wearing?"

"Uh." She stuffed her things back into the tote. "Normal boring ones?"

"Colour?" He walked out of the closet with a shirt on a hanger. "Bra?"

"Black. And a black sports bra."

"Good enough." He handed her the hanger. "Take that shit off and put this on over your underwear."

"Right here?" she joked, hoping to ease the strangely intense look in his eyes.

His expression softened instantly, his lips quirking up. "Not this time. Save it for the studio. Now get your cute butt into the bathroom so I can do your hair. Do you have any makeup in your bag?"

"No." She hopped off his bed and walked into his en suite. "I did it before I left."

"Okay." He suddenly spun her around, palming her hips and hoisting her onto the bench, her back pressed against the mirror. "I can work with this, too. What did you do?" He squinted at her face. "It's hard to tell with you."

She sucked in a deep breath, her hands shaking so much she decided to sit on them, focussing on the cold marble beneath her instead of the steadily increasing blush that fanned over her skin. Kilian was very *hands-*

on, and she didn't exactly hate it, but that only made it even more nerve-wracking.

"Lip stain, mascara, some foundation." She avoided looking at him until he pinched her chin, turning her eyes back to his.

He reached to the left, turning on his tap and wetting some tissue before he was back in her face, so close she could feel his breath and smell the calming woodsy scent that clung to him.

"Close your eyes," he muttered, his touch so soft, so gentle as he ran his thumb over one of her closed lids and then followed it with the wet tissue. He carefully smudged her mascara and then had her open her eyes as he fixed it exactly the way he wanted it.

She didn't think anyone had spent so much time touching her face, and her chest grew tighter the longer he worked. His fingers were so smooth, so sure, everything he did full of ease and confidence. It made her feel like whatever he was doing, it would work. Because it was Kilian.

He threw out the tissue and returned, pushing her legs apart with a distracted grunt as he focussed on her mouth. She stopped breathing entirely, and it was like he didn't even notice. He set his thumb against her lower lip, pressing in against the soft swell as he dragged his finger out to the edge of her mouth. She wasn't wearing much, only a thin coat of lip stain that was more or less the same tint as her natural lips. He loomed even closer as he reached the edge of her mouth, one hand holding her chin up, and suddenly his heat was everywhere and his breath was against her lips.

Her vision blurred a little, the bergamot scent of his silver hair filling her chest as her breaths turned choppy, and then he was stepping back, the gold of his Alpha ring all she could see, like it had grown larger.

"Yes," he murmured huskily. "That's perfect." He stepped back into her space, loosening her ponytail and finger-combing her hair. "This is what you should look like while you're singing about heartbreak. You should look like you just rolled out of their bed— whoever they are. You should look like you either cried yourself to sleep or ..." He stopped, his fingers trailing out of her strands. "Or you've been *kissing* all night." He snorted, walking backwards with a weird laugh. "Sometimes I forget how young we are."

"Um." She hopped off the bench. "You forget how young you are?"

"That's what I said." His tone wasn't sarcastic. It was more surprised. Either at his own words, or that he had spoken them out loud. He folded the shirt into her tote, which he gently slipped over her shoulder.

"Now go tell Theo to wear something white. And don't leave without me."

She quietly shut the door as she exited the room and looked both ways down the hallway before sneaking toward Sato's room. She knocked as quietly as she could manage, but there was no answer. With a small groan, she checked the hallway again and then tiptoed upstairs, deciding to see if he was on the rooftop. It seemed like something he would do—summon her and then perch somewhere he might have a good view of her approach.

Thankfully, she didn't run into Ashford, Niko or the two professors as she searched the rooftop, but there was also no sign of Sato.

"Not as innocent as you seem, hm?"

The voice shocked her still, and then she turned toward the corner of the balcony where a large daybed with an arched overhang faced away from her. She crept around it. "What do you mean?"

Sato was stretched out long, one leg bent, one arm folded behind his head, his shirt slipped up a few inches to show a brief peek of his hard stomach. His skin was a smooth topaz, a type of golden-brown that was burnt maple in some lights, and lighter honey in others. Right now, it was darker, hidden away by the shade of the overhang.

"You're saturated," he said, his dark eyes landing on hers.

She swallowed, her heart stopping. "What?"

"In Kilian's scent." He pulled up, slinging his arm over his bent knee, his nostrils flaring.

"How does Kilian count?" She folded her arms tightly, her thighs pressing together. She hadn't realised before, but she was ... well ... *damp*.

Not quite saturated.

It was hard to tell, but something weird was definitely going on. It was *wrong* to let Kilian affect her that way, even if he did look like an actual angel. Even if he was the most beautiful boy she had ever seen.

"How doesn't he count?" Sato's lips quirked, his eyes flicking to her thighs, like he had caught the shift in her posture, which was *really* not cool. "You're in an Alpha den right now, little Sigma. They might call it a dorm, but you can't put so many Alphas in one place without it becoming a den. And in a den, we're very sensitive about smells. Kilian's sexuality doesn't even come into it. You don't saturate someone unless you're claiming them."

"Right." She rolled her eyes, folding her arms tighter. "He was just helping with my makeup and hair for a dance I'm about to record."

"I heard," Sato drawled, his focus touching on her

face as she waved a hand at her smudged makeup. "There's a lot of dancing going on around here. Dancing around secrets, dancing around issues, and dancing at the end of your silky little strings."

"And dancing around the reason I'm here," she pointed out blandly. "What's your favour?"

"Oh, you're so unbothered, aren't you?" He laughed, knee-walking to the edge of the daybed. Even on his knees, he towered over her. His thumb brushed against the edge of her mouth, probably smudging her lip stain even more. Some of the bravado slipped out of her, and she knew he could feel the way she trembled as his chest pressed against hers. "I need you to steal something for me."

"What is it? From who?" As she spoke, her lips brushed his thumb since he hadn't pulled it away entirely.

He brushed the side of her mouth again, his chest swelling as he took a deep breath.

"I need you to steal Renee Wallis' phone and bring it to me." He collapsed back to the daybed, resuming his earlier position, stretched out, lazy, unbothered. "It's Cian's birthday in a few weeks. He'll host a party the weekend before, and she'll be there. You can do it then."

"That's impossible," she spluttered, clutching the handle of her bag with white fingers.

"It's compulsory," he told her calmly. "You'll take it without her noticing, bring it to me, and then return it to her without her noticing."

"How the hell am I supposed to do that? She hates me."

He shrugged, examining his fingernails. "Suggest a threesome with Theo."

"She *hates* me."

"It's the only way she'll get any action from him, though."

"Ugh." She shook her head, pinching her nose. "We're just friends. I'll figure something out."

"Good." His eyes drifted lazily up to hers again. "Break a leg today."

She gripped her bag so hard her nails were cutting into her palm. "Why does it sound like you mean that?"

He only bared his teeth, his hard lips peeling back to flash teeth that likely weren't any sharper than anyone else's teeth, but they still made his smile look deadly. She sucked in a breath and hurried away from the daybed, escaping down to the lower level and pushing into Theodore's room after quickly knocking.

He was inside his closet, calling out to her. "I don't really have much ... but I can do casual or formal?"

"How'd you know it was me?" She perched on the edge of his bed, crossing her legs and resting her chin on her palm.

He emerged from the closet, his smile easy and bright, melting all the way into her. "I smelled you. What did Oscar want with you?"

"How did you—"

"Oleander." Theodore rolled his eyes. "He's on you."

"I ran into him."

"Hm. I'm happy to see you." He shocked her by suddenly scooping her up, pulling her into a bone-crushing hug, his hands pulling at her waist. "I love your makeup look. Very angsty."

"Thanks." She giggled. "Kilian helped."

He squeezed her, setting her back down on his bed, and then he began to trace the messy strands of her hair. He touched her chin, lightly thumbed the edge of her mouth, and eventually set his hands on her shoulder. "Better," he muttered, even though he hadn't changed a thing. "Now ... help me."

"Okay." She jumped up and wandered into his sparse closet. He had a loose, thin white button-up like the one Kilian had given to her, so she handed him that and then chewed on her lip, cutting her eyes back to him.

He was wearing black pants that were possibly a little too small for him, because they hugged him in places she shouldn't be focussing on, but she loved that he had tried to find something formal for her.

"Those are great," she said, pointing to the pants.

"Great." He tugged off his shirt right then and there, and even though it wasn't the first time she had seen him shirtless, she still sucked in a small breath, averting her eyes from his muscles as he pulled on the shirt, half-buttoning it in a haphazard way. "Let's go. Is your friend meeting us there?"

"Yeah, she was just grabbing the recording equipment. She's really excited."

"Are you excited?"

"I'm petrified."

He laughed, tucking her under his arm. "You'll do great." He paused on the way past the lounge room. "Who's coming?"

Kilian threw down his controller, jumping up to join them, but he wasn't the only one.

Reed stood, stretching his long limbs before pulling out his phone. "I'll text Niko and Cian to meet us there."

Spade got up without a word, punching Moses'

shoulder on his way past. "Go upstairs and get Oscar. Meet us there." He gave Isobel a short, assessing look that told her he had seen Theodore's upload of her dare. She got the distinct impression that he didn't like that he had been dragged into it, but he was keeping his opinions to himself for the time being.

She waited for Moses to say something snarky, but he surprised her by standing and walking off toward the hallway without so much as blinking.

"This is a pretty big deal," Kilian whispered to her, stopping on her other side and bending close to her face. "It's basically Theo's debut."

She nodded tightly, trying not to panic as they left Dorm A in a silent pack. If it had just been Theodore, she might have felt like she was on her way to do something scary with the support of a good friend.

Instead, it felt like a pack of Alphas were marching her off—possibly all the way to the academy gates— and she wasn't the only person thrown off by them. When they reached the training room, Eve almost dropped the recording equipment she was setting up.

"Hi," she squeaked. "Um ... everyone."

"Hi," Theodore responded with a warm smile, immediately putting her at ease. "Thanks for helping us do this—Indie, right?"

"Yes. Eve Indie." She was staring at him with eyes as wide as saucers.

"It was her idea," Isobel reminded him out of the side of her mouth.

He only smirked at her, moving over to the piano and sitting down.

"Am I good here?" he asked Eve, motioning to the camera. "I can move the piano."

"No." Eve was still choking on her tongue. "You're perfect, obviously. I mean you'd look great wherever, so. Wow." Her gaze shot over to Kilian. "I mean you're all perfect."

Isobel decided to shake off Eve's weirdness. The poor girl was clearly in shock.

She dropped her tote on the bench as the other Alphas all walked out of the room, Spade muttering something about chairs.

She extracted the shirt Kilian had given her and laid it on the bench, quickly pulling off her shirt and tights.

"Jesus, Illy," Theodore growled. "Warning next time."

"Sorry," she rushed out, wiggling into the shirt. She was so desperate to get changed before the others came back that she didn't even look at him as she buttoned the shirt all the way from the hem to the neck. It fell down to her thighs and was soft and billowy as silk—the perfect thing to dance in.

Kilian came in first, his chair hitting the ground with a thump as he saw her. A laugh burst out of him, and he crooked a finger at her. "No no no, young lady. Come here."

She dragged her feet all the way over to him, frowning as he unbuttoned the shirt enough that it was hanging open at the top and the bottom. "You're not dancing for a job interview," he teased.

She grunted a sound in reply, since she couldn't really argue with him, and then walked over to the ballet bar to begin her stretches as Theodore played through the song on the piano, warming up.

She heard the door open a few times, but she decided to ignore it, focussing on her stretches and the slow melody sinking into the back of her mind.

"Ready?" Eve asked nervously, sliding up to Isobel's side. "I'm so nervous I could drop the camera."

"Why—" Isobel paused, her eyes on the chairs that had been set up along the back of the room.

Every Alpha within the walls of Ironside Academy had been corralled into the back of the dance studio. Including Professor Easton and Professor West—who ironically looked like night and day. Mikel Easton was slighter than the giant standing next to him, but he looked rougher, meaner, those scars mottling his face. His sharp features, strong nose, and clean, arched brows might have made him handsome, but all of it was tagged by jagged white lines. People online were calling him ugly, saying that even his hair looked like dark blood, though Isobel didn't agree. It was mostly a rich dark brown, but there were a few russet tinges. She couldn't discern the black splotches in his blue eyes from so far away, but his sharp gaze was unmistakable. He was looking at her like she was about to fuck this up for Theodore on a significant scale, but there wasn't a thing he could do to stop it. Like he was watching a car crash in slow motion.

Kalen West, on the other hand, was huge. His face was broad and chiselled, his dark mahogany hair cropped short, containing the hint of a curl against his collar. He had yellow-amber eyes, like gems, like the eyes of a tiger. The colour merged with his golden Alpha ring, making his eyes appear to glow from where he stood across the room. He had his hands tucked into his pockets, and from the bulges straining against the material, she assumed he was curling them into fists.

The two professors stood behind the other seven Alphas, who were seated in a neat row, languishing in shadow. Ashford, Sato, and Moses were all slouched, legs spread, arms crossed, expressions guarded. It was hard to look at them, so she quickly moved on, taking in Niko, whose head was cocked to the side, one hand tucking the wavy strands of his hair behind his ears. He had bleached it at the start of the year and it was now several shades lighter than the light honey tint of his skin. His well-shaped brows jumped up, like he was challenging her about something, but the smile on his lips was easy and light. It was a mask. She had seen it on the show a thousand times. Nobody ever got past the social mask Niko Hart put on. She blinked, casting her eyes over Kilian, whose lips lifted into a soft smile, and then Spade and Reed, who sat there like robots, ready to analyse her every move.

Which ... made sense, actually.

If they thought she was actually trying to *win* the game, then they would be her competition, out of the Alphas.

She shrugged off the odd sensation of so many eyes on her and so many emotions fluttering up against her chest, turning to Eve.

Those Alphas *really* liked to stick together, every single one of them turning up to support Theodore. It was beyond strange.

"Ready," she muttered, moving to the centre of the room.

Eve switched on a second floodlight, directing it to slant over Isobel—the other lighting up Theodore—and Isobel gave her a nod. The Alphas had positioned themselves at the back of the room instead of the front, which meant they would all be in most of the shots, but they were cloaked by darkness. If they were trying to intimidate her, it wasn't working, because her brain had already switched from Sigma to choreographer, and she thought they added a brilliant depth of mystery and malice to the atmosphere. She lowered herself to the ground and then curled onto her side, the spotlight burning into her cheek as she closed her eyes.

"On three," Eve called out. "One, two ..."

Theodore started to play, and she started to stir, each note of the piano pulling at a part of her body, though she didn't become fully animated until his voice sounded, low and haunting, creeping through the shadows of the room to force her eyes open.

"I never dreamed that I'd meet somebody like you."

She rolled and arched and stretched, her body like a bow fighting against the pull of his voice, fighting against the power that wrapped all around her until she was forced to her feet, until she was dancing like a broken ballerina who only wanted to soar.

"No, I don't want to fall in love."

She acted like she was tugged around the room, spinning and spinning and extending painfully, reaching for freedom.

"No, I don't want to fall in love with you."

Her face was torn, her hands pulling desperately at the billowy shirt, like she might pull it clean from her body, and then she was tumbling to the ground again, focussing on keeping her lines clean and sharp, her extensions taut and beautiful.

"What a wicked thing to do, to make me dream of you."

She was being consumed, ripped apart right there on the floor while she twisted her body into positions that hurt like hell but appeared effortless—she had made sure of that, practising until the pain became numb, until the expression that stared back at her in the mirror was exactly what she wanted to portray, until the physicality of her movements became secondary to the emotion of her choreography. She made her movements smaller again, returning to that fight against the pull of the haunting melody, stretching and releasing, sharply reaching and rapidly withdrawing, her arms and legs stiff but pliant, pulled up and away by invisible forces.

"It's strange what desire will make foolish people do."

She was tugged up to her feet again, one little bit

at a time, each movement driven by a vibration from Theodore's perfect voice, and then finally, she was released.

"And I don't want to fall in love."

She was flying.

"No, I don't want to fall in love."

She moved fast, leaping and soaring and spinning and spinning, like before but different. Because she was finally free, but freedom changed nothing.

"With you."

The pain was still there.

"With you."

She collapsed.

She stayed prone as the final notes died off, and silence filled the hall, thick and weighted by judgment, until Eve let out a loud *whoop* and Theodore was tugging her up, pulling her into another crushing hug. He was getting good at those. Less stiff, his hands warmer, holding her so close that she could feel the breath that filled his chest.

"You were *so* good." His words brushed her temple, his heart pounding against hers. "You're the one who should win this game."

"How could you even see?" she panted out, hitting his back.

"I watched every second—*no*." The last word was a

growl, and she realised there was another hand against her back.

Kilian's familiar smell wrapped around her. "Theo," he said calmly.

Theodore set her down, and Kilian quickly pulled her away, his mouth set into a firm lime. Theodore winked at her, strolling off to the other Alphas like the weird moment hadn't happened at all.

"Iz!" Eve threw herself at Isobel, knocking her out of Kilian's hold. "Oh my *god*, that was brilliant. I still have goose bumps, look!" She shoved her arm into Isobel's face, making Isobel chuckle.

"I'm glad I didn't mess up," she admitted.

"Oh, you messed up alright," Kilian tittered. "The last video of you dancing wasn't anything like this. Now people are going to know what it looks like when you really try, and it is *not* good news for you. Unless you like death threats and extreme hazing."

"You have no idea," Isobel murmured, earning her a sharp look from Kilian. "Anyway, thanks for all the help." She grinned at him and wound her arm through Eve's, just in case any other Alphas tried to grab her. "Let's go," she whispered low to her friend.

Kilian bit back an amused smile. "Run, little Sigma."

"Don't think I won't," Isobel shot back, flicking her

tangled hair over her shoulder before quickly grabbing her tights out of her tote and pulling them on.

"Are we actually making a run for it?" Eve asked, casting a nervous glance to the other side of the studio. "What about Kane? Shouldn't we thank—"

"I'll thank Theo later." Isobel grabbed her hand and dragged her out of the room. "Let's get that video edited before something happens to it."

"Like what?" Eve asked, hurrying to keep up with her.

"I don't know!" Isobel released her, throwing up her arms. "You never know *what* those Alphas are going to do next! Let's just get it uploaded!"

Eve skipped ahead, suddenly reanimated now that they were out of the oppressive air of the studio. "Deal! Race you back to my room! There's no way they'll set foot in Dorm O."

"You'd be surprised," Isobel sighed out beneath her breath before running after Eve.

Kilian had to admit, things were getting complicated. As soon as the Sigma and her Omega friend escaped the hall, the friendly look dropped right off his face, replaced by one of concern as he turned to face the rest of the room. Gabriel, Moses, and Oscar were still in their seats, still in the exact same position. Arms crossed, legs spread, lips frowning. Moody bastards. Cian was up with Niko, both of them talking in low voices and casting blank looks toward the door Isobel had disappeared out of.

"Save it," Kalen barked, not that anyone had said or done anything. He had addressed the room at large, but he was looking at Theodore, making it seem like he didn't want the second-youngest of their group to run after Isobel, since he was already halfway across the room. "Dorm meeting tonight. Don't be late."

Kalen stalked out, Mikel his dark shadow. Moses and Oscar escaped next, leaving Gabriel and Elijah to saunter off like none of this bothered or threatened them in the least. They were pretty good actors, actually.

Niko and Cian cornered Theodore, herding him out while pretending not to herd him at all, their arms around his shoulders and their fingers poking his ribs as they teased him about being an angsty, piano-playing fuck.

Kilian was left alone in the studio, something he was used to. People tended to overlook him in a crowd, and the Alphas were certainly a crowd. The Ironside show had labelled him "untouchable," but that couldn't be further from the truth.

Most of the time, he was starving for touch.

He turned everything off and closed the door of the room, slipping into invisibility as he left the fitness centre. That was how he spent the rest of the day— hidden from the eyes of the students he stalked. He didn't do it with any intention, he just liked it better that way. He walked around the grounds before ducking into the Beta dorm and prowling through Ironside Row, since Kalen would ask him for an update on what the top contenders were doing later. After a while, he got bored and stopped by the tennis courts.

Niko was so predictable.

He had remained the most ambivalent toward Isobel, while she seemed to have everyone else either annoyed, amused, or curious—which meant they were completely up in arms compared to their usual blindness to anyone who wasn't an Alpha. But today she had shown her true colours, and Niko had noticed her for the first time.

And now here he was. Pounding out balls against a brick wall like he was trying to write out *what the fuck is going on* in braille. Kilian leaned up against the fence looking down over the courts, folding his arms and surveying his friend with a frown. So, Niko was bothered, too.

Interesting.

He stepped away and found himself wandering toward Dorm O just as his phone rang. He pulled the old Nokia out, frowning at the beat-up screen and the name displayed there.

"Aron," he answered, his steps quickening as he moved away from the main pathway. "What do you want?"

The husky laugh on the other end sent a pang through him. "Oh, so it's like that, Kil?"

Kilian slowed further and then stopped, leaning up against one of the fences on the far side of Jasmine Field. "Sorry." He closed his eyes, pinching his nose. "It's … been a day."

"Hmm." Aron's deep voice hummed. "And a week. I watched Ironside on Friday."

The Valentine's party. Where Isobel had spent a significant amount of time glued to his side or perched on his lap.

But he didn't have to explain anything.

"You're the one who broke it off," he said, but there was no bite to his tone. If anything, he whined a little bit.

Kilian wasn't sunny like Theodore and Niko, moody like Moses and Oscar, stupid-smart like Gabriel and Elijah, or tough like Mikel and Kalen.

Maybe he was like Cian, but Cian was wily and

guarded his heart behind a ten-foot wall of mystery, which was guarded by a twenty-foot wall of charm. Kilian was softer than the rest of them.

He was fucking sensitive, dammit.

"So, who is she?" Aron asked conversationally.

"As if you don't know," Kilian scoffed. "She's the Sigma."

"Who is she to you, Kil?"

"What is it to you?" Kilian shot back too quickly.

"You've only ever been with guys, that I know of." For the first time, Aron sounded ... unsure. *Concerned?* "I ... guess I just wanted to let you know I'm here if you need to talk. It's clear something is going on."

"With me and her?" Kilian barked out a soft laugh. "Nobody thinks that. It's not clear at all."

"Nobody knows you like I do."

"Alright, well, this has been fun—"

"Is she your mate?" Aron rushed out, like he couldn't hold it back any longer.

"Jesus. Fuck," Kilian swore. "Are you insane? Good*bye*, Aron." He quickly ended the call, shaking his head as he stuffed the phone back into his pocket.

He walked back to the main path with a heavy frown, hugging his invisibility even closer as he teetered, torn about which direction to go in. With a short, sharp breath, he turned in the direction of Dorm

O and soon found himself in Isobel's empty room. He wandered around, touching the neat little piles of her folded clothes before sinking down against the wall beside her bed. She always folded her pyjamas up under her pillow, and he lifted the pillow now to check that she was still sleeping in one of the shirts he had given her.

She obviously liked it. It was a faded yellow, with *good vibes* scrawled across the front in a '70s font. The material was so thin, the cotton almost silky, because it had also been his favourite, once upon a time.

Back when he was a scrawny little Alpha who everyone looked down on because he cried when he hurt himself, and Alphas weren't supposed to cry.

"Mate?" he asked the silent room, the word dying off on an exasperated laugh.

Bonding was rare. *Very* rare. So rare that it had only happened three times at Ironside over the years, and only twice since he had been alive. He remembered when Braun Carter announced to the world that he had found his Sigma match, and then subsequently hid her—and his daughter—away from that same world. He never spoke about them in the press, or released photos of them. It was almost like they didn't exist, until Isobel came to Ironside.

But that was all after Carter graduated, so none of

it was on film. What *was* on film was censored, because of course, a mate-bond couldn't start without someone coming *very* close to dying.

He pulled out his phone again, picking at the old buttons until he finally navigated to the number he had saved but never used. He wanted to message her. He wanted to be *friends* with her. Was that really such a big deal? She was sensitive just like he was. She was more similar to him than any of the Alphas, and he had been cooped up with them for almost two years already without any external stimulation.

He just wanted to ...

The phone vibrated in his hand before he could form the thought.

Theodore: Where are you?

Theodore: Say "boo" if you're standing right next to me.

Kilian: Very funny, loser.

Theodore: Don't forget charismatic.

Kilian: If it were true, it wouldn't be so easy to forget.

Theodore: She was amazing, wasn't she?

Kilian: You were amazing.

Theodore: Kalen isn't happy. She's good enough to win.

Kilian: But she won't.

Another name flashed up on his screen, and he switched to the other message.

Cian: Come to the dining hall and stop skulking around Dorm O. The Sigma is here. And we're here too, by the way. If that counts for anything.

He groaned, stashing his phone away and walking over to the dining hall, where he found Theodore, Moses, Cian, and Niko stashed away in one of the booths. He didn't make himself visible until he had shoved Cian aside to make room for him on the seat.

"Thought so," Cian muttered, shifting to the side and lifting his lips in a cocky grin, his tattooed fingers rubbing his chin as he looked Kilian over. "Find anything interesting?"

It was hard to tell when Cian was guessing and when he *knew*. This was one of those times. Did he know how often Kilian went to Isobel's room?

Kilian fucking hoped not.

"Not really," he replied easily.

"Where were you?" Theodore asked, his eyes on his phone.

"Around." Kilian stole a sausage from Cian's plate, pointing it at Niko. "Bad form today. What's got you all twisted up?"

Niko, who hadn't even showered yet and still had sticky strands of bleached blond hair matted to his forehead, forced a smile. "An opponent surprised me, but that's okay. I'll demolish them like I've demolished all the others."

Kilian dropped the sausage, his stomach twisting. He snatched up a napkin, wiping his fingers. "Just do it gently," he whispered, keeping his eyes on the table.

15

CHAOS AT DAWN

Isobel dug through the collection of eight-second videos and photos that Eve had helped her prepare over the past week, choosing one at random to post. She could never come up with anything clever to say, so as always, she just set her description for the image as the Sigma emoji. People seemed to like it, because the Sigma emoji was trending—along with her collaboration with Theodore. The clip of her and Moses at the Valentine's Day party still hadn't been knocked out of the top five trending spot, so she was actually starting to accumulate quite a lot of popularity points.

She set her phone down on the table, looking around for Eve, who was supposed to meet her for breakfast, but it wasn't the bubbly brunette who slipped into the chair opposite her.

It was Crowe.

His hair was oily, like he hadn't washed it, and he winced as he tried to sit in the chair, a big hand settling across his ribs. The other pushed oily tendrils of his hair back, revealing deep-set eyes ringed in shadow.

"Sigma," he huffed out. "Been a minute."

"You look like shit." She crossed her arms, pushing back the instinctive fear that tried to sprout up in her stomach. They were in a packed dining hall. What could he do?

"And you look good." He flashed his teeth, his eyes darting off to the side for a moment.

She followed his line of sight, recognising Bellamy frowning back from a table of bustling Betas. Bellamy jerked his head as though to call Crowe over to his table, but Crowe turned back to Isobel.

"You didn't tell anyone about what happened." He spoke plainly, staring at his palms as he turned them upwards, his forearms resting against the table. After a moment, he turned them over, pressing his hands halfway across the table as he leaned forward, silver-ringed eyes focussed with a strange intensity on hers.

"You can't," he hissed. "Because *you're* the villain of that story. I didn't do shit to you, but you tried to fucking *kill* me. Except you couldn't even do that properly. You tried your best and it still wasn't good enough."

And just like that, she felt sick. Her stomach was turning, her vision growing blurry. She fought the feeling back, swallowing several times until he eased into his seat again and she was able to clear her head.

"How about you just consider it a warning," she said to her lap. "Don't come near me again."

He laughed, lumbering to his feet. "We'll see. Catch you round, Sigma."

She texted Eve that she was skipping breakfast and pushed away from the table, making a beeline for the exit. The tightness in her chest didn't ease up until she made it out into the hallway, but the reprieve was brief.

"Sigma!"

She paused, closing her eyes and groaning inwardly. Bellamy caught up to her, his hand on her arm. He spun her around, but just as quickly released her before folding his arms and tucking his hands beneath his armpits. He rocked back on his heels. "Did you have something to do with what happened to Crowe?"

"What?"

"He's been out of the hospital an hour, and you're the first person he wanted to talk to."

"Sounds like he needs to get his priorities straight." She shrugged. "Are you jealous?"

He didn't even crack a smirk. In fact, his entire fake-friendly social mask was absent. There were deep lines between his brows and frown indentations either side of his mouth. His hair was mussed, like he had been tugging on it, and his eyes kept darting off to the side, like he was worried about who might see them talking.

"Did something happen between you two at the Valentine's party?" he asked, his voice dropping so low she had to lean forward to hear him.

"Like you don't know," she scoffed.

"What the hell is that supposed to mean?" He reared back.

"Forget it. But next time I see you handing a girl a drink, I'm reporting you."

He grabbed her wrist before she could stalk away, his breath a hiss. "So something did happen?"

"Get your fucking hand off me." She tore her arm away and tried to leave again, but this time she smacked straight into another body.

Heavy hands landed on her shoulders, spinning her around and pulling her back against a wide chest.

"You know she's serious when she uses bad words," Theodore rumbled out. He sounded like he was teasing, his tone light-hearted, but his fingers on her shoulders were stiff, his hard body lined with tension. "What's going on, Bellamy?"

Bellamy's light green eyes flicked from her face to Theodore's. He seemed torn about something before he shook his head. "Nothing."

"Then *leave*," Theodore growled, the last word carrying a hint of command as his Alpha voice crept through. "Come on," he added gently, tucking her under his arm and turning her away. "I was on my way to class, but it looks like you need an escort more than I need *Social Media Management*."

He deposited her at her first class with a sunny smile and an easy wave, leaving her to stare after him in bemusement before heading in and taking her usual seat across from Ashford. He barely paid any attention to her or the professor. He shuffled his cards with a focussed look, his tanned, tattooed hands occasionally flipping a card the other way to glance at it before slipping it back into the deck with an even heavier frown.

He looked up in surprise when the bell rang, his eyes connecting with hers, his hands stilling.

"Like what you see, Sigma?"

She huffed, standing and grabbing her bag. "You're a really great partner, Ashford."

"And you're a sassy one. What's with the frown?"

"Ask your deck." She flounced away, some of the bravado leaving her as she spotted Crowe leaning against the opposite wall to her classroom. He was staring down at his phone, but he turned it so she could see his screen. He was watching her collaboration with Theodore.

Just catching up, he mouthed at her.

Nerves skittered down her spine, and she quickened her step, hurrying off to her next class. But it didn't stop there. She kept seeing him. In the corridors between classes, in the dining hall, outside the training rooms or the bathrooms in the fitness centre. She even caught him out the back of Dorm O. He was always alone unless he was in the dining hall, where he stuck with Bellamy's group—though he never joined in on their conversations, preferring to stare quietly out across the hall.

It was unnerving.

She stopped going to the library at night and stopped fighting against Eve's attempts to drag her everywhere. Not to mention she was still sleeping in Eve's bed.

She was so distracted by Crowe that she forgot all

about the favour Sato had asked of her until a week later, when Ashford leaned across the desk and pulled the teacup out of her hand.

"I'm having a party on Sunday," he announced. "And you're shit at this."

"How can anyone be good at this?" she complained, frowning down at the dregs inside the cup. "I don't see any of the symbols in the booklet."

"It's easy." He rolled his eyes, tilting her cup his way. "You're about to meet a tall, dark, and handsome stranger. Or come into a large fortune. Or die."

She snorted. "I thought it was a flower."

"So you're pregnant then." His lips twitched, those indentations around his mouth disappearing as little smile wrinkles swallowed them. "Aren't you going to ask why I'm having a party?"

"Will it run over three nights? Will you finally be choosing a bride?"

He levelled her with a flat, bored look, but those smile wrinkles were still there. It was astounding how those wrinkles and indentations could make him look like he was smiling or frowning without him ever really moving his mouth.

"You know what?" He folded his arms and kicked out his legs, nudging her chair the way he liked to do. "You're uninvited."

"You can't un-invite me. I already made you a present."

He froze, his eyes flitting over her face before he sucked his lower lip into his mouth. Releasing it, he said, "You're lying. But I want to see you get drunk and start swearing like a sailor again, so you're reinvited."

"You must not know many sailors."

"Not for lack of trying."

They stared at each other, his boots rhythmically hitting her chair.

"What's the party for?" she indulged him, even though she already knew.

"My birthday. So bring a present."

"What kind of things do you like?"

"Sexy things." He arched a brow at her, tipping his chin down in challenge. He also liked to tease her like this, to make it known he thought she was pathetically innocent.

She blushed and grimaced at the same time. "I don't think I'm equipped for that kind of present."

"Practice makes perfect," he said easily, but he didn't really mean it. As much as Ashford liked to tease her, as much as he liked to dazzle her with his dusky skin and the silky golden hair that brushed his neck and chin before hypnotising her with the strange, thin symbols on his knuckles as he tucked those silky strands behind his ears ... As much as he did all of that and then gave her knowing, hooded looks just to embarrass her, she *knew* that he wasn't actually interested in her. He liked to dance across a line, but he had no intention of crossing it.

He was the same with the other girls, too, which was interesting. He was always seen with a girl or five wrapped around him or hanging off his every word, but none of them had any personal tales of him. Nobody spoke about what he was like in an intimate situation or what his dorm room looked like or any of his private hobbies and quirks.

Nobody really seemed to know him at all. And he hadn't been caught in any *actual* intimate moments on camera at all.

"What kind of things do you like?" She dug her heels in, lifting her chin to meet his stare despite the stain of colour blossoming along the tops of her cheeks.

"I like when things go my way, I like the way the sun rises in the desert, and I like *very* strong coffee."

"Noted. I'll do my best."

"You do that." He smiled at her, and it was a little condescending. It was almost like a pat on the head and a "good Sigma."

She scrunched up her nose and then pulled out

her phone, googling what time the sun was supposed to rise on Sunday, before pausing and shaking her head. *Why would she go to that kind of effort for Ashford?*

"No no no." He leaned forward, his eyes narrowing. "Whatever you were thinking, don't chicken out. It doesn't suit you."

"But it does though, doesn't it?" she shot back before she could censor herself. *Sigmas are weak. Sigmas are meant to be felt, not seen or heard.*

"Tsk." He wagged a tanned finger at her, shaking his head, those aquamarine eyes disappointed. "And I thought you were finally stepping up to play the game."

SHE SNUCK OUT OF EVE'S ROOM WHILE IT WAS STILL DARK ON Sunday, returning to her own room after a quick shower to consult her shelf of neatly folded outfits. She was sick of Ashford challenging her, pushing her, teasing her, underestimating her. But she was still nervous. He obviously didn't want a present. They were in their second year of Ironside—only close family and friends did presents, and she was neither to him. She could have gotten him something stupid just to shove into his chest and meet his challenge out of spite, but she couldn't. It wasn't in her nature.

She wanted to do something nice. It was his *birthday*. So she pulled on denim shorts and a loose, faded shirt that actually belonged to Kilian, but she wasn't giving it back until he asked for it, because she secretly adored the way all his shirts felt so soft and well-loved. Her father was so wealthy that the minute her clothes showed any sign of wear, they were immediately replaced. She never had the chance to wear something that had softened to her, shaped to her. Before she came to Ironside, her clothes hadn't even *smelt* like her.

She stuck her sunglasses on her head, tucked her phone into her pocket, and stepped into a pair of sandals before making her way to the dining hall. Breakfast hadn't been set up yet, but drinks and snacks were always available, so she grabbed two takeaway cups and put four shots of coffee in one of them, since she didn't know what *very* strong coffee consisted of.

She dropped two wrapped chocolate chip muffin-bars into her tote and then made her way to Dorm A, making a big show of carrying the two takeaway cups. She might as well win a few popularity points from the encounter. Even if Ashford took the coffee and laughed in her face. People would still watch it. It would still get her closer to her goal.

She took the steps up Alpha Hill, navigating carefully in the dark, and made her way around to the side of the dorm, counting out the big bay windows. She was pretty sure she remembered which was Ashford's room, but she still gritted her teeth in preparation for a big mistake as she balanced one cup on top of the other and rapped on the glass. She had to do it a few times before Ashford appeared in the window, jerking back the curtains so that the moonlight glowed over his skin. His eyes were heavy and confused, his hair messy, his chest bare. She tried not to look at that.

"Carter?" His voice carried through the glass.

"Come outside," she said, leaning so close to the glass that her breath misted against it because she was too terrified to raise her voice.

He stared at her and then flicked his eyes to the coffee cups, and then stared at her again. Thankfully, there didn't seem to be any cameras around the back of the dorm, but it was still embarrassing enough without them. He leaned forward, unlatched the window, and shoved it open.

"Oh." She stumbled a step back, quickly palming

both cups before she dropped them. "Didn't know you could do that. Here. Happy early birthday."

He kept staring, but the coffee seemed to gradually draw his attention, and he finally took it gingerly out of her hand, taking an experimental sip before coughing and breaking into a tight grimace. "Holy *hell*, are you trying to kill me?"

"Ugh, I knew I messed it up. Have mine." She tried to switch the cups, but he held his out of her reach, forcing her to lean through the window, her chest pressing to the window seat he was braced over.

"No. I like it. Even if it is the middle of the night."

"It's not." She extracted herself from the window. "It's almost sunrise. Put a shirt on and let's go."

"Are you seriously stealing me away to watch the sunrise?"

"Stay if you want." She sipped her coffee, squinting up at the sky. "I'm sure you'll get other presents."

He chuckled, and by the time she dragged her eyes back to the window, he was pulling a shirt over his head. He stepped into sneakers, tightening the drawstring on his sweats at the same time.

She stepped back when he knee-walked over the window seat, pushing his legs through the window and jumping out before closing it securely behind him. He took long drags of his coffee, following her silently as she made her way to the library. She led him to the top floor where a fire door was tucked behind a few shelves of unpacked books.

"Come here often?" Ashford finally spoke up as they climbed the dark stairwell to the roof.

"Not really," she said. "I didn't even check what was behind here until this year." She pushed open the door at the top of the stairwell, holding it with her back as she waited for him to pass. "There aren't any cameras, so you can drop the Ashford-act for a while if you like."

"Here I was thinking you were doing this for views." He planted a bronze hand against the door above her head, refusing to let her hold it open for him.

She shrugged, peeling away from the door and walking over to the edge of the rooftop. The concrete edge had a low metal handrail above it. She stepped over the handrail, sitting on the concrete as her legs dangled off the edge.

"Over there." She pointed out over the eastern point of the campus, toward Alpha Hill. "It's rising."

She could feel him behind her, but he didn't really join her. One of his hands curled around the railing to the right of her shoulder, the other resting to the left of her other side, his coffee balanced against the metal.

"This is the first time I've seen you act like a Sigma," he admitted lowly, his words landing on the top of her head. "Sometimes you bark at me like you think you have Alpha voice."

"How diminishing." She crossed her arms, her mouth setting into a hard line, her empty cup tapping agitatedly against her bicep.

"Yeah, just like that." He chuckled. "Did you really organise this for me just because I told you to give me a present?"

She caught sight of something below just as the first glow penetrated the sky. A hulking form was winding his way around the lake toward Dorm O, his walk a little off kilter. Crowe.

"Yes," she said simply.

"Hmm." He reached down, plucking her empty cup from her hand, bending to place both cups on the inside of the concrete barrier. "My cards told me that I would be surprised today. I was expecting something else."

"What else did your cards say?"

"That people weren't what they seemed."

She kept watching Crowe, barely nodding in response to Ashford.

"Carter ..." He trailed off, and she felt more than saw his hands re-grip the railing on either side of her shoulders. "Can you come over to this side of the barrier?"

"Scared of heights?" she asked, smirking a little as she cast a look over her shoulder, catching sight of the rooftop door opening. "Oh, damn."

A cameraman crept through, followed by another and an assistant holding a big fuzzy microphone. They motioned her to ignore them. She tipped her head back up further, meeting Ashford's hypnotising eyes, the vibrant, blue-green hue reminding her instantly of coral-filled oceans. "They sent spies."

"Of course they did." He closed his eyes. "I better make out with you so they don't think anything weird is going on."

She jumped a little, like he was threatening to grab her right then and there, and his eyelids flew open in alarm, both of his hands snatching at her shoulders and snapping her back against the barrier. His breath hissed out between his teeth. "Shit, don't do that," he demanded. "The hell is wrong with you?"

"There's an arch beneath me," she said dryly, kicking her feet in the direction of the large, tiled window arch.

"And then below that there's a whole lot of fucking nothing."

She tried to lean forward. "Actually, there are more arches ..."

He jerked her back again, leaning down as one arm wrapped around the front of her chest completely. She felt his breath stir her temple as he turned his head to the side, looking away from the view.

"Hey," she tried to sound soothing. "I'm sorry. I'll come off the ledge."

"You're a magnet for disaster," he groaned, his arm tightening when she began to move. "Just *wait*! Give me a moment."

Cian ... The voice floated into her mind, tinkling and musical. *I'm sorry, Cian.*

"W-what the fuck," she stuttered out. She didn't know that voice. "L-let go."

"I ... can't." He was breathing even heavier, his fingers starting to shake against her shoulder.

Cian ... I'm sorry.

"Ashford!" She tried to pry his arm off. He was too big, and his trembling was actually shaking through her chest.

"Fuck," he gasped. "I can't."

He's having a panic attack. The voice in her head was louder this time, more insistent. *Help him. Help my Cian.*

She immediately stopped prying at him, her

touches flattening out, stroking over his arm. "It's okay," she whispered, her chest cracking open a little.

The panic she hadn't even noticed battering up against her—since she had been panicking herself—filled her, flooding in through her walls to slosh sickeningly in the pit of her stomach. *Despair, loss, guilt, fear.*

The strangest thing was ... none of it felt new. These feelings were deep-seated, like the anger she felt from her father.

His breathing evened out, but hers grew choppy. She cut off the flow because she couldn't afford another fit.

Cian ... "Cian," she echoed, tears gathering in her eyes. *I'm sorry.* "She's sorry."

He hauled her over the railing, snatched her hand, and dragged her back to the stairwell. She immediately tipped her head down, letting her hair fall over her face as they passed the cameras. She knew her cheeks were wet, and that was unacceptable. She swiped away the moisture as he pulled her out of the library.

"You can let go," she insisted, her free hand braced against her stomach as she hurried to keep up with him.

"Stop talking," he ground out, his strides growing

longer until it felt like her arm was about to pop out of its socket. "Oscar!" he snapped once they reached the pathway. He stopped and spun them both around.

She jumped out of her skin, coming face to face with Sato. He stared with shadowed eyes, his tall, muscled form hidden in oversized clothing, his tightly curled hair showing surprising licks of gold within the inky strands beneath the sun.

"Well, that was interesting," he drawled, his voice husky.

"Dorm," Ashford growled, spinning around again and resuming his fast pace, his grip still tight around her hand.

THAT *HAD* BEEN INTERESTING.

Oscar had been awake and sitting against his window when the little Sigma appeared like an apparition at the top of Alpha Hill. He tossed aside the book he had been contemplating turning the light on for, and leaned forward, catching sight of the cups in her hand. A growl built up in the back of his throat. This was a whole new level of *not allowed*. He considered storming into Theodore's room and threatening the younger boy with violence, but decided instead to tug on a hoodie and slip into Kilian's room.

"Wake up." He jostled his friend. "Make us invisible."

"*Piss off*," Kilian muffled into a pillow, trying to roll over and push Oscar away.

"Now." Oscar tucked his hands under Kilian's arms and unceremoniously hauled him upright, dumping him on the window seat overlooking the lake. "Cian is sneaking off with the Sigma."

"What now?" Kilian immediately whipped to his feet, groaning at an apparent dizzy spell as he shook his head and leaned into the glass. "Well ..." he murmured lowly. "That's a new development."

Oscar grabbed his arm. "Invisible. Now."

Kilian rolled his eyes, escaping again to pull on a shirt and step into flip-flops before taking hold of Oscar. They hurried to catch up, confusion growing as they entered the library.

"When was the last time Cian stepped foot in this place?" Kilian asked under his breath.

"I didn't bring you along to chit-chat," Oscar snapped back.

Kilian delivered another eye roll but fell into silence as they stalked the others onto the rooftop. A small camera crew arrived a few minutes later, everyone just standing around and watching ... nothing.

Cian and Carter were barely even talking.

"Are they watching the sunrise together?" Kilian whispered, utterly confused. "For his birthday? How is Cian standing so close to the edge?"

Cian was almost touching her. His arms braced either side of her. And Oscar was ... angry. He wanted the inherent mistrust and suspicion he had for the Sigma to be warranted. He didn't want more evidence that she was just as soft and fucking pure as everyone seemed to think she was.

"This is bullshit," he breathed out, careful not to speak loud enough to alert any of the other rooftop occupants.

"Don't," Kilian warned, his head suddenly whipping to the side, shaking vehemently. "Oscar ..."

Too late.

Oscar shrugged off the wave of chaos like it had been desperately gathering around him the longer he looked at her, and he felt it ripple away from him, a pebble tossed into a small pond. This felt like the perfect powder keg moment. It would be rude *not* to.

He dragged Kilian back to the door.

"They could get hurt—" Kilian's protestations were cut off as Oscar hauled him down the stairs. "She was on the *edge*!" Kilian broke away, shaking his head as they spilled out of the library. "You stay away from her!" He pointed at Oscar, stabbing him in the chest. "You pull one more stunt like this, and I'm dragging your ass to Kalen."

"Why wait?" Oscar smirked. "Run to daddy."

"Apologise." Kilian's bark was acidic, strong with Alpha command. The soft-hearted boy almost never used it.

Oscar strained against it, the Alpha inside him immediately rising to the challenge. He beat it down, sucking in a long draft of air.

"I'm sorry." He offered his hand, and Kilian stared at it for a moment before slapping his pale palm against Oscar's.

"I'm out of here," Kilian muttered, realising they were at an impasse. Oscar couldn't be controlled, but he also couldn't step too far out of bounds, or it might risk everything they were trying to do at Ironside.

He waved Kilian off, rubbing a rough hand over his face as he moved around to the side of the library where he had a good view of the pathway back to Dorm A. Cian would have felt his chaos.

Maybe a confrontation was what Oscar really wanted.

And he usually got what he wanted.

16

YOU KNOW WHAT HAPPENS

THE SUN HAD FULLY CRESTED BEHIND ALPHA HILL BY THE time Ashford pulled her onto the roof of Dorm A. She heard doors opening as they stalked through the hallway, so she wasn't surprised to see Spade and Moses appearing at the top of the stairs as Ashford released her, pointing a finger in her chest.

"Just ... stay there," he ordered.

Her mouth thinned, her eyes narrowing. But he was already turning and stalking back down the stairs, calling out Sato's name again.

"The hell?" Moses grumbled, ruffling his sleep-mussed hair.

Spade seemed to be carefully cataloguing her. "You've been up a while," he noted. "You smell like coffee and fear."

"I smell like none of your business." She sighed, plucking at the neckline of her—well, Kilian's—shirt. *Was it getting hot?* "Isn't it rude to scent people you aren't close with?"

"It's barely six o'clock and you're in my kitchen," he returned.

"That's all the invitation I need." She tried to skirt past him to escape down the stairs and out of the dorm, but Moses stepped into her path, shaking his head. He didn't even say anything.

"I thought you didn't want me hanging around." She fought the urge to stumble away from him, pushing her chest out and planting her hands on her hips. "Let me make your day."

"He told you to stay. You stay." He glared down at her, those stormy eyes so familiar but so cold. He wasn't anything like Theodore.

"Alright, caveman." She backed up, panic skittering along her spine. "Are there cameras up here?" She scanned the edges of the kitchen overhang.

"Not inside the kitchen," Spade answered. "Move a few feet to the right."

She immediately moved, breathing a sigh of relief as the sunlight slanted over her skin.

"Why?" Moses asked, leaning up against the

kitchen counter, his arms folded. He was acting like some sort of guard dog.

"She wants to feel safe, asshole." Spade rolled his eyes, padding over to the coffee machine and opening a cupboard of mugs. "You look pretty jittery already," he said over his shoulder, "or I would offer you some coffee."

"Illy?" Theodore's voice had *never* sounded so good. He shuffled into the kitchen, a confused frown on his face. "Why do you smell scared?"

She opened her mouth, but her words got stuck inside her throat as Moses looked down at the ground, his frown deepening. His conflicting emotions reached out to her, spidering cracks out along the outside of her wall as a slight flash of darkness crept into the corners of his eyes.

"I ..." Her fists clenched tight. "Sato." She unfurled her fingers, pointing toward the stairwell. "Have you seen him? He's terrifying. I ran into him again."

"Ah." He frowned, looking back toward the stairs, but he didn't appear alarmed, only exasperated. Sato probably scared everyone who came within stone-throwing distance of the dorm. "That would check out. He's not a morning person, or an evening person ... Now, how about the truth?"

He stopped in front of her, his amber scent warm, the sun shining through the stormy colour of his eyes.

"Um." She cleared her throat and tried again. "Well, Ashford told me to get him a present, and I asked what he liked and he said sunrises and bad coffee—"

"Strong coffee," Ashford corrected, stepping onto the rooftop. He appeared much calmer. "We went for a walk, and now I need to talk to her alone." He wasn't asking permission.

None of the others moved.

Ashford tipped his bright eyes up to the sky, like he needed to pray for patience, and then he held out his hand. "Come talk to me, Sigma."

"I have a name." She folded her arms, staring at his hand.

"Please, Carter. We need to talk about what happened."

"What happened?" Theodore and Moses demanded at the exact time, but in entirely different ways. Theodore's tone was furious. Moses sounded horrified.

"It's not my thing to tell." Isobel shrugged a little, looking at the ground. She wasn't about to blurt out that Ashford had a panic attack because he was scared of heights.

"It's not my thing to tell either." Ashford dropped his eyes to hers, looking confused.

The voice.

So maybe they did need to talk after all. She scooted around Theodore's body. "Excuse me. Sorry."

He grabbed her wrist before she could pass, but his eyes were on Ashford.

And they were growing dark.

Moses immediately jumped off the counter. "This conversation is over. Carter, you need to leave."

Isobel tried to pull her arm free, but Theodore's grip was too tight. "I can't," she whispered.

Spade pulled out his phone and held it up to the camera, while Theodore slowly lifted his fingers from her arm, one-by-one.

"I'll catch up with you later," he croaked out to her, but his attention was still on Ashford.

She edged toward the stairs, but when she turned back, all she could see were the three other Alphas stalking toward Theodore, and the bleeding darkness that was starting to take over his eyes.

"Run away," Moses barked at her, his Alpha voice carrying a harsh command.

Her body immediately jerked to obey, but her heart stopped her, her wall crumbling as she reached out to Theodore with her ability.

Stay right where you are, Isobel. That was the Alpha command she was used to fighting against. That was the memory that seized her as Moses' order fissured along her limbs and she tried to fight it off. Her father would force her still, force her to stay in place to take his beatings.

She would fight it with all she had.

She was used to resisting the Alpha command ... but defying Moses and sucking in Theodore's darkness at the same time was a different story. She focussed on Theodore's pupils when his eyes swung to hers. She fixated on the wavering darkness as it paused, surged, and ebbed, a silent tug-of-war going on. Her knees buckled, bile rising into the back of her throat. Sweat gathered on her forehead. Theodore's arms were trembling, and Moses looked torn between marching over to force her down the stairs or going to his brother.

Isobel let out a low, pained whine, and it seemed to whip every head in her direction.

"What are you doing?" Spade demanded. "Stop. Carter—Isobel. Stop."

"*Stop.*" It was someone's Alpha voice again, doubling the effect of Moses' command, the weight of it forcing her lower against the stairs, forcing her head to the side, forcing her to bare her neck and back in submission and whimper, but she never broke eye contact with Theodore.

She wasn't sure if her position was a reaction to the compounding Alpha command or if her body simply remembered the way her father preferred her to position herself for punishment.

"Isobel?" The voice was soft, calming, soothing. Hands were stroking her hair back from her face. "Isobel, it's okay, you don't have to obey." Alpha voice again, but this time it was spoken lowly, smoothly, and the iron will forcing her to bend eased somewhat.

"K-Kilian," she cried, recognising his gentle scent and the soft way he gathered her up.

"What is she doing?" Moses sounded shaky. Panicked. "Theo? Theo! Make her stop! She can't! You know what happens!"

"Carter?" This time it was Sato. He swore darkly. "Again? Seriously, this fucking girl."

"Again?" Moses' voice was getting louder, his panic increasing.

"Moses, you need to calm down," Spade ordered. "I've texted Mikki, he's coming. Just stay calm. Focus. Moses. Look at me. Focus, okay?"

Theodore fell to his knees, breaking eye contact just long enough for her to notice that Spade was holding Moses back from both her and Theodore ... and that Moses' eyes were also starting to bleed black.

She tried to draw her walls back around her, tried to separate herself from Theodore, desperately gathering the pieces of her barrier even as the dizziness took hold, but it was too late. Her chest was already cracked open, already lined with darkness —*demanding* it from Theodore. So when the flood of Moses' emotion knocked against her, it wasn't met with any resistance.

With Theodore, she had pulled, like she had one end of a rope and all of his demons were dragging along at the other end as she corralled them into her body ... but this time, she was the one being pulled. That same rope grew taut in her hands, wrapping her wrists and dragging her toward a bigger darkness than she had ever experienced.

Let go.

She knew that voice. That calm, safe voice.

Mama. She almost sobbed the word out loud. The first time she heard it, she thought she was going crazy. But now she was just desperate, because she had never been so afraid before in her entire life. Not when her father had beaten her so badly they needed to rush her to the hospital. Not when, three months later, he had a drunken breakdown, overflowing with grief over what he had done to her, and she sucked away too much of that grief, inadvertently stopping her own heart. Not when Crowe cornered her in the chapel, or when she thought she might have killed him.

This was true, pure fear.

It was a fear so consuming it spiralled her all the way back to her childhood, to the very first time she ever felt fear, and how utterly awful it was. Just like then, it tingled all the way through to her feet. It blocked her throat, made it hard to breathe, made her head swim and her thoughts turn into vapour.

Let go, Illy.

There was so much talking going on all around her. So much shouting, but all she could hear was that steady voice inside her head.

I can't, she tried to say, reaching desperately for the voice, wanting nothing more than for her mother to whisk her off to the hospital like all those other times.

Afterwards, the doctors would say she was lucky to have an Icon for a father, to have access to the human services, and she would nod shyly and agree while her mother's hand shook around hers.

The more she reached, the more the sensations all around her began to change, the sounds becoming louder, more demanding, like her tugging was drawing her in the wrong direction—back to the rooftop instead of toward her mother.

She tried to open her eyes, but she was swimming in darkness. Everything around her was black and full of menace, tearing and ripping away at her insides. Her heart was so frantic, her chest heaving as she tried to pull in air.

You're dying, love. It's time. Let go.

Her mother was there, in the darkness with her. Isobel had thought that she was urging her to fight, to live, to *let go* of the darkness, but that wasn't it at all. She wanted her to let go of the light. To surrender.

"S-s-scared," she wheezed out, wasting precious breath in a desperate bid for help. Suddenly, she wasn't so sure about that voice inside her head.

"I'm here." A deep voice pierced through the fog of sound around her, like a call through the wall of a waterfall. It was familiar in this hazy, foggy place, like she had heard it before in a state just like this one.

Kalen West. The man who could take her body back in time.

"I can't," his voice continued, answering someone else's frantic question. "It isn't working. It's like ..." He trailed off, and she heard a fresh uproar of sound, forcing him to finish his sentence.

"It's like she's already dead."

413

. . .

THEODORE FELT LIKE HE HAD CRAWLED OUT OF ONE nightmare and into an even bigger one. He remembered locking eyes with her. He remembered the ebb and flow of the vicious beast inside him frantically trying to claw its way out while she drank and drank all the poison that fuelled him, sedating him over and over again. And then he remembered her eyes drifting closed. Her whimpers, her cries. The scrunch of her brow, the way she panted for breath.

Moses had collapsed, Mikel holding him down even though he didn't seem to be moving. Cian, Oscar, Gabriel, Elijah, Niko ... everyone was there, crowded around where Isobel had fallen, like they didn't know how to help her. And Kalen was striding to the top of the stairs, barking questions, fire in his eyes. When the others scattered, he saw Kilian cradling Isobel. He was crying, his tears dropping onto her cheeks. He wiped them gently away, repeating to her that she was going to be okay and she didn't do anything wrong.

"Reverse it." Oscar dragged Kalen down beside Isobel, shoving his hands onto her chest. "Take her back, quickly!"

Theodore fought off the lingering clutches of ferality, crawling toward them, his eyes fixed on her.

"I can't," Kalen's voice was ghostly, like Theodore was starting to lose conscience, but he held tight, watching as Moses struggled to his feet and almost collapsed, caught by Mikel. Moses didn't go feral either.

Isobel had taken it all.

The taste of ash hit the back of his throat, but he swallowed it down, biting his tongue and spreading the copper taste of blood across his tongue.

Not again.

Not her too.

"It's like she's already dead."

Theodore stopped trying to pull himself toward them, his eyes wide, ash spilling all the way to the back of his teeth. Darkness flashed, and he lost the battle completely.

Kilian swept up her body, pulling her back from the hands of everyone else as a loud roar ripped across the rooftop.

"Theo's fucking lost it." Niko jumped in front of Kilian, his hand rubbing across his chest as Gabriel quickly turned and set their shoulders together, forming a barrier between Theodore and Kilian, whose chest was also hurting. He wanted to rub it like Niko was, to ease the sharp burn, but he didn't dare shift Isobel.

Theodore was tearing things off the kitchen counter, smashing them everywhere, while Mikel and Oscar tried to subdue him. Moses was standing on the sidelines, trembling, fighting his own battle against the surging ferality. He was also rubbing his chest, but Kilian wasn't given any time to dwell on it as a toaster was suddenly flying toward Gabriel. Elijah knocked it out of the way, almost falling into Gabriel before righting himself and adding his body to the wall protecting Isobel and Kilian.

Kalen had stepped up to Moses, a hand on his shoulder, muttering low and blocking his view of Theodore, but his voice rose suddenly loud and ferocious. "Downstairs. Everybody. Mikki, can you handle him?"

"Got him," Mikel gritted out, forcing Theodore back against the fridge, which now had a person-sized dint in it, the door hanging unevenly on its hinges.

Kalen's Alpha bark was forcing them all to the lower level of the house, where Kilian sank into one of the common room couches, still clutching Isobel against his searing chest. Kalen grabbed his face, staring right into his eyes, and that was when Kilian noticed.

Kalen's eyes weren't the same.

One was his usual yellowed amber, but the other was pale honey with gold specks. The exact same shade as Isobel's. Kilian pulled her closer, pinching her even tighter against his burning skin.

"You're her *mate*?" Kilian rasped out, his voice shaky. He could feel the tears slip down his cheeks again. "She's going to live?"

Kalen released him without answering, grabbing Niko by the shoulders and repeating the same examination. They were all looking at each other now, all noticing the same thing.

Their eyes had changed, exactly like when a mate-bond is found. Kilian stopped breathing, flicking his attention between his friends. Niko. Cian. Oscar. Moses. Elijah. Gabriel. They all had a single gold-flecked eye.

"No no no no no." Moses stalked off, horrified, in disbelief, presumably to consult a mirror.

Kilian didn't need to. He could feel it in his chest. The burning, the pain, the things that the Gifted hardly ever talked about—but they *did*. They talked about it just enough for him to know exactly what was happening. He was forming a mate-bond. With the soft little Sigma who refused to stray far from his mind.

"Theo?" He sucked in a deep, unsteady breath. "Mikki?"

"We'll know when Mikki gets a hold of him," Kalen answered before frowning, turning to stare at Kilian. "Wait, what do you mean *Mikki*?"

Fuck. Kalen didn't know. He didn't know his eyes had changed. He hadn't been paying attention to what Kilian had said. He wasn't thinking about himself, only them.

Kilian didn't answer, looking back to Isobel's pale face. She could have been sleeping if it wasn't for the blood dripping from her nose. He used his shirt to wipe it away as gently as he could.

Kalen was frozen in the middle of the room, staring at the small body wrapped up in Kilian's arms. Gabriel and Elijah had collapsed into chairs of their own, eyes wide and unblinking, like they had decided to temporarily vacate their minds. Cian looked disturbed, but not exactly surprised.

They had all quietly considered that Theodore might have been her mate, even if they didn't admit it out loud. But *this*? Nobody could have expected this. This didn't make sense in the slightest. He had no idea if anything like this had ever happened before.

"She almost died with me." Oscar's face was dark,

his brows heavy as he stared at the floor. "She stopped breathing. I resuscitated her."

"What are you trying to say?" Moses demanded, striding back into the room. He had blood dripping from his knuckles. He must have punched something. "That mating can't possibly be a coincidence?"

"It's not important right now." Kalen was still staring at Isobel. "Is she breathing?"

They all immediately turned to hear Kilian's answer.

He nodded silently. He could feel her breath stirring against his collarbone.

"Kil." Cian finally collapsed into a chair, his eyes heavy on Kilian's face. "I'm sorry."

Kilian winced, cuddling her closer. He didn't need pity. Isobel had made him wonder ... made him think things ... but being *forced* to feel a certain way about one person, about one gender? That was a whole other thing.

"I don't want to talk about it," he said firmly.

"Does she need medical attention?" Niko asked, guiding the topic away immediately.

"None of us can take her." Elijah winced, waving at his face. "The second the authorities find out that a Sigma has bonded to eight—possibly *ten*—Alphas, our lives change. Ironside is important to them, but not as important as understanding how the bonds form. They'll pull us out of the academy and have us strapped to lab tables before sunset. They might even fake our deaths, and it won't be hard with Theo trying to tear through the fucking dorm. They'll say one of us had an illegal ability, that one of us was explosive and dangerous, and killed the rest of us. And they'll use the story to tighten restrictions in the settlements. We'll lose decades of progress."

That helped to bring things back into perspective. Gabriel visibly pulled himself up taller, some of the numbness creeping out of his expression. "We need to come up with a plan. No matter what, this can't affect what we have going on here."

"Agreed," Kalen grunted. "Oscar? Go help Mikki. We've got a long day ahead of us, and we need both of them conscious when ... *she* wakes up."

He couldn't even say her name.

17

SPOKEN FOR ... AND AGAINST

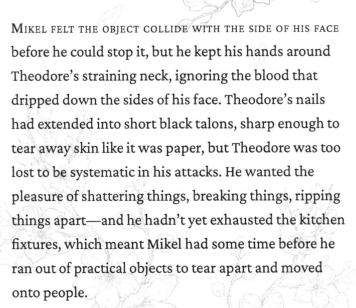

MIKEL FELT THE OBJECT COLLIDE WITH THE SIDE OF HIS FACE before he could stop it, but he kept his hands around Theodore's straining neck, ignoring the blood that dripped down the sides of his face. Theodore's nails had extended into short black talons, sharp enough to tear away skin like it was paper, but Theodore was too lost to be systematic in his attacks. He wanted the pleasure of shattering things, breaking things, ripping things apart—and he hadn't yet exhausted the kitchen fixtures, which meant Mikel had some time before he ran out of practical objects to tear apart and moved onto people.

"Get off me," Theodore growled, every word from his mouth spoken in Alpha voice. Ferality was forbidden for a reason. Perhaps it was the *only* ability the government had good reason to extinguish. Spit flew from the sides of Theodore's mouth, his eyes dark pools of ink, spidery black veins shooting out from that cold black stare. Mikel pushed off Theodore's influence, disregarding his command. Theodore's struggles intensified, but Mikel only tightened his grip, grunting at the impact of something crashing into his shoulder.

It was difficult to ignore a command, even amongst Alphas, but when too many of them cohabited for too long, a ranking system inevitably formed. Mikel was second from the top, and Theodore was second from the bottom. His orders barely had any hold on Mikel.

"Enough," he snapped, lifting Theodore's neck and smacking his head down against the hard ground.

Theodore had been trying to hit along his right side with a heavy blender, but he tossed it into the broken kitchen counter instead, releasing a litany of curses as his talons finally began to tear away at Mikel's torso.

"Allow me," a hoarse voice offered, a dusky hand appearing over Theodore's face, covering his nose and mouth. Oscar grabbed one of Theodore's lethal hands, using his body weight to pin it to the ground as Mikel did the same with his other hand, trapping it against the ground with his knee.

"Pass the fuck out already," Oscar demanded, continuing to cover Theodore's air passages for a good minute even after his body went limp. Theodore was known to pretend to pass out when he was pinned down, and it usually ended in carnage when they underestimated him.

"So you too, then." Oscar quickly lowered his face when Mikel glanced up, something dark in his expression.

"What are you talking about?" Mikel stumbled up, lifting his shirt to check the damage Theodore had done before swiping a hand towel from the ground and shaking glass out of it. He folded it up and pressed it to one of the gouges in his neck.

Oscar stood and lifted his eyes properly to Mikel's, revealing one dark eye, and one pale gold eye, lit from within like sunlight passing through dripping honey. He hadn't paid much attention to the Sigma, but it didn't take a genius to figure out whose eye colour that was.

"You have a mate." Mikel was so shocked he could barely speak.

That poor girl.

Holy fuck, that poor, poor girl.

"Not just me." Oscar shrugged, dropping that bomb before he walked off. "Come downstairs. Leave him." He nodded his head toward Theodore. "I don't need to check to know his eyes have changed."

"The hell are you talking about, Oscar?" Mikel wanted to stalk after him, but he couldn't just leave Theodore to bleed out on the rooftop—especially if the production team decided they were tired of waiting for the Dorm A cameras to "reset" and decided to deploy drones. He hoisted Theodore up, grunting at the weight as he carried him to the stairs. He deposited the unconscious boy onto his bed and then stepped into his en suite. He tore off his shirt since it was already in tatters and switched out the bloodied hand towel for a fresh one, cleaning himself in the sink as best he could before rummaging around for a first aid kit.

It wasn't until he was all bandaged up that he decided to wash the sweat from his face, and it wasn't until he was staring directly into his own mismatched eyes in the mirror that Oscar's words finally made sense.

So you too, then.

One of his eyes was a pale, honeyed gold. He

quickly pushed away from the sink, his stomach dropping, his hands shaking. His phone was already burning a hole through his pocket, and he resisted the urge to reach for it.

She doesn't need to know. Not just yet. Not until they figured out what was happening.

He burst out of the room and swallowed his dread as he congregated with the others. Kilian sat with his head in his hands, his shoulders hunched and tense. Cian looked like he was staring into the eyes of a demon only he could see, but he was the only one who didn't look entirely shell-shocked, his arm looped around Kilian like he didn't know quite how to console the other boy. The Sigma was stretched out along the couch, everyone avoiding looking at her or approaching her.

"Is she—" Mikel started, but Kalen cut him off.

"Alive. Just. From what I know of the Death Phase, she probably isn't going to wake up anytime soon."

Mikel froze, meeting his best friend's gaze. Kalen stared back with mismatched eyes, one more yellow than gold. They all had it. The gold eye. Like some sort of plague that had rapidly burst through the dorm.

Moses looked like he was on the verge of a mental breakdown, and Mikel kept him in his sights, watching for signs of ferality. Gabriel and Elijah were standing together in the corner, huddling in like they could step into a bubble and be invincible against this situation. Niko was staring straight at the door, a blank expression on his face, like he was trying to decide if he should just leave. Give it all up.

But it was Kilian he was most worried about. Kilian and Kalen.

And goddammit ... himself, too.

"Obviously, no bonds are going to be completed," Kalen finally announced, his tone husky.

Mikel had never heard him sound so unsteady.

"We're all too old for her," Oscar added. "Just in case you were floundering for reasons."

"Bro." Cian groaned, his arm dropping from Kilian's shoulders. "Shut the fuck up."

"I'm literally her age." Moses rolled his eyes at Oscar. "And Theo is only a year older. Cian, Niko, and Kilian are ... what? Three years older? Even Kalen is only seven years older. Stop stirring, Oscar."

Mikel looked down at the girl laid out across the couch. Her knees were bruised. Her hair was tangled. Her name was Isobel. She had honey-coloured eyes. She could dance well enough to make him hold his breath. She was six years younger than him, and she was his ... *nope*. He stopped trying to think of everything he knew about her. She was a problem. That was all.

Granted, she was a significant problem.

"She's eighteen. Bonding doesn't happen to underaged people," he said, lifting his eyes to the window instead. "Moving onto the real issue ..."

"We could kill her," Oscar suggested casually.

There were a few exasperated sighs around the room, and Mikel was glad Theodore was still unconscious, or another fight might have broken out.

"I don't have to do it *directly*." Oscar offered. "I could wait for the chaos to cause an accident. Then there's no blood on our hands, and the problem is dealt with. She's the Tether, right? We're the Anchors? That's how it works, since she was the one who almost died? That means her connection to us is the only thing keeping her alive. If she dies, nothing happens to us."

It was disturbing how much he had thought it through already. Disturbing, but unsurprising.

"The blood will most definitely be on our hands," Kalen shot down the idea just as calmly as Oscar had brought it up. "There's only one way forward. We need to hide what happened—not just from the world but from ... her."

"She has a name," Kilian muttered, still unable to lift his head.

"Isobel," Kalen relented, only wincing a little. "We need to keep Isobel in the dark for now. Until we figure out how to deal with this situation."

"Oscar is right," Elijah spoke up. "The only way out of this situation is if she dies. Even half-formed bonds are unbreakable."

"Then we will all live with half-formed bonds," Kalen shot back, his voice a little too heavy. He straightened up, taking a deep breath to steady himself. "Murder isn't an option."

"I wasn't suggesting it." Elijah folded his arms, looking beyond pissed off. "I was just pointing out the obvious. Her bonds are half-formed, and the longer we resist it, the more the bonds will act up. You've all heard the stories of couples trying to ignore or resist the mate-bond. It isn't patient and it isn't gentle. It will force her to us and us to her. It will broadcast our thoughts at the most inappropriate moments. It will rip us from where we stand and drop us at her feet without warning—heedless of whether we're in the middle of class or trying to sleep. It will overwhelm us with dreams of her and drive us all insane trying to make us give in. And those are only the first three side effects I can recall off the top of my head. There are *dozens* of them."

"Then we keep it secret for as long as we can," Kalen ordered. "And we resist until we die, because the alternative is ten Alphas sharing a single mate—and even if we managed to keep that hidden from the government, we wouldn't need them to tear us apart. We would do it ourselves."

"I'll organise contacts to hide our eyes." Gabriel was already on his phone. "But we're going to need to do a lot more than just cover that up. What about *her* eyes? Who's going to make her wear contacts?"

"We could get her expelled?" Oscar wasn't so ready to give in.

Moses perked up, like that might be a suitable solution.

"Tethers can't be far from their Anchor for long," Gabriel replied without looking up. "Side effects include dizziness, shortness of breath, chest pains, and if left for longer, severe flu-like symptoms. Rare cases can lead to hyperthermia and eventually, death. I advise you to stop suggesting we kill her."

Oscar sighed, pushing away from the wall. "I didn't sign up for this shit." He began walking away, but Kalen stepped into his path, shaking his head.

"Wait," he commanded. "Kilian?" He didn't shift

his attention from Oscar for even a second. "You're going to be her shadow until we figure out a better plan. She doesn't sleep alone, she doesn't eat alone, she doesn't shower alone. Do you understand?"

"That's too much. I can't follow her everywhere," Kilian's voice was low, trembling. "I have my own classes."

"Theo will transfer into her classes and be her shadow during the day—"

"Is that the best idea?" Mikel interjected, that hard ball of dread thickening and rolling around inside his stomach, making his throat tighten with nausea. Theodore *liked* the girl. They all knew it. He had better self-control than Moses—and probably most of the rest of them, thanks to his constant battle with ferality —but would it be enough?

"We'll transfer to her dance classes," Elijah offered, his eyes falling to the couch before quickly flicking away. "She does mostly dance anyway."

"She's already in one class with me," Cian offered.

"Theodore should convince her to join one of his vocal classes," Gabriel added thoughtfully. "It might draw attention if we're all suddenly transferring into her classes. And she has a nice voice. It's light as air and kind of husky. If she sounds that nice talking, I imagine she could sound good enough singing."

"Is there anyone else we need to worry about?" The words were out of Mikel's mouth before he could stop them, because Gabriel complimenting *anyone* was a red flag. He tried not to look at anyone in particular. "Anyone other than Theo, I mean."

"No," Moses scoffed.

"No," Cian said, that disturbed look back on his face.

"No," Elijah and Gabriel answered at once, both of them huddled over Gabriel's phone, Elijah pointing out things on the screen.

"I don't even know her," Niko answered with a shrug. He was trying to look like he was above all of this. Like it affected him the least. But Niko had very traditional parents who had formed a small Asian community within Niko's settlement. They would arrange his marriage when the time seemed right and the girl seemed appropriate. This wasn't the right time, and Isobel wasn't the right girl. She was blonde. American. She wasn't even from the settlements, and who knew what her religion was. Even if Niko told his family that she was his mate, they would never accept her—not as she was. Fated mates were very important to people who followed the Gifted religion, but it would take more than that to earn their acceptance. Maybe that did actually make this situation easier for him, knowing it could never happen.

"Cian?" Kalen prompted, as if he hadn't heard him the first time.

Cian brushed his golden hair back, aqua eyes scanning the room. He took a little too long to answer this time, and seemed to be lost in thought before he finally settled his attention on Kalen. "You don't have to worry about me, but you should be worried about her. There's something off about her."

"Yeah, this whole time she was your fucking mate," Moses spat out. "Of course there was something off about her."

Cian only let his attention drift back to the ground as he calmly returned, "It's more than that. But you'll figure it out for yourself. And we all know I'm not the real threat here. Oscar is."

Oscar had fallen back against the wall, his arms loosely crossed, his teeth digging into his lower lip. He was jumpy, the energy inside him making his skin itchy. Mikel knew the feeling. It was like there was some sort of demon inside him sometimes, itching to crawl out of his skin and wreak havoc. Watching Oscar struggle only brought his own irritability to the surface, and he walked over to the window, placing his hand against the glass as he looked up to the sky.

The light blue slowly darkened, clouds gathering.

Only a big storm would explain away the damage Theodore did to the rooftop this time. He closed his eyes with a sigh, releasing the energy inside him, pouring out the restlessness and turmoil until it swirled above them, menacing and heavy. Rain began to fall down in thick droplets, thunder rumbling in the distance. He kept his hand on the window, willing the storm to take form as he turned back to face the room. Everyone had been watching him, but they turned back to Oscar now, not willing to let him escape the question.

"Do we need to worry about you?" Kalen asked bluntly.

Oscar laughed, throwing his head back, his deep-set eyes closing. "You brought me here so you would have someone to tidy up all your messes, and now you have a messy situation, and *I'm* the one you're worried about? Give me a break."

"Give *us* a break," Elijah returned coldly, though he wasn't being unfriendly, only annoyed that they were taking so long to sort this out. Mikel could tell he wanted to disappear into his room and research everything there was to learn about mate-bonds. "You're an independent person, Oscar. You do whatever you want to do. You're not just a soldier who waits around for orders. Are you going to hurt the Sigma or not?"

"My sister is back home *dying* without the right medicine," Oscar whispered darkly, his brows drawn down. "I sacrificed everything to come here. To carry out our plan. If she threatens to expose us, I *will* get her out of the way, and I won't be gentle."

"But you won't go out of your way to hurt her?" Gabriel was making more of a statement than asking a question.

Oscar grunted. It seemed to be an affirmative, so Kalen sought out the only person who had yet to speak, other than Mikel.

Mikel couldn't possibly be a problem, just like Kalen couldn't be.

They were both spoken for.

Kilian looked up, his face drawn. "I don't know if you have to worry about me," he admitted softly. "I'm worried about myself. I really liked her, and then … it seemed like …"

"She's fine, Kil." Cian wrapped his arm around the other boy again. "She's going to be okay. And so are you. You won't be completing the bond, and it can't *force* you to feel anything. It might make you think about her a lot and want to be near her and all the other wacky side effects, but it can never change what's in your heart."

"Murder is in my heart," Oscar pointed out. "You're all making me change that."

"He's joking," Moses added, unnecessarily. "But it's also in my heart to get her expelled. Or to ignore her completely. We could stay just close enough that she doesn't get hyperthermia and die, but she might have to put up with a little light hay fever or something."

"Idiots," Mikel muttered, walking over to the couch. Everyone shut up immediately, holding their breath. He knelt down beside the Sigma, his hand hovering over her face.

He didn't want to touch her.

"Check her eyes," he said, dropping his hand again.

He couldn't do it.

It was Kilian who unfurled, walking over to kneel next to him. He pulled open one of her eyelids, and they both stared at the colour of her eyeball, even though it was half-rolled into the back of her head. It wasn't a warm honey anymore, but it wasn't any other colour, either. It was green, blue, yellow, gold, black. It was dark and pale, uneven and splotchy, like some sort of optical illusion that changed when you shifted your head to look at it a different way.

"She has all our colours," Mikel announced, standing up. "It will be impossible for her to tell who her mate is—only that she has one—and she won't suspect any of us from the colour."

"Not until the bond starts pushing us together, at least," Elijah added. "So we're doing this, then? We're lying to her?"

"For now." Kalen stepped out of Oscar's path, and Oscar immediately strode off, his fingers agitatedly tapping against his thigh. "Eventually, we will need to tell her the truth," Kalen added. "But only when she's ready for the *whole* truth. Only when we can trust her not to expose us and destroy decades' worth of meticulous planning and hard work."

"Then it's decided." Mikel stood, looking down at the sleeping Sigma. *For your sake, I hope the bond doesn't draw you to me,* he thought before turning and leaving the room.

Isobel reached for her blanket with aching fingers, almost too weak to grasp the material.

"Here." The blanket was tugged to her chin, careful hands tucking it around her arms.

"Kilian?" She blinked her eyes slowly open,

wincing at the stabbing pain that ricocheted through her head. "Oh god," she groaned, hitting her forehead. "I really messed up. Big time."

His hand caught hers, holding onto it like she was made of glass. Her vision cleared, and she looked around at his room and then down at his bed, which she was tucked into. There were bowls and cups and spoons piled on a tray, decorating a small table that had been pulled up near the bed, and Kilian looked ... different.

She couldn't quite put her finger on it, and the emotion that usually thumped against her chest was all confused and muddled, like even he didn't know what he was feeling. He looked down at their hands, and his shoulders suddenly slumped forward, his head landing on the bed beside her thigh. His entire body shook as he let out a long, broken sigh.

"You're awake." He spoke into the blanket, his tone distorted. "You're finally awake."

"How long have I been out?" She frowned down at his tense, broad shoulders before plucking open the top of her T-shirt with her free hand. There were no bruises on her chest this time. "Wait." She pushed back the blankets, shivering a little. "I wasn't wearing this ..." Her denim shorts were gone, replaced with *nothing*. Only the long, faded yellow shirt that was thin and soft against her skin, and what felt like clean underwear. In other words ... what she usually wore to sleep.

But she didn't usually sleep in Kilian's bed.

"It's been a few days." He slumped back in his chair, his eyes rising to meet hers again. His thumb began tracing small circles along the back of her hand, almost distractedly, like he didn't even realise he was touching her. "I changed your clothes. I hope that's okay."

"*Three* days?" she spluttered, accepting the glass of water he handed her.

She sipped it slowly as he gave her a tired nod, the liquid like knives going down her sore throat. She set the glass aside, rubbing at her chest.

"Why didn't you take me to the hospital?"

"We couldn't." He pulled his hand away from hers, his eyes switching between hers, like he didn't quite know where to focus. "There was a storm. It was too dangerous."

She rubbed a little harder at her chest, memories slowly seeping back to her. "Theo ..." she croaked, her vision blurring as she remembered the look on his face.

And then Moses' desperate pleas.

And West's deep voice.

It's like she's already dead.

"No, fuck, don't cry." Kilian was suddenly leaning over her, his hands on her face, brushing her tears away. "You're okay, sweetheart. You're okay. Theo's okay, too. Everyone is fine." His voice broke, like that was a lie, and his emotion was a heavy weight against her chest, making it hurt even more.

He wasn't okay.

"Shh." He tucked her hair behind her ears and kissed her cheeks gently, and just as she lifted her face, overwhelmed by the gentle affection, his mouth suddenly brushed against hers.

The pain in her chest eased, but her breath halted. She grew hot, her entire body flushing, her hands shaking in her lap.

"Your eyes changed," he muttered against her lips. "You have a mate." He pulled back, letting her see his eyes. "But it isn't clear who it is. Your eyes don't match any of ours."

"Did you just kiss me?" she asked numbly.

Mate.

She had a mate?

Her eyes had changed?

"No." He was staring at her mouth, his hands still firmly holding her face. "But I'm about to."

"Why would you do that?"

She had a mate?

"To see if I feel anything." He came back to her slowly, his thumb touching her lip just before his mouth pressed to hers, lush and soft, his breath sweet and warm, stuttering as his lips parted.

Her heart was racing so fast it felt like she was in danger of passing out again, but he held her up, he held her firm, he seared her with his breath so that she couldn't slip away, forcing her to pay attention.

"I don't know how to kiss," she mumbled against him, awkward and panicking and so hot she could feel a droplet of sweat gathering along the centre of her spine.

His hand slipped around to the back of her neck, some of the softness leaking from his grip as he took hold of her.

"Open your mouth." It was a gentle command, tinged with a strange note of despair.

Stop, she was on the cusp of saying. *You don't have to do this. Of course you aren't my mate.* But as soon as she opened her mouth, his tongue pushed inside, brushing against her own, tasting her.

The fingers against the back of her neck flexed, his grunt vibrating against her tongue. She must have moved it instinctively, chasing his taste. His mouth slanted over hers, pressing harder, his tongue driving deeper as he loomed closer, his chest brushing hers, like he was about to press her down into the pillows, and then he was tearing himself away.

"It's not me." His chest was heaving, his eyes bright and tortured. "It can't be me, you understand?"

She could only croak out an unintelligible sound of shock.

She had a mate.

Kilian had kissed her.

Kilian wasn't her mate.

The facts rolled around and around, refusing to stick.

"I don't understand," she finally rasped, her fingers fluttering back to her chest, where the ache had sprung up again.

Kilian's light eyes followed the movement before flicking back to her face. His tongue ran across his lips, his nostrils flaring. "Isobel ..." His chest expanded, his breath uneven. "I shouldn't have done that. I just needed to know."

"If you were my mate?" It still wasn't sinking in.

His eyes drifted to the side, like he didn't know how to answer, before moving back to her. "You almost died. We think you *did* die, but it was only the Death Phase. You came back, and your eyes had changed." It was like he was speaking from a script, his voice too numb to properly broadcast his feelings.

She struggled up, her limbs weak as she tried to stand. He turned slightly like he was about to scoop her up, and she quickly skidded away, her steps unsteady as she pushed into the bathroom, leaning against the sink.

The first thing she noticed was that she wasn't dishevelled, as she had expected. She was clean. Her hair was smooth and shiny. She smelt nice.

"You've been taking care of me," she muttered, raising her eyes in the mirror.

Kilian came up behind her, his posture hunched, his arms tucked protectively across his chest. "We thought you would be most comfortable with me, but it almost earned me a broken rib from Theo."

She barely heard him.

She could see it now.

Her eyes were multicoloured. She was staring into a galaxy. Black splotches decorated the centre, filled with specks of yellow, green, blue, and grey in several different shades. And between all the colours were the golden flecks that were her own.

It wasn't one of her eyes that had changed.

It was both of them.

"Who has eyes this colour?" she baulked, gripping

the counter harder. "I don't know anyone with eyes this colour!" Her voice was rising in a panic. "You have to be *beside* your mate in the Death Phase! Does this mean ..."

Her mate didn't exist?

She was finally coming to terms with what Kilian had said.

With what he had done.

"You were worried it was you?" She spun, her heart hurting for him.

He didn't move. He just stared at her. "I ... just needed to know."

"But you know now, right?" She felt her whole body lock up, her mouth going dry.

She could still taste him. Still feel him. His weight as he tipped her backwards, his hot breath as it stuttered, his deep grunt. She had always thought Kilian was beautiful. He had always taken her breath away. She just didn't need to be admitting that to him right now.

"I do." He stepped back. "And I think ... I think there's something I need to tell you." He did a quick check over his shoulder, his mouth firming into a determined line as he seemed to make sure the door to his room was shut. "I'm terrible at keeping secrets."

"You are," she agreed automatically, numb with shock.

"There's something else you need to know." He took a deep breath, holding her gaze as all of the emotions battering against her chest evened out, morphing into one.

Her hand was pressed to her chest again, and Kilian's emotion settled beneath it, stark and painful.

Guilt.

To be continued ...

BONUS SCENE
GUILTY

Don't do it.

She was *crying*, for fuck's sake.

But he couldn't stop thinking about it. For days, Kilian had cared for her. He had brushed her beautiful hair until the ripples of strawberry gold were smooth as silk, until all she needed were flowers tucked into the ripples and she would have looked like a Disney fucking princess. He had kept her hydrated and carefully fed her soup with her head propped up, one tiny little spoonful at a time. He had made sure she was comfortable and monitored her like a goddamned mother hen.

And the whole time, he thought about one thing.

He thought about kissing her.

Like she was a science experiment. Or ... like he

was a morbid scientist who already knew the consequences of his experiment, but he couldn't just leave it alone.

And now she was crying, and it hurt to see her so upset, but there was something broken inside him because he wasn't *just* sorry for her. He was also sorry for himself and still driven by that same incessant, niggling thought. He kissed her cheek, tasting the sweet cherry of her skin mixed with the bitterness of her tears, and maybe that should have been enough, but it wasn't, so he kissed the other cheek.

He was just making it worse.

She lifted her head and he didn't move his away, allowing their lips to brush together. He could hear her breath halt and feel her wide-eyed shock.

"Your eyes changed." His lips brushed hers again as he spoke. "You have a mate." He shifted back. "But it isn't clear who it is. Your eyes don't match any of ours."

His lips were tingling. He wanted to lick them, to draw her taste into his mouth, but she looked so shocked.

"Did you just kiss me?" she asked.

"No." *God*, it felt like he was on an edge, and he could give in to this impossible need, or he could give in to the panic. He still hadn't let go of her face, and he gently pulled her an inch or so closer, his stomach curling with heat at how she swayed toward him. "But I'm about to."

"Why would you do that?"

Good question.

"To see if I feel anything." He was lying. Fuck. He was lying, *right*? He tried to convince himself to back off, but his thumb brushed against her lips, and they parted slightly, the movement a straight shot to his gut.

He couldn't help himself.

He kissed her, dragging his thumb out of the way and pinching her chin to keep her there in the moment, to stop her giving in to the shock.

"I don't know how to kiss," she whispered against him. She was shaking, her skin ratcheting up in temperature, and he needed more of it. More of the innocent reactions she didn't even bother to hide.

She was soft and pliant as he slanted his mouth over hers. Her lips seemed to be dusted with sticky cherry syrup, and he felt the danger of addiction in that moment. He wasn't sexually inexperienced, but her scent, her taste, was ...

He had never experienced anything like it.

"Open your mouth." He tried to sound gentle. Not

like his world was falling down in ruins all around him. Not like his worst fears were confirmed.

For most people, being attracted to their mate was a given, not just a blessing. But for them? It would be a soul-deep curse.

He would have to push it down.

He needed to switch it off.

He had to …

She opened her mouth, and he forgot all about what he had to do. *Just one taste* … He drove his tongue between her sweet lips, trying not to lose himself in the potent sensation of her little tongue licking back curiously against his. It was just attraction. She was just … attractive. He liked most things about her, and she was so *fucking* responsive. That's all it was. He could ignore that.

He grunted, his body growing heavy, his fingers itching to reach down and haul her up against him, to weigh her back down and part those trembling thighs so he could ease some of the ache springing up through his body.

But he didn't.

Because he wasn't for her, and she wasn't for him. Not *Just* him.

"It's not me." He tore himself away, his chest

heaving, his body aching. "It can't be me, you understand?"

She was touching her chest again, and he could feel a corresponding pain in his own. They would all feel it. They would know she was awake.

"I don't understand." Her voice was rough, her doe-eyes rounded, her cheeks tainted with colour.

He ran his tongue across his lips, breathing deep to fill his lungs with her scent, savouring what would be his first and last taste. "Isobel ..." He struggled to bring himself under control. "I shouldn't have done that. I just needed to know."

"If you were my mate?" She looked so confused. *Fuck.*

How could they do this to her?

But they had to.

For now, it was her or them.

Until the mate-bond gave them away.

'I HOPE YOU ENJOYED PLIER!

If you want to chat about this book or catch all the teasers for my next book, scan the code below to check out my reader's group!

If you enjoyed this book, please consider leaving a review. Indie authors rely on the support of our incredible readers, and without you guys, we wouldn't be able to continue publishing. Thank you for everything you do for the indie community!

Thank you!!
Jane xx

CONNECT WITH JANE WASHINGTON

Scan the code to view Jane's website, social media, release announcements and giveaways.

Milton Keynes UK
Ingram Content Group UK Ltd.
UKHW021804270524
443037UK00001B/42